FALLEN FEATHERS

Best wishes

Romy x

Fallen Feathers

Nessa & Ophelia Book One

Romy Morgan

This novel is entirely a work of fiction. The names, characters and events portrayed in it are the work of the author's imagination. Any resemblance to actual persons, living or dead, events or situations is entirely coincidental.

First published in 2025 by Jupiter Cloud Books

Copyright © Romy Morgan 2025

Romy Morgan asserts the moral right to be identified as the author of this work.

ISBN: 978-1-0685863-0-9

All rights reserved. No part of this publication may be reproduced or transmitted, in any form or by any means, electronic, mechanical, photocopying, recording or otherwise, without the prior permission of the publisher.

This book is sold subject to the condition that it shall not, by way of trade or otherwise, be lent, re-sold, hired out or otherwise circulated without the publisher's prior consent in any form of binding or cover other than that in which it is published.

For my beautiful, amazing mama,
my best friend and biggest inspiration in life!

Please Note
This is a fantasy story. This book is not based on, or supposed to represent any genuine religion or belief. It depicts an entirely fictitious version of religion and while some well-known names are used, these characters and events are not intended to actually resemble any actual religious figures. This is purely a fantasy version of God, Heaven and Hell, and the angels and demons that live there. There is no intention to cause offence to any individual or group.

Contents

Chapter One
The First Sin..11

Chapter Two
Seven O'clock on a Wednesday....................................26

Chapter Three
Archangel Zadkiel..40

Chapter Four
We're Off to Burn Down a Monastery!........................59

Chapter Five
Somewhere in the Middle...76

Chapter Six
What Heaven Are Planning..90

Chapter Seven
An Angel in Hell..104

Chapter Eight
Not a Real Demon..120

Chapter Nine
Sorry I Couldn't Save You..135

Chapter Ten
A Heavenly Warning...157

Chapter Eleven
The Biggest Scandal in History..........................178

Chapter Twelve
Heaven or Us?...197

Chapter Thirteen
Bad Angels Go to Hell....................................223

Chapter Fourteen
Upon Your Sacrifice We Shall Build a New World.........246

Chapter Fifteen
An Angelic Taxi..266

Chapter Sixteen
God's Perfect Creation....................................290

Chapter Seventeen
No One Survives This!.....................................314

Chapter Eighteen
Beautiful Love Filled Angels..............................337

Chapter Nineteen
On the Same Frequency.....................................369

Chapter Twenty
Hell's Hit Squad..394

Chapter Twenty One
You're Not Nessa..420

Chapter Twenty Two
Soulmates...443

Bonus
Ezra and Beelzebub's Guide to Heaven and Hell...........467

Hello From The Author

I started writing this book at the end of December 2023, inspired to write an angel and demon love story after watching and falling in love with the TV programme 'Good Omens'. By the end of February I had finished writing it. I hadn't planned a sequel, but I missed it, so I started writing another. In eight months I had written three books about these characters, who I came to love a lot. I guess you could say I'm obsessed? I have written parts of this on holiday, while travelling, backstage at a theatre show I was in, basically anytime I had a spare moment, I'd be writing. I can't wait for you to explore the world I have created and fall in love with the characters as you follow them on their journey.

I'd like to thank my family for being the first people to read/listen to this story, and for always being my biggest supporters, not only with this book, but in life in general. Thank you to my wonderful mum for editing, and to my little sister for her help when I come to her saying "help, I need *insert thing* to happen, any idea how that can work?"

If you love Nessa and Ophelia's story and want to chat about it and keep up to date with the release of the next books, join me on Facebook in the *'Fallen Feathers Fan Club'* group! I'd love you to join us!

Chapter One

The First Sin.

(Six Thousand Years Ago)

As night fell in Eden, Ophelia sat on the floor and looked up to the sky, as she did every night. She thought of Zadkiel again. She always did whenever she saw stars; after all Zadkiel had created them. Lots of angels had become demons since then, but she was the one Ophelia thought about all the time. She wondered what Hell was like. She couldn't imagine anything very terrible, but then she was an angel, and so far she had only witnessed good things.

Ophelia wondered whether the humans were enjoying looking at the stars. She knew that the idea of stars existing just for humans to look at upset Zadkiel, but if that was the case then she certainly hoped they liked them. She wondered if she should point them out to the humans, in case they hadn't noticed them yet, but she supposed they were likely going to sleep now, as humans do.

Ophelia lent back against the wall, stroking the soft grass beside her, wondering whether anything interesting was going to happen. Eden was all well and good, but it had only been a few days and Ophelia already felt a little bored. Plus, if Adam and Eve were asleep right now, she couldn't even talk to them. Not that she really should be talking to them she knew... Was this it? Nothing of interest was happening. Ophelia wished for any sort of excitement. During creation there had always been something interesting going on; something new that God thought of, or another little job to do. She'd been excited about Eden, she was one of the first angels to volunteer to oversee things there and she did enjoy teaching the humans about the world; telling them about all of the animals and other creations they had been working so hard on. Only, the garden was actually quite small and they had already discussed most of the things there, plus humans slept a lot longer than Ophelia imagined. There were other angels there of course, but she had already tried speaking to them and they dismissed her, telling her that they had an important job to do, guarding the gates. Ophelia did secretly wonder whether guarding the gates was a little pointless. Sure, there were dangerous animals outside, but realistically how likely was it that any would try to come into Eden? Ophelia wondered whether any of the other angels ever doubted things? She supposed not; angels were required to do as they were told. If they didn't; well, that's when things go terribly wrong...

    She sighed and looked back at the stars. She wished she could see all of them, but only a few were visible from earth. She remembered that Zadkiel once told her that she had hidden pictures in the stars; that certain ones would create a shape when viewed from Earth. That was a secret that the other angels didn't know, because it didn't work from Heaven. Ophelia wondered whether the humans would ever notice. It would be a fun little game for them to try to find them all. She glanced around, looking for the patterns. She had suggested an image of an angel and she wondered if Zadkiel had made one. She knew there was definitely a bear and a lion; Zadkiel had shown her the sketches of those ones. Ophelia had only met her twice. Zadkiel was the Leader of the Archangels and created the whole universe, while Ophelia just worked as an assistant in the Earth department, so they were barely acquaintances, but she found her truly fascinating. The last time she saw her was when she delivered notes on where the Earth would fit into the universe, and it wasn't long after that that Zadkiel was banished from Heaven.

Ophelia often wondered exactly what had happened, and whether Zadkiel was alright. The word was that she had a different name and was a big deal demon now; Prince of Hell, whatever that was. Ophelia couldn't imagine her being a demon, she always seemed so sweet, and in fact far better company than any other angel in her opinion.

Ophelia continued looking at the stars, trying to work out if those ones made a bear or a goat. She felt that they could have been more clear, but maybe that was the idea; to use your imagination? Zadkiel always seemed very creative. Ophelia thought she must have a great imagination. She waved her feet slightly, wondering whether anything interesting was ever going to happen.

Suddenly she heard a rustle in the bushes nearby, and her interest was piqued. It definitely wasn't the humans; they were asleep, and the other angels were far too busy with their important jobs to wander about the bushes. Ophelia wasn't one of the guardians of Eden; she wasn't important enough for that, but the other angels were unlikely to notice the sound, so she decided she ought to investigate. Standing up, she nervously walked towards the sound, and was shocked to see a demon! What was a demon doing on earth? Was that allowed?

"Err, excuse me?" said Ophelia quietly. "What are you doing here?"

The demon turned and Ophelia let out a small gasp, she recognised her! Did she? It couldn't be Zadkiel could it? She had the same beautiful long curly hair, but now it was jet black. It had been a soft ginger colour before. The demon's face looked the most familiar though, Ophelia imagined it with a warm smile and that joyous sparkle in her eyes that Ophelia loved so much. The sparkle was definitely gone now though. Zadkiel definitely did not look happy.

"Shouldn't you be guarding something, angel?" asked the demon, spitting out the word *angel* as if it were a bad word.

"Err, no. I don't guard the gates," said Ophelia nervously, wondering whether Zadkiel remembered her. Perhaps not, she was only a small-order angel, and Zadkiel used to be the Leader of the Archangels and of all Heaven. Why would someone so important remember her?

"Right," said the demon. "Well, don't let me stop you; go get on with *not* guarding Eden then!"

Ophelia was a little taken aback by her sarcasm; it wasn't just her hair that was different now... "I'm not sure that demons are permitted in Eden..." she said uncertainly, painfully aware that, though she was different now, she was talking to someone who was several ranks above her as an angel.

"Who said?" asked the demon with a slight toss of her hair.

"The Almighty?" offered Ophelia, realising she wasn't sure.

"Did The Almighty actually say that?" asked the demon. "You see, I don't think there are any rules about demons coming in, and if there are, your colleagues are doing a pretty shit job of guarding Eden, aren't they? If I'm here, legions of demons could easily come pouring in, to corrupt the poor helpless humans couldn't they?"

"Are they going to?" asked Ophelia worriedly.

The demon looked at her with an expression that Ophelia couldn't quite read. "Nah, it's just me," she answered after a pause. "Anyway, it doesn't matter if I'm *permitted* or not, I don't obey God's rules; that's being a demon! Plus, humans have equal capacity for good and bad, what goes on here is just as much in Hell's interest as Heaven's..."

"What are you going to do? Are you planning to tempt the humans to stray from God?" asked Ophelia, glancing around in concern, wondering if she should do something.

"No. Couldn't give a shit what they do," said the

demon simply. "I'm just observing." She sniffed slightly and looked at her surroundings. Ophelia couldn't help gazing at her, she looked gorgeous, Ophelia thought, staring off with a wistful look; dressed all in black with the breeze gently blowing her hair, her big black wings moving slightly as she breathed.

The demon turned and caught Ophelia's gaze, her eyes narrowing slightly in confusion, or else perhaps suspicion. Ophelia wondered whether there were any rules about angels talking to demons, even if not she shouldn't be so fascinated by her right? She considered how to politely end the conversation. Being this close to a demon was making her feel strangely uncomfortable, and she had been assured that she wasn't planning anything untoward; not that Ophelia really had the authority to stop her if she was.

"Then I shall leave you to observe," she said, "If that is truly what you plan to do."

The demon said nothing, but rolled her eyes slightly and walked away, disappearing through the trees. Ophelia watched her go, wondering what could have possibly happened to Zadkiel since she saw her last. That was definitely her, but she seemed so different now...

The sun rose in Eden and Ophelia didn't see Zadkiel again. The sound of the humans, now done with their sleeping, made the garden feel more alive. Ophelia wandered among the flowers, trying to count all the varieties. Her favourites were roses, they looked so pretty, yet for some reason God had added sharp thorns to them. Ophelia found that interesting, that there can exist something that is both delicate and fierce at the same time. Things ought to be either good or bad, yet roses seemed to be both, that was intriguing. Suddenly Eve came running up to her, interrupting her musings.

"Angel Ophelia!" Eve said, seeming very distressed.

"Eve, are you okay?" asked Ophelia in concern; wondering what could possibly be wrong. Nothing bad could happen could it? Not in Eden.

"We have eaten all the food that God provided," explained Eve. "There is nothing left and we are so very hungry…"

Making humans rely on consuming food for sustenance was a little inconvenient in Ophelia's view. It was inevitable that they would soon run out.

"I'm sure there must be something to eat…" said Ophelia, glancing around the garden thoughtfully.

"I don't know," Eve sighed. "Adam suggested that we stab one of the rabbits and eat its flesh!" she said; a disgusted look on her face. "He said The Almighty gave him authority over all animals, but I'm not sure we ought to eat them?"

Ophelia was horrified by the thought. It hadn't occurred to her that anyone might look at that fluffy, friendly-looking creature and consider eating it! The rabbit was one of God's most adorable creations, why would that thought even enter someone's mind? Then again, Ophelia remembered what the demon had said the night before, about humans having equal potential for good and bad. Ophelia felt it was her Heavenly duty as an angel to ensure that the very first humans made good choices. It would look very bad if they ended up straying. That would mean humans were hard to control, and if that were true the demons may well take hold of them. That would be a nightmare, especially as The Almighty had already given humans power over all the other animals... If it starts with one little rabbit, where might it end? Ophelia shuddered at the thought. She knew that some of the plants around the garden were edible, and tried desperately to remember which ones were. She spotted an apple tree in the corner.

"Apples can definitely be eaten!" she said excitedly, pointing in their direction. Eve suddenly looked worried.

"Oh no!" she said, "I am fairly sure that Almighty God told us not to eat those..."

"Why ever not?" asked Ophelia, taken aback.

"I'm not certain," said Eve. "I do believe it was a rule though."

"Well if you have run out of food what choice do you have?" said Ophelia. "I am certain that The Almighty would far prefer you to take an apple than kill one of her innocent animals!"

"I suppose you are right," said Eve doubtfully, looking at the tree as though it were some vicious animal threatening to tear her apart.

"I'm sure nothing bad will happen if you eat one apple!" Ophelia said encouragingly. "Perhaps God meant you can't eat *all* the apples? You know, in case they run out?"

"Thank you Angel Ophelia, you are always so kind to us!" said Eve with a smile.

"Of course I am!" said Ophelia. "I'm an angel!"

"You are the kindest!" insisted Eve. Ophelia felt joy

well up inside her. She really was trying to be the very best angel she could be.

Eve set off towards the apple tree and Ophelia smiled. Eve was finally convinced, and the poor little rabbit was safe for now. A job well done, she thought.

She suddenly felt as though she were being watched. She turned to see the demon standing among the trees, staring at her. Neither said a word and the demon looked her up and down with a stoney face, giving nothing away in regards to her thoughts. After a strange moment where the two stared in silence, the demon moved off back into the trees. Ophelia was left feeling odd. A sensation she couldn't begin to describe, but one that made her feel mightily uncomfortable. As though something terrible was going to happen.

Eden was supposed to be perfect; nothing bad should happen there, so Ophelia spent the rest of the morning stressing about why she couldn't shake that strange feeling. She wondered whether it was the presence of a demon in the garden. Perhaps she could pick up on the demonic energy? She wasn't sure, but whatever it was, she didn't care for it!

By the afternoon there was some kind of commotion in the other end of the garden. Ophelia couldn't make out anything being said, but one of the voices sounded oddly like God's... She was about to go and find out what was happening, when a dazzling golden light shone down on her. That meant only one thing, The Almighty was going to address you. Ophelia gulped in terror. God never really spoke to anyone unless it was absolutely necessary.

"Angel Ophelia!" said God. Her voice filled Ophelia with terror at the best of times, but she sounded especially angry right now.

"Yes my Lord?" said Ophelia nervously.

"Did you tell Eve to eat the forbidden fruit?" asked God, her voice full of accusation. "Did you lead a human to temptation?"

Ophelia was horrified by the suggestion that she might have *tempted* Eve. Tempting was something that she knew demons could do; she didn't think that angels had the ability to tempt. If she had done something wrong she hadn't meant to, she'd simply tried to help. Was The Almighty really angry at her? She noticed the demon standing nearby looking at her, and was filled with terror. She didn't know what Zadkiel had done to fall from Heaven, but if Ophelia was in trouble now, what if she ended up falling too?

"Are you going to answer me Ophelia?" asked God irritably.

Ophelia knew she should answer, but she felt that she somehow couldn't quite say the words, any words! She was rooted to the spot, filled with fear.

Before Ophelia could force herself to speak, the demon stepped out from the trees into the golden light.

"The angel didn't do it," she announced, shocking Ophelia greatly. The demon had been watching her conversation with Eve, she knew full well it was she that suggested the apple. Ophelia stayed silent, wondering where this was going.

"Zadkiel?" said God questioningly.

"My name is Nessa now," answered the demon,

sounding slightly nervous, Ophelia thought, which was odd for a demon; or for Zadkiel who was so very confident as an angel. "I tempted Eve to eat the apple," she continued. Nessa glanced at the floor as a snake disappeared into the bushes. "I enchanted a snake to persuade Eve to taste the forbidden fruit. I came to test the humans' sense of righteousness. To see if they would stray from your sacred rules, oh mighty God, and apparently they would?"

Ophelia stared at the demon, completely stunned. Was she lying to...protect her?!

"A snake?" said The Almighty, genuine confusion in her voice.

"Yeah, I was feeling creative..." said Nessa quickly, with a little uncertainty.

"Is this true Ophelia?" asked God, snatching Ophelia's attention back from Nessa. She was completely torn, she should *never* lie! She was an angel! And especially not to God. But if she admitted it now, then both she and Nessa would get in trouble. A demon wouldn't likely get in trouble for tempting, not if that was what they were supposed to do.

Nessa looked at Ophelia encouragingly, and she felt she saw a glimmer of Zadkiel's kindness on her face.

"It is..." Ophelia said, her face burning with shame and fear. Nessa gave her a small smile and she took a rather shaky breath.

"Very well," said God after a pause. "Eve and Adam have been sent out of Eden as punishment for their disobedience, they are not to return..."

Ophelia took in a short gasp of air, the humans

were kicked out because of her?! She wondered what The Almighty would have said if Adam had killed and eaten that rabbit. Would she have been more angry, or was eating the apple somehow worse?

The golden light vanished; The Almighty had left Eden. Ophelia was left feeling a strange sense of emptiness she had never felt before.

The demon started to back off into the trees.

"Wait!" said Ophelia desperately.

Nessa stopped and gave Ophelia a look which was a little mean for someone who had just protected her from God.

Though she had stopped, Nessa was clearly not intending to say anything.

"Thank you…" Was all Ophelia could think to say.

"Don't!" snapped Nessa.

"That was very kind," said Ophelia nervously.

"No!" Nessa said quickly. "Don't you dare say that word! Demons are *not* kind! Lucifer will have my head mounted on his throne room wall if he hears about this…"

Ophelia's eyes widened. She wasn't sure if Nessa was being serious or not. She had no idea what went on in Hell, but she supposed it could be anything…

Nessa noticed the angel's look of horror and rolled her eyes. "Not really," she said, "But not far off… If there is one thing demons can get in trouble for, it's doing good! So that's why I didn't!" She shot Ophelia a pointed, warning look.

"But…" Ophelia hesitated, not certain how to continue. "Why did you do that then?"

"Purely a selfish action, so don't flatter yourself!" Nessa said, refusing to meet Ophelia's eye. "I saw an opportunity to pass that off as my own work, stealing if you will. The Devil will be thrilled to hear that the very first humans got booted out of Eden for taking temptation and straying from God, and if he thinks I did it, I'll get in his good books! Or, bad books I suppose!" She said with a small laugh.

Ophelia wasn't sure if any of that was true; supposedly demons were known for lying. Either way though, this demon had likely just saved her, and she was very grateful.

"What do you suppose will happen to the humans now?" asked Ophelia, not really wanting to know the answer.

"Who knows," Nessa sighed. "In Eden they were guarded by angels, out there they are all alone." Nessa looked sad, as though she knew what it felt like to be abandoned like that. Ophelia wished she could comfort her, but decided against it. Instead she thought of the poor humans, cast out because of her.

"Do you think I'll go to Hell?" she asked Nessa in a small voice.

"Nah. At least not for this," said Nessa. "You're an angel, I'm sure you had good intentions. Right?"

"I suggested it to save a rabbit..."

"Of course you did!"

Nessa laughed slightly, and Ophelia felt that was a little uncalled for.

"But..." Ophelia urged, her guilt still bubbling at the surface, ready to make her cry at any moment. "I sinned! I tempted Eve away from God's path! I must be a demon now!"

This time Nessa laughed heartily, as though Ophelia had told the funniest joke. Ophelia couldn't help but feel that her genuine terror was being unfairly mocked, but then Nessa was a demon...

"Sorry for laughing... you think you're a demon?" Nessa said through her giggles. "You're practically glowing with angelic goodness! As if you're a demon, with your soft light bouncy hair and your sweet innocent angel eyes! They'd eat you for breakfast down there; if demons ate, that is!"

Ophelia looked at Nessa carefully. She did look like a demon now, but she didn't used to. Zadkiel had soft light hair and angelic eyes too!

"Are you sure I'm not a demon?" asked Ophelia quietly.

"Absolutely, categorically, no!" said Nessa. "You're practically the advert for all that is good and pure. I can't imagine you doing anything wrong, not on purpose anyway! Forget about the whole apple thing, it doesn't matter now."

Ophelia smiled. She felt very comforted, but then remembered that Nessa was a demon, and felt rather uncomfortable instead.

"Thank y—"

"Ah!" Nessa cut in. "Don't say it Ophelia, I don't want to hear it!"

Nessa turned and disappeared from sight before Ophelia could say anything else. As she swept off, one of her sleek black wing feathers floated to the ground beside

Ophelia. She picked it up and stroked it, finding herself strangely fond of a supposedly evil demon. Then again, she had been very fond of Zadkiel; and Nessa was still the same person underneath, right? As Ophelia turned the feather around in her hand, she wondered whether she would ever see Nessa again. Probably not; they were on opposite sides, they shouldn't really talk at all.

Chapter Two

Seven O'clock on a Wednesday.

(21st Century)

"The usual please!" announced Nessa, leaning against the bar.

As the barman prepared her drinks, she casually traced an 'N' with her finger in the spilled beer on the bar. A girl across from her was staring, Nessa wondered why. The girl gave her a very flirty look when she caught her eye and Nessa sighed. She shot the girl a look that she hoped said *I can't go out with you, I'm a demon, and even if I was going to date someone it wouldn't be you*. Or words to that effect.

The barman presented her with the drinks and she sat down at the table that was always miraculously free at seven o'clock on a Wednesday. Nessa glanced at her phone; Ophelia was late, but then she often was. Ophelia had an aversion to most modern inventions; a trait that Nessa found very amusing and quite sweet. The only timepiece Ophelia owned was a pocket-watch that Nessa gave her in the Victorian Era. Nessa had enchanted it to tell the time in all of Ophelia's favourite countries. When the angel was, quite rightly thrilled with the gift, Nessa had quickly claimed she only got it because Ophelia was annoying her by always being late. In truth, Nessa secretly loved making her angel smile. Not that she could ever admit that of course...

The crash of the door heralded Ophelia's chaotic arrival. She had several shopping bags and bustled past the other patrons, apologising profusely for knocking into them. Nessa should have been embarrassed, and she was a little, but she couldn't help but smile at Ophelia's chaos. Usually Nessa was the chaotic one, but Ophelia certainly had her moments.

"Hi!" announced the angel, sitting opposite Nessa, letting the bags spread under the table. "Sorry I'm late!"

"And you brought the contents of every shop in York with you?" Nessa asked, looking down at a bag which had fallen against her leg.

Ophelia rolled her eyes. "I was actually early in the city centre, so I thought I'd look around the shops for a bit, but true, I might have got a little carried away..."

"And lead us not into temptation..." Nessa said sarcastically with a playful smile.

"I really don't think it counts as temptation!" said Ophelia indignantly.

"Oh it does. You didn't need this stuff, but you were tempted by their lovely shop displays. Score one to Hell!" grinned Nessa, raising her glass slightly towards Ophelia before taking a sip.

"You didn't invent shopping!" said Ophelia, picking up her drink.

"Oh we did!" said Nessa. "Why else would

everything humans need not be provided for them, like in Eden? Plus, this kind of shopping where you absolutely don't need any of the things you bought screams demonic work, don't you think?"

Ophelia narrowed her eyes slightly at the demon. "Well then, I suppose you don't want your present if you are going to mock me!"

"A present?" asked Nessa in interest, putting her glass down.

"Yes, but since you disapprove so much, I shall have to return it!" said Ophelia, raising an eyebrow.

"Hey, it is up to God to judge you, not me! Anyway, why do you care what a demon thinks?" Nessa grinned.

"I don't," said Ophelia, reaching into one of the bags. "There's a new chocolate shop near the Shambles and they had these, which I think are super cute, and of course you love chocolate!"

She presented Nessa with a box of chocolates in the shape of an 'N'.

"Aww, thank you!" Nessa took it and looked at the box, turning it in her hands. As she turned it sideways it suddenly looked like a 'Z' instead of an 'N' and she was reminded of her former life. She quickly turned it again. "That's very nice and thoughtful of you," she said after a moment.

"Of course!" said Ophelia. "You're my best friend, I always think of you!" She then quickly took a rather large drink of her wine, likely feeling that what she said may be far too friendly for an angel to say out loud so casually to a demon.

Nessa said nothing, but raised an eyebrow.

"So!" announced Ophelia, obviously trying to change the subject. "What have you been up to this week?"

Nessa and Ophelia had met up at seven o'clock on a Wednesday every week for thousands of years to update each other on what they'd been doing. Nessa pitched a lot of her demonic inventions to Ophelia before suggesting them to Lucifer. Her most successful inventions over the years had been chocolate, coffee, social media, horoscopes, public transport and rap music. If Ophelia thought they sounded too innocent, Nessa had to work on justifying why they were demonic. It was always helpful to get the opinion of an angel. She might be the enemy, but the enemy can be useful. Plus she was also her best friend of course, which helped!

"Oh, the usual," said Nessa in response to Ophelia's question. "You know how it is, bit of tempting, making general chaos and disharmony... The bare minimum to keep them off my back."

"Ooh! I have something you can tell them you did!" announced Ophelia excitedly. "It's really the sweetest story, but Heaven really wouldn't be very pleased about it..."

"Go on..." said Nessa, intrigued.

"Well, I found out that the two vicars at the church near my cottage have been secretly in love with each other for *ages*! But they never admitted it because, well, they are vicars. That kind of thing breaks my heart, when people can't be together because of duty or whatever. So I may have helped to nudge them towards temptation and they snogged under the big crucifix and ended up leaning against the statue of Jophiel!" Ophelia started giggling as she said the last bit, and Nessa burst out laughing at the idea.

Jophiel used to be Nessa's sister long ago, back in Heaven when she was an angel. Of course, angels don't truly have relatives like humans, but Nessa and Jophiel were considered sisters, as they were created together, the very first angels in fact. Jophiel was a very serious angel and had been the leader of Heaven for thousands of years, the idea of her statue being sullied by the passions of priests was hilarious.

"That's brilliant! Well done," laughed Nessa. "They'll love that down there! Ooh, especially Beelzebub! She'll laugh her head off!"

"Why thank you!" said Ophelia with a grin, giving Nessa a mock-bow with a roll of her hand. "Needless to say they are not vicars anymore... But they are together, so that's a win for love right?"

"Absolutely!" smiled Nessa, taking another drink of her cocktail.

The angel and demon had been occasionally helping each other out with the odd good deed or temptation for years. As long as neither strayed too far into the territory of either good or evil, and the other could pass it off as their work, then no harm was done right? In fact, Nessa had often joked that Ophelia made a better demon than her, as some of what Hell considered to be Nessa's best demonic work, was actually that of Ophelia. Being an angel was very important to Ophelia though, and she did live in constant fear of God and the idea of becoming a demon. Nessa occasionally had to reassure her that she was not actually doing evil. Nessa was a strong believer that there was no such thing as good and evil anyway; at least it wasn't so simple or absolute. Of course she had to keep up the demonic facade, but after thousands of years it all seemed a bit of a burden; especially when she had never really agreed with Hell's values in the first place.

Whenever Nessa and Ophelia met up at the pub, what started as a quick catch up would always turn into hours of laughing and chatting about absolutely nothing. Several rounds of drinks would be had and they would never run out of things to talk about, despite it being their latest weekly meeting in several thousand.

As Ophelia laughed at one of Nessa's completely hilarious jokes, Nessa was reminded for the hundredth time how beautiful the angel was; extra gorgeous when she laughed, Nessa thought. She stared at Ophelia, as she always found herself doing, wondering how it was possible to love someone so much. Nessa had loved Ophelia for thousands of years. It was that painful, all-consuming love that you don't quite know what to do with. Especially if you cannot actually tell the other how you feel!

There were so many reasons that Nessa could never tell Ophelia how much she meant to her. Among them was the fact that angels and demons were not even technically supposed to be capable of love, not like that anyway. Nessa had always been told that love was dangerous. In a way it was love that caused God to cast Nessa from Heaven in the first place. The strongest reason that Nessa could never admit her feelings however, was that she wasn't sure if Ophelia felt the same way about her. They had always been friends, but even that was a stretch for an angel and demon. Officially, to their respective rulers they were mortal enemies; rivals; both sent to represent their realms in the North of England, and both meeting up simply to keep an eye on the opposition. Nessa was fairly certain that the whole of Hell and Heaven knew without a doubt that they were best friends though, but no one ever really brought it up. They were probably too worried to mention it, in case it caused drama, most things you brought up to either realm caused drama.

After a little longer, and another drink or two (alcohol doesn't affect angels and demons as quickly as humans, but they were, at this point, rather tipsy), Ophelia became a little quiet. She held her drink and swirled the wine around in the glass thoughtfully.

"Remember all the fuss when Jesus turned that water into wine?" she said randomly, obviously choosing to muse on an anecdote to delay bringing up whatever had caused her to turn quiet. "It was such a big deal, but I could do that easily! I mean, it wouldn't be very angelic, but I could!"

"I'll tell you a secret Phee," said Nessa, leaning closer to her angel. "Jesus didn't turn the water into wine, I did it for him!"

"You did it?!" exclaimed Ophelia in genuine disbelief.

"Yeah!" said Nessa. "He might have been God's son, but he was still a human! Humans can't do magic. I'm surprised everyone fell for it."

"That's crazy!" said Ophelia.

"Uh-huh, and you know Moses? Never parted that bloody sea. What was it called?"

"The Red Sea."

"Are you sure? That's a damn silly name, because it wasn't remotely red!" Nessa sighed. "Your lot have had some weird ideas over the years! By the way, needless to say, don't tell anyone about the wine thing or the sea..."

"Of course," said Ophelia. "Speaking of *my lot*," she continued, suddenly regaining her air of quiet concern. "I'm not sure what, but I think something is going on up there at the moment."

"What?" asked Nessa, noting the angel's serious tone.

"Err, I literally just said I don't know what!" Ophelia sighed. "Weren't you listening?" She gave Nessa's foot a playful, yet rather hard, nudge with her own. "I wasn't sure if I should bring it up, because I'm aware it's not mightily helpful to say: 'Something's happening, sorry, that's all the information you get!' But I felt like I should tell you, just so you can keep an eye out."

"Right... What exactly am I keeping an eye out for? Aren't you angelic lot likely to be doing good?" said Nessa, slightly sarcastically. She took another drink as she remembered a particularly smug look on her former sister Jophiel's face, the last time she saw her all those years ago.

"Well, you would think," Ophelia sighed. "But we both know that Heaven's version of good isn't always very obviously good. Plus I heard someone mentioning Hell when discussing, well, whatever this is. So that's why I'm telling you. I don't want you to get hurt."

Nessa smiled and raised an eyebrow at the last comment. Perhaps slightly more obviously flirty than she intended, but she had had rather a lot of cocktails. Ophelia said nothing, but frowned slightly, with a cute, but disapproving look.

"I'll bear it in mind," said Nessa after a moment. "Let me know if you hear anything else, yeah?"

Later, when the two finally decided that they had been at the pub for long enough, and, more importantly, there was no more room on the table with all the empty glasses, Nessa waved Ophelia off as she got into her taxi. She always had to make certain that Ophelia was safe before she would consider heading home herself. One time, she had sent away a taxi and called for another when she decided the driver had bad energy.

Nessa walked through the dark and drizzly streets. It was eleven o'clock at night on a Wednesday, so there was hardly anyone around. She thought about what Ophelia had said regarding Heaven. Generally speaking Heaven and Hell got on with their own stuff and didn't tend to bother each other. So the thought that Heaven could be up to something worried Nessa the more she thought about it.

Suddenly she heard a voice in the darkness call out her name. There were fewer streetlights in this area and Nessa couldn't see anyone around. "Nessa!" It came again, the voice sounded unfamiliar, eery and chilling. Who on earth could be calling her. She sensed demonic energy from a particularly dark alleyway. She looked down it and a pair of eyes flashed red for a moment.

"Hello?" said Nessa, as she started towards the alley, wondering what another demon was doing in York. As she got closer she recognised the figure leaning nonchalantly against the wall. Her green hair and signature fishnet tights were the only clue to her identity, until she got close enough to see her face. "Beelzebub?" she asked, half wanting confirmation it was her, because it certainly didn't sound like her.

"Yeah, hi," said Beelzebub in her normal voice.

"Why the fuck did your voice sound like that?" asked Nessa.

"I was trying something," said Beelzebub with a grin. "Was it scary?"

"Well, I'm also a demon, so no. But to a human I'm sure it would be terrifying?" offered Nessa, not wanting Beelzebub to know that, while she wasn't scared, she was a little startled.

"Hmm, I'll take it," said Beelzebub, rubbing dirt off her fingers from the grubby wall. She looked Nessa up and down with a disapproving look. "You're drunk," she said.

Nessa laughed. "Not really! I've been drunker. *You've* been drunker, so don't give me all that!"

Angels were not supposed to eat or drink human food, they were far too pure for that, and technically neither should demons. Most of them didn't, apart from Nessa, but some of them could occasionally be persuaded to consume alcohol. Alcohol was the very first thing that The Devil invented in Hell, so it was only right. Nessa and Beelzebub had had more than a few drunken nights over the millennia. Beelzebub was the only demon that Nessa could tolerate. She wasn't exactly sure she would describe her as a friend, she maintained that Ophelia was her only true friend, but they got along well enough. Beelzebub was basically The Devil's right-hand demon. Back at the beginning, she and Nessa shared that job, helping Lucifer to shape Hell into what it became. They were both Princes of Hell, but somewhere down the line Nessa and Lucifer had a disagreement, and Nessa was demoted to Duke of Hell instead. Now technically Beelzebub outranked her, but since Nessa was an Earth representative, she wasn't really fussed about ranks back in Hell. After all, she tried to avoid going back there as much as possible.

"Have you been hanging out with that angel again?" asked Beelzebub with a sniff of disapproval.

"We meet up so that I can keep an eye on her! She's been up to all kinds of good this week, it's sickening really," said Nessa quickly.

Beelzebub raised an eyebrow. "Right..." she said, obviously knowing full well that Nessa and Ophelia were very good friends, and probably knowing that Nessa loved the angel too.

"Anyway, how are you? What are you doing up here?" asked Nessa, really wishing she could go home instead of standing in a dark alley in the rain.

"*How am I?* What are we, humans meeting up for a little coffee and a natter?" said Beelzebub sarcastically. "I'm a demon, that's how I am! Anyway, believe me I wouldn't be up here if I had a choice. Lucifer seems to think I'm some damn messenger he can just order around." It was true, while Nessa had grown to love the

Earth over the years, Beelzebub had never been fond.

"So do you have something to say then, oh great messenger of Satan?" smiled Nessa.

"Don't push it!" Beelzebub said irritably, flexing her fingers and allowing a few sparks of fire to fly from them in a clear attempt to appear both threatening and cool.

Nessa wasn't that impressed by theatrics; not when she was freezing cold and soaking wet. She suddenly noticed that despite the rain, Beelzebub was completely dry; damn why didn't Nessa think of that? Of course she could use magic to stay dry! She had been on the Earth too long, some would say. She had spent too much time around humans.

"The boss has a job for you apparently," sighed Beelzebub. "A bit of a waste of time for a talented demon such as yourself, but he is pretty insistent. He wants you to destroy some monastery or something?"

Nessa sighed. Sometimes their boss would get a mad idea in his head and it would become the most important thing in Hell, even if it wasn't, and no one could rest until it was done. Then of course he'd likely think of something else straight away. Luckily, living on Earth, Nessa tended to sidestep most of Lucifer's crazy plans, but if for some reason, he seeks you out, you can't escape.

"Why me?" asked Nessa through gritted teeth.

"No bloody clue! 'Cause it's in the North of England?" said Beelzebub.

"Ugh, why can't *he* do it if he wants it destroyed so badly?"

"Are you seriously asking that question?" said Beelzebub with a slight laugh. "When has His Majesty ever done anything himself since the fall?"

"Good point," smiled Nessa. There was one thing that she and Beelzebub never failed to agree on, and that was that their boss was a nightmare; and a bloody idiot too!

"Anyway, I'm off home. Here's the information," said Beelzebub, taking some crumbled paper out of her pocket and shoving it into Nessa's hand. "Get it done. He's got a right bee in his bonnet about it, no idea why."

"Right, okay," sighed Nessa, looking at the paper and wondering if she could decipher Beelzebub's writing. "See you soon!" but when she looked up, the demon was gone. She didn't even have chance to tell her about the priests kissing in the church.

Nessa rolled her eyes. She hated all these stupid pointless jobs almost as much as she hated being ordered around by Lucifer in Hell. Over the years he had become known as The Devil or Satan to humans, but to Nessa he would always just be plain old Lucifer underneath all the bravado; a fallen angel just like the rest of them. He wasn't even the first angel to fall, Nessa was. Only, Lucifer's fall was the result of his stupid war, so it seemed to get more attention. He soon decided that he was in charge, clearly trying to create for himself the power that he didn't have in Heaven. Lucifer liked to act as though he was as powerful as God under his great Satan persona, but he was no more powerful than any other demon, he just somehow ended up in charge.

Nessa stuffed the paper into her jacket pocket and

set off home. Back in Heaven Nessa was the Leader of the Archangels, and Lucifer started off as a small order angel who occasionally assisted The Almighty. How did he end up as her boss?

Chapter Three
Archangel Zadkiel.
(Before Eden

Long before Nessa the demon, there existed Zadkiel the angel. She and her sister Jophiel were particular favourites of The Almighty, entrusted to lead the archangels, and by extension Heaven in general, and head up the creation of the universe. Zadkiel was extremely creative and often came up with ideas that even God hadn't thought of. Therefore she was given command to put into motion all their plans and actually create the stars and planets.

Zadkiel and Jophiel stood at the edge of the universe, watching the sky light up, and the stars and planets their department had worked so hard on designing, appear before them. Zadkiel was the one that actually made them come to be, Jophiel was there to observe, and help where needed. Zadkiel could hardly contain her excitement at seeing the once empty space now full of her beautiful creations. She couldn't wait to know of God's reaction, she would be so proud, Zadkiel thought, and likely reward her greatly. Though in truth, The Almighty had been rather busy of late, focusing on some new department that Zadkiel didn't have time to find out about.

"Isn't it amazing sister?!" said Zadkiel, her eyes shining with joy.

"Indeed. It is an honour to carry out God's work," said Jophiel, showing far too little emotion as usual.

Zadkiel felt everything very deeply, perhaps because she was created to be the Archangel of Justice, and she often found it strange how little the other angels seemed to say or show with regards to their feelings. There was Jophiel, witnessing the creation of the entire universe, and all she could say was that it was an honour! *Tell that to your face!* Thought Zadkiel, but she decided against saying anything at all. They had been planning all this for ages, and the time had finally come, why did no one else seem excited?

She looked over towards Jupiter, that was her baby; her creation. The Almighty had realised that she had an extra space for another planet, so had asked her favourite angel to design one with leftover star materials. Zadkiel spent years planning its design; she was proud of its beautiful swirling pattern. It was the biggest planet, and the most interesting looking, Zadkiel thought, though she would never tell The Almighty that!

"We ought to go." Jophiel said suddenly, startling her sister after the long silence. "Or else we shall be late for the meeting."

Zadkiel couldn't believe that Jophiel was concerned about the meeting when they had the whole brand new universe to explore. But she knew Jophiel, like all the other angels she had an obsession with rules and duty.

Of course Zadkiel knew the importance of those things too, but she also couldn't help but think that they were not quite the priority right now. After all, the universe was only ever going to be created once. Was she not permitted to enjoy the occasion at all?

Zadkiel took her seat at the meeting with less enthusiasm than usual. The Seat of the Archangels was a table at which all the archangels gathered to make decisions and plans. As the Leader of the Angels, it was Zadkiel's job to head up the meetings, with her sister beside her acting as her second in command.

Zadkiel looked down and absentmindedly rubbed her finger along the rough edge of the table. Jophiel nudged her and shot her a look which said *what is wrong with you? Get on with it!* Zadkiel sighed, she wanted to see her beloved Jupiter up close, and she wanted someone, *anyone* to be interested or care that she had just created the universe! But no one did.

The meeting seemed to go on far longer than usual, but it likely didn't. Zadkiel was simply highly distracted with thoughts of her creation. Jophiel chose to recount their day creating the universe to the group. She said it was because Zadkiel had to focus on leading the meeting, but really Zadkiel knew that her sister thought she would get too excited, so didn't trust her. Angels didn't really show emotions, not properly, their purpose was simply to serve God; but Zadkiel always felt things fiercely and the others didn't care for that.

Midway through the tale, Zadkiel tried to add a point to Jophiel's story, but her sister gave her a rather nasty sideways glance and hurried on with the next part.

Zadkiel experienced a feeling she never had before. She felt a little like everyone in the room disliked her, and as though nothing she had to say mattered. She was supposed to be their leader, how could she continue on with her Heavenly duty if the other archangels didn't respect her?

She was barely listening when Gabriel was discussing the Earth department's progress with their 'human' designs, and as soon as the meeting finished, she left, not even turning back when Jophiel shouted after her asking where she was going.

Zadkiel walked down one of the endless corridors, feeling strangely empty. She had been so excited about this day, yet now the deed was done, no one cared... She stopped walking and leaned against the wall. Pretty much since she was created, she had been working on the stars and planets, and now it was all over in a moment. What next?

She suddenly experienced something very strange; her eyes began to sting, and Zadkiel discovered water when she touched them. She was both fascinated and terrified. Humans would one day cry all the time of course, but angels shouldn't; crying hadn't really been invented yet. No angel had ever cried before, and Zadkiel wasn't sure what it was or what was wrong with her.

Soon though, she had to force herself to stop, as she heard footsteps approaching. She furiously wiped the water from her eyes, still unaware that they were tears, and stood up straight, adjusting her robes slightly. An angel came into view down the corridor, she looked to be a small-order angel, and Zadkiel was surprised to see that she was actually smiling. Most angels didn't smile, not with genuine joy like that anyway! As she approached, the angel noticed Zadkiel and her eyes widened, she almost looked frightened, Zadkiel thought.

"Hello!" called Zadkiel. After feeling so unwanted by the other archangels, she decided she might as well attempt conversation with this angel, whoever she was.

The other angel looked truly startled, and glanced behind her to see if there was anybody more important that Zadkiel could be addressing. She turned back, having confirmed that she was quite the only angel around, and blinked at Zadkiel, obviously taking in her archangel regalia.

"Are you talking to me, Your Highness?" she asked uncertainly.

"Yes," Zadkiel replied softly, moving closer, as she realised the other angel wasn't intending to take another step in her direction. "Are you busy?" she asked, knowing full well that angels are always busy. Apart from her perhaps, now that she had finished her job.

"Indeed not…" said the angel nervously. "I am an assistant in the Earth department, but rather a lot of that is simply standing around without much to do when the higher angels don't need help…" she paused, meeting Zadkiel's eye shyly where she had been looking at the floor. "Ought I be doing something? Do you, need something, Your Highness?"

Zadkiel considered the question. She knew that small-order angels were always rather frightened of her, in command as she was, but that meant that they would do whatever she asked of them. Right now all Zadkiel wanted was to show someone, anyone, her magnum opus that the others had shown no interest in.

"Can I show you something?" she asked, still finding herself nervous for the rejection she knew wouldn't come from an angel like this one.

The other angel let out a small gasp. "Of course Your Highness!" she said, trying not to show how much joy and excitement was bubbling up inside her.

"Brilliant! Come on then!" grinned Zadkiel, taking the angel's hand. They both looked at their hands for a moment. Neither angel had held the hand of another before, it felt strange. Zadkiel gulped uncomfortably, before hastily drawing her hand down to miraculously transport the two of them close to Jupiter.

The angel looked truly startled. Once she got over the initial surprise of the sudden change of location though, she stared around in awe at all the stars and planets around them. There was silence for a moment, as she fully took in the sight. Zadkiel watched her intently, a warm feeling spreading through her, as someone enjoyed her creation.

"What is this? It's truly amazing!" asked the angel.

"It's the universe!" announced Zadkiel proudly. "Those are stars, and those ones are called planets!"

"Did you create all this?" the angel said in wonder.

"Yes! Well, me and God, oh my sister helped too, but not so much with the design..." She, in fact, struggled to think of anything that Jophiel had contributed to the project, but she would never say that out loud of course!

"This is the most wonderful thing I have witnessed, Your Highness! It is glorious!" said the angel, her eyes shining with joy.

Zadkiel smiled, the warm feeling now welling up inside her almost unbearably, but somehow in a good way, as if she may well explode, but with happiness?

"Thank you!" she said proudly. "And there is no need for 'Your Highness', that makes it sound like I'm better than you... I am Zadkiel."

"Oh I know who you are!" said the angel, almost indignantly as though she were offended that Zadkiel would doubt it. "And you *are* better than me! By far... I'm just an unimportant assistant!"

"Everyone's important!" said Zadkiel, horrified that this angel thought so little of herself. "What is your name dear angel?"

"My name?" said the angel, shocked that the leader of the archangels would care to know her name. "My name is Ophelia..."

"That's a beautiful name, it suits you," said Zadkiel, feeling especially inclined toward kindness now that someone had taken an interest in her work. "Tell me Ophelia, which part do you like the most?"

Ophelia smiled at hearing her name spoken so warmly by the leader of Heaven. "Oh well it is all simply stunning!" she smiled. "But I believe that orange-y planet is particularly fascinating, the biggest one..." Ophelia pointed towards Jupiter and Zadkiel smiled excitedly.

"That's Jupiter!" she announced proudly. "That's my planet. I designed it. I'm so glad you like it!"

"It's incredible!" said Ophelia. "Will it be visible from Earth?"

"Earth?" questioned Zadkiel. "Err, I should think so, but it would most likely simply appear as a small dot from that distance. Why?"

"Because Archangel Gabriel said that The Almighty wants the humans to be able to enjoy looking at the stars at night, that's what they are for! I hope they can see Jupiter too."

"That's their only purpose?" asked Zadkiel. "God has been quite busy with a new project recently, is that the Earth?"

"I believe so," Ophelia said, clearly nervous to upset the mighty Zadkiel. "She is quite taken with it. It is to be the only planet that can support the humans, after all her experimenting with these planets, she has finally got the temperature and gravity right and all that. Not that I understand any of it! The Earth to be the centre of the universe in God's eyes I believe…"

Zadkiel was stunned, she suddenly wished she had paid attention to Gabriel detailing the Earth department's work. She hadn't thought that the Earth was going to be all that important, in fact she had wondered why it needed its own department. It was tiny compared to everything else they had been working on. Did God truly view all of this as experiments?! She glanced over to the space where the Earth was going to be.

"It's not in the centre of the universe though is it? And it's going to be tiny compared to some of the others!" She gestured towards her beloved Jupiter. "Why is that one planet such a big deal?"

"Truthfully I don't know," Ophelia said. "I suppose

it is part of God's plan? All I know is that it's important that the humans enjoy the stars..."

"Thank you for coming to see all this," said Zadkiel. "No one else seems that bothered, and even The Almighty hasn't had time to come and look at it..."

"I am truly honoured Zadkiel," said Ophelia, seeming nervous to call her by her name. "As I said, it is the greatest thing I have seen. Thank you for allowing me to witness it."

"Aside from me and Jophiel, you are the first angel to see it!" smiled Zadkiel.

Ophelia took in a breath and looked about once again, enjoying the honour.

Zadkiel looked at Jupiter, even she hadn't seen it up close yet. "Ophelia!" she said, excitement almost consuming her. "Shall we be the very first beings to see Jupiter up close? To stand upon it?"

"Is it safe to stand on?" Ophelia asked doubtfully, obviously knowing the Earth was to be the only planet suitable to live on.

"Absolutely not! It's mostly gas!" smiled Zadkiel, her eyes shining with an almost mad sense of possibility. "But I will keep you safe. I promise no harm shall come to you while you're with me." She offered out a hand to Ophelia, who took it nervously.

Zadkiel transported them onto Jupiter and used her magic to ensure they could safely stand on it. They both looked around, they had never seen anything so vast, it stretched out for as far as they could see. The planet made them both seem rather small and Zadkiel was overcome with the thought that *she* made it.

She glanced towards Ophelia and suddenly realised that she still had Ophelia's hand in hers. She panicked, not wishing to make her new friend feel uncomfortable; angels barely ever touched one another. She quickly released the hand and Ophelia looked down at it as she did. Zadkiel wished she could tell what she was thinking, but she couldn't. After a moment Ophelia caught her eye and smiled shyly again, then hastily continued looking out to space. Zadkiel shifted her gaze out as well, taking in all the stars. This was a little like what they would look like from God's precious Earth. Was all this really just pointless? Was it all just to be looked at?

The angels stood together on Jupiter staring out at the stars in silence. Both lost track of how long they had been standing there, but it didn't matter.

Aside from that first meeting, which meant a great deal to both of them, Ophelia only met Archangel Zadkiel one other time before her fall, but it somehow meant almost as much.

The chance to see the archangel again came during one of the Earth department's many gatherings where Ophelia had nothing to do, as usual. She was gazing out towards where she knew all the stars and planets were beyond the clouds.

"Angel Ophelia!" called Archangel Gabriel, startling her out of her daydreaming. There was always so little for her to do that her mind often wandered like that.

"Yes, Your Holiness?" she said, quickly scurrying to his side.

"Can you handle an important task?" Gabriel

asked, rather patronisingly in Ophelia's opinion.

"Yes, Your Holiness…" Ophelia answered suspiciously.

"I need you to deliver these notes to the Archangel Zadkiel," said Gabriel, presenting a folder of papers. "They detail how the Earth shall fit into the rest of the universe."

"To Zadkiel?" Ophelia quickly took the notes, excitement spreading across her face.

It was Zadkiel she had been daydreaming about. It was the greatest honour that she was chosen by the archangel to see the universe, and since that day she had been hoping for a chance to see her again. There was just something about her that Ophelia couldn't quite put her finger on. Well of course there was the power; she was the most powerful archangel, the one that worked with The Almighty to plan the entire universe! The angel who put in motion matter, gravity, light and all that other important stuff that Ophelia didn't really fully understand, but knew were vitally important.

Ophelia clutched the notes tightly to her chest as she navigated the many Heavenly corridors in search of Zadkiel's office. She found herself a little nervous. It definitely wasn't just Zadkiel's power that Ophelia found fascinating, there was certainly something else… She couldn't possibly begin to understand what it was though.

Ophelia reached the door to the office. Even though she was there on official business, she almost felt that she would be inconveniencing the archangel. She knocked softly on the door.

"Come in!" came the cheery voice from within.

Ophelia hadn't been expecting the Head of the Archangels to be sitting on the floor drawing, but there she was. There was a perfectly good desk behind her at which she could sit, but the choice to sit upon the floor instead made Ophelia smile. Zadkiel looked up and grinned when Ophelia came in.

"Ophelia right?" she said cheerily. "How can I help you?"

"Oh, well I've been asked to deliver these notes to you," Ophelia answered nervously, slightly flustered that Zadkiel remembered her name from that one meeting. She had no doubt met almost every angel, and many were of far more importance than her.

"What are they?" asked Zadkiel, continuing to draw.

"Err, it's information about the Earth?" said Ophelia, glancing at the notes slightly. Truthfully she wasn't entirely sure what they were, she was just the messenger. She wasn't ever involved in any decision making, and she wasn't important enough to be told anything. "I think it's getting closer to the time now, when they'll be starting it all up, you know?"

"Okay thanks, I'll take a look in a minute," Zadkiel said, putting out her hand to take the notes, but not looking up from her drawing. Ophelia handed them to her quickly, and of course planned to leave straight away, but then she noticed something familiar on the floor beside Zadkiel.

God had a set of very detailed plans for each of her strange creatures; all were fascinating, and all were rather odd in Ophelia's opinion. There was the kangaroo with a pocket in which they shall keep other kangaroos; there was the hedgehog, all over with sharp twigs; and the ostrich, which was a bird that could not fly, but could run unnecessarily fast. Ophelia often wondered how God came up with them all.

"Are those The Almighty's animal plans?" She asked, recognising the images of a crab and goat among the papers.

"Yes, I'm just borrowing them," smiled Zadkiel, her eyes shining in an excited yet angelic way that Ophelia found rather beautiful and endearing. "Look, I'm designing pictures in the stars!" She proudly held up strange sketches of a lion and a bear with shiny dots over them.

"Ooh, lovely!" said Ophelia encouragingly. "What exactly for?"

"Well, you mentioned before that God wants these humans to enjoy looking at the stars, so I thought it would be fun to add some little hidden details for them to find!" Perhaps it was this bubbly, impulsive, almost cheeky element that Ophelia found so interesting in Zadkiel.

Ophelia smiled. "That is a lovely idea! Perhaps one could be in the shape of an angel?" she suggested. "To remind the humans who created the stars?"

Zadkiel said nothing, but smiled as she put the drawings down and picked up the plans that Ophelia had brought.

"Sorry, I should probably go," Ophelia said hurriedly. "You are obviously very busy, and Gabriel gets rather annoyed if I'm not quick enough with my tasks..."

Zadkiel laughed. "I bet he does! Thanks for bringing these."

"You are most welcome!" smiled Ophelia. "I look forward to seeing your, err, what do you call those star pictures?"

"Constellations!" said Zadkiel, flicking through the Earth notes. She stopped on one page near the back and frowned.

"What's wrong?" asked Ophelia in concern.

"Oh, err, nothing..." Zadkiel said in a very unconvincing way.

Ophelia wished she could push further, but she knew it wasn't her place. She took a step backwards towards the door, but hesitated. Zadkiel must have noticed her look of concern, because she gave a rather forced smile.

"Truly, everything is fine... I am sorry, you have work to do, I don't want to keep you or for you to get in trouble."

"I actually don't really have anything to do at the moment..." said Ophelia, worried about her new favourite angel. She had never seen an angel look so sad. Angels should never be sad, everything was supposed to be wonderful! Ophelia wasn't certain if it was appropriate to ask, but after a pause, decided that she would regret it if she left Zadkiel without knowing what was troubling her. "Please, whatever is wrong?" she asked shyly.

"Honestly, it is rather silly," Zadkiel said. "Only, I cannot believe that all we worked for, all I poured my passion into, all I was created for, is largely meaningless..."

"Whatever do you mean?" asked Ophelia, moving towards Zadkiel, wondering whether she ought to kneel beside her or not.

"I worked with God to make the stars and the planets, the whole universe, yet it all clearly means nothing to her! This *Earth* is the only thing that is important now. That's where the humans will live, and all these animals!" She glanced down at the animal plans in front of her. "The rest of the universe is just pointless... Just to look at! And guess what, it won't look nearly as impressive from Earth anyway! The stars will be little shiny dots, and most of the planets won't be seen at all!"

"But it's all very impressive though?" suggested Ophelia, unsure of anything remotely useful to say. "I am certain that The Almighty will give you a new task now. Perhaps you could come and work with us on the humans? The designs are almost done, but there's still plenty to do!"

Zadkiel didn't look impressed by that suggestion. "I don't want anything to do with Earth or humans," she sighed. "God is far too obsessed with them! It's ridiculous! What makes the Earth so special?!"

Ophelia gulped. "I don't think it's wise to talk about The Almighty like that..." she said, glancing around worriedly. "We are not to question her! Everything she does is part of her great plan."

"What great plan?" said Zadkiel. "Does she even *have* a plan?! It all seems a bit random to me!"

"Of course it seems random to us," Ophelia said,

feeling rather uncomfortable by Zadkiel's questioning. "But to God it all makes sense." Ophelia paused, rather terrified by the thought of questioning God. "I actually really must go... The Archangel Gabriel really will be angry if I take much longer..."

"Of course," said Zadkiel, clearly aware that Ophelia looked uncomfortable. "Don't worry Ophelia, honestly. Everything is fine."

Ophelia nodded quickly, gave Zadkiel a warm smile, and then hastily backed out of the room.

That was the very last time Ophelia would see Zadkiel; as an angel anyway.

During the next monthly archangel meeting Ophelia was sitting in the Earth department offices among the other angels in her rank, the ones that tended to ignore her. With the archangels busy, all the other angels had time off, not that angels knew what to do with time off of course!

Ophelia was thinking of Zadkiel again, but specifically of all those worrying things that she said about God's plan. There was an ever-present threat in Heaven. When God created it, she also created another realm known as Hell. It was currently empty, but it was said to be a place where disobedient angels might be sent. There were all kinds of rumours about what could be down there, and what would happen to an angel sent there. It hadn't happened yet, and everyone assumed it never would, angels were pure beings after all, but the threat was still there.

As Ophelia continued to daydream, a strange dark feeling suddenly spread throughout Heaven. Everyone felt it. Everything fell silent and all the angels looked up from whatever they were doing. The room then erupted in confused chatter, as they all questioned what just happened. A few minutes later the Archangel Jophiel swept in.

"Good day angels!" she announced, addressing them with a strange, smug tone. "I am simply here to inform you that I am now your commander. I am the new Leader of the Archangels, and of Heaven in general. Please, continue on with your day." She began to sweep out as dramatically as she had arrived, and Ophelia quickly stood and ran after her, panic filling her. She followed her out into the corridor.

"Wait! Your Highness!" she called, reaching out and taking hold of Jophiel's robes. An inappropriate thing for a lesser angel to do, but she wasn't thinking straight.

Jophiel stopped and turned, staring Ophelia right in the eye. "Hello?" she said disapprovingly. "Is there a problem? Is something not clear?"

"If you are the leader of the archangels, then what happened to Zadkiel?" asked Ophelia, barely wishing to know the answer.

"The former Archangel Zadkiel is an angel no more," answered Jophiel simply, as if it were not her own sister she were referring to, or indeed any fellow being. "She is a fallen angel now, the very first demon, and unless you wish to join her in Hell I would advise that you forget about her."

"But, what happened?" Ophelia's voice was barely audible and choked with panic, she was so shocked and concerned. She didn't know that fallen angels became demons! There were none yet, but demons were said to be the antithesis of an angel, they represented everything bad. They were dark and evil, a nightmarish story that angels told each other, a little like humans would one day tell each other ghost stories. Zadkiel couldn't be a demon! She was the kindest angel Ophelia had met, and that was quite a feat as angels were created to be kind and loving.

"Zadkiel's true nature was revealed to us today," said Jophiel with a sad sigh that sounded a little fake in Ophelia's opinion. "She is evil and corrupt. She cannot be forgiven. Just know that we saved you all from such an adversary this day, and Heaven is a better place for it. Now, be off with you, and think no more of the former angel, but in pity. It is a poor damned soul that strays from God, may we be thankful that we remain in light." Jophiel nodded her head slowly towards Ophelia, a little like God did. Rather pompous, thought Ophelia.

Jophiel walked away and Ophelia watched her go, feeling rather strange. Was that true? Was Zadkiel really evil? She seemed so nice, so wonderful. But now she was a demon? Ophelia stood rooted to the spot out in the corridor, not far from where she had first spoken to Zadkiel. She felt a tear run down her face and wondered what was wrong with her. Angels were never this sad, they certainly didn't cry! She found the emotion strange, but oddly not unpleasant. In fact, she found that she wanted to allow the tears to come, as though they would heal her troubles.

In that moment she vowed to be sure to always follow God's plan unwaveringly. The thought of Hell terrified her, and the idea that Zadkiel; the only angel who had ever seemed to care about her, could fall was awful. What could she have possibly done?!

Ophelia stood crying in Heaven's corridor, and somewhere down in Hell, a demon was crying too...

Chapter Four
We're Off to Burn Down a Monastery!
(21st Century)

Ophelia stood in the kitchen, icing the cakes that she had just cooled with magic, because she was far too impatient to wait for them. She glanced out of the window. She could see the top of the church from there and she wondered how her love-filled priests were. She was telling the truth when she told Nessa that it broke her heart to see people unable to express their feelings due to duty, and that was mainly because it hit rather close to home.

She had loved Nessa since the beginning. When Nessa was an archangel, Ophelia couldn't stop thinking about her, a little like the way humans feel about their favourite celebrity. If their favourite celebrity was kind to them when no one else was! When Nessa became a demon, the idea of getting too close to her worried Ophelia, she'd heard terrifying stories about demons. But Nessa had always been nice to her, nicer than the other angels usually. (Even if she didn't always like Ophelia to mention it.) Over the years, she had grown to love her more and more, and Nessa was definitely the most important thing in her life. However, she could never admit how she truly felt, because both she and Nessa would get in lots of trouble. Heaven often used the Archangel Zadkiel as a bad example, her story was a warning to other angels about what might happen if you strayed away from Heaven and God's plan. Ophelia still wasn't certain what exactly Nessa did to get cast out of Heaven; she never wanted to talk about it, but she hated the way the other angels talked about her. Whatever she did, she didn't deserve the hatred she got, especially from Jophiel.

So for that reason, Ophelia had to be careful what she said about Nessa, she didn't want to give either realm more cause to hate her. Plus, on a rather more selfish note, Ophelia was absolutely terrified of falling, and becoming a demon herself.

She thought of when the priests confessed that they fancied each other and began kissing. Ophelia had felt such love in the room. Love that may never have been expressed due to fear of God, a fear Ophelia definitely shared. Angels didn't kiss, it was a human thing and the other angels thought it was very unholy. The thing was, Ophelia enjoyed all the other human things that angels disapproved of, and she knew she would like kissing. She couldn't imagine the scandal if an angel kissed a demon though, that was quite the least angelic thing she could imagine doing! She had once promised Jophiel that she wouldn't cause another scandal. Plus if she kissed Nessa, she was afraid she wouldn't be able to handle the feelings that she currently did a good job of bottling up. She imagined that a kiss might awaken something within her, and that was a scary thought. Or worse, it could somehow ruin everything between them, and Ophelia loved being her demon's companion more than anything.

Ophelia had just finished icing the cakes when there was a knock at the door, she sensed Nessa's energy and a big smile spread across her face. She was filled with that effervescent feeling of joy that she felt whenever Nessa was nearby. She quickly wiped the icing sugar from her hands and rushed to the door. She was always thrilled to see Nessa outside of their weekly meetings. Any chance to spend more time with her was welcomed.

Ophelia opened the door and Nessa stood on the doorstep holding a small bunch of white roses with that adorable smile that Ophelia loved.

"Come on my little mortal enemy, we're off on a trip!" announced Nessa, thrusting the roses in Ophelia's direction.

"What kind of trip?" asked Ophelia suspiciously.

"We're off to burn down a monastery!" Nessa said, almost triumphantly.

"Oh…" Ophelia said quietly, not entirely certain what her response should be to that statement. "And these are?" She gestured the flowers in her hand.

"A present!" Nessa said. "You gave me a present on Wednesday, so I thought I'd get you something. You like roses and the flowers in your vase are all dead, which doesn't really give off a 'welcome to my cosy cottage' vibe. Plus, these are white so they look angelic like you!"

"Oh, well thank you!" smiled Ophelia, trying

not to show how truly delighted she was that her demon brought her flowers like humans bring to their girlfriends. Then she remembered what Nessa had said. "I'm sorry, what's this about a monastery?"

"Oh yeah, it's some bullshit job that Lucifer's got me doing," sighed Nessa. "But I figured it might be kinda fun if you come?" Nessa paused as Ophelia gave her a disapproving look. "I'm not saying that the burning down bit will be fun, but it's up in the Lake District, and we can go on the train if you want?"

"Hmm…" Ophelia paused, looking at the roses. "I do like the Lake District…"

"Exactly!" smiled Nessa. "That's why I thought of you when I saw the address!"

"Very well, I will come," Ophelia said, as if there was ever a doubt she would go anywhere Nessa asked. She would follow her beloved demon to the end of the universe if needed. "I just finished some cakes, so I'll bring them," she said excitedly.

She put the roses on the side table and started heading back towards the kitchen.

"Hey, Phee! Can I come in or what?" Nessa shouted after her.

"Oh, yes of course! Sorry…" Ophelia called back. She still sometimes forgot that demons need permission to enter into Heavenly spaces, and because an angel owned it, her cottage counted as such. It seemed a bit silly to be honest, Nessa was always more than welcome. Though it did protect Ophelia from all the other demons, who were, in her experience, a lot less friendly.

Ophelia packaged up the cakes along with a few

more of her and Nessa's favourite snacks, and when she got back to the hall, Nessa had replaced the dead flowers in the vase with the new roses.

"There you are!" said Nessa triumphantly. "Much more angelic!"

"Oh thank you Nessa. They look lovely!" smiled Ophelia. "It's a shame I won't see them much if we're going on a trip?"

"I'm sure they will miraculously survive until you're back," Nessa grinned.

Ophelia smiled. "You are sweet!" she said.

"Hey! Don't say that, you'll ruin my reputation... A bad reputation's all a demon has, right?" Nessa said with a slight smile. "Think of my feelings, I'm a terrifying Duke of Hell who's come to drag an angel up North via the Hellish public transport system so I can carry out The Devil's work, and all you can say is I'm sweet? I'm a fucking maniac!" she said with a curl of her lip and flash of bared teeth which Ophelia just found cute.

"Oh poor you!" Ophelia said sarcastically with a smile.

Long ago Nessa would have got defensive and angry if Ophelia had described her as sweet or kind, but over the years she reacted less and less aggressively and now just tended to make jokes about it.

When they arrived at the train station, they had a while to wait. Ophelia sat at one of the tables outside a coffee shop, while Nessa went off to buy the tickets. Ophelia watched all the humans rushing about and wondered what they were all doing. Who knew back in Eden when the first humans were wondering whether or not they ought to eat an apple, that humanity would create such a complicated world for themselves. Ophelia couldn't even blame Hell for it, because most of it was down to the humans. Strange creatures… For all their quirks though, Ophelia loved humans and the Earth; she always had, since Eden. In fact since then she had barely been back to Heaven. Even before she had an official job, she enjoyed experiencing life among the humans. There was always something fascinating going on so it was much more interesting than Heaven. Plus of course if she hung out on Earth there was a chance she might occasionally bump into a certain fallen angel who was back then, Hell's sole representative on Earth. Eventually Ophelia had been given the role of Guardian of the North of England, or more simply, as most people called her 'The Angel of the North' and she had settled to live in York. She had been extremely delighted when, not long after she got the job, Nessa announced that she had the equivalent job in Hell and was to live in York too. That was when they started their weekly meetings as official 'rivals'. Sometimes Ophelia wished that they didn't have to be rivals, that Nessa could somehow be an angel again so they wouldn't have to pretend to be enemies. But then, she loved Nessa just as she was, and even angels weren't supposed to care about each other as they did. Mostly Ophelia was perfectly content with her life and her relationship with Nessa, it was just the occasional frustrated moment that annoyed her; if she really thought about the injustice.

Two teenage girls walked into the coffee shop holding hands, then stopped at the back of the queue and gave each other a kiss. Ophelia smiled. She wondered whether life was simpler for humans, they didn't carry the burden of Heavenly duty as she did. She did know that many of them still struggled with morals, and the ones that worshipped her had the same fear of God that she had. However she envied their choice, not all humans lived their lives guided by Heaven, a lot of them didn't even believe in God. That must be nice, Ophelia thought - not to live in constant fear of judgement. And as far as she was aware good people went to Heaven whether they believed in God or not.

Suddenly, Ophelia was startled out of her thoughts by someone's hands on her shoulders.

"Hey little angel, do you want something from the coffee shop?" Nessa was standing behind her.

"You scared me!" said Ophelia.

"That was the intention," grinned Nessa, coming round to lean on the table. Ophelia gave her a mock-disapproving look. "The stupid train is delayed, so we'll have to wait for ages!" Nessa continued. "Bloody transport system!"

"Oh dear, foiled by your own dastardly invention?" smiled Ophelia.

"I know right? I designed it to inconvenience humans, not me! Anyway, do you want a drink or what?"

"Yes please, but not coffee! Your demonic inventions are causing enough trouble already. I'll have a tea please!"

A train announcement proclaimed that their train would be an hour late. Nessa pointed upwards as the tannoy spoke and shook her head before heading into the coffee shop.

Ophelia smiled as she thought about how either one of them could transport them both to the Lake District in seconds, but neither of them were going to suggest it, because they enjoyed taking the train together. Plus it turned a very quick job into a weekend together, so Ophelia certainly wasn't going to complain.

When Nessa returned she had their drinks and a little pot of something else hot.

"They had little soups, so I got you one!" Nessa said proudly.

"Soup?" queried Ophelia, looking at the contents of the pot.

"Yeah, I thought it might be something you'd like, and it's even labelled as vegan! Well, it's vegetable soup so you'd think it would be vegan, but you can never be sure right?"

Ophelia laughed. "Thank you Nessa. Do you want one of the cakes to go with your coffee? They're chocolate."

"I thought you said my demonic inventions were causing trouble? Yet you make cakes with chocolate?" smiled Nessa, taking the cake Ophelia offered.

"Well, that was the one good demonic thing you created," said Ophelia, taking a sip of the soup.

"What an endorsement!" Nessa said. "Hey, speaking of my inventions, let me take a picture of the drinks and stuff for Instagram."

"You have some social media?" asked Ophelia in concern as Nessa arranged the things on the table.

"Yeah I have Insta."

"Do they know you're a demon?"

"Nah, they just think I'm a moody bitch!" grinned Nessa as she took a photo.

"Right, well make sure I'm not in the picture. The angels could use it as some kind of evidence or something…" Ophelia said worriedly.

"Angels don't have Instagram," Nessa said, picking up the cake to eat it.

"Well, still… Better safe than sorry," Ophelia said as she stirred sugar into her tea.

When their train finally arrived, it was a pleasant trip. One mostly filled by Ophelia quietly reading her book to Nessa, really hoping she wasn't annoying the other passengers too much, while Nessa gazed at her fondly and pretended to be interested; eating most of the snacks.

Eventually the two of them stood on the edge of Lake Windermere. Ophelia looked out to the lake as the sun began to set, admiring one of her favourites of The Almighty's beautiful creations. Ophelia helped to decide the placement of all the lakes and rivers, so she had a particular soft spot for them. While she stared out at the water, Nessa stood beside her quietly muttering about something on her phone.

"Hey, you're an angel!" Nessa said, nudging Ophelia.

"Observant…" Ophelia said, not shifting her gaze, but allowing a small smile to spread across her face.

"Do you know where this damn monastery is?" Nessa continued, not acknowledging Ophelia's sarcastic comment, but failing to hide her smile at her angel's silliness. "The map isn't loading, and if a demon can't get it to work then God help any human trying to work it right now, not that God would care of course!"

"No, she would be far too busy with important matters to help with the Internet," Ophelia said.

"Nah, I was going to go for the fact that she doesn't care about helping anyone!"

"Nessa, please! Be careful how you talk about The Almighty!" Ophelia said worriedly. "You could get us *both* in trouble!"

Ophelia knew that demons wouldn't really get in trouble for bad mouthing God, but she was afraid that she might, by association. Nessa knew that too and quickly stopped, seeming rather guilty.

"Anyway," Ophelia said. "Which monastery are you looking for, is it near here?"

"Yes, but I don't know the name, Beelzebub has got notoriously bad handwriting…" Nessa handed Ophelia the crumpled note.

Ophelia studied the scruffy piece of paper. "St Jophiel's Monastery?" she said after a moment. "You can't destroy that!"

"Why not? I'll enjoy destroying anything that bears Jophiel's name!" Nessa said with a grin.

"It's sacred!" Ophelia said, handing the note back with perhaps a little more aggression than she intended.

"All monasteries are sacred," Nessa said.

"But that one is a particular favourite of The Almighty! And Jophiel for obvious reasons… It's very old and rather important. Heaven won't like it at all!"

"That's probably the point," said Nessa. "Any chance to piss off The Almighty, you can bet Lucifer will be on it!"

"Yes, but..." Ophelia struggled to think of anything that might convince Nessa. "It was the first monastery! Jophiel herself protected it back when that King Henry was destroying them all!"

"Yeah, well I was the first angel. Things get ruined!" snapped Nessa.

"Come on, that's not fair!" Ophelia protested.

"Do you know where this bloody monastery is or not?" asked Nessa, starting to sound rather angry.

"I do, but I'm not going to tell you!" said Ophelia curtly. "I am the Guardian of the North, I cannot aid you in destroying God's favourite monastery!"

"Oh come on Ophelia! You're already here, you knew what I'm here to do, you might as well help now!" sighed Nessa.

"No!" said Ophelia firmly. "I won't stop you destroying it, but I absolutely won't help!"

"For fuck's sake Ophelia, don't make me *take* the information from you!" Nessa had lost her temper now, likely from annoyance at having to do the job rather than at Ophelia. Ophelia still took it personally though, and was horrified by the threat.

Demons have the ability to extract information from people, and particularly angels. It is a mild form of possession, and the only type that can be done on angels. Nessa had only done it to Ophelia once, way back thousands of years ago. She used to threaten it quite often, because she knew it was something she had over Ophelia, but she hadn't threatened for hundreds of years now. Ophelia had assumed that now they were as close as they were, Nessa wouldn't threaten her like that anymore. Rather than matching Nessa's anger, Ophelia chose to try to reason with her demon, appeal to her kind side.

"Don't you dare," she said calmly, stepping away from Nessa. "I'm not being unreasonable. It is already a risk my coming here with you, but I wanted to. However, if I am found to be helping you to destroy that place, Jophiel will absolutely lose it! I already can't imagine her reaction to you destroying it, but if I help you? Good Lord, Jophiel's wrath rivals God's… Please Nessa, don't put me in more danger."

Nessa took a long sigh as she looked at her angel's pleading eyes. She glanced over towards the lake cruise kiosk. "I'll ask them," she said after a pause.

As Nessa walked towards the kiosk, Ophelia let out a small sigh of relief. She knew that no matter how much of the evil demon was showing, underneath it all was someone who would always protect her. She never doubted it, but she felt that Nessa had taken things a little far just then.

Ophelia didn't speak to Nessa the whole way to the monastery, and as they neared its gates, Nessa grabbed Ophelia by the arm, stopping her.

"Phee, listen. I'm sorry!" she said, still gripping Ophelia's arm, a little too hard in truth. "I shouldn't have threatened you, I was just getting frustrated."

"It is not okay to forcibly take information from someone. Even to threaten it. Invading someone's mind is not right. And you're hurting my arm." Ophelia pulled her arm from Nessa's grip.

"I know, I'm sorry," Nessa sighed. "If it helps I wasn't actually going to do it. I will never do that to you, I promise!"

Ophelia looked into Nessa's eyes. She saw kindness, as well as desperation; a desperation not to lose Ophelia over a silly argument.

"I forgive you," Ophelia said, after making Nessa wait a few moments. Nessa looked relieved. Demons were known to be unforgivable to angels, by their very nature, so Ophelia knew how much it meant to Nessa whenever she said that out loud.

"Now, I am sorry dear angel, but I really must destroy this thing before Lucifer throws me into the ninth circle!" Nessa said, walking towards the monastery gates. She commanded the gates to open with a flick of her hand and stood on the threshold.

"You can't go in there, it's consecrated ground!" Ophelia said, knowing it would hurt Nessa.

"It won't be for long!" said Nessa, rubbing her hands together, preparing for large-scale demon magic.

"What are you going to do?" asked Ophelia nervously, glancing at Jophiel's name adorning the gate.

"This!" said Nessa theatrically. She swept her hands upwards, drawing power from Hell, and in a moment the North side of the monastery was engulfed in flames.

Ophelia gasped in horror. "Nessa!" she cried. "Monks still live there!"

"Well then you'd better go and warn them!" yelled Nessa, using her hand to guide the flames.

Ophelia rolled her eyes and dashed towards the South side of the building. She noted as she ran, that the side that Nessa had set fire to was the chapel, and no monks would be there right now as it was evening. Of course Nessa didn't really want to hurt the innocent monks.

Ophelia rushed into the monastery. It had been over two thousand years since she had performed a proper divine message, but this seemed to call for it.

"Be not afraid!" she yelled, in perhaps not the most angelic way, but then the building was actively burning down and humans were notoriously flammable. "For I am an angel of The Lord come to guide you devoted souls to safety!"

The monks stared at her in utter bewilderment.

"Who are you child?" asked one of them. Apparently not one had noticed that their monastery was on fire.

"I am an angel of The Lord!" repeated Ophelia. Surely if anyone would believe she was an angel it was monks! However they all continued to stare at her as if she were insane.

"Listen love, we might be monks, but we're not stupid," said a monk.

"Brother David, please! Be kind," said another.

"Please listen to my message! You are in grave danger!" Ophelia said, glancing worriedly towards the door that led to the North Wing. She wondered why none of the monks had noticed the burning smell, or heard the cracking of heated wood.

"You don't look like an angel..." said a monk. In

truth Ophelia was a little offended by this remark. "I thought angels had wings!"

"I do have wings, I just don't tend to have them on Earth!" Ophelia sighed before continuing. "If I prove I have wings will you heed my warning?" She felt that people were far more open to divine messages back in the day.

"It would help!" said the same monk with a laugh.

Ophelia let her wings sprout for the first time in many years. She stretched them as they ached after all this time. The monks stared in amazement at Ophelia's soft feathery white wings.

"Now!" she said, spreading her wings in an attempt to make herself look more impressive and commanding. "Your monastery is alight as we speak. The fire shall soon spread. A demon seeks to destroy your home this night!"

"A demon?!" said one of the monks in fear. Clearly deciding that, if angels truly exist and roam around on Earth, why not demons?

"Yes, The Devil himself has condemned this building to destruction," Ophelia said.

Before she could say anything else, the door to the North Wing fell down with an almighty crash. Behind it was a raging inferno, and a demon standing directly in the middle of the flames.

"She's right! I am a demon, come to destroy this place, and anyone still foolish enough to remain inside!" Nessa bellowed in a scary demonic voice. The monks all began screaming and made their way rather clumsily outside. Nessa looked Ophelia up and down and raised an eyebrow. "Nice wings!" she said with a small bite of her lip. Ophelia thought that Nessa looked oddly striking and beautiful in the doorway amidst the fire, flames licking around her body. However, a demon standing in a burning monastery was just about the least angelic image Ophelia could imagine, so she really shouldn't be as impressed as she was. The two stood gazing at each other for a few moments, then there was a crash from behind Nessa as part of the building collapsed.

"Shall we go?" Nessa said quickly.

"Indeed!" said Ophelia, noting the faint sound of a fire engine approaching.

Ophelia's wings disappeared and they ran out around the back in order to avoid the monks, though they were understandably terrified of Nessa by this point so it wouldn't have mattered much anyway.

"I didn't think you'd come in," said Ophelia. "I thought it would hurt you."

"Once enough of it is destroyed, it's no longer consecrated," Nessa said as they slipped through the back gate.

Once they were well away from the building, they stopped to look at the blaze. Ophelia felt that it was a great shame. Not because it was God's favourite monastery, more generally. It was a beautiful building that had stood there untouched for a very long time compared to a lot of buildings. She wondered why Lucifer was so desperate to destroy it.

"Come on Phee!" said Nessa, startling the angel. "Let's go get something to eat before we go to the hotel! I hear there is a new place that has lovely vegan meals.

Then tomorrow we can look for some good for you to do, to balance all this out if you want?"

Ophelia nodded and reluctantly followed Nessa away from the burning site. She wondered how The Almighty and Jophiel would react when they found out about this. Not very well she imagined.

Chapter Five

Somewhere in the Middle.

(Four Thousand Years Ago)

The Demon Nessa and the Angel Ophelia had been working together on the odd job since they discovered that, surprisingly, their morals tended to align. Both would likely trace the origins of their partnership back to the story of Abraham. The Bible stated that the Archangel Zadkiel was involved in the tale, which was true, only, said archangel had been a demon for a considerable amount of time by this point.

As Hell's sole representative on Earth, it was Nessa's job to keep an eye on things and report anything of interest back down to Lucifer. She had always hated the Earth, and she wasn't keen on humanity either. After all, the Earth and its stupid humans were entirely to blame for Nessa becoming a demon! Well, that's what she said anyway. She and Beelzebub shared the job of being Lucifer's right hand demons, and one of them had to stay to run things in Hell, while the other went to Earth. Neither demon wanted anything to do with Earth, but Nessa drew the short straw and was still extremely bitter about it all these years later.

On this particular day, Nessa was sulking around looking for any hint of trouble among the good God-fearing humans. The problem was, Nessa found a lot of God's own ideas to be questionable, hence her being a demon. So it was rather hard to tell what human activity concerned Hell and what was considered Heaven's business. For example, Nessa would never have guessed that the very first human action to evoke The Almighty's wrath would be eating a piece of damn fruit! That was a long time ago; almost two thousand years, but Nessa sometimes thought about that angel. She really hoped that The Almighty believed her and that Angel Ophelia didn't get into trouble. Whilst Nessa told Ophelia that she had taken credit for selfish reasons, in truth it had been for Ophelia. As a demon she wasn't supposed to be particularly nice to angels, and to most she wouldn't be. Smug, self-centred little things! But Nessa had two motives for helping Ophelia that day. Firstly, underneath it all, as an angel Nessa had been created to be the Archangel of Justice, and though she was now a demon, she found it hard to shake that part of herself. If anything she had stronger feelings regarding justice as she had suffered the worst injustice herself. She found it mightily unfair that the angel would be punished simply for trying to help. The second reason that she stepped in that day was that, whether Ophelia remembered or not, many years ago, she was once kind to her when Nessa felt that no one else was, so it was only right that she return the favour.

Nessa noticed a man she recognised as Abraham,

one of Heaven's particular favourites she believed. He was loading a cart with exactly the kinds of things one would require for a sacrifice. Nessa paused, thinking this was rather unusual, and she sensed some strange negative energy. Abraham's son Isaac came out of the house and tapped his father, asking him a question. Abraham nodded as he answered, but as his son skipped away, his face turned sad and remorseful. Nessa decided to approach him, something odd was definitely happening here.

"Excuse me?" said Nessa. "I was simply wondering what you are doing with all those supplies this fine day sir?"

Abraham was startled by Nessa, as though he were deep in thought as she spoke.

"Oh, good day child," he said.

Nessa looked him up and down slightly. It seemed strange for this human to refer to an over two thousand year old demon as 'child', but then what did she expect, she was disguised as a human.

"Who are you?" asked Abraham with an air of suspicion.

"A concerned citizen of Earth," said Nessa. Which of course is rather an unusual way for a human to describe themselves, but Nessa hadn't been masquerading as one for very long. Abraham obviously noticed this strange turn of phrase, but he smiled kindly nonetheless.

"I am simply preparing for a day journeying up the mountain. I am to make a sacrifice to Almighty God," he said, an air of sadness clouding his words.

"I see..." said Nessa, noting the materials in the cart

and the sadness in Abraham's voice; not to mention the way he watched his child go with regret. "What kind of sacrifice?" she asked suspiciously.

"The ordinary kind," Abraham said quickly. "I was commanded by a messenger of The Almighty, it is between myself and God. Good day child!" He then hastily continued on with his preparations.

Nessa stepped away. It all seemed highly suspicious. From where she was standing it seemed as though Abraham planned to sacrifice Isaac. Surely not, and after all the fuss he made about wanting a son in the first place! Would God really tell the man to slaughter his own child? That seemed a little far, even for her.

Nessa stayed nearby, her interest piqued by this odd situation. And when Abraham set off towards the mountain, accompanied of course by his son, Nessa followed. At the foot of the mountain, Nessa noticed angelic energy, it must have been the angel that gave Abraham his instructions. Nessa wondered whether it was Jophiel. Based on her sister's behaviour last time she saw her, she wouldn't be too surprised if she was first to suggest sacrificing a child.

Nessa investigated, and discovered a nervous looking angel hiding among the trees. She recognised her at once as Ophelia.

"Angel Ophelia?" Nessa said.

The angel span around in a panic at hearing her name. Of course, she wasn't expecting anyone on Earth to know it. She gasped and took a step backwards when she recognised Nessa. Nessa stared at Ophelia, it had been a very long time since she had been in the presence of an angel, she wasn't sure how she felt. Ophelia certainly looked uncomfortable having a demon stare at her like that.

"Demon Zadkiel…" Ophelia said at last, her voice sounding small and meek.

"Nessa!" the demon corrected her with a snap. There was something horrible about hearing the name Zadkiel placed beside the word demon. That was why Nessa had changed her name, to differentiate between the archangel she was and the dark person she had become.

"Sorry…" Ophelia said. "What are you doing here?"

"Looking for trouble I guess. Same as usual," Nessa paused for a moment as she glanced up the mountain path that Abraham and Isaac were slowly trudging up. "What's his deal?" she asked.

"Hmm? In what way?" Ophelia said, seeming slightly flustered.

"What is he sacrificing?"

"Do not worry about it, it's Heaven's business…" Ophelia said quickly.

Nessa raised an eyebrow at the nervous looking angel. "Why won't you answer me? What's happening here?"

"I am not supposed to talk to demons!" Ophelia said simply. "You are sent to corrupt and tempt us."

"Oh I don't know, contrary to popular belief I wasn't the one who tempted Eve to eat that scandalous apple was I?" Nessa said with a smirk.

Ophelia flushed red with shame and took a step

back. "Please," she said. "I must go and oversee things with Abraham." She began to move away, but Nessa caught hold of her arm. Ophelia gasped at a demon touching her, she looked at Nessa in fear and Nessa just smiled.

"I'm not letting you go until you tell me what's going on here Ophelia!" Nessa could be quite sinister and threatening when she needed to be, though secretly her motives were far from demonic.

"I won't tell you!" Ophelia said, her voice shaking slightly with fear. "Even if I wanted to, I can't tell a demon about God's plans..."

"Well I need to know!" said Nessa.

Ophelia shook her head.

"Well then if you can't tell me, I'll have to force the information out of you! Then you don't have a choice, so it's not your fault!" She pushed Ophelia rather forcefully against a tree. Nessa noticed the terror in the angel's eyes and wondered if she was being a little harsh, but she had committed to the act now.

"What are you going to do to me?" asked Ophelia.

"*Take* the information!" hissed Nessa.

She put a hand on Ophelia's chest and summoned all her demonic power. It took a lot to invade the mind of an angel, that's why they can't really be possessed, angelic power is too strong; it has a higher frequency than that of a demon, and that acts as a sort of protection. As Nessa's power flooded Ophelia, her soft blue eyes turned a deep red. Her mind was under Nessa's control. Nessa was so impressed with herself, having never done this kind of magic before, that she almost lost concentration. She focused on extracting the information about Abraham. She could feel the angel's fear, it was almost overwhelming. She didn't especially want to frighten Ophelia, but the Archangel of Justice inside her couldn't bear to allow little Isaac to be killed by his own father.

"God has commanded Abraham to sacrifice his son to prove his devotion to her…" Nessa heard Ophelia's voice say, though of course no sound was coming from Ophelia apart from that of shallow breathing filled with terror.

Nessa pushed deeper, desperate to know *why* God would do this.

"It is a test to see if Abraham trusts God to bring Isaac back from the dead, as he didn't trust her as he waited to be blessed with a son…" came Ophelia's voice.

Before moving away, Nessa looked into Ophelia's eyes, it was odd to see them taken over by demonic energy. Nessa couldn't imagine this sweet little angel ever being a demon.

As Nessa released Ophelia from her grip and stepped away, Ophelia took in a deep breath and her stiff body relaxed. Her eyes returned to normal and she stood motionless against the tree, staring at Nessa, clearly wondering what the maniac was going to do now.

Nessa paced slightly. "Well that is ridiculous!" she said, her long dress whipping up fallen leaves as she turned. "Is The Almighty really *that* attention seeking?! What is the point, other than to traumatise people and potentially murder a young boy for no reason?" She turned to Ophelia for a response that never came.

Ophelia's gaze shifted to the ground and there was silence.

"Are you okay?" asked Nessa, wishing Ophelia to know that she never wanted to cause her any harm. Which is more than can be said for most demons who would jump at the chance to torture an angel.

"I'm fine," Ophelia said shortly, understandably rather annoyed at the demon.

"As I said, you haven't actually *told* me anything. Therefore Heaven cannot be angry at you!" said Nessa, desperately trying to justify the invasion of Ophelia's mind.

"Hmm..." said Ophelia with a tone that made it hard to ascertain the meaning. "I need to be up there to oversee the event." And with that, Ophelia disappeared, transporting herself to the top of the mountain.

Nessa followed immediately, startling Ophelia by appearing beside her. Ophelia said nothing, but sighed.

Abraham and his son were preparing the altar for the sacrifice.

"Father? Where is the ram that we are to sacrifice?" asked Isaac innocently.

"Almighty God shall provide the sacrifice when the time comes," answered Abraham, not looking at his son as he spoke.

"This is one of the most outrageous things your boss has ever done, and she has done some questionable things over the years!" said Nessa.

"We too must trust that God will save him," muttered Ophelia, though her face was filled with concern as the boy built his own sacrificial altar before them.

"Are you sure?" said Nessa. "What is she doesn't?"

"I don't doubt God," said Ophelia, sounding extremely unconvincing. "I trust in her judgement and her benevolence."

"Do you now?" said Nessa, giving the angel a sideways glance. "I don't!"

"That's why you are a demon!" whispered Ophelia viciously.

"Yes, because I question things. I don't follow blind faith until it's too late!" Nessa answered, rather frustrated at the trusting angel.

The humans finished building the altar and Abraham hesitated, obviously hoping to receive some divine message telling him not to go through with it, but no such message arrived. Nessa glanced at Ophelia, who also looked to the Heavens in concern.

"Where is your God?" whispered Nessa. "Would you really worship one who allows a young boy to be killed to prove a point? And of course that isn't counting all the other times that similar things have been ordered by The Almighty. The Flood for example? To name just one."

"Even if he is killed, God promised Abraham many descendants, so he will surely be resurrected," Ophelia said uncertainly.

"Is that a risk you are willing to take?" asked Nessa, glancing back towards the altar that poor little Isaac had now been tied to. Ophelia shifted nervously but said nothing. "Strange isn't it? How you are supposed to be on the side of good, yet you are all for killing the kid!"

Nessa hissed.

"I'm not!" Ophelia said in a panic as Abraham readied his knife. "But I don't know what to do! I can't disobey God!" She was close to tears now.

"I can!" said Nessa. And in a moment she turned her black dress white and stepped out onto the mountain. Ophelia gasped; she looked like an angel again.

"Halt!" announced Nessa, putting out a hand as she knew angels did when delivering God's mercy. "Do not end the boy's life this day!"

Abraham turned, his knife held aloft, and his eyes filled with tears. "Oh kind and compassionate angel! Is his life truly to be spared?"

"Indeed," said Nessa. "You have proved your faith in God and may make another sacrifice in his place." Suddenly Nessa felt angelic magic being cast behind her and a ram appeared beside Abraham. She smiled slightly, somehow feeling proud of Ophelia for helping, when she made it clear that she was terrified of doing so.

"You see my son!" Abraham said, untying Isaac. "I told you that God would provide the sacrifice. We must both have faith in their gracious heart!"

"But, you were willing to kill me father…" said Isaac in a small voice, clearly, and quite rightly, traumatised.

"Blame not your father," Nessa said. "The fear of God is a very powerful thing. But you are safe this day my child!" Nessa smiled warmly at Isaac, really enjoying playing at being an angel again, even if only for a few moments.

"Who are you kind angel?" asked Isaac.

"I am The Archangel Zadkiel, Angel of Justice,"

announced Nessa, which was only partly true, but it gave her a little bit of a thrill to say it.

Long ago the Angel Zadkiel had been destroyed, but for a moment she lived again. Whilst overall Nessa cared not for humans; blaming them for her troubles, she did wonder in that moment what the Archangel of Justice could have done on Earth if she had been given the chance. Then she remembered that real angels like Ophelia follow orders unquestioningly, no matter their own views. It was clear that Ophelia did not want the child to die, yet if Nessa had not stepped in he would have, and God showed no signs of coming to help. Nessa would far rather make her own judgement, than be bound to serve God, even if that meant being an evil demon.

The father and son thanked Archangel Zadkiel, and as she walked away she was right back to being Demon Nessa; Prince of Hell again. However a real angel was smiling at her and she found herself smiling back. It felt good to do something nice. Not even Heaven's version of nice, but her own version of nice. And the fact that it may well annoy God was just a bonus!

When Nessa and Ophelia reached the bottom of the mountain, Ophelia stopped and looked at Nessa.

"You saved him," she said after a moment.

"Yeah, I guess so," said Nessa.

"You have always been so nice and kind, you shouldn't be a demon," said Ophelia.

Nessa grabbed Ophelia by the front of her robes and pulled her close, desperate to prove she was still a demon. "I once told you not to say that and I absolutely meant it!" she snarled, her face almost touching Ophelia's. "Demons are *not* nice! What I did was defy God, that's demonic!"

Apart from the initial shock at being grabbed, Ophelia didn't look scared this time. In fact she was almost smiling at this wicked demon that had hold of her. Nessa could feel Ophelia's breath on her face and she stopped talking, still staring at her supposed enemy. It felt strange to be this close to anybody, but somehow especially Ophelia. The two stood looking at each other for a few moments, before Nessa suddenly shoved Ophelia away when the strange feeling became too uncomfortable to bear.

"Can I at least say that you are the nicest demon I have met?" asked Ophelia with a smile.

"I suppose so, if you must..." said Nessa with a sigh. "Thank you for the ram. That was quick thinking."

"You are welcome. And no harm came to it either. I couldn't bear to bring about the death of an innocent little creature..." Ophelia said.

"But you would let the child die?" questioned Nessa, confused by the angel's morals.

"Of course not!" Ophelia said indignantly. She hesitated. "Well, there was nothing that I could do. If it was God's will that the boy be slain, then there was nothing to be done..."

"There clearly was, because I did it!" Nessa said with a slight laugh.

"Yes, but I am an angel! I cannot disobey The Almighty. You are a demon, you can do whatever you want."

"You sound jealous, dear angel."

"Of course I'm not!" Ophelia said hurriedly. "It simply wasn't an option for me to help him."

"You did help though," said Nessa. "How about the ram?"

"I know! I'm a little worried... What with that and of course," Ophelia lowered her voice, "the apple thing. The threat of falling from Heaven haunts me!"

"You won't fall!" said Nessa. "I tell you what, anything you do that you think is bad or in any way questionable, tell them I did it, and I will play along. I promise!"

"Really?" said Ophelia in delight.

"Yep! And if I ever do anything good you can absolutely take the credit," smiled Nessa. She had never had a friend before, and she had liked Ophelia since she first met her in Heaven all those years ago. She wondered whether they might become friends.

"Can I ask you something?" Ophelia asked shyly.

"Sure," said Nessa.

"Do you agree with everything Hell does?"

"Absolutely not!" Nessa said. "They're a bunch of evil idiots. I know there are two sides; good and bad, but I sometimes feel like I'm maybe somewhere in the middle? On my own side. You could, join me on my side if you want?"

Ophelia's eyes widened. "I can't be on the same side as a demon!"

"Just on the things we agree on. I think we make a good team, an angel and a demon. We cover both bases, you know? Not officially, but if you agree that Isaac didn't deserve to die, then we were on the same side just then, weren't we?"

"I suppose we were…" said Ophelia nervously. "I'm not sure. Truthfully, I'm terrified of God and the Archangels…"

"Understandable," said Nessa. "That's why it would be good to have someone else on your side keeping an eye on you?"

Ophelia looked torn. She said nothing, but tears started to well up in her eyes.

"Just think about it," said Nessa, gently touching Ophelia's arm, causing her to flinch slightly. "But, no matter what side you are on, why don't we go for a drink to celebrate a job well done?"

"A drink?!" Ophelia said in horror. "A human drink? Angels don't consume human things…"

"Angels don't do lots of things!" laughed Nessa. "Come on, give it a try. I won't tell anyone."

"I think you're trying to tempt me…" said Ophelia.

"Do you now?" Nessa said with a grin. "You know, angels *can* consume human food, they just don't. It isn't a rule."

Ophelia didn't actually verbally agree to the drink, but she did follow Nessa to the tavern anyway. Just as she never explicitly stated that they were to work together, but they absolutely did.

Chapter Six
What Heaven are Planning.
(21st Century)

The stairway to Heaven is a very literal thing, but nowadays there is also a lift, which Ophelia was always grateful for, as a self-proclaimed lazy angel.

As the lift doors closed, Ophelia thought about the monastery. It was all over the news in the human world, and it was very likely a hot topic Upstairs too. Ophelia really hoped that Jophiel didn't know that she was there when it happened. She always found herself feeling a little nervous when making her monthly report to Jophiel and the others anyway. As though the angels might somehow be able to read her thoughts, or she might accidentally announce that she was in love with a demon.

As soon as she exited the lift she sensed something strange; an odd feeling clouded Heaven. As she entered the room where Jophiel and the other archangels waited for her, she detected some kind of bad energy; almost demonic in its negativity. The archangels all stared at Ophelia as she walked in, despite her having knocked and been asked to enter.

"Angel Ophelia!" said Jophiel as though she were addressing an audience full of people.

"Your Highness?" answered Ophelia uncertainly.

"You are close with Demon Nessa aren't you?" said Jophiel with an air of disgust. A wave of panic filled Ophelia. Before she could decide on a response, Jophiel continued. "Are you aware of what she did on Saturday?"

"No..." Ophelia lied.

"She declared war upon Heaven on behalf of Hell!"

Ophelia was stunned by this accusation. "Err, are you sure, your Highness?" she queried nervously. "I'm not sure that she would do that."

"Yet she did," insisted Jophiel. "To destroy Heaven's fondest monastery is to declare war on us! Lucifer knows what he is doing. We shall have to hurry our plan before his legions can form. And rather than simply quashing Hell's Earthly influence, we may have to destroy them all. I fear Heaven and Earth shall not be safe until no more demons remain..."

Ophelia's eyes widened. Surely Jophiel wasn't serious? Heaven wouldn't destroy Hell would they? Of course they have always been archenemies, but that was rather extreme, wasn't it? Was Heaven even capable of destroying Hell? Why now anyway?

"I agree Your Highness," said Archangel Gabriel. "Lucifer and his diabolical minions have corrupted our Earth for far too long! With them gone we can steer humanity back into light."

"St Jophiel's Monastery was the most sacred ground

in England!" said Jophiel. "I do not even know how my former sister was able to destroy it. The consecrated ground there was enough to not only burn a demon, but engulf them in flames!"

Ophelia had to hide a smile thinking of her precious demon standing in the monastery surrounded by flames of her own making.

"Ophelia. Did you know that Nessa was planning to declare war upon us?" asked Jophiel.

"No I didn't!" said Ophelia truthfully. "And I really don't think Nessa knew either. Or at least it definitely wasn't her idea. I believe I heard that she was sent by The Devil to do a mission, but that is all." Ophelia was desperate to defend her beloved friend.

"It doesn't matter if she knew or not, the deed is done!" sighed Jophiel. "And for that reason and many others I shall ensure that she is dealt with myself." She shot Ophelia a rather nasty look.

Ophelia was very aware that Jophiel had never really liked her, and her being so close to Nessa didn't help. Jophiel hated all demons, but it was clear to everyone that she hated Nessa by far the most intensely. Even so, what did she mean 'dealt with'? Ophelia was suddenly rather worried about Nessa. If the Head of the Archangels was after her specifically, she might not stand a chance… Ophelia glanced at the empty seat at the archangels' table. Beneath the moss she knew it bore Nessa's old name. It was always there, left to fall into ruin as a warning, and Ophelia couldn't stand it.

"Uriel, how is the plan progressing?" Jophiel asked the angel to her right.

The Archangel Uriel glanced at some notes on the table in front of her. "I believe everything is almost ready, your Highness," she said, "Michael and I have been working hard on a foolproof way to bring about the end of Hell, but I shall not disclose it now..." She looked in Ophelia's direction as she said the last part.

Jophiel nodded. "Raphael! Have you been in contact with The Almighty to seek authorisation?"

"Err, no Your Highness," Archangel Raphael said nervously. "I haven't seen her or heard from her since the monastery was destroyed. I don't know where she has gone..."

Ophelia found the idea that God had disappeared to be quite concerning, but it didn't seem to faze Jophiel.

"Very well, then we shall use our own judgement as we do when The Almighty is busy," she said. Some of the other archangels glanced at Zadkiel's empty seat and Ophelia wondered what that meant. Surely Jophiel wasn't the one that banished Nessa from Heaven? Only God can cast angels out...

As Ophelia made her monthly report, her mind was swimming with a hundred thoughts. She was utterly desperate to get back down to Earth, so that she could tell Nessa about all this. Surely the archangels couldn't really destroy Hell could they? But if they did, then as Jophiel said, no demons will remain! As an angel of course, Ophelia didn't give two figs about Hell or demons, apart from one. She couldn't let them destroy Hell if it meant destroying Nessa too! But she had absolutely no idea how to stop them.

Ophelia recounted the good deeds that she and

Nessa had done in Windermere on Sunday to make up for the monastery. Though of course she was careful not to mention the location in case the angels guessed that she was with Nessa as the monastery burnt. The more she spoke, the more uncomfortable she felt, so she was thankful when Jophiel eventually waved her away, dismissing her.

As soon as Ophelia exited the archangels' room she began to sprint down the corridor. No one ever runs down Heaven's corridors, unless apparently their best friend is in danger that is. As she ran, she careered straight past another angel, sending all the papers he was holding flying. He squeaked in concern and Ophelia stopped, turning to him.

"I'm sorry!" she said hurriedly.

The other angel looked down at the papers scattered about the corridor. Ophelia clicked her fingers and the papers were back in his hands. He gasped in surprise.

"Thank you..." he said. "Are you alright? Why are you in such a rush?"

Ophelia was very surprised that an angel would ask after her like that. Mostly they didn't seem to give a damn about anyone else, in Ophelia's experience.

"I am fine, thank you for asking," smiled Ophelia. "I just need to get to the lift as quickly as I can to tell my friend something. So sorry for knocking into you, I didn't see you."

"That's fine, people don't tend to notice me," said the angel with a smile that didn't match what he was saying. It was clear that he was a small-order angel like Ophelia was during creation, before she was given earthly duties. She remembered the feeling that she was just one of many and that no one really cared for or noticed anything she did. She smiled kindly at the angel, hoping that a friendly look might make him feel a little more appreciated.

"I'm sorry, I really must go," she said before running off down the corridor, leaving the other angel rather confused.

As soon as Ophelia arrived back on Earth, she rushed to Nessa's flat. Whilst Ophelia had bought herself a beautiful cottage in the outskirts of the city which now looked like the kind of thing you would see on Pinterest, Nessa had never seen the point in getting anywhere fancy. Her flat was in the city centre and she viewed it more as just a base to come back to rather than a house. Neither demons nor angels require sleep, much like they don't require food, but similarly they could sleep if they wanted to. Nessa never did. If she slept she would have nightmares, so she hadn't been to sleep in a *very* long time. The function of her bed was very much to lounge upon, watching Netflix. Ophelia on the other hand had created such a cosy bedroom in her cottage that she loved to snuggle up to sleep in the bed. Perhaps not every night, but most of them. Ophelia could never understand why Nessa lived in that silly little flat. She couldn't imagine spending eternity living somewhere that didn't make her smile.

Ophelia rang the doorbell and waited nervously for an answer that couldn't come quick enough. Nessa would know who it was, as they decided long ago that if Ophelia ever rang the doorbell she would ring it three times to show it was her. This was because as a general rule, Nessa didn't tend to answer the door to anyone else.

Nessa opened the door with a smile, clearly delighted to have seen her angel so many times that week. However, her smile soon disappeared when she noticed Ophelia's look of concern.

"Phee, what's the matter?" she asked worriedly.

"Can I come in?" asked Ophelia, glancing around nervously as though archangels might be lurking in the streets.

"Of course. Are you okay?"

Ophelia didn't answer the question right away. She moved past Nessa into the flat, barely noticing the mess that she usually teased Nessa about. Somehow seeing Nessa's face had made the archangels' threat seem all the more real. What if they really did destroy the demons? Ophelia began to panic. Nessa came through, having closed the door and took Ophelia's hands.

"Talk to me silly angel. What's wrong?" she said with an air of genuine care and concern that Ophelia only ever witnessed from her.

"I know what they're planning!" Ophelia said breathlessly. "Well, sort of. I don't know exactly how, but it's awful!"

"What? Slow down, it's okay," said Nessa. "Sit down. Try to calm yourself a bit and breathe properly." Nessa led Ophelia to a chair and she reluctantly sat down, almost not wanting to calm down when Nessa might be in danger. "Hey, I said breathe properly!" Nessa said, perhaps a little too harshly, when Ophelia's breathing hadn't calmed after a moment.

Ophelia smiled a little in spite of herself at her demon's tough love. Nessa knelt on the floor in front of Ophelia, still holding her hands.

"Now," she said, "When you are calm enough, talk to me and tell me what's going on."

Ophelia tried to steady her breathing a little. "I think this is as calm as I'm going to get right now, because you might be in danger!"

"Me?" said Nessa in surprise. "Why am I in danger?"

"Jophiel and the others want to destroy Hell and all the demons!" Ophelia cried. "They were already planning some sort of attack, but apparently destroying that monastery was declaring war on us!"

"Oh shit. Bloody Lucifer!" Nessa said through gritted teeth.

Lucifer had launched a war on Heaven once before, many many years ago when he was still an angel, but both Nessa and Ophelia had managed to stay out of it.

"That's why he was so adamant about it being done. He's such an idiot!" sighed Nessa.

"Yes, but this isn't going to be a war!" insisted Ophelia. "They are going to kill you all before you can start any kind of attack! Nessa, I'm terrified! Heaven can't really destroy Hell can they?"

"I don't know," said Nessa thoughtfully. "I wouldn't have thought so, but then, Jophiel wouldn't start something unless she was a hundred percent certain about it..." Nessa paused and looked into Ophelia's panicked eyes. "Why do you care about Hell anyway? You're an angel!"

Ophelia raised an eyebrow at Nessa in a way that said *are you stupid?* "I don't care about Hell, I care about *you*!" she said, gripping Nessa's hands tighter.

"I'll be fine!" said Nessa. "I can take care of myself! Anyway, I don't live in Hell, so it's okay."

"Not if the whole of Heaven is out to get every single demon! Nessa, this is serious!"

"I know it is, but you need to calm down Phee. It isn't up to you to stop them."

"But, no other angel is going to care!" said Ophelia desperately. "I can't just calmly allow them to hurt you! You're my only friend, I don't know what I'd do without you…" She was crying now. She hadn't even told Nessa that Jophiel had mentioned 'dealing' with her specifically, but she somehow couldn't bring herself to say it. Tears fell down Ophelia's face and Nessa moved an inch closer a little awkwardly, perhaps wishing she could hug Ophelia, but deciding against it.

"But you are no help to anyone in this state!" Nessa said kindly. "We will think of something, but you need to calm down, you're going to make yourself feel ill! Look, let me make you a tea or something? Yeah?"

Ophelia said nothing, but nodded through her tears.

By the time Nessa emerged from the kitchen with the tea, Ophelia had stopped crying and managed to take control of her breathing. Nessa smiled.

"There you are," she said, presenting the drink to Ophelia. "Do you feel a bit better now?"

"Yes, thank you," said Ophelia. She took a sip of the tea and smiled. Nessa hated tea, so she must have had it especially in case Ophelia came round. She looked at her beloved demon smiling at her. She felt all the love inside her well up, like she might start crying afresh just because she adored her. There was no way she could let anyone hurt Nessa, no matter how much she herself was scared of them. She had always been terrified of the archangels and the threat of falling, but over the years thanks to Nessa, she had slowly become more comfortable with bending the rules for the sake of what she thought was right. Protecting Nessa was definitely right.

"Take me to Hell," she said after a few moments of silence.

"Huh?" said Nessa, her face the picture of confusion. "What was that?"

"You heard me!" said Ophelia determinedly. "I need to warn them!"

"Warn who?" asked Nessa.

"I don't know, Lucifer?" Ophelia said. "If Hell know that the angels are planning an attack, they can be ready for it. Heaven won't be able to completely destroy you all!"

"Are you insane?!" yelled Nessa, clearly horrified by the thought. "Lucifer?! You; an angel, want to saunter on down to Hell to have a little chat with The Devil?"

"I know it sounds crazy, but I can't let them kill you!"

"Yeah, but what makes you think that demonic dickhead will listen to you?"

"I'm an angel!" said Ophelia, almost sounding offended. "He will surely heed my warning."

"You overestimate demons, my dear angel," said

Nessa. "It is far too dangerous for a little angelic being like you to go up in front of a demon, let alone Lucifer! Believe me, demons are awful. I am not exactly a shining example of one, if I was we certainly wouldn't be friends." Nessa sighed. "Do you know what demons hate most of all? Angels! They think your lot are obnoxious and self righteous, and that's a fair enough description of most of them. I know you're different, but to Lucifer and the others, you are just another of those angels they despise. It's way too dangerous!"

"You've taken me to Hell before!" protested Ophelia.

Nessa had once taken Ophelia to a party down in Hell and not one demon recognised her as an angel. It was in the 1800s when Ophelia had persuaded Nessa to join her at a human ball, and in return she had agreed to go to a rather more risky party with Nessa.

"Yes I did, but that was different!" Nessa said. "You were in disguise and it was a busy party. That's hardly the same as trying to reason with Satan! Plus, that was a long time ago and it was silly of me to take you. We are lucky no one noticed."

"I don't care if it's dangerous, I have to try!" insisted Ophelia.

"Phee, it's dangerous in so many ways!" said Nessa. "If Lucifer doesn't do something, then think of what the angels will do if they find out you tried to warn him about their plan."

"It's fine," said Ophelia, but her heart was thumping in her chest and she was terrified. "You are more important than any of that! If you won't take me,

I'll have to find a way to get down there myself!"

Nessa sighed. "If you're really sure about this then of course I'm coming with you! I wouldn't let you go down there on your own! No way! But I really wish you'd reconsider..."

Ophelia shook her head. Both angel and demon knew that if the other gets an idea into their head, they are unlikely to be able to stop them.

"Promise we'll get you out of there if anything goes wrong, yes?" said Nessa, her tone deadly serious.

"Yes yes," Ophelia said, standing. "Come on. Jophiel didn't say *when* they were going to attack, but Uriel said the plan was almost ready!"

"This is completely insane and very dangerous!" sighed Nessa standing to join the angel.

"I know, but thank you for coming." said Ophelia as they headed towards the door.

As they made their way to the lift, which could go down if summoned by a demon as well as up for an angel, Ophelia considered what Nessa had said. This idea was completely insane, but she was haunted by what Jophiel had said about 'dealing' with Nessa. Even if a war broke out between the two realms, at least that would be better than all the demons including Nessa getting destroyed.

When they reached the lift, Nessa turned to Ophelia before summoning it. "Last chance to change your mind you crazy angel," she said.

"No. I won't let you get destroyed, I need to do what I can to save you. Heaven will back off if Hell starts fighting back. That's why they are planning this sneak attack I guess."

Nessa didn't say anything. She just looked at Ophelia with an odd expression on her face. Ophelia felt that the look could mean a hundred different things and she wondered which one Nessa intended.

When they stepped out of the lift into Hell, Ophelia felt strange. The energy was so dark and heavy that it made her feel quite ill. She took hold of Nessa's arm and clung tightly to it.

"Are you okay?" Nessa asked worriedly.

"I'm fine," said Ophelia abruptly. "Take me to Lucifer."

Nessa continued staring at Ophelia in concern for a moment, before reluctantly leading her down the dark corridor. Ophelia shivered. There is a common misconception that Hell is boiling hot, and true, the deeper parts are; closer to the fiery pits, but the first layer is actually rather the opposite. The bad energy probably didn't help the frigid atmosphere either though.

They reached a large set of medieval style double-doors covered in small metal spikes. Nessa sighed and told Ophelia to let her go in first. As the door opened, Ophelia saw The Devil sitting on an obnoxiously large throne, more extreme even than God's. She wasn't sure what she expected him to look like, perhaps the way humans always draw him; some big red monster, but he looked very ordinary, Ophelia thought; like any other fallen angel. In fact, Ophelia remembered seeing Lucifer as an angel, and she could still tell it was him, despite his demonic outfit, new black hair, and dramatic makeup. Then again, most demons looked like that, there was nothing especially scary about him. But regardless of looks, he was The Devil, and Ophelia was about to face him. She was terrified!

Chapter Seven
An Angel in Hell.

Nessa couldn't think of anyone more obnoxious and self-centred than Lucifer, and that's aside from him being downright evil. As an angel, he declared war on God and the rest of Heaven when he had a disagreement with The Almighty. The word was. that Lucifer somehow thought he would do a better job of running things than God. A very bad move! Nessa was the only demon in existence for a while, until Lucifer and the rest of the angels he had persuaded to join his side arrived.

Nessa and Lucifer dealt with the fall in very different ways. Both were angry of course, but Nessa's anger seemed to manifest in sadness and despair, whereas Lucifer's fueled him, inspiring him to take charge of Hell and build up some kind of demonic empire. Another difference between the two was that Nessa chose to change her name, as several of the demons did, and Lucifer didn't. To Nessa, changing her name was a way to preserve Archangel Zadkiel. That way Zadkiel never really became a demon, she just stopped existing.

Nessa was the unforgivable demon, and Zadkiel was the kind hardworking angel. The Devil on the other hand, wanted people to fear the former Angel Lucifer as well as the demon he had become.

Letting Ophelia go up in front of Lucifer was like throwing a lamb into a wolves' den, but what could Nessa do? Ophelia was determined to try to keep Nessa safe by any means. So, whilst Nessa really wanted to stop her, she knew that if it were the other way around she absolutely wouldn't let Ophelia stop her. When you love someone, you'd risk anything for them! She glanced back towards the terrified looking angel standing by the door and she wondered, *did* Ophelia love her? Well, she had no doubt she loved her in a way, but did she love her in the same way she did? Or more akin to a best friend? Either way it felt nice to know someone was willing to go to extreme lengths to try to save her.

"Well well well. Look what the cat dragged in!" said Lucifer in a mocking tone, with an air of genuine disdain. "Duke Nessa!" he said, taking delight in using her demoted title. "Fancy seeing you down here. Aren't you too good for us lot, sauntering around on Earth as you do?"

"Doing my job!" Nessa said through gritted teeth, immediately reminded of *why* she never went down there, as if she could have possibly forgotten. Lucifer was always jealous of Nessa as an angel because she far outranked him, so now he took great pleasure in reminding her that he was in charge.

Beelzebub was standing beside Lucifer as usual. She glanced past Nessa towards where Ophelia stood.

"Something feels... Angelic..." she announced in disgust.

Before Nessa could say anything, Ophelia stepped into the room bravely; bravely *and* stupidly!

Lucifer looked the angel up and down and then laughed. "You brought a little snack did you?" he grinned.

Nessa rolled her eyes. "Quit trying to scare her you idiot! Believe or not she's come to try and help us."

"I choose not!" said Lucifer with a frown. "Why would an angel help us? Help us how, by fucking up all our plans and schemes? Nice try love!"

"Shut up and let her speak will you!" Nessa growled, sick of Lucifer's shit already. Ophelia looked at her in awe, clearly impressed that she was brave enough to speak to The Devil like that. Nessa and Beelzebub were the only demons that could get away with talking to him in such a way; they always had done.

"Go on then!" Lucifer said with a smirk. "I was rather bored, I could do with a bit of entertainment. What do you have to say, fiend?"

Ophelia gulped nervously and shifted her feet slightly. When she caught Nessa's eye, Nessa smiled at her. Ophelia smiled back a little, then turned to Lucifer.

"I have come to warn you about Heaven's plan," she said, "They are going to attack Hell and intend to destroy all demons! They took the destruction of St Jophiel's Monastery as a declaration of war, but they want to destroy you first!"

Both Lucifer and Beelzebub laughed, and Ophelia looked uncomfortable.

"It's true!" she insisted.

"What a load of shit!" Lucifer said, still laughing. "As if I'd believe that!"

"Why not?" asked Ophelia. "I'm an angel. Angels tell the truth…"

"*An angel…*" said Lucifer patronisingly. "I don't care if you're an antelope, I still think you're lying!"

"But she isn't!" Nessa protested, trying to stick up for her beloved angel.

"Do you know Nessa dear, I trust you almost as little as I trust this stupid angel!" Lucifer said with a sneer. "Don't think I haven't noticed your shenanigans over the years."

Nessa and Ophelia looked at each other in horror and panic. What was he referring to? What did he know? Nessa looked over at Beelzebub, who lifted her chin and looked down at Nessa disapprovingly. Nessa wondered whether she had told Lucifer anything. Not that Nessa had ever told Bee that she was helping Ophelia out, but she certainly knew that they met up regularly.

Nessa considered asking Lucifer what 'shenanigans' he meant, but she decided it was best not to say anything at all.

"Come along you idiots," said Lucifer. "Give me a realistic reason that I would believe an angel came down to Hell to warn me about a secret plan formulated by Heaven!"

Nessa looked at Ophelia. He was right. Without outing their relationship, whatever it was, there was no realistic explanation as to why Ophelia would do this.

"I'm waiting," smiled Lucifer. "Tick tock my

dears…" He was so awful and so very patronising! Nessa really wished she could tell him what she thought of him, or better still punch him in his stupid smug face! "Nothing to say have we?" Lucifer said with a look of mock concern. "Deary me… Well, do you want me to tell you what *I* think the best explanation is? Of course you do! I think the reason you're here, is because you are a spy!"

Ophelia gasped, in, unfortunately, exactly the way a spy would gasp if they had been found out.

"This is ridiculous! She's not a spy! Ophelia, let's get out of here, it's not worth it!" Nessa went to grab Ophelia's hand to transport them back to Earth with magic, which could be done if needed, but Lucifer must have given Beelzebub some kind of signal, because in an instant she had hold of Nessa, pulling her hands behind her back.

"Oww, Bee what the fuck? Get off me!" yelled Nessa, twisting in the demon's tight grip.

"Just doing my duty," said Beelzebub, digging her fingers harder into Nessa's wrists.

Ophelia looked terrified, rooted to the spot staring at Nessa in horror.

"Ophelia run!" cried Nessa. "The back stairs are never guarded!"

Ophelia didn't move.

"Oh yes, run! Go 'wee wee wee' all the way home!" said Lucifer. "Unless…" He flicked his wrist flamboyantly and the heavy doors slammed shut. "Oh dear!" he said, staring Ophelia right in the eye. "I guess this little piggy isn't going anywhere…"

"You're insane!" Nessa said, still trying to struggle out of Beelzebub's iron grip.

"Why thank you! I do try…" grinned Lucifer. He stood up out of his throne and advanced slowly towards Ophelia, who began to back away in terror. "Now!" he said. "Why would Heaven send me a spy? Too cowardly to face me themselves are they? Come down here if you have something to say to me, oh great Almighty!" he yelled upwards. He looked back down at the terror filled angel before him and smiled a diabolical smile. "Did I not send enough of a message with the monastery? How foolish and amateurish of me. How is it that those humans send a message in that film? Ah yes, with a horse's head! How about I send a similar message, with an angel's head!" Ophelia had backed up so far that she hit the door and Lucifer gently touched her face and pulled a little of her hair as he said the last part. Ophelia screwed her eyes up and held her breath.

"Touch her again and I swear to, well, whoever, that I will fucking kill you!" yelled Nessa, managing to break away from Beelzebub's grasp in a surge of protective power. She grabbed Lucifer by the front of his shirt and pulled him away from Ophelia, pushing him to the ground.

Lucifer simply laughed, and Beelzebub quickly took hold of Nessa again.

"So the rumours are true!" Lucifer said, standing. "My little former Prince of Hell has fallen again! Only this time fallen in love with an angel!" He laughed as though it were some hilarious joke and frowned at Beelzebub until she started laughing too. "You see, I *hate* love stories. Apart from the ones that end in tragedy! I have a feeling yours might be one I can get behind…" He started advancing towards Ophelia again.

"I said don't touch her!" Nessa yelled.

"Oh dear. Your girlfriend is feisty!" Lucifer said to Ophelia. "Does she act as your big scary guard dog, so that you can walk the streets knowing she'll protect you from any of those nasty little demons? Well, luckily for us, scary dogs like that actually tend to be far too soft and can be easily restrained. Exhibit A…" Lucifer pointed at Nessa who had given up struggling for now and was trying and failing to think of anything she could do.

"I came to warn you," said Ophelia. "I was trying to help!"

"Why? Why would you go against your own people to warn The Devil about your attack?" Lucifer was close to Ophelia again, but she didn't look as terrified this time. Nessa admired her bravery. Ophelia looked over towards her and gave her a small smile.

"Because I can't let them destroy you all. I had to save Nessa. She is my only friend, I need her!" Ophelia was close to tears now. "Don't you understand what I'm risking just coming down here? Heaven would never send a spy to Hell because no angel in Heaven would be willing to do it. I've tried to warn you, now please let us go!"

"Aww, your only friend? How heartwarming!" said Lucifer sarcastically. "But you see dear, I am rather notorious for being heart*less*, and as I said, I'm only interested in the tragic part of love stories!"

"What are you going to do!" Nessa shouted as Lucifer ran his fingers down Ophelia's neck in a sinister way. "Get off her you bastard!"

"You see, at first I thought you were a spy, and so I was going to kill you," said Lucifer, turning so he was addressing Nessa as much as Ophelia. "But now I don't know what you are, but it doesn't matter. I will never pass up a chance to ruin someone's happiness, bonus points if it's an angel! And besides, demons and angels aren't supposed to be friends, you freaks!"

Suddenly, Lucifer grabbed Ophelia and threw her across the room. She landed against Lucifer's throne, with her arm taking most of the impact.

"Ophelia!" screamed Nessa, struggling harder against Beelzebub, who responded by twisting her arms behind her back causing her to wince in pain.

Ophelia held her arm, clearly hurt, and Lucifer advanced towards her. He reached the throne and opened a secret compartment in the arm of the chair.

"I'm glad you dropped by angel, I've been hoping I'd have the chance to use my lovely new invention," he said with a sickening grin.

Nessa panicked. Lucifer wasn't planning to kill Ophelia was he? Of course when an angel's physical body is killed they don't really die, they are sent back to Heaven, but then it takes a lot to persuade the archangels to let them come back to Earth. Then they must be authorised by The Almighty as it is she that provides them with an Earthly body anyway. That had happened to Ophelia once before, and Nessa never thought she'd see her again. Heaven might not let her come back this time... Nessa really wished that Ophelia had listened when she begged her not to come down there.

Lucifer had taken a small ornate bottle out of the compartment, and pulled out the stopper with a flourish. Poison? Really? Ophelia was still holding her arm and she looked over at Nessa in panic when she saw the bottle.

"What is that?" yelled Nessa. "You're going to kill her, you idiot! What's the point in that? Heaven will be angry, you're going to add fuel to their fire, they already want to take us all down!" Nessa was desperate to try to reason with Lucifer, but he was known to be particularly unreasonable.

"Angering Heaven is what I do!" laughed Lucifer. "Anyway, it'll do more than that! This is my new Angel Poison! Trademark pending... It is forged in the very deepest fiery pits of Hell, and it won't just kill an angel's body, it will destroy their soul! Your beloved angel won't go back to Heaven. When this poison takes effect she will just be gone!" He had an evil triumphant gleam in his eye that made Nessa boil with even more fury.

"You're a psychopath! Why would you do that?!" she cried

"I'm The Devil honey, of course am a fucking psychopath!!!" Lucifer laughed maniacally and grabbed Ophelia's face. "Open wide sweetie!"

Nessa screamed in panic and kicked Beelzebub hard in the shins, forcing her to let go. She rushed across the room and yanked Lucifer away from Ophelia, but it was too late, he had already forced the poison into her mouth. Nessa dropped to her knees and threw her arms around her angel, accidentally touching her arm causing her gasp and wince in pain.

"I'm sorry!" said Nessa in a panic. "I shouldn't have let you come down here!"

"You tried to stop me..." whispered Ophelia, already a little weak from the poison.

"There must be something I can do, I can't lose you!" cried Nessa.

"There's nothing you can do!" Lucifer said. "You don't even have time to think of anything anyway. The poison only takes around a minute. Tick tock..."

Nessa looked down at Ophelia in her arms, who was smiling weakly up at her. She had to do something! Suddenly her eyes widened as she remembered something; a power that she often forgot she had. She could temporarily stop time! She could freeze the world around her in a single moment. She never normally needed to do it and she tended to forget about it because as far as she was aware she was the only demon to have that particular power. If she froze this moment then Ophelia would stay alive and she could try and think of a plan.

She carefully laid Ophelia down and clicked her fingers, the quiet buzz of noise that could always be heard in Hell turned silent in an instant. She looked around the eerie room, Lucifer and Beelzebub were frozen in their positions. Ophelia laid beside her, perfectly still with her eyes now closed, but at least Nessa knew that when she started time again she would still breathe a few more times. Nessa had been a heartbroken mess when Ophelia had been killed during the wartime, but at least then she knew that she wasn't really dead and even if she never saw her again she would know that she lived on throughout eternity. But this was so much worse.

Now that there was a moment of calm and Ophelia was safe for the time being, trapped in that second, Nessa's emotions were allowed to come to the surface and she began to cry desperately.

She wasn't sure how long she sat sobbing beside Ophelia; there was no way to know, as time wasn't being recorded, but it felt like forever.

"I love you..." she whispered, able to say it because she knew Ophelia couldn't hear her. "You are the best thing in my life... Why didn't you listen to me? I know you wanted to save me, but if you go, then so goes my reason for living. I can't walk the Earth without you. I am always comforted by you. Even when we are not together I can feel you. Your presence on Earth or in Heaven calms me. What will I do without you?" She started sobbing again.

This kind of self pity wasn't going to get her anywhere, and right now she felt that all she could do is stay in this frozen moment forever, but she wanted Ophelia awake, she needed to restart time with a way to save her.

Nessa glanced over to Beelzebub, she wondered whether she would be willing to help her. As an angel, Beelzebub had been a healer, so maybe she would know of a way to save Ophelia. Nessa might be able to persuade her to help, they were as close to friends as demons could be, they had been since Beelzebub arrived in Hell, along with Lucifer and the others.

Nessa stood up and walked up to Beelzebub. She glanced back at Ophelia, it was worth a try, *anything* was worth a try! She clicked her fingers to wake Beelzebub, who jumped when she saw Nessa so close to her when, as far she was aware, she was across the room by Ophelia an instant ago.

"Fuck, Nessa! How did you get over here? What's going on?" Beelzebub looked around, taking in the eerie stillness.

"I stopped time!" said Nessa.

"You what?! Really?" Beelzebub looked over at Lucifer, looking like a particularly pompous statue. "Dude, that's actually really cool! I didn't know you could do that."

"Yeah," said Nessa. "I don't know how... Anyway, I woke you up because I *need* your help! You used to be a healer, is there any way I can save Ophelia? I'll do anything!"

"You really do care about her don't you?" said Beelzebub, looking over at the poisoned angel.

"Yes I do. More than anything," sighed Nessa. "I don't care if you have to know, as long as I can save her!"

"I already knew. I'm not blind, or stupid! And don't say I am!" Beelzebub smiled. "And I also didn't tell Lucifer, because I know you're wondering if I did. But no, I'm afraid there is nothing you can do to save her."

"But... There must be something! I can't let her die..." Nessa had tears in her eyes again.

"I get it, you've had fun with her, but now forget about her and get on with your life. There's no other option."

"What kind of life would that be? All alone on Earth?" Nessa said, a tear running down her face. "She came here to try to protect me, well all of us I suppose! Please Bee, we've known each other since the fall, if there's anything at all that I can do, you have to tell me! Look, I'm begging you!" She looked searchingly into her fellow demon's eyes.

Beelzebub looked uncomfortable. "Well, there technically *is* something you could do, but you really shouldn't."

Nessa's face lit up with hope. "What? I knew there must be something!"

"There are two reasons why you absolutely can't save her. Firstly you would have to use all your demonic power, and that means permanently sacrificing your ability to perform any kind of demon magic!" Beelzebub said warningly.

"That doesn't matter!" said Nessa, highly determined and indifferent about any kind of sacrifice.

"No I suppose it doesn't, because the second reason is that saving the life of an angel that he put to death is the highest form of treason! I don't think our psycho boss will take kindly to treason, considering he's in the process of murdering your friend just for existing near him!" sighed Beelzebub.

"It's okay. I'm willing to do it, I don't care what happens to me. I can't let her go, knowing I could have saved her!" Nessa said determinedly.

"Very well. As long as you are aware that I am very much against this!" said Beelzebub, obviously realising that Nessa's mind was already made up straight away.

"Yeah yeah, what do I do?" said Nessa irritably.

"Well, you are basically going to give her some of your life force, that's why you sacrifice your magical power. With a bit of a demon's life force she can not only be brought back from the brink of death as she is now, but the demonic energy will neutralise the poison. She also should be immune to it in the future if she does anything else stupid!"

Nessa felt it was a little unnecessary to insult Ophelia now, but to be honest it was very out of character for a demon to assist in saving an angel anyway, so she didn't say anything. Suddenly though, Nessa had a thought.

"If she has some of my life force, does that make her part demon?" she asked worriedly. It had been her number one priority for many years to ensure that Ophelia never became a demon.

Beelzebub laughed slightly. "No, you're either a demon or an angel, you can't be *part* demon! She'll have a bit of demonic energy in her, but she probably already does from hanging around with you. I can certainly always feel a little bit of angelic energy on you after you've been at that pub with her!" she said with an air of disgust. "Anyway, it will just be a small amount so I imagine her angelic power will cancel it out. It's either that, or let her die. I vote let her die, but I'm sure you'd rather pick insanity!"

"Damn right I pick insanity!" said Nessa, rushing to sit by Ophelia. "Now, what do I actually do, specifically? I want to be clear because when I start time again I only have a few seconds..."

"Put your hands on her, and imagine some of your

energy going into her through your hands. Imagine your power filling her and healing her. But not too much or you'll give away too much of your own life force and you'll end up on the floor instead! Just until she opens her eyes." Beelzebub sighed. "I can't believe I'm helping you with this nonsense! Just don't you dare tell Lucifer that I had anything to do with this. I have to pretend to be just as shocked and horrified as him, okay?"

"Thank you!" said Nessa. "I mean it!"

"Don't mention it. Literally! Saving an angel is *so* bad! Especially when Lucifer was the one who wanted her destroyed." Beelzebub looked in concern at their boss.

"I won't." said Nessa. "As far as he knows you are about to wake just the same as him."

Nessa took a deep breath and readied herself, knowing that she didn't have much time once she restarted everything. She clicked her fingers again and the hum of noise returned. Nessa put her hands on Ophelia's chest, like she did when she extracted information from her years ago, but with a far kinder intent.

"What are you doing?" breathed Ophelia weakly, her eyes still closed.

"Saving you..." whispered Nessa.

"I just told you you can't save her!" said Lucifer from behind them. "What's wrong with you?!"

Nessa ignored him. She imagined her energy and love entering Ophelia's body through her hands. Her hands felt burning hot as the power filtered through them into Ophelia's chest. Suddenly Ophelia took in a deeper breath and opened her eyes. Nessa quickly stopped as Beelzebub had warned. She felt a little odd and lightheaded, likely because she had just lost her magical powers and given away part of her life force, but she smiled at Ophelia.

"Nessa," said Ophelia, obviously confused. "What did you do?"

"It doesn't matter what I did. I saved you!" Nessa said, another tear running down her cheek. She wrapped her arms around Ophelia and never wanted to let go.

Chapter Eight
Not a Real Demon.

"How do you feel?" Nessa asked, her arms still wrapped around Ophelia.

"I feel fine," replied Ophelia, smiling at the demon who just saved her life. "Thank you for saving me..."

"That's impossible!" yelled Lucifer. "What did you do?!"

"What I did was stop you from murdering somebody who was just trying to help you!" said Nessa, turning sharply to face Lucifer. "Do you know what one of your *many* problems is? You don't trust anyone!"

"I'm The Devil! Why would I trust an angel? I literally lead the opposition. Tell me angel, would your lot believe a demon that turned up to warn you about something?"

"That is a valid point I suppose." said Ophelia, sitting up and making a pained face as she moved her arm slightly. "But I really did try to warn you. To protect my friend."

"Yes I know, soppy!" Lucifer said with a small

disapproving laugh. "But any angel stupid enough to come down here for whatever reason deserves exactly what they get! Your pet demon may have saved you that time, but you're not getting away that easily!"

Lucifer looked down at the poison bottle still in his hand and took a step forward. Ophelia looked at Nessa in panic. Nessa just gave her a reassuring smile and turned back to Lucifer.

"Don't bother. She's immune to your nonsense now. I had to give her some of my life force, so the demonic energy in her would neutralise that stuff if you tried again!" Nessa gave Lucifer a triumphant look.

"Demonic energy?" Ophelia said in panic.

"It's okay. It won't do anything to you. Other than save your life..." smiled Nessa.

"How the fuck did you know about that?!" yelled Lucifer. "I didn't even know that would work with this poison!"

Beelzebub's eyes widened and she shot Nessa a desperate look.

"I don't know, I guess I heard it somewhere?" Nessa said nonchalantly. "Or maybe it's instinct because I care about Ophelia?"

Suddenly Lucifer's eyes lit up. "Ha! I do know this though! You just sacrificed your ability to perform demonic magic! For an *angel* no less! You fool, what does that make you now? Useless!"

"You did what?!" exclaimed Ophelia in horror.

"It doesn't matter!" Nessa said quickly.

"That's not all, angel!" laughed Lucifer. "Your worthless girlfriend just committed the highest form of treason by saving you!"

Ophelia turned so quickly to Nessa that she hurt her arm again. "Treason?! Oh Nessa, for goodness sake…"

"I couldn't let you die!" Nessa said defensively.

"What a fun turn of events!" grinned Lucifer. "I actually think this is more entertaining than watching the angel get poisoned!"

"Will you shut up!" Nessa yelled.

"Oh dear… Looks like the fun's over, don't you think, Beelzebub? Looks like our former colleague here is getting a little testy…" Lucifer sneered, with a nasty gleam in his eye.

"Look, do what you want with me, but let Ophelia go now!" said Nessa. "You've done enough to her!"

"Very well," said Lucifer. "As you say, there is more important fun to be had concerning *you* now!"

"What do you mean? Nessa!" Ophelia's shout of concern was cut off as she suddenly disappeared, transported out of Hell by Lucifer. Nessa gasped in surprise then turned sharply towards Lucifer.

"Is she safe?!" she yelled. "I don't care what you do to me as long as I know she's safe."

Lucifer rolled his eyes. "For the sake of all that's unholy, you are *so* tiresome! Yes, I just sent her back up to your beloved York!"

"Thanks…" Nessa said quietly. Not a hundred percent certain that she trusted Lucifer's word on anything, but knowing that there was nothing she could do about it. Besides, she could feel that Ophelia was on the Earth, if she concentrated.

"Now!" said Lucifer. "Stand up girl!" He pushed past Nessa to get back to his throne and he sat in a flamboyant yet casual way with his leg over one of the throne arms.

Nessa stood before The Devil, resenting him with every bone in her body.

"Now then!" said Lucifer, tutting theatrically. "What shall we do with you?" He paused for a moment, then obviously decided that a patronising anecdote was required. "Do you remember when you were demoted from Prince of Hell to Duke?"

He stared at Nessa expectantly, wishing her to actually answer the obviously rhetorical question. "Yes..." said Nessa suspiciously.

"Do you remember *Prince* Beelzebub?" Lucifer asked, putting great emphasis on her title. Beelzebub just nodded. "It was way back when. That time when our dear Nessa decided for some unknown reason that she couldn't handle being our sole Earth representative, and wanted to focus her attention on the North of England... Of course, now the mystery is solved; it's all because a certain angel worked there isn't it?" Lucifer tutted again. "First you give up your title for her, then your magic, and now; your life!"

Beelzebub gulped uncomfortably, but Nessa was determined to stay strong and seem unfazed. She didn't want to give Lucifer the satisfaction of knowing he got to her, even though her heart was thumping with terror.

"You see, this is an exciting day! We are getting to try all sorts of new things aren't we?" said Lucifer, addressing the room as though there were a crowd of hundreds rather than just two demons, neither of which he was actually looking at.

"Err, what other new thing are you referring to?" asked Beelzebub in concern. She obviously knew something that Nessa didn't.

"Yes yes Beelzebub dear, the Pool of Destruction!" grinned Lucifer. "I really ought to think of more catchy names for these things shouldn't I?"

"What's the Pool of Destruction?" Nessa asked, imagining (correctly) that she already knew what it would be.

"Oh, well let me show you!" said Lucifer, swinging his leg over the throne arm to stand with a flourish. "It's perhaps my greatest invention! Though I have so many good ones! Let's say it's certainly one of the most diabolical!" He led the two reluctant demons out of the throne room and down the corridor as he spoke.

The corridors in Hell were dark and filthy; a sharp contrast to the pristine white of Heaven's. Nessa glanced at the grubby walls, reminded again why she avoided this place as much as possible. She was aware of Beelzebub staring at her in concern. She met her eye and Beelzebub put a hand awkwardly against Nessa's arm, allowing it to sort of hover, unsure if she should touch her or not. That was uncharacteristically affectionate for Beelzebub, so Nessa knew she was right about what was coming. Pools mean water, and there was a specific kind of water that would turn a pool into a 'Pool of Destruction'. Nessa had feared holy water since she fell. It was a threat that demons loved to give each other, but Nessa had never heard of any actually following through with. Even demons didn't tend to be that evil! A single drop could burn a demon terribly, and anything more than an egg cup full would completely destroy them in seconds. Similar to the angel poison that Lucifer used on Ophelia, their soul would be destroyed, as well as their body, but unlike with Ophelia, there was no one around to save Nessa, and no way to save her even if there was.

They eventually reached a strange little door and Lucifer produced an ornate key with a flourish. He unlocked the door and waved the demons in.

"Ladies first!" he said patronisingly. Nessa gave him a particularly cold look as she walked past him. The room inside was small, with a glass booth in which Lucifer and Beelzebub could stand to protect themselves from the water. The pool was small and round, it didn't look deadly at all, it looked a little like a hot tub or jacuzzi that you'd find in a spa, but Nessa knew this one was far from relaxing.

"Now! Nessa! Tell me, what kind of water do you think is in here?" asked Lucifer, closing the door and almost leaping in front of Nessa and Beelzebub with excitement.

"Is it holy water by chance?" said Nessa, unimpressed.

"Ding ding, correct answer! And do you think a demon can survive a pool full of holy water?"

"No..."

"Another right answer! You're on fire! Oopsie, bit insensitive given that you are about to burn to death..." Lucifer smiled one of his most evil smiles.

"Alright! You're about to destroy her, you don't

have to be even more of a dick!" Beelzebub said disapprovingly. Nessa smiled at her in thanks, not just for that, but for everything, if she was about to get destroyed.

Lucifer chose to ignore Beelzebub's comment, as he carried on talking about his brilliant invention, which was hardly even an invention in Nessa's view, it was just a pool.

"I've been working on it for a while now," he announced. "It took time to ensure the water could be installed safely, not that I would have cared if we had lost a demon or two to its creation, hazards of the job you know?" Lucifer laughed heartily at his own 'joke', then continued. "We haven't had to use it yet, but then along came you! First angel created, first angel to fall and first demon to be officially executed for treason, my my, you are going for all the records aren't you?"

"Are you going to get on with it?" snapped Nessa. "Honestly, death by holy water is preferable to listening to you talking nonsense all day, I don't know how you put up with it Bee!"

Usually Beelzebub would have said something, she would have joined Nessa in mocking their boss; an enjoyable pastime for both of them. But now she stayed silent, even her confidence didn't extend to mocking The Devil in a room full of holy water.

Lucifer didn't respond to Nessa, he signalled for Beelzebub to follow him into the booth. "Right," he said once inside. "It's very simple. You stand on that platform, and then it will disappear from under you and you fall in! Any questions? No? Good! Now, I suppose we should do this right, even though we both witnessed your crime. Duke Nessa, I hereby sentence you to execution by holy water for high treason in the form of saving the life of an angel that I, The Devil, condemned to death. Do you plead guilty?"

"Absolutely!" grinned Nessa.

"Do you regret your actions?" asked Lucifer.

"Nope!" Nessa hoped she was successfully keeping up her air of confidence, when really she felt like screaming and begging for her life. She thought of Ophelia waiting for her back on Earth. She wished more than anything that she could say goodbye. If Nessa got destroyed, Ophelia would be able to tell straight away. Nessa really hoped she wouldn't try to confront Lucifer about it, she might be immune to his poison, but there was plenty Hell could do to an angel without killing them.

Everything had escalated so quickly since Ophelia knocked on her door that afternoon. She almost lost Ophelia, and now due to Nessa saving her, Ophelia was to walk the Earth without her only friend. Exactly the thing Nessa wanted to avoid for herself. She never even got to tell her that she loved her…

"Oi! Quit daydreaming and get on the platform!" yelled Lucifer.

Nessa shot him a nasty look. "I do have one thing to say!" she called. After all she had nothing to lose now. "You are a fucking idiot and I *hate* you!"

She looked over at the two demons, one grinning like a manic and the other with a look of great concern. She looked down at the water, she had never seen so much holy water. It didn't look particularly dangerous, but neither did Lucifer! She took a deep breath and whispered an 'I love you' upwards to Ophelia, then jumped in, causing water to splash onto the glass booth and startling both sheltering demons. Nessa had decided that she would rather jump in than allow the unnecessary extra humiliation of being forced to *fall* in.

As she became submerged, the water felt burning hot, like if you got into a bath having just run the hot tap. It hurt! She thought about Ophelia and how she really wished she could have kissed her, but then suddenly she found herself back at the pool's surface, still very much alive. She was filled with confusion, this was definitely holy water, she could tell. This much should melt a demon in a second, but all Nessa felt was uncomfortably hot.

She hauled herself out of the pool and stood staring at Lucifer with a triumphant smile, steam rising from her skin, as the holy water was heated by the touch of a demon and met the cold air of Hell. Both Lucifer and Beelzebub were, understandably, completely stunned.

After a moment, Beelzebub nervously stepped out from the booth, glancing worriedly at the water still dripping from Nessa's clothes and hair. She must have trusted that Nessa wouldn't splash any on her, she noted.

"How did you do that?" she asked in amazement.

"I didn't do anything..." said Nessa. "I don't know how I survived that." She put her hand on her jacket sleeve, the water sizzled with her touch. "Bee, do you think you could dry me? I lost my magic and I don't want to get any on you..."

Beelzebub smiled and with a wave of her hand Nessa was completely dry.

"I'm glad you survived," she whispered.

Before Nessa could say anything or acknowledge Beelzebub's kindness, Lucifer came out of the booth, his face thunderous.

"What are you?" he yelled.

"Err, a demon? I think?" said Nessa, beginning to wonder that herself.

"Come out here!" Lucifer yelled, marching towards the door, obviously worried that Nessa might get revenge by throwing him into the pool. Nessa and Beelzebub followed him out into the corridor and Lucifer grabbed Nessa, slamming her against the wall.

"Real demons wouldn't survive that!" he snarled. "You're a freak! You are *not* welcome down here anymore! I only employ real demons, you fell in love with an angel, sacrificed your magic to save her *and* survived a pool of holy water! Now I don't know what that makes you, but whatever you are, I know that I don't want to see you here again!"

"Good, because I hate working for you anyway!" Nessa said.

"Ha! What you are now is nothing... unwanted! Not a real demon and certainly not an angel, and no magic on top of that! No one will want you! Now get out!" He turned to Beelzebub. "Needless to say, if you breathe a word about this, I'll chuck you in the damn water! Understand?"

Beelzebub nodded quickly.

"I said *out*!" Lucifer yelled at Nessa.

She didn't need telling again, apart from anything else she was desperate to see Ophelia. She gave Beelzebub a quick look and then ran down the corridor.

When Nessa was back on Earth she was filled with a hundred thoughts and questions; mainly about how she had just survived an execution, and whether or not she was still a demon. But the most important thing on her mind was Ophelia. No matter how or why, she was just given a second chance when she should have been destroyed, and before that, Ophelia had almost died, she absolutely needed to see her. The only problem was she didn't have a clue where she was.

She tried to tune in to Ophelia's energy, wondering whether giving up her magic extended to other kinds of ethereal abilities. As she neared her flat, she suddenly sensed her, Nessa lit up with joy and rushed inside.

Ophelia was sitting in Nessa's living room fiddling nervously with the hem of her skirt, obviously waiting for her. She stood up quickly when Nessa entered the room.

"Ophelia!" Nessa cried, rushing towards her.

Ophelia smiled and pulled Nessa in for a hug.

"Your arm..." Nessa said.

"I healed it." Said Ophelia. "My magic doesn't work in Hell, but it's okay now. It was broken though."

"You are so brave." Nessa whispered.

She melted into her angel's embrace, feeling her soft hair against her cheek and inhaling her sweet perfume. She wanted to stay there forever, to somehow get even closer to her.

"Have you ever had a hug before?" whispered Ophelia.

"Of course not," answered Nessa. "Who would hug me?"

"Neither have I… It's nice…"

"Mmm…" Nessa took in a deep breath. It was as if she could finally relax after being on high alert down in Hell. She suddenly realised something. Something that thrilled her. Lucifer had just fired her, she and Ophelia were no longer enemies! Nessa wondered whether that meant that maybe, there was a chance that they might actually be able to be, *together*? Or at least Nessa could tell Ophelia how she really felt, regardless of whether she felt the same.

Ophelia broke away from the hug and looked at Nessa.

"What did he do to you?" she asked.

"It doesn't matter, I'm fine," said Nessa, sparing Ophelia the details about the attempted execution.

"I was worried," Ophelia said. "I was scared he'd destroy you, and it would be all my fault!"

"No it wouldn't! I wanted to save you!" protested Nessa, suddenly extra glad that she survived and didn't leave Ophelia with that guilt for eternity.

"Yes but I was the one who went down there, you tried to stop me. If I died it would be my own silly fault, but if you died then it would be because of me!"

"You went down there for me though," said Nessa. "So I would have blamed myself if anything happened to you."

"Did you really lose your magic?" asked Ophelia in

concern.

"Yes, but I really don't care about that. All I care about is you!" Nessa found herself caught up in the moment. Perhaps it was her new freedom, or else it was the trauma of nearly losing Ophelia. Whatever it was, before she knew what she was doing, she was leaning towards Ophelia to kiss her. Ophelia's eyes widened in panic and she stepped back.

"No! Don't kiss me, please," she said softly "I'm already going to be in so much trouble for all this."

"But, I nearly lost you; properly this time! And I lo—"

Ophelia quickly covered Nessa's mouth with her hand. "Don't say that either! Thank you for saving my life, and I'm really sorry for all this, but I can't let you say that..."

Nessa's eyes stung with tears that she willed not to fall. She gently removed Ophelia's hand. "Sorry..." she said quietly. There was silence for a moment before she said, "Hey? I got fired. We are not rivals anymore..."

"Again, I'm sorry..." said Ophelia.

"I'm not! I never wanted to be your enemy, we have never really been enemies, but now we don't have to pretend anymore?" There was a desperate plea in Nessa's voice. She really wanted Ophelia to love her back.

"I'm glad we're not official rivals, but you are still a demon, even without your magic, and I am an angel. Angels and demons don't kiss and they don't love each other... We shouldn't even be friends!"

There was another silence.

"Phee?" said Nessa slowly. "If we were humans,

would you love me?" Her tears had betrayed her now, and she had never felt less like a formidable demon. Crying, and begging an angel to love her.

Ophelia turned away, perhaps she was crying too?

"Don't make me answer that Nessa..." she sighed. "I have to go. I'm going to be in so much trouble. They'll know I tried to warn Lucifer about their plan, and that's without almost getting myself killed! I'm an idiot!"

"No you're not!"

"I am! And I'm a bad angel..." Ophelia turned back to Nessa, she *was* crying too.

"You're a very good angel, the best! But more importantly, aside from being an angel you are a good *person*! You always have pure and kind intentions, I've never met anyone else like that!" Nessa smiled at her angel and Ophelia smiled back. "Tell the archangels that I dragged you down to Hell to meet with Lucifer! Then it's not your fault."

"Thank you..." said Ophelia. "As I said I really must go. Thank you for everything, and I'm sorry again... But I magicked your flat tidy," she said, with a small smile. "Lucifer sent me here and I was waiting for you, you know?"

Nessa looked around the room, she had been so focused on Ophelia that she hadn't noticed. She laughed slightly.

"See you on Wednesday..." said Ophelia, leaving the room.

Nessa followed her into the hall to watch her go, she didn't like to mention that they no longer needed weekly meetings if she didn't work for Lucifer.

Ophelia closed the door and Nessa felt oddly empty. She remembered feeling a similar way back in Heaven before her fall. It was the feeling that no one really cared about her or anything she did. She hadn't felt that way since she and Ophelia became friends. As she fell in love with that beautiful, kind, headstrong angel, she had often wondered if Ophelia felt the same way. She had always told herself that she didn't really mind, so long as they could be close friends. But suddenly she found herself desperate for Ophelia to love her. She knew that Ophelia's fear of Heaven would prevent her from admitting even if she did, but she longed to know if she felt it. Nessa had promised never to extract information from Ophelia again, but she rather wished she could have done that just then, to *force* Ophelia to tell her if she loved her or not. But she knew that wouldn't be right, and if Ophelia did tell her she loved her, she wanted it to be through choice anyway, that would mean so much more.

Nessa sat down in her now tidy living room and cried. She had been through a lot and was rather tired out by it. After a while she thought about what Lucifer said, she wasn't a real demon now, she was nothing. She had never wanted to be a demon, but she didn't particularly want to be an angel either, and somehow the idea that she could be something new and different was suddenly quite thrilling. She wasn't nothing, she was Nessa! Whatever Nessa was... She decided that she didn't really care what she was, she could be whoever she wanted now, and that felt exciting!

Chapter Nine
Sorry I Couldn't Save You...
(Second World War)

The Archangel Zadkiel once promised Angel Ophelia that she would make sure no harm came to her, and while that promise was originally made regarding visiting Jupiter, Nessa had spent a long time trying desperately to keep it. The two had been on Earth for around six thousand years and Nessa had only failed to keep her promise once, but it haunted her.

Over the years the humans had started all kinds of wars all over the world, they were good at that, they could always find something new to disagree about, no matter how petty. Nessa had seen a lot of bloodshed during the various wars that she did her best to keep out of. At first it didn't bother her too much; she didn't care about humans back then. But the longer she lived on Earth, the more she became fond of the odd creatures, and the more she didn't particularly wish to see them tearing each other apart for silly reasons. However the Second World War was the one that affected her the most, because that was when she experienced a loss herself. To a human the Second World War was quite a while ago now, but to a six thousand year old demon, it was still painfully recent.

Both Nessa and Ophelia had been very surprised that there was to be another world war, and so soon after the last one. They had listened to the Prime Minister announce the war on the wireless in Ophelia's cottage. It wasn't like Ophelia to own modern technology, but Nessa had bought her one for this exact reason; they knew there would be an announcement. It was a Sunday morning, so not a time the two normally met up, but Ophelia was a little worried about the idea of another war, so Nessa wanted to be with her for the announcement. They had talked for hours about the impending conflict, about how terrible it was to have almost the entire Earth at war again. The First World War had been awful, and though Nessa didn't want to point it out to Ophelia, the humans had created a lot of new dangerous weapons since then. She had a feeling this one would be the worst.

Demons and angels didn't get involved in human wars. They didn't pick sides because all humans had both good and bad in them, and both sides always did questionable things during a battle. Lucifer did however, delight in a war, and often quizzed Nessa on the latest horrors. He didn't care who was doing it, he just loved to hear about suffering. Much as they tried, it was hard for Nessa and Ophelia to completely stay out of this war. After all, it was between Britain and Germany, and if any human asked them they would say they were English as they had lived there permanently for nearly two thousand years. As the war raged on for three years, Ophelia helped out those suffering the best she could. Her excuse was that she was tasked to be guardian of the North, therefore she had a duty to the people there. Nessa on the other hand, illegally sold extra rations and other restricted items. Her excuse was that she was a demon and could do whatever she damn well wanted, and it was always great to get a few extra temptations into the monthly quota. Truthfully though, Nessa felt that the poor humans could do with the odd treat, there had already been three years of this nonsense after all!

One day though, Ophelia's desire to do good led to Nessa almost losing her completely. It started at their weekly meeting. Luckily for them their favourite pub stayed open to keep up morale, and Nessa certainly felt that eight glasses of whisky a week were contributing to the upkeep of her morale.

Nessa was already at the table as usual when Ophelia entered the pub, intently reading a leaflet about the Women's Land Army. She stopped by their table and stood, still reading.

"Hey Phee?" Nessa tugged on her sleeve. "Oi, what you doing?"

"Hmm?" Ophelia slowly looked in Nessa's direction, her eyes remaining fixed on the paper for as long as possible. "Oh, sorry! Hi Nessa!" She sat down and took a sip of the wine waiting for her, closing the leaflet with a little reluctance. "How are you?"

"I'm fine; you?" Nessa swirled the whisky in her glass a little.

"As good as I can be I suppose," said Ophelia.

"Well this might cheer you up," said Nessa, producing a large bar of chocolate from her bag.

Ophelia's eyes widened. "Nessa! I can't take that, chocolate is rationed!"

"It's also unholy, what's your point?" Nessa gently waved the chocolate bar in Ophelia's direction.

Ophelia rolled her eyes and took the bar. "You are worryingly good at tempting!"

"I must be! Supposedly angels are impossible to tempt, but you are my speciality," grinned Nessa.

"I can't decide if that's an insult," said Ophelia, opening the chocolate bar and offering some to Nessa.

"I think it's more a compliment to my skills," Nessa said, taking the proffered chocolate. "But if you want to take it as an insult you are more than welcome to!" Nessa glanced at the leaflet that Ophelia had been so engrossed in before she was distracted by chocolate and her favourite demon. "What's that all about? Do you think you're joining the Women's Land Army, missus? Not very impartial of you is it?"

"What, this? It's just farming, it's not joining the front line," said Ophelia, looking down at the leaflet.

"You can't be a farmer, you don't eat meat! I can't imagine you slaughtering pigs or whatever. Maybe you're a dark horse and I don't know you at all Angel Ophelia..." Nessa raised an eyebrow at Ophelia as she sipped her whisky.

Ophelia shot her a look. "No!" she said, "Anyway of course I'm not joining! A woman was handing out these leaflets at the bus stop. I was reading this inside!" She took a piece of paper out of the middle of the leaflet.

"Apparently this guy is committing crimes during air raids when no one's around!"

"Hmm, not a bad idea to be honest! Clever!" said Nessa.

"Yes, but his crimes are getting worse, and yesterday he shot and killed two wardens who were trying to stop him and make him go into a shelter!"

"Bloody humans, they always take things that little bit too far!" sighed Nessa, taking the paper to read.

"Isn't that awful?" Ophelia said, drinking some wine.

"Well the murder's a bit much," said Nessa. "I might be a demon, but I've never really been down with murder. Then again, people are getting killed by bombs and stuff all the time."

"Exactly!" Ophelia exclaimed. "They have enough to worry about without some mad man out there! That's why I was thinking I should try to reason with him."

Nessa let the paper drop from her hands. "You want to confront a murderer during an air raid?! Are you insane?"

"No, I'm an angel! If anyone can get him to stop it's me. I could teach him the error of his ways."

"No, I don't think you could!" protested Nessa. "He shot the last people who tried to negotiate with him. Some people just can't be reasoned with. It's best to just leave it. There are so many bad things going on right now, what's one more?" Nessa changed the subject to their weekly accomplishments, but she could tell that Ophelia hadn't let go of the idea, and that worried her.

The next time there was an air raid, which was the very next evening, Nessa's first thought was Ophelia. She hung back, hiding in the shadows while everyone else rushed to the shelter. She wasn't afraid of bombs, she could sense where they would land and keep away, the planes above had very dark energy, and Nessa could pick it up easily. However, she tended to follow the humans into the shelters anyway if she was out. She felt that, demon or not, people might find her suspicious if she was wandering around while bombs dropped on the city, and she liked to keep a low profile. Today though, she had more important things to worry about. Ophelia had decided that confronting the criminal was the right thing to do, and so there was no stopping her. Nessa thought it was a very dangerous and silly idea, but while she couldn't stop her, she would never let her angel do anything dangerous and silly on her own.

She manoeuvred the dark streets, dodging wardens and listening to the distant sound of the approaching aeroplanes. Ophelia's leaflet had stated the general area that the crimes had been committed, so that members of the public could watch out for any suspicious activity nearby; Nessa knew Ophelia would be there.

As she neared the area, she felt Ophelia's presence, but she also had a very bad feeling, like something terrible was going to happen. Suddenly Nessa spotted Ophelia in the museum gardens beside the ruins of an old monastery. It was quite difficult to see during a blackout, but the bomber planes' spotlights were scanning the city, providing a little light. Plus, demons' eyes are well-equipped for the darkness; after all hell is quite dingy. Nessa stopped in panic as she made out a shadowy figure standing before Ophelia. The figure was holding a gun. Quite a lot of the human men carried guns during the war, but Nessa knew that this one had murdered two wardens just a couple of days ago. She couldn't hear what they were saying, but the gun was pointed threateningly in the angel's direction. Oh Ophelia! Why did she have to be so damn *good*? She was always putting herself in danger for the sake of what's right. Nessa took calculated risks for what she believed in, but Ophelia was often blinded by her desire to help. She had come a long way in confidence from that angel who was too scared to save Abraham's son, thanks mainly to Nessa's influence, but as Ophelia stood trying to convert a crazed murderous criminal, Nessa wondered if she had gone too far. She did manage to be more intimidating than some of the demons when she wanted to be, but intimidating someone who is pointing a gun at you may not be the best idea.

Nessa was about to intervene, as she often did when Ophelia got herself into this kind of trouble, but as she took a step forward, a bomb landed rather close, startling Nessa and nearly deafening her. Her instinct caused her to turn in the direction of the explosion, temporarily distracted from the worrying scene in front of her. It unnerved her that a bomb had dropped so close and she hadn't sensed it. She had clearly not been concentrating on the planes. It could have killed them...

Suddenly, as Nessa was momentarily distracted by the bomb, she heard a gunshot behind her, along with a scream; a scream she recognised immediately... Her blood ran cold. She could hardly bring herself to turn around. When she did though, she was met with the sight of her beloved angel laid out on the ground, blood staining her dress.

"Ophelia..." she said in what came out as a strangled whisper.

She rushed to her side, but before she could touch her, Ophelia disappeared. When an angel's body is killed, they fade away like that. Suddenly Nessa was alone in the world. She touched the ground where Ophelia had been and began to cry.

"Bugger me, where did she go?! What did you do to her?" came a voice from behind Nessa.

She turned sharply to face the figure, a youngish man who really ought to have joined up by the looks of him.

"*I* didn't do anything to her, you bastard! *You* killed her!" She felt such fury, it wasn't fair, nothing was ever fair!

The man was rather understandably both confused by Ophelia's disappearance, and angry that Nessa had witnessed the murder.

Nessa turned away from him, still crying. Despite her anguish she was hyper aware of his actions. In an instant he aimed his gun to shoot her, thinking she wouldn't notice as she was facing the other way. One should never underestimate a demon though! As he pulled the trigger and the bullet began to travel towards Nessa at lightning speed, she put her hand up and it stopped in mid air, halfway to its target.

"What the hell?" said the man, genuine terror in his

voice.

"Exactly!" said Nessa, turning to glare at him, no longer caring that her face was stained with tears, she could still be terrifying if she wanted to be. Her eyes turned red as demonic rage filled her. The man aimed his gun at Nessa in fear, but before he could pull the trigger again, the gun crumpled as if it were made of tissue paper. His eyes widened and he dropped it to the ground. Nessa turned the bullet in his direction. Despite being a demon, she had never killed anything in her long life, but she was so angry in that moment that she felt like avenging her beloved. But in a split-second she realised that Ophelia wouldn't want her to do that. She had come here to try to reason with the criminal, and while Nessa fully believed he couldn't be reasoned with, Ophelia would be so angry if she knew that she killed him.

Instead she stared him dead in the eye and said, "I'll give you a head start, which is a lot more than you deserve. Run!"

The man didn't hesitate, he ran towards the gates. Nessa sent the bullet in his direction and drove it into his hand with great force. He would live, but he probably wouldn't be able to shoot again. Perhaps Nessa's method was a little more harsh than Ophelia's, but it had the same result. She looked up towards the sky.

"Phee?" she said, knowing she was back in heaven now. "I did it. He won't commit crimes anymore, and he certainly won't shoot anyone else. I had to make sure I finished the job you were doing, for you..." She couldn't see the sky anymore; tears clouded her vision.

She hadn't noticed that the bombs had stopped falling, and she barely acknowledged the all-clear siren. Soon though, the streets began to come back to life, as people emerged from their shelters. Nessa knew she had to leave before anyone asked her what she was doing crying on the floor, but she didn't want to leave that spot. It was the last place on Earth Ophelia had been, leaving it somehow felt like leaving her behind. As a handful of people started entering the gardens though, she had to reluctantly move away.

Later, Nessa sat in her living room drinking copious amounts of the alcohol that she kept to sell, blaming herself entirely for what happened to Ophelia. If only she had got there earlier, or not been distracted by the bomb! She could have saved her. She *should* have saved her. For a very long time Nessa's number one priority had been to protect her precious angel, but now she had failed. Of course, it wasn't particularly Nessa's fault, but she saw it as such. She somehow felt as guilty as if she had shot Ophelia herself.

She wondered what exactly happened to angels that got themselves killed. She knew that nothing on Earth could actually end their life, but if their body was killed then they ended up back in Heaven, which was fair enough for an angel, except that they couldn't come back without their earthly body. Nessa wondered whether Ophelia was hurt, and if she had got into trouble, or whether she was concerned about never seeing her again as well. There was no way Nessa could saunter into Heaven; demons weren't allowed. Earth was their middle ground, the only place they could meet up, but now that might not be an option. Nessa didn't know the specific rules, but she imagined it would be a complicated process to get a new earthly body; if it was possible at all.

Nessa downed her last bottle, she hadn't intended to drink them all but somehow she didn't care, she still wasn't nearly drunk enough to numb the pain or ease the guilt. After a while she went outside, she didn't have anywhere to go and it was the middle of the night now, but she couldn't bear to stay sitting in her sad little flat any longer. It was odd to walk around and not feel Ophelia's presence. No matter where she was on Earth, Nessa could just sense her. Sometimes if she had had a bad day, she would tune into Ophelia's energy, and just knowing she was there on Earth with her made her feel better. Since Nessa's very first day on Earth when she visited Eden, Ophelia had always been there too, and as Nessa fell in love with her, she appreciated it more and more. Now she was alone. She looked up to the sky.

"Ophelia!" she yelled. "Ophelia, can you hear me? Come back! I need you..."

"Will you stop shouting?" a policeman said, pointing a lantern in Nessa's direction. "It's the middle of the night and there's a war on, in case you hadn't noticed!"

The policeman was the only other person around. Nessa glared at him.

"I'm a demon, I can do whatever the fuck I want!" she yelled; and she set fire to the policeman's lantern, causing him to drop it in panic and run away. Nessa watched him go. So much for keeping a low profile!

Perhaps she was drunker than she thought?

She rounded the corner, finding herself near the minster, easily the most sacred ground in York. The closer she walked, the warmer the ground started to feel. Unlike most churches, the minster didn't have an enclosed churchyard, so it was hard to tell where the consecrated ground began. Nessa stared up at the magnificent building. For the first time in thousands of years Nessa wished she was an angel again. If she was she could go up to Heaven to see Ophelia, and maybe she would feel less of a failure. On a bad day Nessa often felt extremely unworthy of Ophelia's friendship. How could a perfect angel like that ever care about a no-good demon like her? If she ever slept, which she hadn't for a very long time, she would always have two nightmares. The first being about her fall, and the second being one where Ophelia finally decides that she is wicked and smites her as she cries and begs for mercy. It was always there, in the back of her mind; if she was an angel everything would be so much easier... Tears pricked her eyes and she began to feel that the large amount of alcohol consumed may have been a hindrance rather than a help. A theory further evidenced by a mad thought that entered her head.

Long ago Ophelia had proudly told Nessa that a statue of her had been placed inside the minster. As the Guardian of the North of England it made sense to honour her in York's own cathedral. Nessa had a sudden thought that if she found it, she would be able to see her face again, even if only made of stone. She set off towards the church, unsure if her plan was fueled by heartbreak, guilt, or alcohol; or more likely a combination of the three.

As she approached the minster, the ground changed from warm to uncomfortably hot. She never normally entered a church, consecrated ground hurt like a bitch, she wasn't insane. However, she felt close to it today! With a flick of her hand the minster doors flew open and Nessa stepped inside. It felt like walking on extremely hot coals and she wasn't sure she could stand it. She leapt up onto one of the pews in an attempt to give her burning feet a momentary rest. It was pitch black and quite eerie in the minster at night. Nessa squinted in the dark, wondering how she would find the statue. It was a strange and mad idea she knew, but for some reason, the more she thought about it, the more oddly important it felt. Creating light sounded more like the sort of thing an angel would do, but Nessa had actually brought the first starlight to be, so surely if anyone could light up the minster it was her. She swept her hands upwards and sure enough, a soft warm glow filled the building, making it seem a lot more welcoming, even for a demon who absolutely shouldn't have been in there.

Nessa knew the statue was on the North side (obviously, what with Ophelia being the Angel of the North), and eventually she spotted it above an archway. Nessa didn't fancy burning her feet by walking all the way over there, plus it was rather high up. She realised that her only real option was to fly to it. Nessa hardly ever used her wings, partly because she lived on Earth among humans, and partly because she always felt a little ashamed of them. She still remembered Ophelia seeming fearful when she first saw her as a demon in Eden. The only thing that had changed physically when she fell was both her hair and wings turning black. Nessa didn't mind the hair, in fact she liked it better that way, but in Eden as that pure white-winged angel stared in fear at her jet-black wings she felt very aware that she was different; something to be feared. She had always resented her wings, but now she needed them. Nessa let her wings spread, stretching them before trying to use them. She actually felt that they looked quite pretty in the warm glow she had created. They were sleek, and the light made the glossy feathers shine almost gold, and when Nessa stretched them out they were bigger than the pew she was standing on. Despite her sadness, she smiled for the first time since losing Ophelia. She hadn't used her wings for a very long time and she had almost forgotten what it felt like to fly. She stepped off the pew and rose upwards, it felt like freedom; it felt like that first time she showed Ophelia her universe, she only wished Ophelia was there…

Nessa reached the statue and landed on the platform beside it, using her wings to steady herself. She smiled at seeing her angel's face, even if it was only made of stone. She touched the statue's arm and gazed at her face. She was overcome with how beautiful Ophelia was and she considered how very lucky she was that she had spent thousands of years in her perfect presence. Nessa felt the familiar stinging of tears, she had lost count of how many times she had cried in the last ten hours.

"Ophelia…" she whispered to the statue. "I'm sorry, I failed. I should have kept you safe! I…" She paused, unsure if she could bring herself to say the next part. "I really think I love you! I'm not just saying that because you're gone, or because I'm really drunk... I think I've been in love with you for a long time. But don't worry, I promise I won't ever tell you. I know you can't love me..." Nessa wiped her tears and stroked the statue's cheek. "Ophelia?" she whispered. "Do you know what humans do when they're in love?"

She leant closer to the statue and gently kissed its lips. She closed her eyes and imagined it somehow really *was* Ophelia, she willed the real Ophelia to feel her love, she wanted her to know she was so, so loved.

Up in Heaven the real Ophelia was sitting alone crying silently as she had been for several hours since Jophiel had told her that there was no way she could go back to Earth. She was completely filled with hopelessness, though 'filled' seems the wrong word to describe it, as she had ever experienced such emptiness. Suddenly though she actually *felt* something! She hadn't experienced a physical earthly feeling since her body was destroyed earlier that day, but suddenly she experienced a strange sensation on her lips. She slowly moved her fingers to her mouth, wondering what it was.

"Nessa?" she whispered. She didn't know why, but she felt like it had something to do with her beloved demon; as if Nessa was somehow sending her a sign. Whatever it was she felt a little bit comforted, reminded that someone down on Earth cared about her. Mostly though, the feeling gave her hope. If she could feel *something*, then maybe she could find a way to go back? Maybe everything wasn't completely hopeless...

"Thank you..." she whispered, her fingers still against her lips.

A week passed and Nessa hardly did anything. She kept hoping to somehow see Ophelia, that everything might be okay, but then she remembered that she would likely never see her again. Even sober, she made it a strange nightly ritual to kiss the statue in the minster, somehow it felt important. It made her feel connected to Ophelia for some reason, though she knew it was only a statue. It was oddly comforting to know that the statue would always be there.

It was seven o'clock on Wednesday evening. Nessa stood outside the pub that she and Ophelia should have been meeting in. She saw their table, empty as usual, but today for the first time since the pub opened, it would stay empty. Nessa wondered whether she should go and have a drink at the table anyway, for tradition's sake, but she couldn't bring herself to.

Nessa was about to leave, planning to go home and have a glass of whisky there instead. Suddenly though she stopped, sure she heard something. She listened intently, trying to hear it again. Was it a voice?

"Hello?" whispered Nessa, moving aside down an alleyway to get away from the passers-by who might think her a little strange.

"Nessa?" came a faint, but familiar voice. "Can you hear me?"

"Ophelia?!" Nessa could hardly contain her joy at hearing her voice, even faintly. Her eyes immediately filled with tears.

"You can hear me!" Ophelia's voice was still quiet,

but it was now filled with excitement, whereas before it had sounded uncertain and nervous.

"You have no idea how pleased I am to hear your voice Phee! Are you coming back?" Nessa asked hopefully, not even caring that she had just said something that hinted at her love.

"No. I can't right now. But I think I might have a way for us to see each other…"

"Really? How?"

"I've been working on something, I've had nothing else to do… But Nessa, do you trust me?" Ophelia's voice sounded a little louder now.

"Yes!" said Nessa without a moment's hesitation. "I trust you…"

"Then close your eyes…" Ophelia whispered.

Nessa did so immediately, and something strange happened; an odd sensation.

"You can open them now!" came Ophelia's voice, but it now sounded as if she was standing right beside Nessa.

Nessa opened her eyes, she was no longer in the alleyway, she wasn't sure where she was, but to her delight Ophelia *was* standing beside her!

Ophelia looked like a proper old-fashioned angel, in robes with her wings spread behind her. She also had a strange ethereal glow surrounding her. She was smiling fondly at Nessa. Nessa thought of all those humans who received divine messages from Ophelia back in the day; no wonder they were awestruck if this was the image that appeared before them. Nessa couldn't imagine a sight more beautiful.

"It worked!" squeaked Ophelia, sounding less like a divine messenger and more like the excitable little angel Nessa loved.

"What worked? Oh I thought I'd never see you again!" said Nessa, wishing she could hug Ophelia, but deciding that might cross some sort of line.

"Exactly!" said Ophelia. "Last week I had lost all hope of ever returning to Earth and seeing you again, but then I received a glimmer of hope and I became determined! I've been reading, trying to learn the rules and hoping I could find a way to communicate with you. I found something better, a way to *see* you!"

Nessa wondered what the glimmer of hope was that Ophelia received, she herself had felt nothing but hopelessness all week.

"Where are we? This doesn't feel like Earth." Nessa looked around at the vast emptiness stretching out before her.

"You don't recognise your own creation?" asked Ophelia with a smile.

Nessa's eyes widened. "Jupiter?" she said looking down at the orange beneath her feet. She hadn't seen her planet properly in over six thousand years.

"You brought me here once, and I wanted to return the favour. I can't go to Earth and you can't come to Heaven, but we can meet here!" Ophelia smiled, obviously thrilled with her idea.

Nessa wondered if Ophelia had any idea how much this gesture meant to her. She looked at her angel, happy to see her face other than in stone. Being on Jupiter with Ophelia actually gave Nessa mixed feelings though.

Long ago two angels stood together in this very spot, and Ophelia hadn't changed a bit; she looked exactly the same, especially right now, but Nessa couldn't be more different. She was constantly surprised that Ophelia wanted anything to do with an evil demon like her. Strangely Ophelia was far more at home with Demon Nessa than she had been with Archangel Zadkiel, her being the head of the Heaven must have made Ophelia feel nervous, Nessa thought.

Being there also reminded Nessa painfully of the promise she made, the one she failed to keep last week.

"I'm sorry I didn't save you..." Nessa said sadly. "I should have protected you, that bloody bomb distracted me! But I was there... I should have thought quicker."

"Don't be silly, it's not your fault!" Ophelia said quickly. "The bomb distracted me too, that's why he shot, when I wasn't looking. Anyway, you told me not to confront him, so you tried to save me before I even went. It's my stupid fault, you're right, I should have left it..."

"You're not stupid, you care about things! And you're very brave! I'm proud of you..." In a way Nessa felt that saying she was proud of Ophelia was almost like saying she loved her. It made her happy to say it.

"Thank you, but you shouldn't be proud." Ophelia sighed. "Nessa I got killed by my stupid attempts to be helpful! How many other times would that have happened if you hadn't stepped in to save me?" A tear fell down Ophelia's cheek.

Nessa reached out to put a hand on Ophelia's arm comfortingly, but strangely she couldn't touch her,

Nessa's hand sort went through her arm, as if Ophelia was a ghost. Nessa gasped and stared at the angel in horror.

"Why can't I touch you? Are you a ghost or something?" Nessa was suddenly filled with anxiety, reminded that Ophelia was technically dead.

Ophelia laughed slightly, wiping her tears. "No silly, you know ghosts don't exist! You can't touch me because my frequency is too high. Your body is on Earth's frequency, I lost my earthly body so now I'm pure angel. That's why I can't come back until I find a way to get an earthly body again, Earth's energy is way too heavy for a proper ethereal being. We were all on Heaven's frequency at the beginning, before the Earth was created, don't you remember?"

"I don't know. By the time we went to Eden I had been in Hell for a while. I lost my angelic energy long before that!" Nessa shifted her eyes down to the ground. Ophelia gave her a comforting smile and mimed stroking her shoulder, though of course her hand couldn't actually make contact. Nessa giggled a little at the silly gesture.

"I'm so happy that I found a way to see you!" Ophelia smiled. "I know it's only been a week like usual, but I missed you. I don't really like being in Heaven, I have always preferred Earth, and the fact that my favourite demon is there is the icing on the cake!"

"Earth isn't the same without you..." said Nessa.

"Well, at least we have Jupiter for now!" Ophelia said. "It's Wednesday and I believe I brought you here at seven o'clock. I've spent this week crying and reading up on angel magic and the laws of Heaven and Earth to try to work out how to do this, how about you, what have you done this week?"

"Big bugger all I'm afraid." Nessa said, smiling at Ophelia's commitment to their weekly meetings. "I've spent this week drinking and generally moping around. I didn't feel like doing anything since my best friend got killed… And of course I totally blamed myself."

"Well don't! Said best friend thinks you had nothing to do with it!"

"But I was there! I could have done something…"

"No you couldn't," sighed Ophelia. "Neither of us could have done anything because of the bomb. It was just bad timing, or good timing on his part."

"Did you know I was there?" Nessa asked in a small voice.

"Not until I saw you come running in the last moment."

"Did it hurt?" Nessa asked, knowing full well the answer and barely wanting to hear it.

"Of course it did!" said Ophelia. "But only for a minute…" she added after seeing Nessa's face. "I was happy to see you coming though, that was comforting, even though it was only for a moment."

Nessa didn't really know what to say. She and Ophelia stared out at space as they had once before.

"I'm optimistic." Ophelia said after a while, breaking the long silence. "Though I shouldn't be able to experience any physical feelings, I occasionally have some sort of earthly sensation on my lips! I think that means I must still have a connection to Earth. So surely that means I will be able to go back somehow. Don't you think?"

Her lips? Nessa held her breath as she wondered whether it could have anything to do with the statue. She had willed Ophelia to feel her love with all she had, what if it worked? Maybe that's why it had felt so important; to give Ophelia hope?

Ophelia wasn't permitted to return to Earth for three years, which happened to be the length of time the war went on for. In fact Ophelia surprised Nessa on VE Day, so while all the humans were celebrating the end of six years of war, they were celebrating Ophelia's return. Whilst they had seen each other; often meeting on Jupiter, it was far better to have Ophelia back on Earth. They immediately went back to their old routine and neither one really mentioned those three years. Neither of them told the other just how much they missed and loved each other. Though Ophelia absolutely would have confessed her love there and then, had she not just agreed to Jophiel's very strict terms of return. Nessa also never told Ophelia that she regularly kissed the statue, and more importantly Ophelia never told her that she knew, and that she loved the feeling of her kiss...

Chapter Ten
A Heavenly Warning.
(21st Century)

Two days had passed since Nessa had saved Ophelia's life, and almost as groundbreakingly, tried to kiss her. Ophelia had spent those two days not only waiting for the inevitable summoning from Heaven, but also replaying each moment from their last interaction. She really hoped she hadn't been too harsh, or upset Nessa too much. She wanted more than anything to let Nessa kiss her. Since she experienced a taste of Nessa's kiss via the statue several years ago, some of her daydreams had included what it would be like to actually kiss her directly. She wondered whether it was because Nessa was a demon that the idea was so appealing. Perhaps it was the temptation of a demon's forbidden lips, designed to put unholy thoughts into an angel's head? Or more likely it was just Nessa... Ophelia was madly in love with her and the fact that she was a demon didn't come into it. Besides, she couldn't imagine kissing any other demon, or anyone else to be honest.

Part of Jophiel's terms when she finally allowed

Ophelia to return to Earth three years after, regrettably, getting shot, was to ensure she never got herself involved in a big scandal again, and that she followed Heaven's will unwaveringly. Though she agreed, she had never been great at following Heaven's will. She had vowed to, when Nessa became a demon, desperate not to follow in her footsteps, but over the years it had been harder and harder. Ophelia and Nessa shared ideals, and they didn't really align with either realm. The two had worked together for thousands of years and Heaven hadn't found out, and though Ophelia still sometimes worried about it, they were always careful, so she believed there was no harm in carrying on. However she often thought about the 'no scandal' rule. She was painfully aware of the outrage that she had likely caused by not only visiting Hell, but also nearly getting destroyed by Lucifer; so though she was also overcome with joy that both she and Nessa survived the encounter, there was no way she could let Nessa kiss her. Ophelia really hoped Nessa wasn't too upset and didn't feel rejected, or worse think that she didn't love her back. It delighted Ophelia that after all these years Nessa was willing to say the 'L' word, but Ophelia was way too terrified to ever say it out loud in case God or the archangels heard her, and she wouldn't let Nessa say it if she couldn't say it back.

    Ophelia was in her living room with classical music on her gramophone, trying and failing to get lost in a book. Admittedly 'Pride and Prejudice' might not have been the best choice of distraction. Elizabeth Bennet rejected Mr Darcy's proposal and Ophelia was right back in Nessa's flat watching tears fall down the face of the person she loved more than life itself, as she pleaded to hear an affirmation of love that Ophelia couldn't give her. Nessa never usually cried, ethereal beings don't tend to cry anyway, and as a demon Nessa liked to pretend nothing ever really bothered her. That's why if felt so horrible to see her cry, especially when Ophelia was painfully aware that she was largely the cause of her tears.

Ophelia closed the book, wondering if there existed a piece of fiction that *wouldn't* remind her of breaking her beloved demon's heart. Before she could consider another title, the gramophone stopped abruptly and the room was filled with strong angelic energy, a little like the wall of energy that hit Ophelia every time she travelled up to Heaven. She glanced around in confusion, looking for any lurking angels, and was almost blinded by a brilliant white light that flooded her cottage, likely shining through the windows for any passing humans to witness too. When the light faded, the Archangel Jophiel was standing before her, looking like a more dramatic version of Gabriel about to tell Mary she was to have Jesus.

Jophiel looked around the room disapprovingly before meeting Ophelia's eye and giving her a particularly nasty look. Ophelia smiled sheepishly, suddenly filled with anxiety. As the leader of the angels, it took a lot for Jophiel to come down there, she usually called angels to her. Ophelia knew she must be in a great deal of trouble to warrant a trip to Earth for the archangel.

"Your Highness?" Ophelia said nervously, trying to break the uncomfortable silence. "Err, welcome to

Earth. Can I help you?"

Jophiel glanced at the window containing the human world outside and wrinkled her nose in disapproval.

"It's very heavy down here," she announced after a moment. "I don't know how you bear it…"

"Oh, you get used to it after a while. It's been long enough!" Ophelia said with a small nervous laugh.

"Hmm…" Jophiel looked her up and down. "Of course, it is not nearly so heavy as Hell I'd wager. Do tell Angel Ophelia, what does Hell feel like?"

Ophelia's face flushed burning hot, as if she were down in the deep fires of Hell right then. Jophiel raised an eyebrow expectantly, awaiting an answer.

"I'm… not certain Your Highness. I should think it feels very oppressive…" Ophelia could tell that her face was red with shame.

"Oh for Heaven's sake Ophelia, do not insult the intelligence of both of us by lying about this!" Jophiel snapped. "I came down here personally to speak with you in the hopes that we do not have to advertise this scandal too loudly." she continued. "Care to explain what you; an angel, were doing down in Hell and why you almost got wiped out of existence by The Devil?!"

Ophelia took a shaky breath. She had been too distracted by the almost-kiss to consider what to say during this inevitable questioning. Nessa had suggested that Ophelia blame her, that did tend to be the angel's way out of most scrapes. It worked because, unfortunately, the archangels were never surprised by anything a demon did.

"Nessa took me down there…" Ophelia said, hating having to blame her, but really hoping Jophiel believed it. "Lucifer tasked her with capturing an angel so that he might ask after Heaven's plan. I believe he knew you were planning something following the destruction of the monastery."

"I see…" said Jophiel. Ophelia couldn't tell yet whether she believed her or not. "I received a message from Lucifer himself stating that he had learned of our plan from you and detailing a new weapon he has at his disposal. He owns a poison that can destroy an angel in only a minute! He easily could have used that on you, you fool!" Ophelia pretended to be shocked by Jophiel's revelation, when of course she knew all too well that particular poison's power. "Now, do not repeat that," continued Jophiel. "That kind of threat from Satan could whip the lower angels into a frenzy of fear."

"Of course," said Ophelia quietly, not wishing to comment on the poison.

"So, did you tell Lucifer about our planned attack?" asked Jophiel patronisingly.

There was no point in denying it, it was clear that Jophiel already knew.

"Yes. I am very sorry Your Highness. As I said, Nessa was asked to bring an angel to Lucifer, and of course as I live nearby I was the obvious choice. I tried to stay quiet, but he is The Devil, he tortured the information out of me!" Ophelia lied, trying to make herself sound as much like a victim as possible, so that little-to-no blame lay at her feet.

"You often cause trouble Angel Ophelia," sighed

Jophiel, clearly ignoring the part where Ophelia had insisted that it wasn't her fault. "You should not allow yourself to get into these situations! Have you any idea how bad it would look if Lucifer had destroyed you with his poison? It would have caused us no end of problems!"

Ophelia noted that Jophiel only cared about inconvenience to Heaven rather than her life. She wasn't surprised though, she was one of many angels and could probably easily be replaced. She wondered what her punishment would be if Jophiel knew that Lucifer *did* use the poison on her.

"I am sorry Your Highness…" she said sadly. "As I said, it was not my fault…"

"You are too close with Demon Nessa!" announced Jophiel with a nasty glare. "You put yourself and the rest of Heaven in danger every time you speak to her."

"She is my enemy!" Ophelia insisted. "My counterpart in Hell. I must keep an eye on what she is doing and attempt to thwart her evil schemes…"

"Do you take me for a fool, Ophelia?" Jophiel said, raising her voice to sound more commanding. "Do you really think I do not know that your friendship spans the millennia?"

Ophelia gasped, almost more terrified of this archangel looming over her than she had been of Satan.

"Now, truthfully I do not care who you associate yourself with," Jophiel went on. "However, I feel it important to remind you oh dear naive little angel, that Nessa is a *demon*, she does not really care about you, she will betray you eventually. That's what demons do! She will destroy you Angel Ophelia!"

"She won't. There is good in her!" Ophelia said recklessly, desperate to finally defend her love. "She was an archangel just like you once!"

Jophiel laughed. "Even Lucifer was an archangel once! The Archangel Zadkiel was entirely at fault for her damnation. You were not there at her fall Ophelia. She destroyed herself, just as she shall soon destroy you! She is a monster, certainly not worthy of an angel's friendship. Why, she almost got you destroyed by taking you down to The Devil. She does not care about you, you are a fool!"

Ophelia said nothing, but shifted her gaze to the ground. She thought of Nessa begging her not to go to Hell and confront Lucifer, and giving up her magic to save her. Jophiel was so wrong about her, if only she could do something to prove it.

"I don't need stupid angels causing scandals," Jophiel said. "That was a condition of your return the last time you did something foolish. Do you remember? You are at risk of such scandals associating yourself with a demon. You may well fall to join her in Hell if she does not destroy you first!"

Jophiel had a way of saying the nastiest things while ensuring her voice still somehow sounded calm and angelic. Her tone almost never matched her words.

"I am sorry Your Highness," Ophelia said again, resenting the number of times she had already had to apologise for what was quite a traumatic event. "Am I to be punished?"

"We have been discussing that subject..." Jophiel

said. "We are giving you another chance. You must be more careful Ophelia. If you continue to put yourself in danger, then we may need to consider replacing you on Earth with a more reliable angel."

Ophelia's eyes widened. They might stop her from seeing Nessa?!

"I recommend that you keep away from that *demon*," Jophiel continued, practically spitting out the word. "And since you can't seem to handle things yourself nowadays, we have decided to send you an assistant."

"What?!" Ophelia was horrified by the thought. Heaven's judgement was bad enough without having another angel running around spying on her.

"He will help you to manage things, and perhaps provide a level head when you are clouded by affection towards *that* demon," Jophiel raised her chin so that she was looking down at the seated Ophelia even more. Ophelia had wondered whether she ought to have stood up, but it seemed more awkward as time went on, so she never found the right moment to move.

"That really isn't necessary," Ophelia said, putting down the book she was still holding, and deciding finally to stand. "I promise I am perfectly capable of running things myself, as I have done for around six thousand years now."

"Clearly you are not!" Jophiel sighed. "It is a very important time for Heaven, we don't need you doing anything else stupid. Now, your assistant will be new to Earth, so teach him the ways, but do not allow him to get corrupted by demons and the human world as you have been!"

Ophelia felt that all these nasty little digs were rather unnecessary. She also *really* didn't want an assistant, especially as Jophiel would likely get them to report back with news about everything Ophelia did, but Jophiel was not someone to be easily reasoned with.

Jophiel clicked her fingers and a bewildered looking angel appeared beside her. Ophelia was a little startled. The angel looked at her shyly. She recognised him as the angel that she had knocked into whilst running down the corridor to tell Nessa about Heaven's plan. That was only two days ago, but it somehow felt much longer, after all that had happened.

"This is Ophelia, our *current* Angel of the North," Jophiel told the angel, with a pointed emphasis on the word 'current', reminding Ophelia that she could quite easily be replaced. "Ophelia, this is Ezra; your new assistant. Now do let us know if you have any issues, and *don't* get yourself into any more trouble, understand?"

Ophelia nodded and in an instant Jophiel disappeared in a flash of light, leaving the new angel standing awkwardly in Ophelia's living room, staring at her in a way that made her feel a little unnerved.

"Err, hello? I'm Ophelia..." she said. She hadn't expected to have a visitor dumped on her like that and she wasn't sure how to proceed.

"I know who you are. You're the Angel of the North! I'm Ezra. I'm just an admin angel." replied the angel, not shifting his eyes from Ophelia.

Ophelia gave him a little awkward nod. "Well, welcome to Earth Ezra. I can give you a bit of a tour of the city in a minute if you want?"

"Okay, thank you..." Ezra said quietly. Ophelia realised that she was an authority figure to him, he was acting nervous in a similar way to Ophelia when she first met Nessa in Heaven. She resented Ezra being there because of what it represented, but as she looked at him, he gave her a friendly, shy smile. It wasn't his fault, he had to do what Jophiel said, just like everyone else, he was probably quite frightened.

"Have you ever been to Earth before?" she asked.

"No never," said Ezra. "I have always wanted to see it though..."

"Well you're in luck I guess!" Ophelia said, giving Ezra a warm smile. "I also suppose you'll have to stay here... I'm sorry I didn't know you were coming."

"Neither did I until around an hour ago," Ezra smiled, as if that wasn't as stressful as Ophelia thought it sounded.

"You had an hour's notice to leave everything you've ever known? Goodness me, that sounds rather abrupt..."

"It's fine," said Ezra quickly, the strange fake smile still plastered on his face.

"Right... Good!" said Ophelia. She was used to talking to humans, or Nessa who was just as worldly. It was odd to speak to a proper, awkward Heavenly angel. "I'll show you upstairs. I guess you can have the spare room."

Ophelia led a nervous but fascinated Ezra upstairs. The cottage came with a spare room, but it had never been used. On the odd occasion that Nessa had stayed the night, they didn't sleep, they spent the night talking. As far as Ophelia was aware Nessa didn't really sleep at all.

Ezra stared around the bedroom as if it was the most amazing thing he had ever seen. Ophelia couldn't help but smile, she thought it might be quite fun to see his reactions to the city outside.

"Miss Ophelia; Your Holiness, what is that?" Ezra asked, pointing to the bed.

Ophelia was a little thrown off by the form of address, but answered nonetheless. "It's a bed," she said. "Humans lay on it to sleep at night, it's what they do to reset their bodies for the next day."

"Do you sleep?" asked Ezra, clearly fascinated.

"Sometimes," smiled Ophelia.

Just then there was a knock at the door. Ophelia's eyes lit up. It was Nessa!

"Err, someone's at the door, I need to go and answer it. Feel free to look around?" she said as she rushed to the stairs, leaving Ezra to investigate the concept of a bed.

Ophelia actually felt a little nervous as she approached the door, she hadn't seen Nessa since she refused her advances and made her cry. She had often wondered whether kissing Nessa would somehow ruin what they had, but now she feared that *not* kissing her might have done just that.

Ophelia opened the door and Nessa looked at her in concern.

"Phee? Is everything alright?" she said quickly.

"Yes, why what's happened?" asked Ophelia.

"There was a massive spike in angelic energy here!

Any demon or angel for a hundred miles would have felt it. I was worried it had something to do with the other day, you know? I wanted to make sure you were okay..."

Thank goodness, Nessa didn't seem angry at Ophelia. She was just as caring and concerned as ever. Ophelia felt comforted.

"It was Jophiel," she explained, glancing behind Nessa at a couple walking their dog past the cottage. "Come in!" she said, practically pulling Nessa through the door.

"What do you mean, Jophiel? She actually came down here?" asked Nessa in confusion.

"Yes!" said Ophelia, closing the door. "She just appeared out of nowhere and started complaining about the heavy energy!"

"Well shit! It takes a lot for Archangel I'm-better-than-all-of-you Jophiel to come down here! What did she want?"

"To tell me off," said Ophelia sadly. "She came here personally to avoid it all becoming a big scandal. I think Lucifer's angel poison has really got her worried, you know?"

"Did you tell her it was my fault?" Nessa asked.

"Yes, but all I got was a lecture about why I shouldn't be friends with you! As if I'm not painfully aware of that all the time!" Ophelia was feeling rather frustrated.

The rules of Heaven always stressed her out and she sometimes wished that she could try to reason with God. Jophiel and the other archangels made their views perfectly clear, but if Ophelia was brave enough, which she absolutely wasn't, she could try to negotiate with the one who was actually in charge. Ophelia refused to believe that God was as unreasonable as Nessa always said she was. Sure, she was formidable, but there must be kindness there; she was God!

"I wish Jophiel could see that you're not like the other demons!" Ophelia went on. "She just told me that you don't really care about me and that you'll eventually destroy me..."

Ophelia remembered how comforting it had been to hug Nessa when she returned from Hell. Since there seemed to be no hard feelings about the rejection, Ophelia put her arms around her demon, desperate for that feeling of comfort. Nessa tensed a little in surprise, but then relaxed and wrapped her arms around the angel. Ophelia felt truly safe; having Nessa's strong arms around her felt like protection. Like nothing in any realm could ever hurt her as long as she was in her embrace. Ophelia laid her head on Nessa's shoulder and Nessa softly rested her head against it; an intimacy neither had felt before.

"She won't ever believe I'm different," Nessa sighed. "Jophiel hates me the way she hates all demons; probably more. But that doesn't matter because she's wrong. I *do* care about you; I always have. You are my only friend, the only being that has ever really cared about me. And doesn't she think if I was going to destroy you I would have done it a long time ago! I will always try to save you, you know that!"

"I do. Thank you," smiled Ophelia. Enjoying being close to Nessa and wishing the hug didn't have to end.

Everything in her wanted to say 'I love you', but she thought about Jophiel's wrath. The threat that she would be replaced on Earth if she caused another scandal, then she might never see Nessa again. Regrettably, Ophelia broke away from the embrace. Nessa smiled and gently moved a piece of hair from Ophelia's face.

"So you're okay though?" she said, "Jophiel didn't do anything to you?"

"No, she didn't do anything..." Ophelia was about to mention Ezra, when he appeared at the bottom of the stairs, glancing into the kitchen.

"Excuse me, Your Holiness, but why do you have a kitchen? You don't consume human food do you?" Ezra asked in wonder.

Nessa raised an eyebrow. "Your Holiness?" she said, looking Ophelia up and down with a smile. "Should I be calling you that too?"

Ophelia blushed slightly and turned to Ezra. "Really, there's no need to call me that, or 'Miss'. Just call me Ophelia. That stuff makes me sound superior to you."

"You *are* superior to me," said Ezra. "I'm just an admin angel, I'm not important like you..."

"Everyone's important!" said Ophelia quickly.

"I remember saying that exact thing to a certain angel long ago during a similar conversation..." grinned Nessa. "And look how far she's come! I wonder if she remembers? I'm not sure, I did have different hair then..."

Ophelia giggled at her demon's silliness. "Of course she does!" she smiled. "Nessa, this is Ezra. He's my new assistant, apparently... Because they don't think I can handle things on my own."

Nessa lent against the wall and grinned at the new angel. "Hello!" she said.

"Hello?" said Ezra nervously. "You are not an angel are you?"

"Absolutely not!" smiled Nessa.

"You also don't seem like a human..."

Nessa raised her eyebrows at Ezra, giving him a slight nod to go on.

"Are you... a demon?" he asked worriedly.

"I might be. What do you think?"

"Are you?"

"Maybe, I'm not an angel or a human. That's the only other option right." Nessa grinned.

Ophelia gave her a playful tap on the arm. "Stop being silly!" she smiled.

Nessa gasped dramatically and held her arm, pretending Ophelia had hurt her.

"I cannot believe you just hit me! That's not very angelic of you," she joked.

"Like I said, silly!" Ophelia said, giving the demon's shoulder a little push. Nessa looked at her in mock surprise again and Ophelia laughed. She noticed Ezra looking extremely uncomfortable. "This is Nessa. Yes, she is a demon, but there's no need to be scared of her, she won't hurt you."

"Ooh, that depends!" said Nessa. "I might if you're particularly annoying..."

Ezra gulped and Ophelia gave Nessa a withering look. Nessa sighed and walked up to Ezra, causing him to back up and stumble against the stairs. She put out her hand and Ezra flinched as if she might hit him.

"For the sake of all that's unholy, I'm just going to shake your hand! That's how humans greet each other, I'm being polite. Give me your hand."

Ezra reluctantly offered his hand to Nessa, who shook it, perhaps a little hard, but with good intentions.

"Nice to meet you Angel Ezra," Nessa smiled. "See, that didn't kill you, did it?"

"Your hand is rather cold…" Ezra said quietly.

"Then I must be a demon eh?" Nessa pushed her curly hair out of her face and gave Ezra a genuinely friendly smile. "I'm Ophelia's best friend. If you're nice to her, I'll be nice to you. Is this your first time on Earth?"

Ezra nodded.

"Has your lovely host offered to give you a tour?" Nessa asked.

"Yes I did!" said Ophelia. "I was planning to just as you arrived." She suddenly remembered Ezra's question about the kitchen. "By the way Ezra, yes I do eat food," she said, "It's honestly one of the most enjoyable things, you should try it!"

"Are you tempting an angel?" grinned Nessa. "Isn't that my job?"

Ophelia rolled her eyes at Nessa, then smiled. "Do you want to come to show him around? Two voices are better than one?"

"Sure! We can show your new friend all the sights and guide him on Earth like a Yorkshire angel and demon on his shoulders!" Nessa grinned. "You can show him the minster; centre of Christianity in the North, you know? And I'll point out where Dick Turpin was hanged and where all those people were killed in that tower, yeah?"

"Maybe not right now..." Ophelia said. "I think sites of terrible bloodshed are the sort of thing we should save for the second outing?"

"Fair enough!" Nessa said, heading for the door. "Roll up roll up for the mystery tour!" she grinned.

Ophelia smiled at Nessa's enthusiasm, nudging the frightened angel to follow her out.

The best friends had a fun afternoon acting as tour guides to their new 'pet angel' as Nessa kept calling him. They showed him all around the city, then to his horror, stopped for something to eat. Ezra refused the offer of any food, as most angels would. Ophelia noticed him watching the two of them intently as they ate and talked about that one time they got locked in the museum and had to use magic to get out.

"Are you sure you don't want to try any?" asked Ophelia, offering the basket of chips in Ezra's direction.

Ezra shook his head violently, as if she had just asked him if he wanted to put his hand in a blender.

Nessa took a chip, showing off, throwing it in the air and catching it in her mouth. Ophelia laughed, but Ezra just looked even more uncomfortable. Ophelia suddenly realised how much being around a demon *had* affected her. Ezra was pure, new to Earth and bewildered by everything going on around him. That's what angels were supposed to be like; ethereal beings, unsullied by Earthly temptations like chips, wine and chocolate. Ophelia had helped Nessa out with so many little jobs over the years that she hardly batted an eyelid when she took her to burn down Heaven's favourite monastery. Ezra would be utterly horrified by some of the things Ophelia had been involved in... Nessa was posting a photo of their food on Instagram and Ezra was staring at her with a definite look of fear. That's how angels should look at demons, but when Ophelia looked at Nessa all she could do was smile. Maybe Jophiel was right... Ophelia hadn't noticed how far she had strayed away from God and Heaven until she spent time around another angel, and it wasn't because she had been on Earth, because she knew of other angels on Earth that remained pure. It was Nessa...

On the way home Ophelia was distracted, obsessing over everything Jophiel had said about hanging out with Nessa eventually leading to destruction or damnation. It was dark, and Nessa was walking with the angels, ensuring they got home safe, even though it was well out of her way. She was being especially delightful, Ophelia thought; in a particularly good mood, especially for someone that she had recently rejected rather harshly. But that didn't stop Ophelia from worrying that she had strayed too far from Heaven. Nessa could be the nicest person in the world, but she was still a demon.

When they reached the cottage door, Ophelia sent Ezra inside so that she could speak to Nessa about her concerns. When they were alone Ophelia quickly took Nessa's hands and stared at her. Nessa jumped in surprise, but then immediately softened and held Ophelia's hands back, interlocking some of their fingers.

"Nessa, I'm a really bad angel! What have I become? It was so gradual I didn't even notice! No wonder Jophiel and the others hate me. I'm more like you than any of them…" Tears pricked Ophelia's eyes as she looked at Nessa, whose face was full of concern regarding this sudden outburst.

"Woah woah, where has this come from?" Nessa asked. "What have you done?"

"Everything? Nothing? Goodness me, I don't know! But I should be like Ezra!"

"What? Boring?" smiled Nessa.

"No! Angelic… Pure… It's honestly a wonder I haven't become a demon yet!"

"But, like you said, you're more like me! You're nothing like demons Ophelia. We've been somewhere between Heaven and Hell for thousands of years. We've always had our own side! Why the sudden doubt?"

"Jophiel is really on to me," Ophelia said sadly. "When I came back after the war I had to promise not to cause any more scandals… She was so angry about the Hell thing today. She hates me for being friends with you, I'm not angelic enough… She told me to stay away from you, but I can't! But if I do anything else wrong they will replace me on Earth, then I won't be able to see you at all!" Ophelia was crying now. Nessa hugged her; their third hug in three days, after never hugging in six thousand years.

"I have an idea," said Nessa after a moment. "What if we kept away from each other for a month or two? Until things cool down with Jophiel."

"Weren't you listening, you idiot, I said I don't

want to stay away from you!" Ophelia said, pulling away from the hug.

"I don't want to stay away from you either. You're all I've got and, well I won't say anything, but you know how I feel about you… But that's why I'm suggesting it. You're right and so is Jophiel, hanging around with me is dangerous, and they'll be on high alert up there right now, so best lie low for a bit." Nessa paused and used her jacket cuff to gently wipe away Ophelia's tears. "It won't be for long. We used to only see each other every few hundred or even thousand years, this only for a couple of months, and we have eternity right? But not if you get banned from Earth! You know where I am if you need me, but there's no need for our meetings at the moment anyway, I don't work for Hell anymore…"

"But, Nessa!" Ophelia wasn't sure what else to say. It was a logical plan, especially with Ezra hanging around, likely tasked with reporting back to Heaven, but the plan being sensible didn't stop it breaking Ophelia's heart. "I'll miss you…" she decided to say after a moment.

"I'll miss you too, and that's why we know that we'll be there, waiting for each other when we meet up again. It's only for a while, to keep you safe!" Nessa said. She stopped for a moment, as if weighing something up in her mind. "This isn't too affectionate, humans did this when they met or parted during the Regency times, do you remember?" She took Ophelia's hand and kissed it gently; looking deep into her eyes as she did. Ophelia felt a strange leap of excitement deep inside her that she didn't really understand. "I'll see you soon, dear Angel

Ophelia," Nessa said, "I can't wait to hear all your news when we next meet." And with that, she turned and walked out of the gate.

"Goodbye!" Ophelia said as Nessa disappeared round the corner. She sighed, wondering when she would next see her love and whether they would *ever* be able to be together like humans when they love each other. She also wondered if she would ever dare to say 'I love you' out loud, or whether her fear would always be stronger.

Chapter Eleven
The Biggest Scandal in History.
(Seven Weeks Later)

"This place really is wonderful!" Ezra whispered, gazing up at York Minster's ceiling. "Why don't we live here? It feels more like home because it's sacred"

"Shh!" said Ophelia, opening her eyes and giving the angel a warning look. "Be quiet and pray!"

Ezra pouted a little and wriggled away from Ophelia slightly, copying the way she and the humans had their hands, and closing his eyes. Ophelia rolled her eyes at him and then continued to pray.

Ophelia had never prayed before, but since she and Nessa parted ways almost two months ago, she had prayed every Sunday. Angels didn't need to pray; it was something the humans did to try to get closer to God and attempt to be more holy; angels were already holy. However, Ophelia was painfully aware that she was not as holy as the other angels, and she decided that The Almighty may forgive her if she prayed in church like the God-fearing humans did. She wasn't really sure if it worked, or if God was listening, but she begged forgiveness for anything unholy she had ever done. She apologised for straying and asked that she not be punished or sent away. She tried to explain to The Almighty that Nessa was truly good at heart and asked to know whether God would allow her to love her. Of course an answer never came, but Ophelia was desperate.

She had tried to focus on being more angelic, but no matter what she did she couldn't stop thinking about Nessa. She loved her with all she had, and in a way she wished she didn't. Her life would be so much easier if she wasn't in love with a demon. Everything would be simple then, and she wouldn't feel so guilty all the time. In Ophelia's life nothing was simple, it hadn't been since that day an archangel asked her if she was busy and took her to see the stars. She wondered what that young angel would have thought if she knew about the thousands of years worth of conflicting feelings that were coming her way after that interaction. Would young Ophelia have decided not to go with Zadkiel, to avoid all the pain? Now, Ophelia would never trade Nessa's friendship for a simpler life, but it sometimes crossed her mind that if she had never met her, then she wouldn't know any different from the life of a good God-fearing angel. At the heart of it all, Ophelia would always be at war with herself, and quite frankly, it was exhausting.

The priest ended the sermon and the humans began to filter out of their seats. Ophelia looked at Ezra beside her. He hadn't been praying, he was squinting at the fine text inside the bible.

"Are you in this?" he asked excitedly.

"I'm not sure, probably not. I think only the

archangels are," Ophelia replied. She glanced at the bible and Nessa's old name leapt out at her among the dense text. It sent a thrill through her body. She loved the thought that even though Nessa had been a Prince or Duke of Hell for thousands of years, the humans still read about the good things Zadkiel did. She wondered whether the bible mentioned Nessa's fall, or if the humans still see her as the Archangel of Justice. She remembered that she had a copy of the book somewhere at home. While she could never be bothered to read it, she had felt it important to own one.

"Come on!" she said, tapping an engrossed Ezra on the shoulder. "I've got one at home if you want to look at it?"

"Ooh yes please!" grinned Ezra, placing the book down and standing alongside Ophelia. They joined the back of the group of people making their way out of the minster.

"All these people are here to feel closer to Heaven," whispered Ezra. "Wouldn't it be funny if they knew that there are two angels right here!"

Ophelia smiled. "Yes, I wonder what they'd say if they knew?" she whispered back.

"I imagine they'd probably start telling us all their life problems like we can do anything about it, and honestly I cannot be bothered with that! For The Almighty's sake I hope praying doesn't work. Can you imagine listening to everyone's petty little problems all day? I'd go mad!" Ezra gave Ophelia a cheeky little smile before glancing across the crowd. "Ooh, look at that!" he exclaimed, and he darted through the crowd before

Ophelia could stop him.

Ophelia smiled. It had been less than two months, yet Ezra seemed so different from that shy little angel that appeared in her living room. He once told her that no one in Heaven took any notice of him, or was willing to speak to him, so he never said much. Ophelia on the other hand actively encouraged him to talk to her, she felt it was important for them to get to know each other properly if they were to work and live together. In fact, after she got over feeling incredulous about being given an assistant because she 'couldn't be trusted', she was quite excited to get to know someone. Aside from Nessa she had never had any kind of friend. She knew that Nessa was somewhat close with Demon Beelzebub, but Ophelia had never really known *anyone* else. She was glad that Ezra felt able to be himself, away from the restrictions of living in Heaven. She felt that all angels would benefit from spending time down there, but then she had always far preferred Earth to Heaven anyway.

She caught up with Ezra who was standing by the font.

"Ophelia, is this holy water?" he asked in interest.

"Yes, can't you feel it?" said Ophelia. "Come on."

"I've never seen any. What do you think it feels like?"

"It just feels like water? I dunno, let's go. Leave it," Ophelia was aware of some staff member glaring at Ezra as if he threatened the very existence of the church.

Ezra didn't listen and put his hand gently in the water. Ophelia sighed, Jophiel had warned her not to let Ezra get 'corrupted' by the human world, but he had certainly been influenced by being there in those two short months. Ophelia liked him better now, even though he often caused trouble, but she wondered whether Jophiel would think she had affected him too much already. Would she prefer Ezra as the silent, obedient, frightened angel that he used to be; rather than this cheeky, chatty, chaotic one he must have always been underneath? Probably…

The staff member headed in Ezra's direction in a moment.

"Excuse me young man, you can't touch that!" he said gruffly.

Ezra looked at the man and shook the water off his fingers. "If I can't touch it, why is it not guarded?" he asked. "It's holy and anyone could take it…"

"What on Earth are you talking about boy?" asked the man, already sounding angry.

"Sorry, please excuse my little brother!" said Ophelia, taking Ezra's shoulders and pulling him away from the font. "He gets a bit confused sometimes… Come on Ezra!" She grabbed his arm and quickly led him away from the man and towards the gift shop exit.

"Little brother?" Ezra asked in confusion.

"Yeah, it's a human thing. It means you're family. That's easier than trying to explain what you actually are," Ophelia said.

"I know what brothers and sisters are from books," said Ezra. Indeed Ophelia had encouraged him to read some of her books to learn more about the world. "Plus, Archangel Jophiel used to have a sister," added Ezra.

Ophelia couldn't hide her smile. "Indeed she did!"

Ezra smiled at Ophelia. "It would be nice if we were family... No one has ever cared about me..."

"No one except Nessa has cared about me either," said Ophelia sadly. "I suppose we are a little like family already aren't we?"

"I like that!" beamed Ezra. He looked down at his damp hand. "It really does just feel like water doesn't it?" He sounded disappointed and Ophelia wondered what he wanted it to feel like. "Do you have any holy water at home?" Ezra asked. "It seems like something an angel would have."

"Absolutely not!" said Ophelia. "I would never go near the stuff. It could destroy Nessa! I could never risk it..."

"I didn't think of that," said Ezra, quickly rubbing his hand on the front of his shirt to dry it. "Can we look at the Earthly objects in the shop today?" he asked, as he did every week when they approached the gift shop.

"Very well," said Ophelia, smiling at her new little brother's chaos. She quite liked the idea of Ezra being her family. She had often thought it would be nice to have some form of family, or even friends. Aside from Nessa, and now Ezra, all the angels and demons Ophelia knew of were awful, and there was no point getting attached to any humans because they weren't around for very long, relatively speaking.

She watched Ezra poring over all the items in the gift shop and wondered whether he would be willing to be friends with Nessa too. He had been terrified of her when he saw her, but so was Ophelia when she first met her as a demon. Eventually, she thought, he might get over her being a demon. She believed they really would get on, and Nessa would probably like a new friend too.

All Ophelia really wanted was for her and Nessa to get back to normal, before she had all this extra guilt, fear and doubt piled on top of her. Maybe if Nessa *did* befriend Ezra, they could get him on their side, then he might not report things back to Jophiel? Ophelia's eyes widened as she realised what a demonic thought that was. What she just considered was technically corruption and bribery… This time away from Nessa hadn't made her any more angelic, despite her attempts to pray; it had actually made her resent the Heavenly system even more. Maybe she was too far gone, maybe there was no hope of redemption, maybe she really would become a demon one day?

"Are you alright?" asked Ezra, obviously noticing Ophelia's worried look.

"Hmm? Oh yes, sorry. I'm fine," said Ophelia, glancing at what Ezra was holding. "What's that?"

Ezra studied the packaging carefully. "A pin badge?" he said uncertainly. "I don't know what it is, but look, it has the minster on!" He presented it to Ophelia excitedly.

"Yeah, you can attach it to your clothes." Ophelia smiled. "Do you want it?"

"To own?" gasped Ezra. "I can have an Earthly object? To keep?"

"Sure, if you want."

Ophelia showed Ezra how to give the coins to the woman on the till and then helped him to attach the badge to his shirt collar when they got outside. He beamed with pride like a little child with a new toy, and Ophelia smiled warmly at him. He was definitely a welcome distraction from missing Nessa and fearing Heaven.

"Now, I fancy some tea and one of those little cakes from the coffee shop. Do you want to try something this time?" Ophelia offered Ezra food and drinks everyday, and everyday he refused vehemently. "I'm only asking because I genuinely think you'll like it," she said.

"I know," said Ezra worriedly, glancing upwards for a moment as if God and all the archangels might be glaring down at him. "I think I *would* like it, that's why I can't try it..."

"Fair enough," said Ophelia. "I'll get you one day!" She had said it playfully enough, grabbing his shoulders in a jokey way, but Ezra looked rather fearful.

The two walked through the city centre towards Ophelia's favourite coffee shop. Ezra kept touching his new pin badge as if he was checking it was still there. Ophelia had been on Earth since the beginning, so took little things like that for granted. It was nice that Ezra was excited by every tiny thing.

They began to walk down the shambles when suddenly Ezra grabbed Ophelia's arm.

"Look!" he said. "Isn't that Nessa?"

Sure enough Nessa was walking in the opposite direction towards the angels. Ophelia gasped, she couldn't see her right now, she didn't know what to say! They were supposed to be staying away from each other for a while. She panicked and grabbed Ezra, pulling him out of sight down a side street. It seemed odd avoiding

Nessa, and Ophelia wasn't really certain why it felt like she should hide.

"What's she doing?" Ophelia whispered to Ezra.

Ezra peeped round the corner onto the main street. "Just walking..." he said uncertainly. "Oh hang on! Now she's gone into that sweet shop."

"Great, let's hurry then!" said Ophelia, rushing back onto the street and walking past the sweet shop as quickly as possible.

"You know we could have gone round the other way?" panted Ezra, almost jogging to catch up with her.

"I didn't think of that..." said Ophelia, stopping for a moment to catch her breath when they had rounded the corner.

"Are you okay?" Ezra asked.

"I'm fine!" snapped Ophelia. "Come on!" She marched on towards the coffee shop, not noticing how hurt Ezra looked to be snapped at.

Ophelia had thought that she sensed something when they got to the shambles, a nice calming feeling. Now she knew it was Nessa's energy she could sense, and it felt like home after being apart from her. Nessa probably felt Ophelia's presence too, she hoped she didn't know that she was avoiding her. Goodness how Ophelia missed her! She would never be happy being a real angel, no matter how much she tried, not if it meant keeping away from Nessa.

Back at home Ophelia searched for the bible that she had promised Ezra could look at. She eventually found it buried under a large pile of more interesting books in the corner of her library. It was a very old copy and humans would probably pay a lot of money to have it. Before she took it through for Ezra she sat down with it at her desk. She really wanted to know what the book said about Nessa. She couldn't stop smiling as she read the lovely stories that the humans must read about her beloved former archangel. It even detailed the story about Archangel Zadkiel sparing Abraham's son, which wasn't even Zadkiel, that was Nessa; Ophelia's precious demon. There was no mention of Nessa becoming a demon, so as far as humans knew, she was still an angel. That fact made Ophelia very happy.

She flicked over to the story of Adam and Eve and read about the supposed serpent that tempted Eve to eat the apple, the story that Nessa had made up to keep Ophelia out of trouble. As Ophelia read the part about God sending the humans away, she suddenly realised something. Jophiel was wrong, even Ophelia had been wrong! She hadn't strayed from Heaven because of Nessa! Sure hanging out with a demon encouraged her to push the boundaries, but the very first sin on Earth was caused by Ophelia! Nessa had nothing to do with it, she didn't even really know her then, and they certainly weren't friends. Ophelia wasn't a very obedient angel, but it wasn't Nessa's fault, it was inevitable from the start. She would have gone her own way with or without Nessa, because she believed so strongly in proper goodness, rather than things that are officially 'good' but with nasty hidden agendas. In fact, being close to a fallen angel caused Ophelia to be hyper aware of the threat of falling, therefore making her rather reluctant to break the rules. She might have been *more* rebellious if she didn't know Nessa. Plus of course Nessa had saved her life countless times over the years. Without Nessa she would no doubt be dead, or a demon at least!

It felt like a revelation. Ophelia had never really blamed Nessa for anything, or resented the way she was, but she had always assumed that she wasn't a pure angel because she was friends with a demon. Everyone thought so, Jophiel said it and even Nessa insisted that everything bad was her fault. Now though, Ophelia had spent almost two months away from Nessa, and despite her best efforts, she was still 'bad' by Heaven's standards. She and Nessa went together as well as if they were made for each other. They were the same; both genuinely good, only, Nessa happened to have fallen, while Ophelia hadn't. Ophelia's heart was thumping; she almost felt like she had suddenly given herself permission to love Nessa, when before it had been forbidden. Maybe she had finally won the war against herself? Part of her had always been afraid that if she fell, or if anything bad happened to her it would be because of Nessa, and she couldn't let it be Nessa's fault, she wouldn't do that to her. But it wouldn't! Ophelia was rebellious all by herself, she always had been.

She picked up the bible and took it through to Ezra in the living room, feeling strangely lighter, as if a weight that she had carried for thousands of years was suddenly gone. Maybe she had always felt a little guilty for loving Nessa, and now she didn't have to.

Ezra was looking at a framed photograph on the fireplace, which regrettably, Jophiel must have seen when she visited. It was a gift from Nessa, a silly photo that they took together when Nessa first bought a colour camera in the 1950s. It was actually the first photo they ever took together, so it was very important to Ophelia.

"You look happy here..." said Ezra when he noticed she had come in.

"Yeah?" said Ophelia, putting the bible down on the coffee table.

"You haven't looked that happy since I've known you, apart from that first day when Nessa was here."

"Haven't I?" Ophelia said, wondering what he meant.

"Why have you been avoiding her?" Ezra asked. "Why did you hide when we saw her?"

"It's complicated... Here, I brought you the bible."

Ezra didn't acknowledge the bible. He carried on looking at the photo. "Is it complicated because she's a demon?" he asked.

"I don't know, maybe? Or because I'm an angel, I'm not sure anymore," Ophelia sighed.

"She doesn't really seem like a demon," said Ezra. "She's a lot nicer than I would imagine a demon to be."

"You were terrified of her!" laughed Ophelia.

"I was scared of you too!" smiled Ezra. "I was terrified of everything. Like you said I had an hour's notice that I was moving here! What do you expect?"

"You said it didn't bother you." Ophelia said suspiciously.

"Of course I said that. You can't complain about things in Heaven, are you mad? You've met Jophiel right?"

Ophelia laughed. "Yes I certainly have!"

She came to stand beside Ezra and looked at the happy Nessa in the photo. She touched the glass, missing her with every fibre of her being.

Ezra looked at Ophelia intently. "Are you in love with her?" he asked.

Ophelia immediately flushed red hot. Though it was of course true, something about hearing it said out loud by someone else panicked her.

"What? Why would you ask that?" she said quickly, fully aware that her flustered reaction gave away the answer straight away.

"Well, I haven't been here for very long, obviously, so up until recently I didn't really know anything about love... But I'm a very fast reader; you have to be to work in admin, and a lot of books are about love! I think it's adorable. I also think you definitely love Nessa. I won't tell anyone, if that's what you're worried about? I promise," Ezra smiled.

Ophelia felt a little choked up. When Ezra arrived she was rather angry about it. He was a Heavenly spy who she imagined would get in the way of her and Nessa's relationship, but there he was genuinely encouraging her to admit her feelings.

"Oh Ezra, yes I love her!" Ophelia said in a sudden burst. "I love her so much it sometimes hurts or I can't breathe, it's unbearable! But it's also euphoric! The best and worst feeling in any realm..." She sighed deeply. She had never said it out loud before. Yet nothing bad happened; she admitted how she felt and fleets of archangels didn't appear to smite her; she just felt happier.

"Have you ever told her that you love her?" asked Ezra.

"Of course not!" said Ophelia, thinking it was rather obvious.

"Goodness, why ever not?!" Ezra paused for a moment. "Maybe if you tell her it will hurt less? How long have you loved her?"

"I don't know exactly when it changed from friendship to love but, a few thousand years I suppose?"

Ezra looked shocked. "Girl, you know humans admit their feelings after a few months or whatever? What's wrong with you?"

Ophelia smiled at sassy Ezra. "Like I said, it's complicated. Neither angels nor demons should fall in love, especially not with the enemy I imagine! Love is a human thing, I don't think we should even be capable of love..."

"Who says?" said Ezra. "There must have been a point where a human fell in love for the first time, and before that they might not have known humans could love. Everything has to happen for the first time once. Even if no angels or demons have loved before, that doesn't make it impossible. It clearly is possible, you're proof of that!"

Ophelia burst into tears. That was so insightful, she'd never thought about it like that. She had always felt like there must be something wrong with her. Loving Nessa was something that she admitted to herself secretly as if it was a crime, but Ezra was right! Ophelia thought about how, up until very recently she and Nessa wouldn't have been able to be together even if they were humans; people didn't believe that two women could love each other, because they had never heard of it before. Just because you think something isn't possible, that doesn't mean it isn't. For example, most humans don't believe that angels and demons roam the Earth, yet there they were.

Ezra put an awkward hand on Ophelia's arm. "I'm sorry, have I upset you too much?" he asked.

"No no, you are completely right. That's why I'm crying. You are very wise Little Brother…"

Ezra smiled. "I have hardly spoken to anyone in my whole life, which is over six thousand years, believe me, I'm *delighted* to help!"

Ophelia took a tissue from the coffee table to wipe her tears.

"Hey, Ophelia! How many times have you cried?" asked Ezra.

"In my life? Ooh, millions of times!" Ophelia said.

"Well, I've never heard of angels crying, but you are proving that wrong too!" Ezra grinned. "I think love is probably the same."

Ophelia considered this. She remembered crying for the first time, when she found out that Nessa had been sent to Hell. She hadn't known what was wrong with her then, she didn't understand the feeling or why water was coming out of her eyes, but now it was perfectly normal.

"Thank you Ezra," Ophelia smiled. "But I still can't tell her how I feel."

Ezra groaned theatrically. "Why ever not?" he asked.

"I don't want either of us to get in trouble. Never

mind whether it's possible; can you imagine the scandal in both Heaven and Hell if they found out? I once promised Jophiel I wouldn't cause any more scandals, and I kind of did, that's why she sent you to keep an eye on me I guess. Loving Nessa would be the biggest scandal in history!" sighed Ophelia.

Ezra thought for a moment. "Well, you mentioned that Nessa doesn't actually work for Hell anymore because she can't do magic or whatever you said. I can't remember exactly, you talk about her all the time!"

"I don't talk about her *all* the time!" Ophelia jumped in defensively.

"Err, you do! I'm pretty sure there are more minutes in the day that you talk about her than those that you don't! And you sometimes sleep for some of those minutes!" Ezra said teasingly. "Anyway, my point is, if she doesn't work for Hell, then they won't really care. All you have to do is make sure Heaven doesn't find out."

"But, you were literally sent to report this sort of thing back to Jophiel!" protested Ophelia. "I'm not stupid, I know that you being my assistant was a load of rubbish. You are a spy really aren't you? Which is fine, except you just worked out my most dangerous secret…"

"I'm not a spy!" said Ezra unconvincingly.

Ophelia raised her eyebrows at him.

"Well, at least I'm not a very good spy if I am!" he said. "I'm too soft to be a spy, literally *any* other angel would be better for the job. I was just excited to have an adventure really. This is way more fun than anything that's going on in admin! I'm insanely jealous that you've been down here since the beginning."

"It doesn't matter if you're a *good* spy or not. If I tell Nessa how I feel, or worse, kiss her, you'll have to tell Jophiel," sighed Ophelia. "That's why Nessa and I haven't seen each other all this time, the archangels are on high alert."

"Don't keep away from each other on my account!" said Ezra. "Like I said I'm a terrible spy, because I don't care if you love a demon. In fact I'm rooting for you to get together! It's really sweet!"

"But, Jophiel..."

"Ophelia! Nothing in Heaven or Earth scares me more than Archangel Jophiel!" said Ezra. "Do you really think I want to be the one who tells her that you two are in love?! Honey I'd want to be in a whole different realm if she finds that out! That's why we make sure she doesn't. Look, if you go off to Nessa's house or whatever and tell her you love her and kiss her and all that, then I won't see it will I? I might technically be a spy, but I don't have to tell her everything. I'm not allowed to lie to her, but if she gets suspicious and asks if you confessed your love or kissed, I can say I don't know. Because even if I *do* know, I don't know a hundred percent if I'm not there to witness it, because technically you could be lying and not go talk to her at all! Do you get it?"

"Err, not really but I believe you. I'm sure it makes sense in your head," said Ophelia with a smile. "Thanks. You're a good little brother!"

Ezra looked a little like he might cry now. "Am I still your brother? Even though I'm a spy?"

Ophelia laughed. "Yes Ezra. I already knew. As long

as you promise you're definitely a bad spy."

"Oh I'm easily the worst!" Ezra said, nodding quickly. "How long have you known?"

"I'm not as naive or stupid as Jophiel thinks," said Ophelia. "I knew straight away that 'assistant' was code for spy. I'm causing trouble and Heaven's busy planning something they don't want me in the way of, of course they send someone to keep an eye on me. I'm just lucky they sent you!"

"So, you've known I was reporting back to Heaven this whole time, and you've still been kind to me?" Ezra asked quietly.

"Of course!" said Ophelia. "I like you. It doesn't matter why you're here, it's not your fault. We all work for Heaven don't we?"

Ezra smiled. "Yes. Thank you. I'm really not spying, I didn't want to spy. I didn't have a choice, but when you and Nessa showed me around the city I realised how amazing this place is, so much better than the Heavenly offices I've been in for millennia. I just wanted to be your friend and try living on Earth. When Jophiel asks, I just tell her about how nice you are and how you're showing me all the cool human things, and about all the good kind things you do for others. Anyway, she wants to know if you're doing anything wrong, and I don't think what you do is wrong. I also don't think loving Nessa is wrong, so go tell her!"

"Really?" Ophelia was overjoyed by Ezra's kindness. He didn't have to be kind, he was scared of Jophiel; he could easily tell her everything. "Ezra you are by far the nicest and kindest angel I have ever met."

"Aww, I think the same about you!" Ezra said. "Thank you for not hating me..."

"I couldn't possibly," smiled Ophelia.

"Great, well go! Talk to Nessa! Then maybe you might be happy again, like in the photograph."

"Thanks Little Brother! The bible is there if you want to look at it," smiled Ophelia, heading towards the door. Suddenly though, there was a strange shift in angelic energy. Ophelia and Ezra looked at each other in concern. Had the archangels somehow heard them, or worse, God?

"This is a message for Angel Ophelia," came a voice that Ophelia guessed might be Archangel Gabriel. "Please report to the Seat of the Archangels at once! We have something important for you to do..."

Ophelia looked at Ezra in panic. "What in Heaven does that mean?" she said.

"I don't know, but you probably ought to go. It doesn't sound like it's about Nessa, so that's something?" said Ezra, almost as nervous as Ophelia.

"Oh Ezra, I think I know what it's about!" said Ophelia, her heart pounding. "They still want to attack Hell! I bet they want me to help! Oh God!" That was half blasphemy, which was very out of character for Ophelia, and half actually begging God not to make her hurt Nessa in any way.

All she wanted was to finally tell Nessa how she felt, but she had been summoned; and if the archangels summon you, you'd better go, as if your life depends on it, because it probably does!

Chapter Twelve
Heaven or Us?

Nessa still thought of herself as a demon, though she wasn't sure if she was one now. She didn't really care what she was, but she wished she could know what it all meant. *How* did she survive all that holy water? If she wasn't truly a demon, then what was she? It was frustrating knowing that she might never get any answers, as the only person who might know was God, and she wouldn't want to speak to Nessa, demon or not.

After six thousand years on Earth Nessa found it rather difficult adjusting to life without magic. She had to live like a human! No more convenient little conjurings or magic touches here and there; things had to be done by hand now. However inconvenient, that was a small price to pay for Ophelia's life though.

It had been almost two months since then; two months of freedom from the bindings of her job in Hell. She hadn't been down there, she hadn't seen a single demon; it was great! But of course it had also been nearly two months since Nessa had seen Ophelia, and that was far from great. Being away from her beloved angel really highlighted to Nessa just how much she adored her, as if she needed reminding.

She had considered Ophelia's recent actions and behaviour, and came to the conclusion that her angel *must* love her back, after all you don't risk destruction in Hell for just anybody. Of course, she knew they were close friends, but Ophelia never actually said she didn't want Nessa to kiss her, she only asked her not to, in case she got into trouble. Surely if Ophelia didn't feel the same way she would have been more horrified by the attempt.

Ophelia would never admit to loving a demon, and Nessa understood why now. She knew full well that Heaven was very strict with their rules, and that there were always threats; after all, Nessa had quite literally been thrown out, back in the day; but she hadn't realised just how much the threats affected Ophelia until she was in tears, clinging desperately to Nessa outside the cottage. Ophelia often spoke about 'getting in trouble', and Nessa knew she was terrified of becoming a demon, but it seemed that it was all getting too much for her. Nessa wondered whether it was since she found out that Heaven planned to destroy Hell, maybe she was finally starting to realise that both realms were as bad as each other? Despite helping to create it, Nessa had certainly never agreed with the values of Hell; and Heaven was often questionable too. Not that they wanted her anyway! But Ophelia had always been convinced that deep down, Heaven was still truly good. They stretch the boundaries of the word 'good', that's what Nessa always tried to tell her. If the people in power say anything with enough confidence and certainty, everyone will believe them.

The thing was, there were millions of angels, if they all followed along unquestioningly, it must be really hard to be the one that dares to disagree. Nessa was used to being the disobedient one, she had been since the beginning, though she hadn't really planned it that way, it was more just something that happened. Now though, Jophiel had spent over six thousand years establishing her strict rules; especially after all that trouble Lucifer caused with the war. It was probably harder to rebel now. It was easy for Nessa to occasionally feel annoyed that Ophelia cared so much about the rules, but then she reminded herself how difficult it must be, and felt proud of her brave little angel for what she did do.

Nessa arrived home, dumping her bags of shopping in her messy hall. It hadn't taken long for her flat to get messy again after Ophelia had tidied it, and Nessa was even less inclined to tidy things away without magic.

She took the little bag of sweets she had bought into the living room. It was Edinburgh rock, which Nessa wasn't particularly fussed about, but it was Ophelia's favourite. She took a piece, then chucked the bag onto the coffee table. She planned to offer some to Ophelia when she next saw her, which would be soon, she hoped. She had been sure that she felt Ophelia's presence as she walked down the shambles to the sweet shop, but she didn't see her, so she might have been imagining it. Maybe she was just so desperate to see her again? Perhaps subconsciously, Nessa had been wandering around the city all day in the hopes of bumping into Ophelia? It wasn't a thought she was aware of; she didn't go out intending to look for her angel, she knew she was supposed to be keeping away from her, but it would have been nice if she did happen to see her.

Nessa was about to see what was on the telly when the doorbell rang three times in very quick succession. There seemed to be panic in the way it was pressed. Nessa's heart leapt; last time Ophelia turned up there in a panic, Nessa almost lost her. What was it now?

Nessa rushed to the door, ironically almost tripping over the shoes strewn all over the hall. She opened the door and was greeted by Ophelia throwing her arms around her desperately. Nessa didn't know what was wrong, but it was clear Ophelia needed this hug. She pulled her closer and brought the angel's head down onto her shoulder, stroking her hair. Nessa felt Ophelia's tense body relax in the embrace and the demon closed her eyes, resting her cheek on Ophelia's hair. She had missed the feeling of being near her. She soon noticed that Ophelia was crying.

"It's okay," she whispered. "I'm here."

"I can breathe now..." Ophelia said quietly, gripping Nessa tighter, as if she couldn't possibly hug her enough.

They were standing in the open doorway. It was December and Nessa was freezing cold in short sleeves, but she hardly noticed. They stayed there, locked in each other's embrace for quite a while, neither one saying anything, until Ophelia broke away and looked into Nessa's eyes. The image must have been blurry, because

Ophelia's own eyes were full of tears, but she kept on gazing at her. After a while Nessa gave a tiny laugh, wondering why she was being stared at so intently.

"What are you doing?" she asked.

"I want to remind myself what it's like to look into someone's eyes and see that they care about me, because I won't see that again where I'm going," Ophelia sniffed.

"What? Where are you going? Look, come in, it's freezing. Tell me what's happening." Nessa guided Ophelia in and closed the door. She was about to go through to the living room, but Ophelia didn't move.

"I've been called back to Heaven!" she said.

Nessa stopped and turned back to Ophelia. "Why?" she said in horror. "Is it that bloody spy they sent you? Has he got you in trouble?"

"No no! Ezra's on our side!" Ophelia protested quickly.

"Phee, no one's ever on our side!" sighed Nessa, a little frustrated by Ophelia's trusting nature.

"It's got nothing to do with Ezra, or what happened in Hell or anything! This is different!'

"Different how?" Nessa asked suspiciously.

"It's the next phase of their plan about taking Hell down. The archangels want me to help! They think I can lead the project because…"

"Because you know a lot about demons?" Nessa finished.

"Nessa, I'm scared! I can't do this!" Ophelia grabbed Nessa's arms tightly. "I want you to come with me! To help. I can't do it on my own. I need you!"

"Ophelia. As much as I dislike Hell, I am not going

to help you destroy it! Plus you know I can't come to Heaven!"

"But you're not a threat to them now you have no magic! They might let you in? I need you..." Ophelia begged.

Nessa sighed. "There is no way. I hate them and they definitely hate me! And without magic I'm not a threat to them because I have no defences!" She looked at her angel's pleading eyes and felt guilty, though she didn't know what to do.

"Nessa. Please! Don't you understand what I'm saying?" There was such desperation in Ophelia's eyes. Nessa wasn't sure what she meant, but it was breaking her heart, she felt so torn.

"Phee, can't you explain? What's really going on?" Ophelia shook her head sadly.

"Then I really can't help you can I?" Nessa thought for a moment, looking at her darling angel's look of despair. "Don't go!" she said, taking Ophelia's hands.

"I have to! You know I don't have a choice!" Ophelia said sadly.

"There's always a choice!" insisted Nessa.

"Not this time. Trust me, there's nothing I can do..."

"There is! We could run away!" Nessa said, her eyes shining with this sudden new possibility.

"What do you mean run away? Run where?"

"Anywhere! I have no ties to Hell anymore, and I'll protect you if the archangels come for us. We could just go and be together! I don't care where we are as long as I'm with you. It's been thousands of years and I love you!" Nessa didn't mean to say the last bit, it just sort of came out. She knew Ophelia didn't want her to say it, but she wasn't sorry about it.

"I know..." whispered Ophelia. "Thank you..." She looked as though she was weighing up what to say next. Like she was scared of saying the wrong thing. "Nessa, I..." There was another pause. "I can't run away with you..."

Nessa tried not to show her crushing disappointment that Ophelia hadn't said she loved her back. Even though Nessa was fairly certain that Ophelia did love her, it still felt like the same rejection she had always had. She was never good enough; there was always something wrong with her. Too troublesome to be an angel, too nice to be a demon, but too much of both for Ophelia to admit to loving her. It reinforced Nessa's view that no one *should* be able to love her. At the end of the day, Ophelia was ashamed of loving her, and that wasn't a great feeling.

"Please run away with me!" insisted Nessa, shaking off the rejection. "Both realms are awful, you know they are! I would dedicate the rest of eternity to keeping you safe. From Heaven, or Hell, or anything! I promise!"

"You can't keep us safe..." Ophelia whispered. "Trust me, not this time. Anyway, I have to go. You can't just run away from your duty!"

"Phee, listen! Even when I worked for Lucifer, you were always way more important than any duty. Which is more important to you, Heaven or us?" Nessa didn't know why she said that. Setting herself up for rejection again like an idiot.

Ophelia had never looked so torn. A single tear

rolled down her face as if she had used all her other tears up and that was all that was left.

"I know you're ashamed of me, but I can't do anything about that!" Nessa yelled, suddenly losing her temper a little. Not at Ophelia; just at life. "It's not my fault that I am a demon, your beloved God did that to me! Ophelia, you have been my number one priority for all these years! It never mattered what Hell or Heaven did to me because I had you! Loving you is what's made this long life worth living... Without you I don't know what I'd be." Nessa broke down in tears. "I know I'll probably never be worthy of your love, but I promise you I will never stop trying to be good enough for you..."

"Oh Nessa..." Ophelia gulped. "I'm not ashamed of you! Please don't say that..." She glanced worriedly upwards. "Follow me!"

Ophelia darted into the living room and Nessa followed, trying her best to wipe her tears with the hem of her t-shirt. Ophelia found some scrap paper and a pencil and wrote something down furiously, as if she were filling the page with desperate emotions. She held up the paper and Nessa gasped. All it said was 'kiss me'. Nessa could feel her heart beating faster; so fast it might burst.

"Are you sure?" she whispered, her voice almost as shaky as her body.

Ophelia took a deep breath and nodded, putting the paper down and closing her eyes.

Nessa walked up to her, suddenly filled with a strange anxiety. She had imagined this moment for years, but now it was finally here she wasn't really sure what to do. Last time she had tried to kiss Ophelia she had been caught up in the moment, she hadn't really thought about it, but this time it seemed different. It felt important that she got it right.

She drew herself close to her angel, hesitating an inch away from her face. Ophelia started to open her eyes, obviously wondering why Nessa wasn't doing it. It was now or never. Ophelia might never ask her again. Nessa was surprised she had now. Before Ophelia could say anything, Nessa began to kiss her.

As soon as her lips touched Ophelia's, all her fear and nerves melted away. This was what had always been missing from her life. It felt like she hadn't realised that something was incomplete, until the feeling of this kiss made her whole. Nessa wrapped her arms around Ophelia and pulled her closer so that their bodies were against each other. She kissed her harder, as if it was the most natural thing in the world, even though she had never done it before. Ophelia gasped slightly and started kissing Nessa back. She wrapped her arms around Nessa's neck, entwining her fingers in her curls. The kiss felt desperate, as if neither one could bear the thought of ever stopping.

After a moment, Ophelia lifted her head slightly away from Nessa's lips and took a deep breath as if she had forgotten to breathe during the kiss. Nessa kissed gently around her mouth, never wanting to stop touching her. Ophelia lifted her head up higher and Nessa gently kissed her neck; showering it with tiny kisses. Then she reached her collarbone and let her lips linger, lightly running her finger along the other shoulder.

Ophelia took in a shaky gasp, as if it caught in her throat, and pulled away quickly, putting her hand to her mouth.

"Are you alright? Did I do something wrong?" Nessa asked after a moment.

"No, but Angels don't do that!" Ophelia said after a pause.

"It felt like Heaven to me…" Nessa said quietly. "What people think Heaven is…"

"The wrong kind of Heaven…" whispered Ophelia. "I have an obligation to the other Heaven…" She paused, wiping away a tear. "I have to go, I don't know when I'll see you."

"I wish I wasn't a demon, I wish I was something you could love…" Nessa said, feeling as pathetic as she sounded.

"Oh Nessa stop it! You are perfect… I'm sorry if I made you feel like you're not!" said Ophelia.

"Angel's aren't supposed to lie…" whispered Nessa.

"That's why I'm not."

"I won't believe an angel could love me unless I hear you say it, I won't let myself believe it." Nessa said quietly.

Ophelia sighed. "Please don't…"

"I'll come! I'll come with you. I don't care what they do to me, as long as we're together!" said Nessa quickly. Letting Ophelia go was unbearable, especially now she had had a taste of kissing her; of what things could be like.

"No! No, you were right. Stay here. You'll be safer here, I won't let them hurt you." Ophelia leant closer to

Nessa and whispered in her ear through tears. "I'll try to fix all this. I don't know how, but I promise you I'll do my best..." She paused. "Nessa? If I'm ever desperate and I ask for help, do you promise to help me?"

Ophelia sounded deadly serious and Nessa felt rather worried.

"Of course I will..." she whispered back, wondering what exactly Ophelia needed to 'fix'.

"Thank you," smiled Ophelia. "You are wonderful! I hope I can come back to you soon. I hope you'll wait for me..."

"I've got eternity..." Nessa sighed, wishing she could stop Ophelia from leaving, but knowing she couldn't. Ophelia clearly knew something she didn't, and it worried her.

"I've really got to go," Ophelia said sadly. "They only let me come back down to tell Ezra how to run things while I'm away. They'll get suspicious soon. Oh, talking of Ezra, please look after him, he's still new."

"Look after him?! He's a spy and he's scared of me," said Nessa incredulously.

"He's on our side, I promise, and he isn't scared of you. I need to go. Goodbye Nessa, thank you!"

Ophelia rushed out of the door, still crying. She stopped on the doorstep and glanced back at Nessa. She mouthed something that looked suspiciously like 'I love you', but Nessa didn't dare to believe it. Ophelia closed the door and Nessa was alone. She fell to the floor, sobbing on her knees. She wasn't even sure which part she was crying about, she was so confused.

After a few moments Nessa jumped as she felt a

hand on her shoulder.

"You really do bloody love her don't you?" said a voice with a slightly disgusted tone.

"Bee?" Nessa said, strangely comforted by her presence. She looked at Beelzebub's hand on her shoulder. "That's quite affectionate for you," she sniffed.

Beelzebub rolled her eyes and moved her hand away. "Fine, I won't go near you then!" she said. "I was trying to help because either, you genuinely seem pretty damn distressed, or I've gone mad working for Lucifer on my own for two months and lost my evil edge, I'll let you pick!"

Nessa smiled and Beelzebub put out her hand to help her up off the floor.

"Thanks, you really are being nice aren't you?" Nessa said.

"Well, you're quite nice most of the time, plus you recently got kicked out of Hell and lost your magic. And, well, look at you, you already seem to be suffering more than most people in Hell, you don't need me adding to it!"

"I'm in love…" sighed Nessa.

"I know. That's my point!" said Beelzebub. "Love is a form of torture that even we keep away from. I'm not sure anything Lucifer could do to you would hurt you more than you're hurting yourself right now."

"I'm not doing it on purpose!" protested Nessa. "Why would I choose to fall in love with an angel? Why would a demon ever do that to themselves?"

"True, even you're not that insane!" smiled Beelzebub. "Are you okay?"

"I'll live," Nessa said, not caring that she sounded awfully dramatic; she was feeling dramatic. "I've lost her again. I haven't seen her for nearly two months and then she just leaves! Heaven will always come first; before a demon who is so crap at everything that they even failed at being a demon! What kind of demon is so shit at being one that they survive holy water? I can't even be murdered properly!"

Beelzebub laughed. "Wow Nessa, you really are a mess! The fact that you survived holy water is an insane miracle. That makes you somehow pretty much indestructible! And you're living our dream not working for that nutjob anymore. Plus you're not crap at everything, Ophelia seemed to think you were pretty decent at snogging!"

"Oh fuck off Bee!" Nessa said, giving her a playful shove. "Were you watching us the whole time?"

"Absolutely!" grinned Beelzebub. "You know she pulled away and got upset because she liked it so much? I think you got her all excited..." Beelzebub raised her eyebrows suggestively and Nessa gasped, shoving her again, harder.

"I said fuck off! Please can we *not* talk about that!"

"Okay okay!" said Beelzebub, putting her hands up in mock surrender. "I'm just reassuring you that you must be good at something!"

Nessa sighed. "Anyway, it doesn't matter if she liked kissing me or not, Heaven have taken her again! They always do..."

"They're not known for being reasonable," Beelzebub said. "They call themselves the good guys!

Ha! Not with what they're planning!"

"Why, what are they planning?" Nessa asked, suddenly concerned.

"Well, I haven't told Mr Angry Pants yet, but there are strong rumours going around Hell" Beelzebub began. "And as the face of the leadership team; or what's left of it without you, I need to know about this stuff. Angels aren't as subtle as they like to think they are, so this is definitely true. You know your girl told us that Heaven were planning to wipe out Hell?"

"Yes?" said Nessa, rolling her eyes, yet secretly feeling thrilled at Ophelia being referred to as her 'girl'.

"Well it's so much worse than that!" Beelzebub continued. "Well, for you anyway, 'cause I don't care that much. Them up there think that we've got too strong a hold on Earth, so they want to basically wipe us out and then start again."

"What do you mean start again?" Nessa asked suspiciously.

"With everything! The humans! They think if they start from scratch, back with the garden of Eden again, only without demons this time, then they can keep the new humans in light."

"By destroying all these ones?!" Nessa asked in horror. "That's worse than anything *we've* done!"

"I know!" agreed Beelzebub. "But they think it's okay because it's for 'righteous reasons', whatever bollocks that is!"

"There's nothing righteous about wiping out a whole planet just to get your own way!" Nessa said, full of rage.

"I agree, but we are always the bad guys. No matter what they do it's never as bad as us just existing!" Beelzebub was the most emotional that Nessa had ever seen her. "As usual life isn't fair! Not for us!"

"No," agreed Nessa.

"And you know what? They didn't just call for Ophelia because she knows about demons, they called her because she knows about *Earth*! My theory is that they want her to help plan the humans' downfall, you know, as an insider?"

"Ophelia would never do that!" Nessa said, horrified by the suggestion. "She loves humanity more than any other angel! She would never have a hand in destroying them."

"Are you sure about that?" Beelzebub said questioningly. "She is one of them after all..."

"No! She is different!" insisted Nessa. "She must not know that they plan to destroy humanity. As soon as she finds out, she'll tell them to stick it up their arse and come home!"

"Wow, humans say love is blind, but apparently love is also stupid!" laughed Beelzebub. "Fear always wins! You know that. That's what most of our methods down in Hell rely on. If she's scared of the archangels, she'll do anything they say. That's a tactic we all use! Hell; Heaven; even humanity! Ophelia could be the Earth's number one fan, but as soon as they put her in charge of destroying it, what choice does she have?"

"My angel is stronger than that!" Nessa said, choking up again.

"I hope you're right, for all of our sakes..." said

Beelzebub ominously.

For a moment the two demons stood in silence.

"I know this is really soppy for a demon, but who cares; I've missed you down there..." Beelzebub eventually said.

"I was never down there anyway. I hate that place!" laughed Nessa.

"I know, but I used to look forward to your monthly reports just so that I could talk to someone cool who I didn't fantasise about strangling every time I speak to them!" Beelzebub said almost wistfully.

"Ooh heck! Things going well with Lucifer then?" Nessa smiled.

"Oh don't!" Beelzebub said, rolling her eyes. "With you gone there's no one for me to mock him with. No one else in Hell is willing to admit that he's an idiot, except us. All my frustration about him builds up. So much so, that the other day when he said something patronising, I had to physically stop myself from ripping off his stupid head!"

"That sounds fair enough!" said Nessa with a grin. "You know; I know you are not keen on Earth, but if you ever need a break or a rant you are welcome to come here for a chat?" she offered. "I've always got alcohol..."

"Thanks," said Beelzebub. "I might come if there's alcohol."

"You should be running Hell, Bee. I've always thought that," Nessa said after a moment.

"Yeah, right!" Beelzebub responded.

"No, seriously! You'd do a way better job than Lucifer," insisted Nessa.

"Well that's not hard is it?" smiled Beelzebub. "But thanks... Anyway, speaking of His Royal Stupidness, I'd probably better go. Are you okay?"

"I'm fine, thanks Bee. You're a good friend. One of the many reasons I'm glad I survived the holy water is that I wanted to tell you that."

Beelzebub looked genuinely taken aback. "Demons aren't supposed to have friends..." she said after a moment.

"So? We're not *supposed* to do a lot of things, but what I've learnt over the years is just because we don't usually do something, doesn't mean we can't. It's good to have a friend in Hell; helps you keep a little bit sane. Plus, what's more demonic than breaking the rules?"

"You're right, I've never really thought about it before, but I suppose we *are* friends..." Beelzebub looked delighted.

Before Nessa knew what she was doing, she hugged Beelzebub. She was devastated about Ophelia and needed comfort, plus her friend could likely do with a hug too, as she'd never had one.

"What are you doing?" Beelzebub asked suspiciously.

"It's a hug!" Nessa announced. "It's what friends do."

"It's not what demons do," Beelzebub said uncertainly. "Physical touch is a human thing..."

"It doesn't have to be a human thing," said Nessa, releasing Beelzebub from the embrace. "But if you don't like it that's fine."

"I didn't say I didn't like it," Beelzebub said

sheepishly, and she awkwardly put her arms around Nessa to hug her again.

Beelzebub's hug wasn't as warm and loving as Ophelia's, but it was still comforting. Her friendship was a welcome distraction from Nessa's broken heart, but as soon as Beelzebub left, Nessa's feelings came flooding back to the surface and threatened to engulf her.

She took a piece of the Edinburgh rock as she considered what to do with herself. Usually she turned straight to alcohol in times like this, but she didn't even feel like doing that. Another thing she tended to do was move; get out of the house and go somewhere, anywhere that wasn't her lonely flat. She decided that was the best option and grabbed her coat, heading out into the dark wintry streets.

She wasn't sure where she was going, but something made her head towards the Minster. She hadn't been there since Ophelia returned from Heaven after the war; she didn't especially enjoy torturing her feet like that. The Minster did however, make Nessa feel closer to Ophelia when she wasn't there.

As she approached, strangely the ground only began to get warm when Nessa was right next to the building, she was sure that the boundary started earlier last time she came. She glanced around at the humans milling about, illuminated by the Christmas lights. She wanted to feel closer to Ophelia, but there was no way she could break into the minster in front of them; they'd call the police. The last time she had been there it was the middle of the night during a war, and she had magic then too! It was harder this time.

Instead of trying to open the main doors, she slipped around the side and eventually found a small door with a very old looking lock. She pulled it hard and it opened suspiciously easily; almost as if she had used magic, but of course that wasn't possible. Once inside she manoeuvred through the back corridor that she found herself in, until she emerged into the nave.

As she gazed around the church she suddenly realised that standing there wasn't unbearable this time. When she last stood in the building back in 1945, it hurt far too much to walk around, but now it just felt like those heated floors humans sometimes have. Nessa crouched down and touched the warm floor with her fingertips. What was happening to her? As a fallen angel she had always felt like something about her must be fundamentally broken, but now something different was wrong with her, and she wished she knew what it meant.

She made her way over to Ophelia's statue, marvelling at how strange it was to be walking across consecrated ground, pain free. The warm floor actually felt quite pleasant. Nessa gazed up at the Ophelia statue, which was looking out across the minster, watching over the people of York.

"Ophelia?" she called. "Ask your God what is happening to me! What's wrong with me? Am I somehow broken? Did I do something wrong? Or maybe right?"

She glanced at the floor, considering whether too many good deeds had somehow made her less of a demon, and sighed.

"Ophelia I love you!" she said, looking back at the statue. "Why did you leave me? You'll come back, right? When you realise what they are really doing. I wish I wasn't a demon! I wish you weren't an angel, I wish we could just be *us*..." Nessa's eyes welled up with tears. She wanted to kiss the statue again, in the hopes that Ophelia could feel it; to remind her that she was thinking about her. She didn't want to fly, because she wasn't sure if flying counted as magic, and if she failed to fly; a fundamental thing that all demons and angels could do, she would feel even more useless. Instead she began to climb up the archway, using the intricate stone carvings as hand and footholds. While Nessa was quite good at climbing, this was still a rather foolish idea as the statue was pretty high and beneath her, the ground was solid stone.

She got about half way up before a voice yelled out to her.

"Nessa! What are you doing?" it echoed..

Nessa was so startled by a stranger knowing her name, that she almost slipped. She heard a worried gasp from below.

"Who are you? How do you know my name?" Nessa shouted back, once she'd steadied herself, not able to turn to look at them.

"I'm Ezra. We met when I arrived in October! Please come down, it's dangerous!"

"Oh. Go away Ezra!" yelled Nessa, continuing to climb.

"No. You're going to get yourself killed!" Ezra shouted in concern.

"Why do you care? You're an angel spy!" Nessa snapped viciously.

"I'm on *your* side!" called Ezra. "Ophelia trusts me!"

"Well *I* don't! No one's ever on my side, I'm a terrifying demon!"

"But right now you're a demon without magic to save yourself when you fall to your death! Please, think of how upset Ophelia would be if anything happened to you!" Ezra's voice sounded pleading. Nessa found it odd that he cared. She also wondered how he knew she didn't have magic, but before she could ask, her long trench coat got caught on a piece of the masonry and she slipped.

She heard Ezra squeak in panic as she fell. She closed her eyes, wondering what would happen to a strange mutant-demon like her if she died. Suddenly though, she wasn't falling anymore. She dared to open her eyes and found herself hovering a few feet from the ground, caught by a net of angelic magic. She was gently lowered to the ground and there was Ezra, standing in front of her, breathing heavily with fear in his eyes.

"That was terrifying!" he exclaimed. "Are you okay? I didn't know I could do magic that quickly."

"I'm fine!" Nessa snapped, a little shaken by the near death experience, and more than a little embarrassed about being so foolish. "Thank you..." she added, seeing Ezra's slightly hurt expression. He somehow looked a bit more Earthly than the first time she saw him, Ophelia had certainly influenced him. "Why are you here?" she asked after a moment.

"I was looking for you!" Ezra grinned. "I followed your energy here, but I was pretty surprised to find you in a church though. I didn't think demons could enter churches…"

"We shouldn't really," said Nessa. "But I've been here loads of times. Why were you looking for me?"

"Ophelia asked me to look after you…" Ezra said quietly. "And I was so scared just then that I would fail already… You could have died…"

Nessa didn't know what to say. Ezra looked sad and she felt a little guilty. "Sorry," she said eventually. "What do you mean *look after me*? She asked me to look after *you* because you're new, why do *I* need looking after?"

"Because she knew you'd be sad and you'll need a friend!" Ezra smiled. "I promise I'm on your side! I thought I'd be scared of demons, but if Ophelia loves you, then you must be nice…"

"Okay… Thanks…" said Nessa, deciding to trust Ophelia's judgement on the angel.

"You're welcome!" grinned Ezra.

"How do you know she loves me? Did she tell you?" Nessa asked, desperate for some sort of confirmation or validation after never hearing it from Ophelia.

"Yes!" said Ezra with a smile. "She was about to come and tell you that she loves you and maybe kiss you, but then the archangels called her, and when she came back she was really upset. I don't know what they said to her, but whatever it was they scared her again after she was finally feeling brave enough to tell you…"

"Really?" Nessa breathed, equal parts delighted that Ophelia was planning to confess her love, and concerned by what archangels might have said to her.

Before either could say anything else, the two heard the sound of a door opening in the east side of the building.

"Oh shit, we shouldn't be here!" Nessa whispered. "Come on!" She grabbed Ezra's sleeve and they ran towards the main entrance to the west.

They dashed down the middle aisle, between the chairs, but their footsteps must have alerted whoever had entered the building, as they heard a far-off voice yelling something. Nessa turned, still running, to check that the person hadn't seen them. She tripped on the uneven ground, causing her to stumble against the font. Not only did she wind herself by hitting the solid structure, but her hands had instinctively tried to break her fall, splashing holy water all over her.

"Fuck that's hot!" Nessa gasped, shaking the water from her steaming hands. Ezra looked utterly stunned, but Nessa didn't have time to explain, they had to get out of there.

As soon as they were safely away from the minster, they stopped to catch their breath. Nessa's ribs felt bruised where she had hit the font.

"Are you hurt?" Ezra asked, seeing her wince as she moved.

"I'll be fine," said Nessa. "It's my own fault, but it could have been a lot worse!"

Ezra flicked his hand downwards in front of Nessa, and the pain was gone. She gasped in surprise.

"You didn't have to heal me!" she said, "Thank you though..."

"You're welcome. You'd might as well not be hurt if that's an option right?" Ezra said with a smile. He glanced at Nessa's sleeves, the ends of which were still steaming from the water. "That was holy water..." he said. "How? I thought that would destroy demons."

"It should," said Nessa, watching the steam rise. "I don't know why it doesn't kill me. The Devil tried to execute me by dropping me into a pool of the stuff when I saved Ophelia's life recently, but I survived. It just feels really hot..."

"Wow, that's *so* cool!" said Ezra, his eyes shining. "You're like a super-demon or something!"

Nessa smiled. She hadn't expected that kind of reaction. Maybe she would like Ezra after all.

"Yeah, but don't tell anyone or I might have to kill you!" she said, raising an eyebrow warningly, knowing full-well that she would never really kill anyone.

"Woah, you really don't need to add the threat!" said Ezra. "I wasn't going to tell anyone. Like I said, I'm on your side! I'm absolutely terrified to be betraying Heaven, but I promise I'm on your side."

"Thanks," said Nessa. "You're alright for an angel you know?"

"You're nice for a demon," Ezra smiled back.

Nessa looked to the night sky. It was sweet of Ophelia to ask Ezra to look out for her too. Ezra followed her gaze.

"The stars are so pretty from Earth," he said, in awe.

Nessa took in a breath, taken aback by the comment. She swallowed hard, trying not to cry for the hundredth time that day.

"I made them…" she whispered, still looking at her beautiful creations.

"Really?! You actually created the stars?!" Ezra was completely amazed.

"Yeah, and the other planets," said Nessa. "I don't think any other angels know, but there are pictures hidden in the stars. See, if you look carefully, those ones are in the shape of an angel. That was Ophelia's idea. Those ones are for her…"

"That's really sweet!" sighed Ezra, gazing around looking for more pictures. He must have suddenly realised something and turned to look at Nessa in wonder. "*You* made the stars and planets? Goodness! Are you, Archangel Zadkiel?!" he asked.

Nessa smiled, though tears were filling her eyes. "I used to be. A very long time ago," she said, still looking up.

When Ezra didn't say anything straight away, she turned to look at him. He was staring at her as if she were God herself, his eyes wide and his mouth open a little.

"What?" said Nessa, laughing despite the tears.

"You are a legend!" he said in awe. "I've always wished I could have met you!"

"Why would you want to meet *me*?" Nessa asked, genuinely confused. "I'm not a legend, I'm a legendary bad example. A cautionary tale to little angels like you."

Ezra shook his head. "I read a lot as an admin angel, there's not much else to do, and I've always found you fascinating! I think you're really cool and I've often wondered what happened to you. That part of the

Heavenly files has always been missing…"

"Has it?" said Nessa, intrigued by the idea, Heaven's files were watertight. They loved records up there. It was odd, and a little suspicious that something would be missing. "Anyway, I don't like to talk about the fall," said Nessa.

"That makes sense," said Ezra. "I can't believe you're Archangel Zadkiel!" He suddenly gasped in excitement. "Wow, I saved Archangel Zadkiel's life, that's so cool!"

"No, you saved a demon's life," said Nessa quickly. "Archangel Zadkiel hasn't existed for a very long time!"

"You're still the same person!" insisted Ezra.

Nessa was a little stunned by that. How could this angel still see her as the archangel she used to be? Well, he didn't know her as a demon. He might not think like that if he did. She wondered whether Ophelia ever thought of her former identity. Did she ever see a glimpse of Zadkiel in her?

Nessa looked at Ezra; he was still smiling at her.

"There's this restaurant that Ophelia and I like, around this corner. Do you want to come with me?" Nessa said. She didn't feel like going home to be on her own just yet, and she felt like pasta and wine might help.

"Err, I won't eat any, but I'll come with you…" Ezra said after a moment's consideration.

"Great! Come on!" Nessa said, comforted by the presence of a new friend. "Are you sure I can't tempt you to try some though?" she said as they started walking.

Ezra looked concerned. "Absolutely not!" he said.

"I'll get you one day!" grinned Nessa, and Ezra gave her a strange smile because Ophelia had said that exact thing to him that very morning.

Chapter Thirteen

Bad Angels Go to Hell.

(Nessa's Fall)

Nessa had spent six thousand years trying very hard to forget about her fall from Heaven. She pushed it down, and sometimes she felt like she might have managed to block it out, but then it would creep back up on her like a horrible recurring nightmare. She hated sleeping, because on the rare occasions that she did, she was troubled by actual nightmares about it; forcing her to relive the trauma. The event haunted her, it was the reason she had always felt like a failure; like something was wrong with her.

It had all started when Angel Ophelia had delivered notes to Archangel Zadkiel, unwittingly throwing her entire existence into question.

The day of the next archangel meeting had arrived, but Zadkiel's mind was elsewhere. She paced her office, occasionally glancing at the Earth notes on the table. She couldn't stop thinking about it, and she had really tried to. She had attempted to distract herself with the constellations, but they were all done now, and God hadn't even noticed… Zadkiel hadn't seen or heard from The Almighty since before she had created the universe. Not one word of thanks, no little 'well done Zadkiel' or any kind of reward. It was as if she hadn't just performed the biggest miracle; bringing to be all the vital things that make up the whole damn universe! Without all that stuff, God's precious little humans couldn't live, not that that seemed to matter a jot to the Big Boss!

Zadkiel picked up the notes and read the section again; the one that troubled her.

And so it is that the Earth shall be our centre, and the humans thereupon shall be of paramount importance within the lives of all angels. Humans are to be devoted worshippers of Almighty God, and shall be nurtured by Heaven and kept upon the righteous path. You must ensure that the humans never falter from God's grace, that they love God above all else; for that is their purpose, while an angel's purpose is to serve them.

Zadkiel wasn't a fan of any of that, to put it lightly. The idea that she ought to serve these new animals was ridiculous to her, and the thought that they are made simply to love God seemed silly too. Was God really that egotistical that she needed to create an entire species, just to ensure they all adore her? And what about all the angels who had already been serving her for ages, doing all her work for her, while she sits around and does nothing! And she didn't even care about any of the work in the end anyway!

Zadkiel took a deep breath, she shouldn't feel like this, she shouldn't think any of this. Her purpose was to serve The Almighty. God had absolute command, what else was there? She looked down at the notes, realising she had been gripping them so tightly that they were crumpling. The rest of the notes bothered Zadkiel almost as much. They were all about how the Earth was important and all of Zadkiel's creations weren't. She wished she didn't have all these strange feelings. Everything was so much easier before, when all her thoughts had been about creating the universe. Before it occurred to her to question anything. An angel's life was simple, they went about their day quite happily; fulfilling any tasks that they were set. Gladly obeying and absolutely never doubting anything. Zadkiel wondered if there was something wrong with her, perhaps she was somehow broken?

She put down the notes and left the room, intending to do something she wasn't certain was all that advisable, but the only thing that might help relieve her of these troubling feelings. She had to speak to God!

She reached The Almighty's gates after bypassing the unnecessary about of stairs by flying. God loved stairs... A particularly pompous angel leaned absentmindedly against the gate, supposedly guarding it, but staring off in entirely the wrong direction, and clearly not even noticing someone approaching. Zadkiel couldn't see his face, but she didn't need to.

"Lucifer..." she said, unimpressed.

He jumped in surprise at hearing her voice. "Goodness me!" he said, turning to face her. "You can't just sneak up on people like that!"

Zadkiel watched as Lucifer made a big deal out of adjusting his robes as though she had somehow caused him the greatest inconvenience.

"Err, you're, supposedly, guarding the gate. I shouldn't be able to sneak up on you…"

"And yet you still managed it!" said Lucifer irritably, still sweeping some sort of imaginary dirt off his sleeves.

"Are those robes new?" asked Zadkiel, noticing the gold trim that wasn't normally there.

"They are!" grinned Lucifer triumphantly.

"You know only Archangels should have gold trim?"

"Oh really?" said Lucifer in mock surprise. "Well that's alright then, because just this morning The Almighty promoted me!" Lucifer's eyes shone with an almost mischievous look.

Zadkiel rolled her eyes. "Of course she did! To what? And more importantly why?"

"Ugh don't worry Your Highness. You still outrank us all!" said Lucifer, giving Zadkiel slight side eye. "I've been named Archangel of Light; a brand new title! *And* I've also been asked to guard God's gates, so she must trust me!"

"I bet she's regretting it already," laughed Zadkiel. "Especially since you didn't notice me coming!"

"Ha ha, amusing…" said Lucifer sarcastically. "Anyway, as for why, I think it has something to do with creation? I have helped quite a lot haven't I? And she likes me!"

"You are The Almighty's servant, that's your job,"

said Zadkiel, unimpressed. She had always found Lucifer rather annoying.

"Are we not all God's servants?" Lucifer said in a self righteous way. "Anyway, never mind about my robes, or rank. What are you doing here Zadkiel?"

"I came to see The Almighty. Is that not rather self explanatory?" sighed Zadkiel. Honestly, give this man a bit of power and he thinks *he's* the centre of God's universe.

"What do you want with her? She is very busy," said Lucifer.

"It is none of your business!" Zadkiel snapped. "I am the leader of the angels, if I want to speak with The Almighty I do not need permission from someone who thinks they're the King of Heaven just because they have a shiny new dress! Move!"

Lucifer looked stunned, and to be honest, Zadkiel was rather taken aback by her own temper too. She had never shouted at anyone before. It was as if all of the complicated feelings inside her had just bubbled up to create a flood of frustration, aimed at Lucifer because he happened to be the one in front of her.

"Sorry..." Zadkiel said after a pause. "I really don't know where that came from..."

"Is everything alright?" Lucifer said, seeming as genuinely concerned as an angel, or specifically he, could.

"Yes, thank you. If you'll excuse me..." said Zadkiel as she pushed open the gates, slightly ashamed of getting angry, and desperate to get away from Lucifer as quickly as possible.

Zadkiel tried to calm herself before she faced God. She couldn't imagine the trouble she would be in if she spoke to The Almighty anywhere near the way she had just spoken to Lucifer.

God was on her throne, unsurprisingly, and she had her eyes closed. Zadkiel nervously approached, wondering what she was doing.

"Archangel Zadkiel…" said God, not opening her eyes. "I did not call for you. Why are you here? I am very busy."

"Yes my Lord, I can see that," said Zadkiel uncertainly, wondering in what way this classed as being busy. "I simply wished to speak with you, perhaps ask a few questions, you know?"

The Almighty opened her eyes slowly and looked Zadkiel up and down, making her feel highly nervous. "As I said I am busy!" God announced. "I do not have time to answer questions right now. It is growing ever closer to the sacred time when we shall bring to be the Earth, much is still to be done."

"Of course my Lord, only—"

"I do not have time Zadkiel!" snapped God, interrupting the angel mid speech. "If you have any problems, discuss them with your fellow archangels. I believe you have a meeting tonight, do you not?"

"Indeed…" said Zadkiel meekly. "So sorry to have disturbed you Almighty God."

"You are forgiven, angel," said God, commanding Zadkiel to leave with a wave of her hand, her golden robes shining in the light as she moved, forcing Zadkiel to squint away. She had annoyed God; Zadkiel should have felt scared, and she did, a little, but she also felt rather angry. The word 'forgiven' stood out to her as particularly infuriating. She had done nothing wrong, nothing at all to warrant forgiveness. In fact, she hadn't even been able to say anything before The Almighty sent her away! Little did she know that things were about to get a lot worse though.

As Zadkiel headed back towards her office, Lucifer was knocking on Archangel Jophiel's office door.

"Who is it?" Jophiel called.

"Err, Lucifer. I was newly promoted to Archangel this morning. I have something important to discuss with you, Your Holiness…" Lucifer sounded nervous, but also very determined. After a moment Jophiel's door opened and Lucifer entered. Jophiel was sitting at her desk organising some notes for the meeting that evening.

"You're The Almighty's butler aren't you?" Jophiel said, looking Lucifer up and down disapprovingly.

"I am her closest assistant!" Lucifer said hurriedly, attempting to make his job sound more important than it was.

"Right…" said Jophiel, unimpressed. "What did you want Angel Lucifer? I must prepare for the meeting."

"Yes, and I shall be there! As I said, I was promoted!" grinned Lucifer.

"Yes, congratulations…" said Jophiel flatly. "Look, I really am busy. Zadkiel is actually the one in charge, why don't you go and tell her about whatever it is you have to say? I'm sure she'd love to listen to the issues of The

Almighty's butler."

"I can't, because it's *about* her!" Lucifer insisted, either ignoring Jophiel's sarcasm or not noticing it.

"Oh?" Jophiel questioned, suddenly taking more interest.

"Yes. Why is she in charge anyway? The two of you were created together and you have worked together since then. Why does she outrank you?"

Jophiel seemed taken aback by the question, as if she had never considered it before. "I suppose because The Almighty said so?" she said uncertainly.

"Well, I think *you* ought to run things!" Lucifer said. "I don't think Zadkiel is fit for the job. She shouted at me a minute ago! All I did was ask her what business she had with God, as I was guarding the gates and she completely lost it! I for one have never seen an angel snap at anyone like that…"

"Intriguing…" Jophiel said. "She has always been so joyous and kind; too joyous some might say. What could have happened?"

"I don't know, but it starts with losing her temper at me. Where does it end? What if she begins treating everyone like that?" Lucifer said dramatically. "She could strike fear into the hearts of every angel if she becomes some angry tyrant. That would certainly upset the harmonies in Heaven wouldn't it?"

Jophiel thought for a moment. "I wonder what has caused her to be angry? Come to think of it, I feel that she has been acting a little strange since we created the universe."

"I have no idea!" Lucifer said. "As I said, when

I tried to ask her why she wished to speak with The Almighty, she just got angry... Who has she spoken to recently? They may know what happened."

"I believe the only angel apart from me that she has had any interaction with recently was an assistant in the Earth department that delivered notes to her from Gabriel a few weeks ago," Jophiel said thoughtfully.

"Do you know who that was?" Lucifer asked, excited to uncover the mystery.

"I believe her name is Ophelia. I will summon her," Jophiel said, and with a click of her fingers, a startled looking Ophelia appeared in the room. Ophelia jumped in surprise when she saw Jophiel.

"Archangel Jophiel!" she gasped. "Good afternoon..." she said uncertainly, wondering what Jophiel could possibly want with her.

"I'm Lucifer! I'm a new archangel, as you can see from my robes!" said Lucifer, attention-seeking as ever.

"Nice to meet you?" said Ophelia, slightly unnerved by him.

Jophiel rolled her eyes at Lucifer. "Angel Ophelia. I believe that recently you were tasked with delivering notes to the Archangel Zadkiel. Is this true?"

"Yes..." said Ophelia suspiciously. "Archangel Gabriel asked me to."

"Do calm down dear angel, you are not in any kind of trouble," laughed Jophiel. "All we wish to know is whether anything happened, if she said anything to you. We are very concerned for Zadkiel, she has been acting rather strangely. Do you know of anything that could be wrong?"

Ophelia looked uncertain; as if she wasn't sure whether she should say anything in case it got Zadkiel into trouble. She had found what the archangel had said about questioning God rather worrying, but she wasn't sure which was worse; lying to Jophiel, or potentially causing Zadkiel problems.

"We assure you that Archangel Zadkiel won't get in trouble for whatever you say," said Lucifer, trying his best to sound reassuring, when affection wasn't his strong suit. "We just want to help her! Don't you want to help your angelic leader too?"

Ophelia considered her response for a moment. "She did seem a little upset when I delivered the notes…" she eventually said.

"About what?" Lucifer asked with perhaps a little too much enthusiasm.

"Err, I think she feels a little disheartened that her creations don't seem to matter as much as the Earth," Ophelia said tactfully, choosing not to mention the part about questioning God's plan. She wasn't lying, she was just leaving that bit out.

"So, is it doubt?" Jophiel asked. "Zadkiel doubts her role in Heaven?"

Ophelia's eyes widened slightly. "I really don't know. I don't think I'm the best person to ask, I don't know her very well. Surely you know her a lot more than me as she is your sister?"

"Yes, but she has not spoken to me about any of this," said Jophiel.

"Why don't you just ask Zadkiel?" offered Ophelia. "She is the only one who can give you a truthful answer, all I know is what she said, and I've told you that..."

"Very well," smiled Jophiel. "We will ask her. Thank you for your help Angel Ophelia, you are dismissed."

Ophelia nodded her head nervously at both archangels, before leaving the room.

"Doubt!" announced Lucifer triumphantly when he was sure Ophelia was out of earshot. "God warned me about doubt once! I don't think any angels have expressed doubt yet, but it could be dangerous."

"So what do we do about it? We can't have her acting like this, not if she's in charge..." Jophiel said in concern.

"Well, if you doubt in Heaven's work and will of The Almighty, that makes you a bad angel, and you know where bad angels go?" Lucifer grinned, full of far too much glee.

"Hell..." whispered Jophiel.

"Exactly!" said Lucifer. "She could be the first angel to fall from Heaven, the very first demon!"

"But no one actually goes to Hell," said Jophiel uncertainly. "It's more of a warning isn't it?"

"It doesn't have to be! Then *you* would be in charge!" Lucifer said almost theatrically. "After Zadkiel disturbed her, The Almighty told me to keep an eye on things until she finishes working on the Earth, and obviously that includes taking any disciplinary actions! If we find Zadkiel guilty, we won't need God's permission to cast her out."

"Lucifer? Why do you care about this so much?" asked Jophiel suspiciously.

"Because she snapped at me!" said Lucifer as if it

was obvious. "It is the first time someone shouted at me and I have found that I don't take kindly to that kind of thing. Plus she didn't seem very remorseful. She just pushed me aside when I tried to express concern as any good angel would. I think she should be punished justly!"

"It is worrying," agreed Jophiel. "We shall speak to her at the meeting tonight."

"Yes, and I will be there!" grinned Lucifer. "My first archangel meeting shall be an interesting one!"

"Yes, well done..." said Jophiel rather irritably, which might have bothered Lucifer, had he noticed, but he hadn't.

"The Almighty might reward me even more for saving Heaven from a dangerous angel in her absence!" he smiled.

"Maybe," said Jophiel, picking back up the notes she had been working on. "I am rather busy, I will see you at the meeting."

"You certainly will!" Lucifer said happily as he left the room.

Meanwhile, Zadkiel was back in her office, the Earth notes still before her, feeling even more despondent. This had all started, she decided, when she cried. That was the problem, angels don't cry, so when she did, it ruined her whole life! Since then she had felt all kinds of strange emotions, and her head became filled with doubts and concerns. She wished more than anything that she could go back to that time when she didn't feel that way; back before she cared. She used to get on with life, not considering for a moment that there were any kind of problems. Everything was perfect. It should be perfect, so why wasn't it? Maybe it was. Maybe she was overthinking it... She gathered the notes and set off begrudgingly to the archangel meeting, hoping it might possibly help to put these strange feelings to rest. As she closed her office door, she had no idea that she would never again reenter the room, no idea that at least two archangels were out to get her.

When Zadkiel arrived at the meeting, all of the other archangels were already gathered around the table. Lucifer was sitting in Zadkiel's seat and everyone was talking in hushed tones, Zadkiel swore she heard her own name being mentioned, but as soon as she entered and Jophiel noticed her, the table fell silent. Every archangel turned to stare at Zadkiel. She felt her face burn and was certain she must have turned red. What was happening? Had she missed something?

"Zadkiel!" said Jophiel, as if that were a sentence all by itself.

Zadkiel glanced among the angels nervously. "Yes?..." she said uncertainly, holding the notes tightly to her chest, as if they might somehow provide her with some kind of comfort and protection.

"Stand before us, if you would be so kind. We need to have a little conversation..." Jophiel said, ominously.

Zadkiel took a few steps forward so that she stood in front of the table, still wondering what in heaven was going on.

"Is there a problem?" Zadkiel asked in concern, placing the notes on the table.

"You have been acting strangely," said Jophiel. "We

have all noticed. It is since we created the universe. You have changed…"

"How have I changed?" asked Zadkiel, feeling uncomfortable. It was true, she did feel as though she had changed, but the idea filled her with terror.

"We are not certain," said Jophiel. "Why don't you tell us?"

Zadkiel didn't know what to say. She really wanted to change the subject and get on with the meeting, but all the archangels were staring at her expectantly, waiting for her to speak.

"The only thing I can think of that has changed is that now that I have fulfilled my duty to create the universe, I feel a little uncertain of my new purpose?" Zadkiel shifted slightly, feeling as though a million angels were staring at her, rather than the seven that were.

"Your purpose is to serve God. As is all of ours," said Jophiel. "Do you think because you were placed in charge that you ought to have special treatment?"

"Exactly!" Lucifer butted in. "Plus, as Archangel Jophiel said, you are, supposedly, our leader. Is that not enough for you?"

"I didn't mean it like that!" Zadkiel said quickly, feeling even more panicked. "It really doesn't matter, I'm fine. If this is about me snapping at you earlier Lucifer, then I am very sorry. I didn't mean to…"

"It is not about that, though that is very concerning…" Jophiel said. "No, we believe that you are doubting Heaven's work and The Almighty's will… You think that God should only care about what you have been doing, rather than her new Earth project don't you?"

"I *never* said that!" Zadkiel said in horror, wondering how the archangels knew about her strange new feelings. "I was simply surprised that God views our creations as experiments. It sort of feels like our work was rather pointless... Like the Earth is the only thing that matters now... And I'm not sure why The Almighty needs these *humans* when we already serve her! Are we not good enough? She should love us!" Zadkiel didn't mean to say all that, but somehow as soon as she started talking about her feelings, they all flooded out.

Jophiel and Lucifer looked at each other in a way that Zadkiel found rather suspicious.

"This is a very serious issue!" said Jophiel, turning back to Zadkiel. "You are obviously full of doubt, and you know what happens when people doubt things? They start to disobey... We cannot take that risk."

"What are you saying?" Zadkiel asked worriedly.

"I believe that this has been a sufficient trial. You know what is to happen to disobedient angels, don't you, sister?" Jophiel said, nonchalantly arranging some of her papers on the table.

"They would go to Hell..." whispered Zadkiel.

"Exactly!" grinned Lucifer. "Not only that, but they become demons! The Almighty was telling me about it recently; if an angel falls from Heaven they become an anti-angel, everything that is wrong and evil."

"But... I can't be a demon, I've done nothing wrong..." Zadkiel felt almost numb, she hadn't expected this to escalate so quickly and she was terrified. They wouldn't really send her to Hell would they?

"You are doubting God's divine plan," said Jophiel simply. "We cannot have angels in Heaven who question things; particularly those in charge. Heaven would soon fall into anarchy."

"Then take my title!" Zadkiel said desperately. "You be the leader of the archangels! I don't mind... I'll keep away from you if you want, but please... Please don't banish me!"

"You are dangerous Zadkiel!" Jophiel said. "You shouldn't have these feelings. None of us question The Almighty, do we? God created you. You should be grateful! You owe your existence to her."

"Yes, and I tried! I am trying, but God doesn't seem to care about what I do anymore..." Zadkiel sighed.

"You've always been her favourite, what more do you want?" Jophiel said, infuriatingly calm as ever.

"I can't be a demon, demons are said to be awful creatures, full of hate! I don't hate anything, in fact I love everything! I always have," Zadkiel pleaded. "I love our creations, that's why it is disheartening that God views them as meaningless..."

"Love can be a weakness Zadkiel!" Jophiel announced. "It is blinding you to your duty. It's a powerful emotion. It can destroy everything if not stopped..."

Zadkiel felt the now-familiar sting of tears in her eyes. She couldn't cry now! Angels shouldn't cry, it would likely give the archangels more fuel for their fire. Suddenly she thought of something.

"Only God can cast angels out!" she said, hoping she'd found a flaw in their plan. "The Almighty is the one that judges us..." She considered whether God *would* cast her out or not. She had seemed pretty annoyed when Zadkiel tried to speak to her earlier that day, but surely that wasn't enough to banish her, was it?

"The Almighty is busy! She asked me to oversee things in the meantime and remove any threats! She wants you out. She's just too busy to do it herself!" Lucifer lied.

Jophiel shot him a look, knowing he was lying in a very un-angelic way. Lucifer narrowed his eyes, as if daring her to say something. She just looked away.

"She does?..." Zadkiel said in a small voice, knowing she had been defeated.

"Oh yes..." Lucifer said ominously.

"Archangel Zadkiel, we charge you with heresy! The punishment for which is banishment from Heaven," Jophiel said, as if it was nothing, as if she wasn't referring to her own sister. "Do you have anything to say?"

Zadkiel should have been sad or frightened, and she was, but a strange new emotion felt stronger; fury. Complete rage overcame her! Before she knew what she was doing, she charged forward to face Jophiel, leaning over the table and scattering her papers to the floor.

"You are my sister!" she yelled, causing Jophiel to recoil in shock. "Why would you do this to me? I would *never* do this to you! If you and God turn against me, then what will I have left?! I've done nothing wrong!"

There was silence for a moment as Jophiel just stared at her, expressionless. Somehow that made Zadkiel feel even more furious.

"Well..." said Jophiel calmly. "If we needed any more

proof that Zadkiel is a danger to Heaven, then there it is!" She was looking at Zadkiel as she spoke, so using her name felt awfully patronising. "Sister, rejecting God's plan is unforgivable. When an angel cannot be forgiven, they become a demon. I do not make the rules. Unlike you, I am simply following The Almighty's great plan. Raphael, Michael, please restrain our former leader before she becomes even more aggressive..."

"I'm not going to hurt you!" said Zadkiel, horrified by the suggestion.

"We cannot take that risk. You have become rather unpredictable..." Jophiel said. "Position Zadkiel in the place of judgement!" she ordered the two archangels that now had hold of Zadkiel.

As Raphael and Michael led Zadkiel to the edge of the meeting place, which also happened to be the edge of Heaven, she noted a particularly smug and triumphant look on Jophiel's face. Zadkiel and Jophiel had never really been very close, but Zadkiel never imagined she could be so hateful. At the end of the day, despite their differences they were sisters and work partners. For a while they had been the only angels. Did their years together mean nothing to Jophiel?

As the other archangels backed off nervously, Zadkiel looked at the ledge behind her. She had been at the Seat of the Archangels hundreds of times, but she had never really thought about the edge, and how ominous it was. Probably because she never dreamt that she might one day be thrown off it. Only bad angels should become demons, and Zadkiel really didn't think she was bad. All she could see was clouds below; she had no idea how far the drop was, but she knew she was about to find out.

She turned back to face the archangels, and Jophiel stood up as if to appear more commanding.

"Zadkiel, you are hereby banished from Heaven and shall reside in Hell for eternity as a demon!" she announced.

Before Zadkiel could say anything; not that she knew what to say anyway, the ground beneath her started to crack, and in a moment she was falling.

She seemed to be falling faster than it should be physically possible to fall, so her wings were useless, there was absolutely nothing she could do. She closed her eyes, screwing them up tightly, hoping that somehow if she wished hard enough she would be back in her office in Heaven when she opened them, and this would all just be something horrible she imagined. Even her vivid imagination couldn't conjure this up though. She had been completely blindsided by the whole thing.

When Zadkiel did eventually open her eyes, she found herself laying on the cold damp ground. She squinted in the darkness, trying to make out her surroundings. All she could see was stone; tall stone walls and what looked like an even darker passageway. She winced in agony as she sat up, she didn't actually feel the impact of hitting the ground; she must have been unconscious, but she felt bruised and she noted cuts on her arms. Her beautiful white angel robes had turned deep black and were terribly torn, her wings were black, even her hair was black; she definitely wasn't an angel anymore. All she had ever known was Heaven and angels, that's all there was so far, so it felt odd to know she was now something completely different, something *bad*...

She felt hopeless, she was going to live forever, but she couldn't imagine the pain of spending eternity feeling like this, she also couldn't imagine ever feeling happy again. She thought of how warm she had felt when she showed that other angel her universe. She had been full of joy and pride then. What if that's as good as life was ever going to get for Zadkiel? If so, she wished she could have somehow known at the time, to try and appreciate it more, because now it was gone. When she looked up she couldn't even see any of her stars, it was just darkness. That seemed like a metaphor for how pointless all her work had been.

She brought her knees up to her chest and wrapped her new demonic black wings around herself to try to get some form of comfort. When she began crying, her cheek stung and when she wiped it, her fingers were covered in blood from what must have been a deep cut. She felt that as a demon, she must somehow deserve that.

Zadkiel had expected to feel different as a demon, but she was still Archangel Zadkiel inside, except she had lost her joy and zest for life. Dark days merged seamlessly into weeks, months and then lonely years. She spent her days wandering the dark empty corridors of Hell, wondering whether she would ever see another soul, or if she would spend eternity alone. She wasn't sure how long she had been down there, but it felt like decades of miserable existence. In reality, it must have been over a year at least since her fall; since she had seen anyone. On this particular day though, as she wandered, Zadkiel was startled by a big commotion coming from the other side of Hell. Up until then it had been deafeningly silent. She wandered in the direction of the sound, wondering if she was brave enough to see what it was, deciding that, after absolutely nothing happening in Hell, anything would be worth investigating.

As she neared the strange place where she had landed after falling from Heaven, another demon stepped out to face her. She gasped in shock, she wasn't the only demon anymore? The other demon seemed a little surprised to see her too.

"You must be Zadkiel?" the other demon said after a moment.

"Err, yes, but I was thinking of changing my name," answered Zadkiel nervously. "But obviously no one was down here to talk to so it didn't matter what my name was because no one would say it..."

Zadkiel was about to cry for the thousandth time since her fall just thinking about how lonely she had been.

The other demon looked at her carefully, probably noticing she was about to cry. "What's your new name then?" she asked simply.

"Oh... I was thinking Nessa?" she answered, feeling strangely touched that this other demon cared what her name was.

"Cool!" said the other demon. "I was thinking of changing mine too, to something more demon-like if I have to live down here now. Like Beelzebub. That sounds pretty scary don't you think?"

"Beelzebub?" questioned Nessa. "Is that a name? It just sounds like random letters..."

"What and *Nessa* doesn't? That sounds like a noise I imagine one of The Almighty's animals will make!" smiled Beelzebub teasingly. "Anyway, all names are just random letters. And I don't want an angel name anymore, so I have to make up a completely new one."

"Good point," Nessa said. "Why are you here? In Hell I mean?" she asked uncertainly.

"Good question!" laughed Beelzebub. "Because Heaven is corrupt? Because God has abandoned us? Take your pick!"

"Us?" said Nessa. "Are there more of you?"

"Yeah, there was a war. And what do you do when the other side are getting too strong? Damn them all for eternity apparently!"

"A war?!" Nessa said in horror.

"Indeed!" said another voice approaching them. "Headed up by me!"

"Lucifer?!" gasped Nessa in surprise. "You're a demon too?" It was him alright, only with black hair, red eyes, and a face like thunder. A small, rather mean part of Nessa was quite pleased that Lucifer had fallen, it seemed quite funny after how he had treated her, all the nasty digs he had made about demons.

"The *former* Archangel Zadkiel!" Lucifer said sarcastically. "Fancy seeing *you* here!"

Nessa rolled her eyes, but before she could say anything Beelzebub spoke.

"Her name is Nessa now!" she said. "Anyway, you

wanted me to be your second in command right? Well, I want Nessa to work with us too!"

Nessa was surprised that this new demon wanted to work with her. She was so sure everyone would hate her now. It was the closest to a positive emotion she had felt since arriving in Hell.

"You don't have the right to order me around!" said Lucifer sharply. "I already proclaimed myself King of Hell!"

"It's your fault we're all down here you idiot!" snapped Beelzebub. "And you made me heal your cuts, even though I didn't want to, because you totally deserve them! You owe me!"

"Fine!" sighed Lucifer. "Even though I don't like Zadkiel or whatever you said she's called now. I'm the King and you two can be Princes of Hell. Happy?"

"Happy's a bit of a stretch, we're in Hell..." said Nessa.

"Yes, and I'm fucking furious about it! God wasn't supposed to throw *me* out!" snarled Lucifer. "Come on Princes, I'm going to invent a new substance that will make us all feel better! I'm calling it alcohol, you'll love it!" With that Lucifer swept off down the corridor.

"He's a bit annoying isn't he?" whispered Beelzebub as she and Nessa followed him.

"That's putting it lightly!" smiled Nessa. She hadn't smiled for quite a long time, but she felt a little cheered. Much as she hated Lucifer, at least Hell wouldn't be so boring now!

Chapter Fourteen

Upon Your Sacrifice We Shall Build a New World.

(21st Century, One Year Later)

It had been a year since Ophelia had left for Heaven, and it had felt like the longest and worst year of Nessa's life. Of course she had lived through well over six thousand years, many of which had been rather bad, and many she had spent without Ophelia; especially at the beginning of their friendship. Somehow though, this had felt a lot worse. Nessa didn't think it would be possible to miss Ophelia more than she did during the war, but now she missed her so much it hurt, and that was with the distraction of friends, which she had never had before. It was probably because of how close they had come to finally being together. Ophelia had planned to confess her love and they had actually *kissed!* After all those years, finally knowing for certain that Ophelia felt the same way, even if she couldn't say it, felt cruel, if the angel was just going to be taken from her straight away. Nessa really wished Ophelia had been able to admit things years ago, or sometimes she wished she had never kissed her at all! Maybe it would have been better not to know how things could have been?

Nessa and Ophelia had developed such a specific routine on Earth that it was hard to get used to doing anything without her. Of course they had their weekly meetings, which Nessa replaced with visiting Ezra at Ophelia's cottage, and while he refused any kind of alcohol because it was made by The Devil, after several months Nessa did persuade him to try tea and biscuits. They would share news over tea and coffee, as Nessa and Ophelia used to do in the pub; after all Ezra had Ophelia's job now.

Since she no longer worked for Hell and wasn't really a proper demon, Nessa tried to do as many good deeds as she was able to, without magic, hoping that enough random acts of kindness might somehow make up for spending the rest of the world's existence being 'bad'. She let Ezra take credit for them and often helped him with his duties where she could.

It wasn't just the Wednesday meetings that Nessa missed. She and Ophelia were creatures of habit, and things weren't the same now. For example, Christmas came painfully soon after Ophelia left. As a demon Nessa shouldn't celebrate Christmas, and indeed she didn't really understand why everyone celebrated the birthday of one single long-dead human; though in truth Nessa had been quite fond of Jesus. Ophelia on the other hand *adored* Christmas, and as the humans invented new traditions, she would make Nessa do them with her until she looked forward to Christmas almost as much as she did. For Nessa it was an excuse to spend even more time with her angel, she would celebrate it no matter who's birthday it was!

That year she cheered herself up by introducing Ezra to all the fun festive things they always did, like visiting the Christmas Market, ice skating, watching Christmas films, decorating Ophelia's tree, and making gingerbread houses, (though at the time Ezra still refused to try food, so Nessa begrudgingly ate both). It was nice to see his childlike joy at the whole thing, but it wasn't the same without Ophelia. Nessa kept imagining how they would have laughed when Ezra got tangled up in the decorations, or how they would have argued over which was the best Christmas film and certainly would both have agreed that 'Buddy the Elf' reminded them of Ezra.

Though she had dreaded it, Christmas hadn't been that bad; she had Ezra to thank for that, he was exactly what she needed. Plus, despite missing Ophelia even more, two things had made Nessa tear up with joy. The first was when Ezra tied a piece of Golden tinsel around her head and told her it was a halo. He insisted she keep it on while they decorated the rest of the tree, and he even let his real halo show so that they were 'matching'. He told her they were both Christmas angels now, and nothing apart from Ophelia had ever warmed Nessa's heart so much.

The second thing that had made Nessa cry was when she found a present from Ophelia on Christmas Day. It was a little bottle containing something orange with a label that said *'You have always been an angel to me. I miss you. Lots of love from Jupiter.'* Nessa was truly stunned by every part of it. The bottle itself contained a little piece of her beloved Jupiter to keep with her on Earth, which meant a great deal to Nessa, but it was the note... Ophelia called her an *angel*, and wrote down the word 'love'. Nothing in six thousand years had ever meant so much! She wished she could have sent Ezra with a gift for Ophelia when he made his next report, but it was far too risky. The other angels would notice straight away if Ophelia had any kind of Earthy object in Heaven. She hoped that her angel knew she was thinking about her every day, even if she couldn't return the kind gesture.

In the summer Nessa had taken Ezra on holiday to the beach. She and Ophelia loved their annual seaside holidays and she knew Ezra would too. She had tried to persuade Beelzebub, who regularly visited Nessa to complain about Lucifer and drink her beer, to come too as she insisted that her friend only hated Earth because she hadn't experienced enough of it. Beelzebub refused, saying it was far too human-like, and especially not if a horrible little angel would be there! Nessa thought that was a fair enough view for a demon to have and just went with Ezra. It was there that she first managed to get him to try human food. It was particularly hot, and Nessa insisted that a nice ice cream was the only thing that would cool him down. Now of course that wasn't technically true as Ezra could have easily used magic to cool himself, but either he didn't think of that, or he welcomed a valid excuse to finally try food; either way, once he tried an ice cream he was completely obsessed!

Now it was a Thursday morning in December, and Nessa stood outside Ophelia's cottage with a packet of custard creams. She and Ezra hadn't been able to meet the day before because he had been called by Jophiel for some reason or other. He had been quite upset to miss their weekly meeting, so Nessa promised him that she would come first thing in the morning to make up for it. She smiled at the sight of Ophelia's cottage. It always reminded her of her sweet angel.

"Morning my darling!" she announced, smiling up at the sky, wondering if Ophelia ever heard her when she spoke to her like that.

It gave her such a thrill to call Ophelia 'my darling'. Since Nessa knew that Ophelia had planned to tell her how she felt, were it not for those ever meddling archangels. In her mind they were a couple now. Now that she knew Ophelia wanted to be.

"I hope you're doing good things up there, and more importantly staying safe," she continued to the sky. "I miss you as much as ever, I hope you miss me? You know, it's been a year? I thought you'd be back by now... I love you!" Nessa felt herself choke up a little. She really had thought that Ophelia would come back when she found out that Heaven planned to destroy the Earth as well as Hell, but now Nessa supposed that she must have known all along. If that was what she promised she would 'fix', she must have been terrified by the responsibility of saving the world all by herself, and from the inside too! That must have been why at first she begged Nessa to help her. She hadn't been asking Nessa to help destroy Hell after all. She had been asking her to help save the Earth! If only Nessa had known, she might have gone with her... Then again, as she said at the time, she knew she really wouldn't be welcome up there anyway.

Nessa knocked on the cottage door and a concerned looking Ezra answered after a moment.

"Good morning Ezzy, what's wrong?" Nessa asked, her cheerful demeanour slipping at the sight of him looking worried, especially after being called to Jophiel yesterday.

"It's *a* morning, but I'm not sure it's a good one... Come inside!" said Ezra.

"Why, what's going on? Did something happen in Heaven yesterday?" Nessa asked, going through to the living room and putting the biscuits on the coffee table.

"Yes, kind of," said Ezra. "I've been worrying about it all night, waiting for you because I don't know what to do!" Ezra sat on the sofa and took the biscuits, quickly putting a whole one in his mouth as if they were pills that would make him feel better.

"Okay, you're freaking me out now!" said Nessa, sitting beside him. "Anyway, you know you could have come to my flat, I'm never asleep, trust me!"

"I know, but I was scared that I would get lost if I went looking for it in the dark!" said Ezra, his mouth still full of biscuit. "They called me and all the other Earth angels to give us 24 hours warning that the world was going to end!"

"They what?!" Nessa was horrified. "Ezzy, that's so much worse than anything I thought you would say! 24 hours? So the world's going to end this evening?!"

"Yes!" said Ezra, taking another biscuit. "All the humans will be destroyed and I will have to go back to Heaven. But you can't go to Hell because they plan to destroy that soon after, so you have to run away somewhere! To the stars and planets you made, you have to live there! That's the only place you can go."

"I'm not going to live on a different planet!" said Nessa. "There's nothing there, can you imagine how boring that would be? I once lived in Hell when it was empty, but I've lived here for far too long, I'd go mad all alone with nothing to do. Plus I don't have magic to get there…" She glanced out of the window as a young child walked past the cottage with her mum, both obviously blissfully unaware of their impending doom. "A few thousand years ago I wouldn't believe I'd ever say this, but I won't give up on the humans. I can't run away; that would be selfish. We have to stop this, we can't let them destroy the humans, most of them are totally innocent!"

"I know, but what can we do?" sighed Ezra. "Ophelia's been up there this whole time and she loves the Earth more than anyone, if she hasn't stopped it what hope do we have?"

"Did she say anything to you yesterday?" asked Nessa hopefully, as desperate as ever to hear anything about her angel.

"No, she wasn't there," said Ezra. "She's always there for the monthly reports, because she's basically an honorary archangel while they work on their plan, but I didn't see her at all yesterday. I tried to ask Gabriel where she was, but he just told me to go away. Which he always does, but still…"

Nessa's stomach knotted with anxiety. What

if Ophelia was in trouble? With Heaven so close to implementing their plan, maybe they found out that Ophelia was trying to sabotage it?

"Oh fuck! What do we do?!" yelled Nessa, ever frustrated by Heaven's nonsense. "How do we help Ophelia, how do we save the bloody world?! You know, when I found out about this stupid planet, I never imagined one day I'd be so desperate to save it!" Nessa picked up the packet of biscuits, as if that might cheer her up.

"I don't know what we can do..." said Ezra sadly. "I'm starting to think there's nothing we can—"

Nessa didn't hear the rest of Ezra's sentence, as suddenly everything turned to bright white; Nessa had to close her eyes in case they burned with the intensity. When she opened them, she found herself facing the archangels' table!

She hadn't been in Heaven since the fall, and she had rather hoped she never would again. Much less here, right where her entire world fell apart. Whilst she had headed up meetings here hundreds of times, it stopped being a meeting room the moment it became a precipice from which innocent angels could be thrown to their doom.

Nessa also hadn't seen the archangels since then either, yet there they were before her. Jophiel somehow had an even nastier look this time, not that Nessa would have guessed that was possible. That didn't bother her so much though, because to Nessa's horror, right in the middle of the archangels, in Zadkiel's seat, looking at her with a similar look of disapproval was Ophelia!

Nessa let out a small gasp and almost felt like she stopped breathing for a moment at seeing her. It had been a year; she was half overjoyed and half terrified. Why was Ophelia looking at her like that? She gave her a small smile, but Ophelia just narrowed her eyes slightly.

"Good morning evil twin!" announced Jophiel, startling Nessa when she had been focused on Ophelia.

"Hello Jophiel... Long time no see," she answered, trying to push aside her concerns about Ophelia so that she could keep up the cool air she liked to have.

"Yes, hasn't it been nice?!" Jophiel said with a slight smile. "So good of you to drop in!"

"Yes, it's always a great start to a Thursday morning; getting kidnapped!" said Nessa sarcastically. "Custard cream?" She smiled, offering the packet still in her hand to the table of archangels, revelling in their horrified looks. She swore she saw the stoney faced Ophelia bite her lip to hide a smile. She didn't know what was wrong with Ophelia; why there was no hint of affection when she looked at her, but she knew that if there was one thing she was good at, it was making her angel laugh.

"What is that?" asked Jophiel in disgust.

"A peace offering!" smiled Nessa. "Oh sorry, you meant literally! It's a biscuit, humans sometimes have them with tea." She got out a biscuit and pointedly took a bite, staring at Jophiel as she did.

"You are trying to tempt archangels to eat human food? What's wrong with you? You are insane!" Jophiel glared at the biscuits. Nessa had never seen anyone look at a biscuit with quite that much hatred, it seemed almost comical, and she had to stop herself from laughing.

"Why thank you! Insanity must run in the family, eh?" Nessa grinned, raising an eyebrow at Jophiel.

Jophiel glared at her. "You are an anomaly Nessa, I truly believe it. Some mistake in God's creations; doomed from the start."

"An anomaly?! Why thank you! If I had a CV I'd put that on it!" Nessa smiled and took another bite of the biscuit.

"Enough Demon Nessa!" said Ophelia suddenly, with a horribly cold tone to her voice. "We did not bring you here to insult our great leader!"

Nessa gasped as the packet of biscuits dissolved into nothing in her hands. She looked at Ophelia in horror. Why was she being nasty? What happened? And in what universe would Ophelia *ever* describe Jophiel as their 'great leader'?

"Quite right Ophelia!" smiled Jophiel. "Now Nessa, I suppose you're wondering why we brought you here? Well, we were hoping you could help us put the finishing touches to our lovely new machine!"

Nessa looked between Jophiel and Ophelia suspiciously. "What's that supposed to mean?"

"Oh, Ophelia won't help you now!" Jophiel smiled calmly. "She has finally made the correct choice; to commit to our cause. The righteous decision."

"What did you do Ophelia?" Nessa asked.

Jophiel began to answer. "Oh, she simply—"

"No!" Nessa interrupted. "I want to hear it from her!"

Ophelia shifted slightly in the chair, but remained oddly confident and certain. "I had to choose between

Heaven's righteous cause and the life of a single demon. It is hardly a dilemma when you are all to die this evening anyway. Plus of course you are nothing compared to the promise of eternal peace and tranquillity without *your* kind!"

Nessa wasn't sure what was going on, but she felt a bit sick. She should have been devastated to hear her beloved angel saying such hateful things to her, and in a way she was, but she was also certain it wasn't real. Those things sounded so odd and alien coming from Ophelia that there had to be something else going on. She couldn't believe that Ophelia would ever turn against her like that. She looked at her in confusion rather than upset, and for a moment she felt she saw Ophelia's eyes change to give her a hint that she didn't mean it. Nessa decided to play along and seem unfazed.

"So what are you going to do to me?" she asked.

"You are to be sacrificed," Ophelia said slowly. "But it shall be in the name of creating a better world…"

"Sacrificed?" said Nessa, looking Ophelia dead in the eye. "By you?"

"The Archangel Jophiel believes it to be fitting; an appropriate way for me to prove my loyalty to Heaven and repent for my sins. Sins caused by you!"

"I see…" said Nessa, still studying Ophelia suspiciously. One indicator that this was some sort of act was the actual words she was saying. Ophelia wouldn't talk in that obnoxious, self righteous way. It all sounded kind of scripted.

"Michael, restrain our demon prisoner and take her to the cell until she is required!" said Jophiel, holding up some odd white handcuffs.

"Wait!" said Ophelia quickly, before Michael could move. "Your Highness, may I have the honour? After all this evil demon has done, corrupting me over the years, I would like to be the one to finally defeat her..."

"Very well," said Jophiel, handing Ophelia the handcuffs. "You may yet prove yourself and earn forgiveness. Who would have thought? We all believed that there was no hope for you!"

Ophelia smiled at Jophiel, then stood. Nessa watched her as she approached. The angel took her arms, gently pulling them behind her back, and slipped the handcuffs on; rather loosely Nessa thought. Ophelia then hesitated for a moment, gently stroking Nessa's hands. Nessa curled her fingers around Ophelia's, and Ophelia squeezed them lovingly. Nessa breathed a small sigh of relief, her instincts were right. Of course Ophelia didn't really hate her, of course it was an act. Whilst Nessa had never really doubted it was staged, it was still nice to have confirmation.

Ophelia suddenly grabbed Nessa harshly by the shoulders, making her jump, and led her from the room.

Nessa glanced around at the Heavenly corridors as they walked, she hadn't seen them in over six thousand years, but they hadn't changed. They turned a corner to a stretch of corridor Nessa would always remember.

"This is where we met," she whispered. "Do you remember?"

"I think it's best if you don't talk!" Ophelia snapped harshly, but she lovingly stroked Nessa's shoulders that she still had hold of with her thumbs, in a way that said she did remember.

Eventually they reached some strange little prison cell and Ophelia pushed Nessa inside, but also followed to stand in front of her. Nessa looked at her, wide eyed, wondering what she was going to do. Ophelia took a small piece of paper out of her pocket and held it surreptitiously, looking at Nessa expectantly. Nessa gave her a confused look, not certain what she was doing. Suddenly though, words began to appear on the paper.

'I need you to take information from me!' it said.

Nessa looked at Ophelia, who was still staring expectantly.

"What? I promised I would never do that!" whispered Nessa.

Ophelia looked down at the paper and Nessa followed her gaze. The words were replaced by new ones.

'But now I'm asking you to. I give you permission to enter my mind. If you don't, you might die, and I can't let that happen!'

"I don't understand..." Nessa whispered. Horrified by the thought of possessing Ophelia when she promised she wouldn't.

'DO IT!' the paper said. *'Make it look like you're attacking me! The handcuffs are loose. Do you still trust me?'*

Nessa nodded, of course she still trusted Ophelia, and she desperately wanted to know what was going on, but it felt odd to extract information from her beloved angel, even if she specifically asked her to. Possession was separate from other forms of demonic magic; in fact it didn't count as magic at all, it was just something demons could do, so Nessa could still easily do it without her powers.

She looked at Ophelia uncertainly, and Ophelia gave her an encouraging look. She quickly slipped the handcuffs off and grabbed Ophelia's collar, pushing her up against the wall of the prison cell as aggressively as she could whilst ensuring she didn't actually hurt her. Ophelia gasped in surprise, then smiled at Nessa. Nessa pushed her harder against the wall until Ophelia made a small noise that suggested she was feeling squashed. Nessa realised that she was only around an inch away from the angel's face, she could so easily kiss her. Ophelia must have thought the same as she was staring at Nessa's lips, taking in shallow breaths, though some of that might have been because of how hard Nessa was pushing her into the wall...

After a moment Ophelia quietly cleared her throat, reminding Nessa that she was supposed to be doing something, not just pinning her against the wall and gazing at her. Nessa took a deep breath, trying to remember how to do it, as it had been thousands of years. She put her hand on Ophelia's chest and stared deep into her eyes, trying to enter her mind.

In a moment Ophelia's body stiffened and her eyes turned red, but she was still smiling at Nessa. Nessa smiled a little back at her, then focused on finding out what was going on.

"They plan to destroy both Hell and the Earth tonight! But they need you, you are the final ingredient..." came Ophelia's voice.

Ingredient? thought Nessa. *What do you mean*

ingredient?

"They need the life force of a demon to make their weird machine thing work!" she heard Ophelia say. "They want me to take your life to use to prove that I'm on their side! They obviously don't trust me, because they did something so that I can't physically tell you any of this if I tried, though I suppose that's understandable as I've spent a year trying to stop them…"

Nessa thought possession was actually a very brilliant and creative idea, as Ophelia knew she wasn't able to talk freely to her. Nessa closed her eyes, pushing deeper; wondering what else Ophelia wanted her to know. When she had taken information from her before, back in the time of Abraham, Nessa had felt overwhelmed by Ophelia's fear, but this time it was love that engulfed her. It was incredible. Nessa could feel just how much Ophelia adored her, and she felt a little foolish for ever having doubted her love.

"I got in trouble and they made me choose between being the one to kill you to prove loyalty to them, or having my memories of you erased. Obviously I chose the first one because I can save you, and I would far sooner let them destroy me for treason than give up my memories of you. Here's what we're going to do, this bit is very important. I will pretend to take your life force, and you have to play along; you know play dead for a bit? Then at the moment that your body should disappear, I will send you back to Earth where you'll be safe! They won't have a clue! Don't worry, I promise you're not in danger. I'm not actually powerful enough to extract your life force, even if I tried. You would need the power of about 20 angels to do that, but the archangels know surprisingly little about their own lore..."

Nessa felt that this was a pretty well thought out plan; a little crazy, but a good idea. Though she couldn't help but worry what could happen if the archangels found out that Ophelia wasn't actually going to kill her.

Suddenly Nessa heard Ophelia's voice again, only this was a little different, for one thing Nessa wasn't actually asking for information at that moment.

"Nessa! Nessa, I don't know how this possession thing works or whether you can hear this, but I want you to hear it more than anything! I love you! Nessa, my beautiful demon, I love you with all my heart and soul and I have done for a very long time. I'm sorry I could never say it, and I hope I can say it out loud soon, but in the meantime I need you to know!"

Nessa was completely stunned by the outpouring of love, it filled her with such joy to hear it after all this time.

I love you too my darling! Nessa thought, hoping Ophelia could hear it.

She released her angel, and after a moment to recover, Ophelia began acting mean again; reattaching the handcuffs tightly, but it didn't matter. Nessa felt like she was floating with happiness after finally hearing, and feeling, how much her beloved angel loved her back. Ophelia grabbed Nessa by the jacket collar and yanked her close, in what was her best attempt at being threatening, which Nessa was confused to find herself oddly aroused by.

"Wait here until we are ready for you!" Ophelia said

nastily, their lips almost touching. Nessa just smiled and mouthed 'I love you'. Ophelia bit her lip slightly then mouthed back 'I love you too', before suddenly pushing Nessa away so forcefully that she almost fell without her hands to steady her. Ophelia winced in concern, before closing the door and disappearing down the corridor.

Nessa watched her go with a sigh, feeling the happiest she had ever felt in her life, which was odd for someone who was awaiting supposed execution by the love of her life.

Nessa stared at her surroundings, hating being in Heaven. She thought of Ezra and hoped he wasn't too worried that she had disappeared like that. Eventually, two Heavenly guards arrived to take her back to the archangels.

Now only Jophiel and Gabriel sat at the table, Nessa wondered where the others were, but then she remembered she couldn't give a damn about them or what they do. Though it did worry her a little, due to the looming threat of apocalypse. The only person in Heaven that Nessa actually cared about was standing opposite her, nervously holding some sort of empty vial.

"I am sorry it must end this way," said Jophiel, with fake regret. "Upon your sacrifice we shall build a new world; one guided by goodness and light. Surely as former Archangel of Justice, that gives you a hint of peace?"

"Nothing about this is just!" Nessa protested. "This is perhaps the most unjust thing I have ever witnessed, and I lived in Hell for a long time! Your whole plan, to wipe out the humans just because you don't think they're doing a good enough job at being humans? You know what people need when they're doing a bad job? Help! You don't destroy them and start again when they are causing trouble; you help the humans you have! Your problem is that as soon as someone is struggling and actually needs you, you abandon them! Then we'll just keep on fucking up over and over again, and we won't ask for help because we don't feel worthy of it!"

Jophiel raised her eyebrows. "You're not talking about the humans, you're complaining about your own problems…"

"It's the same problem!" sighed Nessa. "Fine, whatever! I know you don't care what I have to say. Get on with killing me, Ophelia…"

Ophelia looked so sad. Though of course as she had assured Nessa, she wasn't actually going to hurt her, it still wasn't a great situation.

"Are you ready to get what you deserve, Nessa?" asked Ophelia.

Nessa had to stop herself from smiling, obviously what she 'deserved' was to be spared from this nonsense, and that's exactly what Ophelia meant.

"I am…" said Nessa, letting Ophelia know that she was ready to play the part. "It's been lovely knowing you all, even you Jophiel!"

Jophiel narrowed her eyes and said nothing. Ophelia stepped closer and opened the vial, waving her hand over Nessa. Some sort of black mist appeared as if it were coming from her chest and into the vial Ophelia was holding, turning to liquid in the glass. Nessa stared at it, wondering if her life force really would look black like that. Maybe so; she was a demon after all. She suddenly noticed Ophelia giving her a warning look and remembered that it should be hurting her, so she quickly put on her best performance; ending with her laying motionless on the floor as the last of the black stuff entered the bottle. She stayed perfectly still as she heard Ophelia hand the vial to Gabriel.

"What happens now? Does she just stay there on the floor?" asked Jophiel. "Ophelia, you read a lot about our lore during your time here when you got yourself killed, what happens to her?"

"She will only be destroyed when the vial is put into the machine," said Ophelia. "Right now the life force could technically be returned to her."

"Right, well Gabriel, go and add it to the machine at once!" said Jophiel.

"Yes Your Highness," said Gabriel, and Nessa heard him leave the room.

"Have I proved my loyalty to Heaven, Your Highness?" Ophelia asked Jophiel.

"Well, I am glad that you have seen the error of your ways Ophelia, but your countless crimes cannot be ignored," said Jophiel simply. "Do not think we have not noticed that you have attempted on more than one occasion to sabotage The Almighty's great plan this past year. However in helping us to eliminate an old enemy you have earned the mercy of being charged with heresy rather than treason."

Nessa panicked. Staying still right then was the hardest thing she had ever done, because everything in her wanted to react. She knew what happened to angels charged with heresy, because it had happened to her once; they became demons and went to Hell!

Before Nessa could hear anything else she found herself back in Ophelia's cottage, sitting beside a terrified Ezra, who gasped in surprise when she appeared back where she had been. Nessa wished she could have stayed in Heaven, much as she hated it, to somehow try to help her precious angel, because now she had no idea what to do. She couldn't let Ophelia fall…

Chapter Fifteen
An Angelic Taxi

"Nessa! Where on earth did you go? That scared me so much!" cried Ezra.

"Not on Earth Ezzy, I was dragged to bloody Heaven!" Nessa said, slightly distracted, trying to think of *anything* they could do to help Ophelia.

"You went to Heaven?" Ezra gasped. "Did you see Ophelia?"

"Yes, and I need to get back up there! She needs help, I think she is going to be sent to Hell!"

Nessa had never seen Ezra look so full of terror. "She can't become a demon!" he whispered. "She's not evil, she hasn't done anything wrong!"

"Neither did I!" sighed Nessa.

Ezra looked close to tears and Nessa felt bad. She thought of the first time she questioned things; the first time she realised Heaven wasn't as amazing as she thought it was, that angels could be thrown out just for being themselves. It was like the biggest betrayal, your entire worldview and everything you thought you knew starts to wobble, then of course it all comes crashing down! Nessa didn't want that for Ezra. Ophelia was a perfect angel, but she had always had an edge, Nessa had often said she would make a worryingly good demon. Ezra on the other hand was like a tiny little puppy dog, he wouldn't last five minutes in Hell.

"Ophelia hasn't done anything wrong, but angels don't become demons because they do something bad; they fall when they lose faith in Heaven and God's plan," Nessa said carefully, trying not to scare their adopted little brother too much.

"Oh, so you can do what you want as long as you believe in Heaven?" Ezra asked, sounding a little more hopeful. "I will always believe in the goodness of Heaven and God!"

Nessa wondered how he could possibly think that, after spending a year with her, but for his sake she hoped he hung onto the belief. She didn't have time to quiz him on his faith, though she was very intrigued, she had to get back to Ophelia.

"How do I get back to Heaven?" she asked Ezra desperately.

"I'm not sure... Are you going to be able to stop them from casting her out, if that's what they're planning?" Ezra answered, eating one of the biscuits that Ophelia must have sent back down when they disappeared from Nessa's hands.

"I don't know, but I need to at least be there with her! When you become a demon you feel as if everybody has abandoned you and that the whole universe hates you. I need her to know how loved she is!"

Ezra nodded and thought for a moment. "They don't let demons in without a very good reason, and I don't know about you, but I can't think of anything creative right now. I think that happens when you know the world's going to end in a few hours! But they'll probably let me in? Is there a way I could secretly get you in?"

"I'm highly limited without magic…" Nessa said. It had been over a year, but living like a human didn't get any less annoying.

"I have magic. What were you thinking?" Ezra smiled.

"I need to hide somehow…" Nessa said thoughtfully, standing and pacing slightly. "In theory, the only way I could hide like that without magic would be to possess you, but I can't properly possess angels and I wouldn't do that to you anyway! Ugh, I have no ideas!"

"Wow…" said Ezra, looking a tiny bit uncomfortable. "I feel like that's a bit extreme. Like you've jumped past multiple options that make more sense and chosen violence instead. Well luckily, like you said you can't possess me, and even more luckily there are other options. Like I said, I have magic!"

"What do you suggest then?" snapped Nessa, very aware that the more time that passed, the less chance she had of seeing Ophelia before she was thrown out of Heaven. "I'm a demon, not a little mouse or something! How can I hide?"

"You could be?" said Ezra thoughtfully.

"What, a mouse?" said Nessa, wondering what he was on about.

"Well yeah, if you want? I'm pretty sure we only look like humans because it's easier, and God modelled us on her and humans on us, but you're not a human; you're a demon. Magic can turn you into whatever you want. You're right, if you were small you could fit in my coat pocket and no one would see you!"

"Wait, you're not actually going to turn me into a mouse are you?" Nessa asked in concern.

"Why not?" said Ezra. "You want to get into Heaven don't you? Once we're inside I'll turn you back!"

Nessa really wasn't a fan of this idea. Of course demons and angels technically had the power to look however they wanted, but why would Nessa want to be anything other than a normal human-looking demon? Nobody wants to be a mouse. Nessa was sure even mice wouldn't particularly want to be mice if they were given the choice. They're not the most sturdy of creatures and almost everything is out to kill them.

Before Nessa could try to think of a better, less mousey plan, Ezra had already waved his hand over her and in an instant she was a whole lot smaller. She gasped in surprise, then looked up at Ezra, wondering whether mice had the capability to look as pissed off as she felt she looked.

"Yay, it worked!" smiled Ezra, sounding a little too relieved for someone who had transformed someone into a mouse without waiting for them to agree.

"There was doubt?" Nessa said in horror. "Don't seem so confident about a mad idea like this and then act surprised when it works! I don't appreciate being used as your magical guinea pig!"

"Technically you're a mouse!" grinned Ezra, trying not to laugh at his own joke. "I've never done that kind of magic before, there's no call for anything mouse-related in admin. That was big magic, can't I be pleased with myself?"

"Yes, fine. Well done! Though you could have let me pick a cooler animal!" sighed Nessa. "Now can we go?"

"Yes, of course! I'll get my coat. Stay there!" said Ezra, starting towards the door.

"Are you kidding?" Nessa said. "I have no magic and almost every animal on this planet would want to eat me right now. I'm not moving a muscle!"

As Ezra fetched his coat, Nessa suddenly realised that the archangels would be more than a little stunned to see her, as they thought Ophelia had killed her less than ten minutes ago. Maybe she would be able to somehow intimidate or scare them? It was clear that Jophiel didn't know the rules because she was asking Ophelia questions about angel lore. She'd probably believe anything they said.

Ezra reentered the living room wearing his coat and looked down at Nessa.

"What?" she said irritably.

"I need to put you in the pocket... Are you okay with that?"

"Do I have a choice?" said Nessa, hoping she was giving him the most disapproving mousey stare possible.

Ezra knelt down and picked Nessa up in perhaps the most awkward way someone could possibly pick up a mouse, and slid her into the coat pocket.

"I hated that!" called Nessa as Ezra began walking towards the door. "And this is going to make me feel sick! It's like that rollercoaster we went on at the seaside, but so much worse!"

"You know you don't have to be a talking mouse!" said Ezra with a little smile.

"You're lucky I didn't bite you!" Nessa said. "Oh I *so* resent the fact that I have no magic so you are completely in control here! I *hate* letting other people make decisions for me, I *need* to be in control! The only times I haven't been in control have been when I am being punished… It's not a nice feeling…"

"Well you'll just have to trust me! Because right now that's the only option you've got, unless you fancy your chances of surviving the day as a mouse, let alone when the Earth is destroyed later!" said Ezra. "You're not being punished. I'm helping you, which you know, I don't *have* to do. It's super dangerous to smuggle a demon into Heaven, so I must love you eh?"

Nessa had a comeback planned, but stopped in shock. "What do you mean you *love* me?" No one, not even Ophelia had ever said they loved her out loud… How could this sweet angel say it so casually?

"You're one of my big sisters, of course I love you!" said Ezra as if it were obvious. "If I've learnt anything from books it's that we do crazy things for the people we love, like smuggle them into Heaven disguised as a mouse! There is no one I would betray Heaven for apart from you and Ophelia… I wouldn't even do it for myself… For over six thousand years the other angels treated me like I was nothing, but I didn't do anything about it. Doing things for you is easier than doing them for me."

"I get that," said Nessa sadly. "I've always found it easier to fight for Ophelia than for myself. You know what, I love you too, my sweet little brother. And I will make a promise to you like I made to Ophelia; that I will do everything I can to keep you safe forever. Because if there's one thing *I* know about love, it's that when I love someone, I love them fiercely. I protect them with all I have, I would give my life for them in a moment..."

"Well I hope it doesn't come to that!" said Ezra nervously. "But thank you!"

"You're welcome. Now, I really am not going to be a talking mouse anymore, because I'm actually starting to feel sick with all this swinging, and I ate quite a few biscuits! Especially for a mouse..."

Ezra smiled, probably half at Nessa's silliness, and half at hearing that after all those years alone, someone would be willing to fight for him; his old archangel hero no less!

When the Heavenly lift that Ezra summoned arrived, he gulped nervously.

"Nessa?" he whispered worriedly.

"Yeah?" said Nessa, poking her head out of the pocket.

"I think Heaven's on lockdown... They do that when something really big is happening to make sure Hell doesn't get involved... I'm quite scared now..."

"It's okay!" said Nessa, trying to be as reassuring as a tiny mouse could be. "You'll be alright! I'm so proud of you, you're really brave!"

"You're proud of me?" Ezra squeaked excitedly.

"Very!" said Nessa. "And Ophelia will be too, when she hears how far you've come! You can do it Ezzy. I promise I won't let anything happen to you!" Nessa really wasn't sure how she would keep that promise, as a non-magical mouse, but Ezra seemed cheered by it nonetheless.

When Ezra stepped out of the lift, he was stopped by an angel guard. Nessa could tell that he had tensed up in fear and she squashed herself down as low as possible to ensure she stayed out of sight.

"Who are you?" asked the guard.

Whilst Ezra's first response to that question had always been 'no one', now he was someone; and he was on a very important mission for his beloved sisters. He smiled confidently.

"I'm the deputy Angel of the North, and I have something important to discuss with the archangels!"

"Something seems, dark... There is some heavier energy here..." said the guard, glancing around Ezra suspiciously.

"Oh... That will be my clothes!" Ezra said, thinking fast. "They were made by humans, and humans are both good and bad. Maybe the person who made these was especially dark? I'm not thinking like serial killer level, but maybe they don't pay their taxes or something? I don't know? Please let me pass."

Nessa had to stop herself from laughing. She was impressed with Ezra's wit and quick thinking.

The guard glared at Ezra disapprovingly. "So you want to see the archangels? I'm afraid they are quite busy at present."

"I know, but they called for me!" Ezra lied.

"How do I know you're telling the truth?" asked the guard suspiciously.

"I'm an angel! Angels don't lie!" Ezra smiled sweetly at the guard and they let him pass. Nessa felt so proud; how she imagined big sisters must feel when their little brothers walk for the first time, or get into university, one of the two.

Ezra rounded the corner and stopped to catch his breath. Nessa popped her head out of the pocket.

"Well done Ezzy! That was brilliant!" she said.

"That was the scariest thing I've ever done!" Ezra said, leaning dramatically against the wall. "I'm such a bad angel!"

"No, you're one of the best angels, the others are bad," Nessa insisted.

"Thanks, the archangels would disagree though!" Ezra grinned. "You know? I've been hanging out with a demon far too much, because I don't actually care that I'm a bad angel. It was quite exciting lying to that guard! This is how people end up in gangs Nessa!"

Nessa laughed. "I'll make sure you don't end up in a gang! Now let's get to Ophelia."

"Where is she? Heaven's a big place, and this bit's just the offices." Ezra desperately looked around.

Nessa focused on Ophelia's energy. "That way!" she announced.

"Which way? Hun this is why mice don't give directions!" Ezra said, looking down at Nessa in his pocket.

"Left…" sighed Nessa. "Promise me you'll turn me back to normal as soon as we get to Ophelia! I'm sick of this!"

"Absolutely," said Ezra, setting off down the corridor.

They navigated their way through the Heavenly corridors, with Nessa shouting directions, until they reached the same prison cell that Nessa had been put in earlier that day. Ophelia was sitting in the corner. It looked like she had been crying. She quickly rose to her feet and wiped her eyes when she heard Ezra approaching, obviously thinking it was a guard coming to take her away. Her face lit up with relief and joy when she saw Ezra.

"Ezra!" she cried. "What the heck are you doing here?"

"Well, I'm sort of the delivery person!" Ezra smiled. "Like an angelic taxi!"

"What are you talking about?" Ophelia said in confusion.

Ezra put his hand gently in the pocket. "Don't bite me or I won't turn you back!" he said, carefully scooping Nessa out and placing her on the floor.

"What's that?" asked Ophelia suspiciously.

"It's the demon you killed earlier!" Nessa smiled. "Come back to haunt you in the inconvenient form of a mouse!"

"Nessa?!" Ophelia said in surprise. "I thought I felt your presence. What are you doing here, and why are you a mouse?"

"Believe it or not, I'm like this because I'm trying to

save you, or at least be with you. It's a long story," Nessa sighed. "Ezra? I'd really appreciate *not* being a mouse anymore."

"Right, yes of course!" said Ezra. He waved his hand over Nessa, and in a flash she was back to normal. Well, almost normal…

"What the fuck am I wearing Ezzy? It's way too white for my liking!" Nessa said in disgust.

"I don't know… I didn't do that, I just turned you back to normal…" Ezra said quickly.

Ophelia was leaning against the bars, staring at Nessa in complete awe. "Nessa… I know what that is! Your archangel robes! You look like Zadkiel again!"

Nessa looked down at the outfit in horror. Ophelia was right, it was the white and gold robes she had worn as an angel! But, this very garment turned black and was torn as she fell, it became her demon rags. Only God can create archangel robes, so it was impossible that it was here now…

"Is my hair still black?" she asked in concern, hoping she hadn't fully become Zadkiel.

"Yes," said Ophelia. "You still look like my Nessa. You are perfect… Come closer."

Nessa walked up to the bars and took Ophelia's hands, pulling her close.

"I love you," she whispered.

"I know, but you're silly!" Ophelia whispered back. "I sent you safely back to Earth. You're like some sort of fly getting caught in a web again even when you've been freed! Why would you come back?"

"Because I heard Jophiel sentence you to heresy,

and believe me I know what that means. I had to be with you! I won't let you face that alone," Nessa said, feeling close to tears.

"You are so lovely!" Ophelia said, putting a hand on Nessa's neck and pulling her as close as the bars would allow. She closed her eyes, and before Nessa knew what was happening, her angel was kissing her! It was a soft and simple kiss, but one filled with so much love and adoration. Ophelia was running her fingers through Nessa's hair and Nessa had her hands on Ophelia's waist. Suddenly though, they were interrupted by a worried squeak from Ezra.

"Someone's coming!" he gasped.

Nessa and Ophelia parted quickly; letting their hands linger together for an extra moment.

Archangel Gabriel was striding down the corridor, followed by two heavenly guards. He stopped in his tracks and gasped when he saw Nessa in her archangel robes.

"Heaven preserve us! Archangel Zadkiel?!" he said in horror.

Nessa grinned, remembering her plan to mess with them.

"Archangel Gabriel..." she said with a self-righteous nod of her head

"How... How are you here?" Gabriel asked in terror. "You were dead! Demon Nessa was dead..."

"Indeed!" Nessa smiled. "Yet I returned as Zadkiel! I cannot be destroyed by you, not for your petty plans to destroy the Earth! I am too powerful to get rid of that easily!"

Both Ophelia and Ezra were smiling proudly at Nessa, and she felt very pleased with herself for terrifying the Archangel Gabriel like that; especially bragging about how powerful she was when actually she was totally useless in most ways right now without magic, but her outfit alone was enough to strike fear through Gabriel's heart.

The two guards glanced nervously at Nessa as they opened the prison door and tied Ophelia's hands behind her back. They were obviously concerned that she would do something, but Nessa wouldn't make a scene right now even if she had magic, not when they had Ophelia as their prisoner. Ophelia smiled at Nessa lovingly and Nessa forced herself to smile back in a way that she hoped was convincing, though she was terribly worried about the whole situation. Being back in her angel robes was reminding her of one of the worst things that ever happened to her; an event she would pray wasn't about to repeat itself with Ophelia, if she still believed in God at all. She had spent six thousand years ensuring that Ophelia never fell from Heaven, and now she had to stand there and watch helplessly as her worst nightmare came true.

"You cannot interfere Zadkiel…" said Gabriel, still sounding nervous.

"I won't," said Nessa, not taking her eyes off Ophelia. "And Nessa is fine!"

Nessa and Ezra followed as the guards led Ophelia down the corridor back towards the archangel meeting room.

"Ezzy? Can you turn my clothes back to normal

please?" Nessa whispered. "It feels really awkward wearing this..."

"Of course," said Ezra. He waved his hand over Nessa, but nothing happened. His eyes widened and he tried several more times as they walked down the corridor, but still nothing happened.

"What's going on?" Nessa asked.

"I don't know!" Ezra said in panic.

Suddenly some chocolates appeared in his hand and Nessa looked at him in confusion.

"What's with the chocolates?" she said.

"I was just checking my magic wasn't broken, because it's not working when I try to change your outfit!" said Ezra quietly. "And I went for chocolate because this whole thing is highly stressful and I somehow feel like chocolate might help... Want some?"

He offered the chocolates to Nessa and she took one, sighing at the absurdity of everything that was happening that day.

Ezra glanced at a door as they passed. "That's where I used to work," he whispered. "It's funny, if you had told me when I left there with an hour's notice to move to Earth that the next time I walked past this door I would be sharing human chocolate with a demon who happens to be Archangel Zadkiel and is also my sister who I had to smuggle into Heaven disguised as a mouse to try to save my other sister, I don't think I would have believed you..."

"And that would be fair enough!" smiled Nessa.

"And the world's going to end!" Ezra sighed. "This is a weird day..."

"It certainly is," said Nessa, stroking the gold on her robes, feeling how soft they were. She had absolutely no ideas. Maybe Jophiel was right, maybe it was inevitable that Ophelia would eventually fall, because she was so close to Nessa. Perhaps all Nessa could do was be there for her beloved. She considered how much less traumatic her fall might have been if someone had loved her. Now that she knew Ophelia loved her back, Nessa wanted to ensure her angel never had to face anything alone.

They entered the meeting room and Nessa took a proper look around, resenting being there for the third time that day, after thousands of years. It hadn't changed a bit; it looked just the same as when Nessa was thrown from the ledge. The other archangels weren't there yet, only Gabriel, who was overseeing the guards leading Ophelia into position opposite the table, and occasionally glancing nervously at Nessa.

Nessa walked up to the archangels' table. She didn't particularly mean to, but it almost felt like it was pulling her, like whichever part of Nessa was still Zadkiel longed to retake her seat. Well, even if Zadkiel wanted to, Nessa certainly didn't! She ran her fingers along the moss that covered the top of her seat. It was like a neglected tombstone dedicated to her old life. She pulled at some of the moss and revealed the word 'Zadkiel' etched deep into the stone. Usually any mention of her old name, or sometimes even the letter 'Z', filled Nessa with an odd sadness. But seeing her old seat actually gave her a strange calm feeling. As if she was somehow finally at peace with being both Nessa and Zadkiel, when all this time she had tried to push the archangel away, far into the depths of her mind. Maybe to protect her from the demon she had become? Who knows…

Ezra put a hand on Nessa's arm, startling her a little. "Are you okay?" he asked.

"Hmm? Yeah, I'm fine…" answered Nessa, rubbing a little more moss off her name.

"Yours is the fanciest seat," Ezra smiled. "I like the patterns."

"Yeah, because I was in charge," Nessa smiled.

"Was it fun? Being an archangel?" asked Ezra.

"It was all I knew," Nessa sighed. "Until it was gone…"

"I always thought you were brilliant!" Ezra said. "You signed all the best documents; I mean, to pass all the good rules. Since your day not many good rules have been passed… All the best stuff happened when you were in charge!"

Nessa laughed slightly. "I didn't do anything! It only seems more interesting because it was during creation, when everything felt more exciting…"

"No!" whispered Ezra. "It's because Jophiel was never supposed to be in charge! I've been thinking since I met you, I really don't think it's a coincidence that the last bit of your file is missing! There's information about all the other fallen angels, showing that their banishment was approved by The Almighty, but there's nothing about yours!"

Nessa's heart thumped as she thought of Lucifer sitting in that very seat, telling her that The Almighty had authorised him to banish bad angels while she was busy. What if he was lying? It wouldn't be out of character, he went on to become the bloody devil after all! Maybe Nessa was never supposed to be a demon? She wasn't sure how she felt about that, so she decided to push the idea away and focus on Ophelia. She was the most important thing right now.

"I'll be back in a minute!" Ezra said suddenly, and he rushed out of the room.

"What? Where are you...?" Nessa stopped because he had already gone. She looked over at Ophelia who was smiling warmly at her. Ophelia's expression suggested that Nessa was the most amazing thing she had ever seen, and Nessa felt like she might tear up seeing such adoration on her darling angel's face.

Suddenly their little moment across the room was interrupted by Jophiel sweeping in.

"Gabriel! Is everything ready for..." she trailed off when she saw Nessa. "Oh for Heaven's sake! I really thought we got rid of you! What are you doing here, and why are you dressed like an archangel you meddling fool? Ophelia, did you somehow *pretend* to kill her?"

Ophelia opened her mouth to speak, but Nessa jumped in, scared they'd give her a worse punishment if they knew. "No, she did!" she said, carrying on the act that she started with Gabriel. "I cannot be killed by your silly plans to end the world. I have come back to life as Zadkiel!"

Jophiel looked worried. "Fallen angels are exactly that; fallen. It cannot be reversed! You will always be a demon Nessa."

"Maybe? Maybe not?" smiled Nessa. "Maybe there's a lot we don't know about the rules of Heaven?"

"Shut up Zadkiel, or Nessa, or whoever you are!" Jophiel hissed. It was clear Nessa was getting to her. Maybe Ezra was right, maybe Jophiel and Lucifer damned Nessa without God? Perhaps Jophiel was scared that someone would find out? "Anyway, the time of Angel Ophelia's trail of judgement is upon us," Jophiel continued, regaining her calm air. "Any uninvited guests must now leave. If you do not you shall only make Ophelia's punishment more severe, and I'm sure you don't want that, do you? You know well enough how bad things are already going to be for Ophelia, now don't you Nessa?"

Nessa clenched her fist. She wanted more than anything to punch Jophiel in her stupid patronising little face. She hadn't realised just how much she resented her until she was face to face with her again, for the first time since Jophiel smiled smugly whilst throwing her own sister to oblivion.

Nessa couldn't bear to leave Ophelia on her own. She glanced over to her and Ophelia gave her a nod that said *it's okay, you can go*, but she was still torn.

"Are you leaving?" said Jophiel irritably. "Or do you want to cause Ophelia more trouble? And we will be keeping an eye on you, Angel Ezra!" she said, glaring at Ezra who had reentered the room without Nessa noticing. "Don't think we haven't noticed how pally you are getting with a demon! Nessa, you really can't help but corrupt innocent angels, can you? I advise you leave Ezra alone. Lead not another of our Angels of the North to damnation. One is quite bad enough..." Jophiel shot Ophelia a look and Nessa was furious. Ezra took her hand and she stared down at it in surprise; forever shocked that anybody cared about her.

"Come on Nessa. We should go…" he said quietly.

Jophiel looked at Ezra in surprise. "Did you not hear my warning to stay away from her?" she asked.

"I did, Your Highness, but there are no rules about being friends with demons. You are in charge, perhaps you could make one?" Ezra smiled sweetly.

Nessa and Ophelia looked at each other across the room, equally impressed with their brother's bravery.

"Just go!" said Jophiel irritably.

Nessa gave Ophelia a quick reassuring look and then let Ezra lead her out of the room.

As soon as they were outside, Nessa grabbed Ezra by the shoulders, probably a bit too aggressively.

"Go back to the cottage!" she said. "I'll come back and I'll bring Ophelia, I promise!"

"What are you going to do?" Ezra asked worriedly.

"I don't know, nothing really. There's nothing I can do… But I won't leave Ophelia. Listen Ezzy, can you disguise me again somehow? Just *not* as a mouse this time! Perhaps make me invisible or something? I know I won't be able to undo it, but either you or Ophelia can eventually… I *need* to go back in there!"

"No, listen to me first! I've got something important to tell you!" said Ezra desperately. "You *can* do magic!"

"No, I gave it up to save Ophelia, I've told you the story a hundred times," said Nessa quickly, anxious to get back inside with Ophelia.

"Yes I know, but you gave up your demonic magic! And it turns out you've had angelic magic this whole time!" Ezra insisted.

Nessa paused, suddenly interested. "I haven't been an angel for over six thousand years..." she said.

"I know, but when we were looking at your seat I noticed something. When you touched it, your hand was glowing slightly with angelic energy, and I could feel it, so I had an idea. I checked in the admin room. The certificate of authorisation to expel you from Heaven definitely isn't there, I'm starting to think you never had one at all, but on Lucifer's it specifically says that by signing it, God was taking away his angelic powers! So because she never signed one for you, you still have your old magic! You just haven't used it because you didn't know! Maybe that's why you are immune to holy water?"

Nessa was completely stunned. She focused on trying to feel angelic energy, and sure enough she felt her hands fill with light power. Had it really been there all along, deep inside her? She just never tuned into it, because why would she try to use angelic magic if she wasn't an angel?

"See! I'm right, aren't I?" Ezra said in excitement at seeing Nessa's face.

"You are..." said Nessa slowly. "Thanks Ezzy... Now, amazing as this is, I really must get back in there! You go home and promise me no matter what happens or how long we take, you wait there for us okay? We won't abandon you!"

"Okay..." said Ezra. "Though I can only stay there until seven, because that's when the world's going to end..."

"Oh yeah... Shit, I forgot about that... We'll be back before then! Go!"

"Alright, be careful. I love you!" Ezra said, giving Nessa a quick hug; their first ever.

"I love you too Ezzy," Nessa smiled, and she watched him run down the corridor, out of sight.

Nessa used her new-found angelic magic to turn herself invisible, then slipped silently back into the meeting room. The archangels were all seated now, and Nessa felt that her own empty seat stuck out like a missing tooth. A permanent reminder of the archangel that failed... Nice to make a lasting impact, Nessa supposed.

Ophelia was still standing facing the archangels, and Nessa wished she could let her know she was there. Just to have the knowledge that she wasn't alone would be so comforting, Nessa imagined. She willed Ophelia to somehow sense her, even though she knew she couldn't see her. Ophelia glanced around the room with a slight look of confusion and stopped at Nessa, staring directly at her. Nessa had to nervously check that she actually was invisible. She was, but Ophelia was looking right at her, smiling as if she knew exactly where she was. She smiled back, even though she was invisible.

"What are you looking at?" Jophiel called to Ophelia irritably.

"Nothing... Sorry Your Highness..." said Ophelia, looking back at the archangels.

"I should think that that part of the wall is not more interesting than your trial of damnation?" Jophiel said sarcastically.

Ophelia didn't say anything. Nessa wondered whether she was more important to Ophelia than the horror of becoming a demon. Ophelia had always been scared of the threat, how did she feel now that it was actually happening?

"It has been some time since an angel has fallen, and since you are so obsessed with Demon Nessa, it is amusingly ironic that you now stand where she stood; about to join her in Hell." Jophiel said.

Nessa suddenly realised, this was *just* like her fall! Where was God? She wasn't there! If Jophiel and Lucifer *did* damn Nessa without authorisation, Jophiel was about to do the same to Ophelia! Maybe Ophelia would keep her angelic magic too?

"Did you plan to do this?" Ophelia asked. "Did you call me here and make me help you for a year *and* make me kill the person I love most, knowing you'd just send me to Hell anyway?" She sounded angry rather than scared, but Nessa was a little distracted by Ophelia admitting she loved her in front of the archangels to think about it.

"Well, we *hoped* you would learn the error of your ways and join us," sighed Jophiel, sounding fake as ever. "What we did was give you a chance, Ophelia. We all hoped you would rise to it…"

"But I haven't done anything bad!" protested Ophelia. "I did all the stupid stuff you said, even though I really don't want to destroy anything, let alone the Earth! I want the Earth and all the humans to be saved because I love them! You can't punish me for caring about things…"

"Oh we can," said Jophiel. "As I once told your precious little demon, love *can* be dangerous when it gets in the way of your Heavenly duty! Anyway, angels become demons when they lose the last of their faith in Heaven, and we can tell you doubt us. You are lost to scepticism."

"So that's it?" said Ophelia. "In the back of my mind I've been imagining the day that I might fall for over six thousand years, but I never thought it would be like this! I thought it would be because you found out I am in love with a demon, or that I sometimes help her with her demonic missions, or more recently that I went down to Hell to warn Lucifer about your plan because I didn't want to lose Nessa and The Devil gave me deadly poison! But it isn't any of that… It's just because I don't agree with you?!"

Nessa held her breath. Did Ophelia really just confess to nearly every Heavenly crime she had ever committed. Nessa was scared for her, but admired her bravery; she had been terrified during her own trial!

"That was a lot of information…" Jophiel said after a pause. "You are lucky I'm feeling generous today," she continued. "I am fairly certain that a lot of what you just mentioned would actually count as treason. Wouldn't you agree archangels?"

The archangels quickly nodded their agreement, perhaps all a little scared to say anything at all to Jophiel right now.

"The punishment for which is, as I'm sure you are aware, execution. But as we had already decided to charge you with heresy, we shall honour that. Angel Ophelia, you are hereby banished from Heaven and shall become a demon, and I really don't think Lucifer likes you very much so I doubt you will enjoy life in Hell!"

Cracks appeared beneath Ophelia, and Nessa gasped quietly, despite her efforts to remain hidden. She knew what happened next, the ground would crumble completely and Ophelia would fall.

Ophelia's eyes widened. "I have one thing I absolutely have to say while I'm still an angel!" She turned and looked directly at invisible Nessa. "Nessa, my darling, I love you with all my heart! I'm sorry I never said it before!" And with that, the ground gave way and she was gone.

Nessa panicked. She dropped the invisible disguise and ran to the edge of the precipice. "Ophelia!" she yelled.

She shot the shocked archangels, and particularly Jophiel, the nastiest look she could as her wings sprouted. Jophiel opened her mouth to speak, but Nessa didn't stay to listen. She spread her wings and plummeted after her angel.

Chapter Sixteen
God's Perfect Creation.

Nessa didn't remember her fall being this long, but it must have been. She knew that at one point she had blacked out, because she never actually felt the impact of landing.

She couldn't catch up to Ophelia, and there was absolutely nothing she could do to stop it. Eventually she landed in the same strange place that she had found herself all those years ago. As Nessa had been flying down, she was in control, so landed gently, whereas Ophelia had fallen and was lying unconscious beside her.

"Ophelia! My darling!" Nessa cried. Rushing to her love's side and sitting beside her, taking her head into her lap.

Ophelia always wore pale colours, in a style that she excitedly described as 'cottagecore', Nessa didn't especially know what that meant, but her angel always dressed exactly how you would imagine an angel in disguise to dress. Like some beautiful woodland fairy from a book, always breathtakingly beautiful Nessa thought. Nessa on the other hand was happy trying to look cool rather than beautiful. She wore dark clothes; mainly black with the odd dark red and purple, though purple was Zadkiel's colour, so she was never sure how she felt about that. Nessa *didn't* look like she lived in a cottage, she looked like she was the mysterious one from a rock band. Now though, Ophelia's outfit had turned black with the fall, and Nessa had managed to turn her clothes back to normal, as she was no longer in Heaven, so they were the closest to matching they had ever been. Clothes turn black on those who fall, it's a visual symbol that suggests that a fallen angel is now evil. Never in a million years would Nessa ever describe Ophelia as evil though, she was the nicest person in any realm.

So far Nessa couldn't see anything else different about Ophelia, apart from the cuts and bruises from the fall; her hair hadn't changed, as some demons' do. Nessa wiped a little blood from her angel's forehead. How could this have happened? She was completely distraught, and the image of her perfect angel's beautiful face all broken like that sent an indescribable feeling of anguish through her body. Nessa loved that angel more than life itself, she had sworn to protect her all those years ago, and now there she was; a *demon*, and she was hurt! Nessa was sure the image would haunt her forever...

No one was there to heal Nessa after her fall, so she was damn certain she would heal Ophelia now she knew she had magic again. She couldn't bear to look at the face she loved so much that hurt; it was breaking her heart. She gently waved her hand across her angel's body, and in an instant Ophelia's wounds were healed, and she looked peaceful, but Nessa couldn't undo what Jophiel had done to her... She was a demon now! To Nessa though, she would always be an angel; the purest being to ever exist.

She gently kissed Ophelia's forehead. She was pleased that Ophelia wouldn't wake up there alone. For a very long time, waking up in Hell after the fall had been the worst thing to ever happen to Nessa. She had felt so alone, so abandoned; as if she could never possibly be happy again. But now being with Ophelia made her happier than she could have ever imagined, so if Ophelia woke up to love, it might not be so bad for her?

Nessa looked at her beautiful sleeping angel and wondered whether, if she had gone to Heaven with her last year, or better still Ophelia had agreed to run away with her, this could have been avoided. Maybe not, maybe it really was inevitable because she was close to a demon? As usual when anything bad happened, Nessa blamed herself. Though perhaps it should have been Jophiel that she blamed? Or God, Nessa blamed a lot of things on God and her supposed great plan.

"You're all bastards, you know that?" Nessa yelled to the sky. "I don't know why you all hate me... Even you God! So maybe you didn't cast me out, maybe you didn't sign anything, but you also didn't help me! You could have saved me... All I wanted was for you to be proud of me..." Nessa choked up. All this Zadkiel stuff had brought up feelings she had tried very hard to push away. "I worked so hard on the universe, I was so proud of myself, why were you not proud of me? All you cared about was your stupid Earth! The Earth that, by the way, despite all of that, I am desperate to save from the idiots you've let run Heaven all these years! Even if it wasn't specifically your doing, you're God! It's your fault you didn't care..." Nessa paused and looked down at her precious fallen angel, laying in her lap, looking like the subject of some beautiful oil painting. She continued addressing God, even though she knew she wouldn't be listening. "I was proud of our universe," she whispered. "But now any amount of stars and planets would pale in comparison to my love for Ophelia. She is your most perfect creation, an angelic masterpiece that I am in love with, and who somehow loves me back, though I can still hardly believe that. God, if you hate me that's fine, I don't really care, but please leave her out of it..." She gently stroked Ophelia's cheek and pulled her closer so that she was right in her arms, she held her tight and rested her head on Ophelia's, kissing the top of her head as she did. Nessa closed her eyes, enjoying being this close to her angel, even if not in the best situation. Her wings wrapped around them both, as if shutting out the dank surroundings.

"I love you," Nessa whispered into Ophelia's hair. "I love being near you. God did one thing right in creating you my angel. It has always been an honour and a privilege to be the one allowed to be with you." Tears were now falling into Ophelia's hair.

"You've stopped..." mumbled Ophelia quietly. "Please keep saying lovely things..."

Nessa smiled, relieved to hear her voice. She kissed her soft hair.

"My beautiful angel," she whispered into her hair. She found herself subconsciously rocking Ophelia a little, not sure who she was trying to comfort more.

"Not anymore," sighed Ophelia.

"You'll *always* be my angel," said Nessa, tightening her grip around her.

Ophelia turned so that she was facing Nessa, still laying on her. Nessa looked into her eyes, they were shining with love and kindness. Further proof that demons being evil was a load of shit. Ophelia's eyes widened.

"My love," she said, sending a thrill through Nessa's body with the name. "Your wings!"

"What about them?" asked Nessa.

She hadn't noticed her wings, she had been focused on Ophelia, and cursing God. But they were grey... They should be black, but they were grey! Not even a particularly dark grey either, more a light grey, closer to those of an angel than a demon. Nessa hadn't used her wings since the wartime, when did this happen?

"What does that mean?" she said, turning a wing slightly to look at it.

"I don't know," said Ophelia, "But they are beautiful!" She reached out and stroked Nessa's wing gently. No one had ever touched them before, it felt special... "I think it must mean you are very unique," said Ophelia. "They are gorgeous; just like you!"

"Oh, I love you!" said Nessa, trying to gather Ophelia closer in her arms. After not daring to say it for thousands of years, Nessa was determined to tell Ophelia that she loved her so often that it would likely become annoying.

"I love you too Nessa!" said Ophelia.

Nessa could hardly believe that Ophelia had just said it so casually, as if it were just a normal fact, not something to be ashamed of; but then she was a demon now too. That probably made it easier to love her.

"I wish I had been brave enough just to tell you I loved you, even when I thought you couldn't possibly love me back," Nessa said sadly. "You deserved to know how much you have always been loved..."

"What are you talking about you silly thing? I have always known how much you love me!" said Ophelia, almost sounding offended. "I didn't let you say it because I was scared they would take me away from you if I said that I love you out loud, and I really didn't want you to say it out loud if I couldn't say it back... Which ended up happening in the end anyway and I'm very sorry about that..."

"It's okay, I understand," sighed Nessa. "I'm a no-good demon; hard to love. You could only admit to loving me when you had nothing left to lose..."

Ophelia sat up sharply. "Come now darling, that's not fair!" she said. "I was trying to protect what we had! If there's one thing that has been confirmed today it's that Jophiel is an absolute psychopath! If she knew I was in love with you, don't you think she would have done everything she could to keep us apart? When Lucifer found out you were in love with an angel he tried very hard to kill me! I couldn't risk it... Plus, the only way I was allowed to come back to you after I got shot during the last war was to agree to Jophiel's rules, which included promising to never create another scandal. I didn't know what would happen if I did, but that's when I knew I could never say it out loud. And that's not even because you were a demon, it's more because I was an angel! Angels aren't supposed to be in love, we weren't made for that. You heard Jophiel, love is dangerous. That's what angels think…"

Nessa was silent for a moment as she tried to process what Ophelia had just said.

"So… You loved me this whole time? Since the last war?" said asked in a tiny voice, tears in her eyes.

"Since *long* before the war!" sighed Ophelia. "I really thought you knew, I knew you loved me without you saying it! Why didn't you know I love you?" she implored. "Have I not shown you enough affection over the years? Have you never noticed the way I have always looked at you? The things I do for you? The delight that must be visible in my eyes every time I see you? Yes I only said it out loud then, because if I was to be a demon, then they can't take me away from you because we are the same! But before that I wanted you to hear it from an angel, just once… I have been madly in love with you for a *very* long time!"

Nessa sniffed, tears falling down her face. Ophelia used her jacket sleeve to wipe Nessa's tears, frowning at the black fabric as she did so.

"I think it will take me a while to get used to the idea that you actually love me," Nessa whispered. "I was once sent a pretty strong message that no one could ever love me… I'm never good enough for anything, why would I possibly be good enough for something perfect like you?"

Ophelia sighed. "Nessa, do you really want to know how much I have always loved you?" She reached into her pocket and seemed relieved that something was still there. Nessa stared at her, wondering what she was doing. In a moment Ophelia produced a sleek black feather. Nessa's eyes widened. It was definitely a demon feather, the colour hers were the last time she saw them, before they were weirdly grey.

"You have my feather in your pocket?" Nessa asked in wonder.

"I do, always," Ophelia smiled sheepishly.

"But, I don't even remember the last time you could have seen my wings, you must have had that for ages!" said Nessa in disbelief.

"Longer than ages, I'm afraid," said Ophelia. "You dropped it in Eden…"

"Eden?!" Nessa gasped, almost laughing. "You've had it since Eden?"

"Yes, that day meant so much to me!" Ophelia said. "You saved me from God! No one had ever done anything nice like that for me before. Even though you pretended it was for selfish reasons, I knew it wasn't. I kept the feather to remember the moment someone did something kind for me, because I didn't know if I would ever see you again; but as I fell in love with you, it felt even more important…"

Nessa was crying even more now. It felt odd to know that she meant enough to Ophelia that she was willing to carry around her silly little feather for thousands of years.

"That's very sweet and angelic, and a little bit soppy..." Nessa smiled through the tears.

"I'm afraid it gets worse."

"What do you mean?"

Ophelia took out another feather, this time a white one.

"Aww, you keep it with one of your feathers?" asked Nessa. "That's sweet."

"No..." said Ophelia. "I don't need to keep my feathers, I have plenty of them on my wings. This is also yours..."

This time Nessa was truly mind blown.

"That's an angel feather," she stated, knowing it was obvious.

"Indeed..." said Ophelia. "This is from when you took me to Jupiter. You dropped this feather, but didn't notice, and I couldn't leave it on Jupiter, so I picked it up. It meant everything to me that you chose me to see it, and I'm afraid I was quite the Zadkiel fangirl, so I kept it." Ophelia paused as Nessa stared at the feathers. "I really hope you take this as the sweet romantic gesture I intended it to be, rather than something creepy and stalkerish, which I've just realised it might come across as..." she said uncertainly.

"Oh it's definitely romantic!" said Nessa, pulling Ophelia closer and giving her a little kiss.

Ophelia gasped in surprise, then smiled, stroking Nessa's hair. "I was so in awe of you back then," she whispered. "And I still am! After all these years I am still honoured and amazed that that beautiful, incredible archangel became the one I love, and who loves me. I'm the one who isn't worthy!"

Nessa was shocked. "But, I'm not Zadkiel anymore…" she said.

"I don't care what your name is, silly!" smiled Ophelia. "I am in love with *you*! Not as an angel or as a demon, just as a *person*!"

Before Nessa could respond, Ophelia grabbed her and kissed her hard. So hard that she knocked her over backwards and ended up laying on top of her. They both held each other tightly as if they never planned to let go, and Nessa wrapped her wings around Ophelia like a blanket of love and protection.

After the kiss, they lay still for a moment. Nessa spread her wings out on the floor, looking as dishevelled as a bird that had flown into a window. Ophelia laughed softly and ran her fingers gently through Nessa's hair.

"I adore you," she whispered.

"I adore you too, my little feather collector!" Nessa smiled. "With all I have!" She paused, looking at the feathers still in Ophelia's hand. "Do you have any other feathers in your collection my darling?"

"No, only yours," said Ophelia with a smile.

Nessa looked at her strange new grey wings, then carefully pulled out one of the feathers, wincing slightly at the pain.

"What are you doing? You'll hurt yourself," asked Ophelia in confusion.

"Here," Nessa said, presenting the feather to Ophelia with a flourish. "You need to complete the set. But this one is different. It hasn't fallen out, I am giving it to you. So in a way I am giving you part of myself to have always." She paused for a moment as Ophelia took the feather. "But the feathers are just a token, I want to give the rest of myself to you too, if you would have me?" she said nervously.

Ophelia was stunned. "What are you saying?" she said, obviously wanting to be certain of her meaning.

"I'm saying that I love you, and I want us to be together!" insisted Nessa. "You can have the feathers, but *I* want to belong to you too! I have already dedicated my life to you for a very long time, I want to spend the rest of eternity knowing that I am completely yours…"

"You *are* mine, and I'm yours," Ophelia smiled, leaning down and kissing Nessa gently on the cheek. "I would love nothing more than to be your girlfriend! In my mind we have been as good as girlfriends for years, it would be nice to be able to actually officially say it."

"Wow, I wish you'd been able to tell me!" Nessa smiled. "Then I could have been a better girlfriend! It's a pretty shit girlfriend that doesn't even know she's someone's girlfriend!"

"Shut up, you've always been perfect!" Ophelia smiled, hitting Nessa playfully in the face with the feathers.

"You can't assault me with my own feathers! If you're my girlfriend then that's domestic violence!" Nessa joked, pushing Ophelia off her and sitting up.

Nessa's wings disappeared and she pulled Ophelia in for a hug, wrapping her arms around her and bringing her close, so that she was curled up on her knee.

"I'm sorry I couldn't save you, again…" she sighed, looking at the white angel feather against Ophelia's black skirt.

"What are you talking about?" Ophelia said.

"I couldn't stop you from becoming a demon..." Nessa was crying again now. "I failed to keep you safe, just like during the war..."

"Well, I don't know about that!" said Ophelia. "I'm here in my girlfriend's arms, I haven't felt this safe for a very long time, if ever! You put so much pressure on yourself to keep me safe, which is really sweet, but then you end up blaming yourself for things that have nothing to do with you! It was my fault I got shot that time, and now it's my fault I have been thrown out of Heaven, you didn't do anything!"

"But everyone has always known if you ever fell it would be because you hang out with your evil, bad luck demon too much!" sighed Nessa.

"But that's not true!" insisted Ophelia. "In the end I became a demon because I didn't agree with what Heaven were doing. I spent a year trying to stop their plan from the inside, and all that did was make me finally realise that they are completely corrupt, just like Hell. No one can call themselves righteous if they are willing to destroy a whole world! You didn't ask me to work against Heaven; I did that myself, so how can it be your fault that I fell?"

Nessa hadn't thought about it like that, she was so used to assuming everything bad was her fault.

"But, even if it wasn't my fault, I feel like I should have been able to do something..." she said sadly.

"But you couldn't! You take on far too much responsibility my darling. Sometimes things just happen, it's not your fault. In fact, one of the things I was planning to tell you last year before the archangels called me back was that I have always been a bad angel with or without you! Think about it; I nearly became a demon right back in Eden when I persuaded Eve to commit the most famous sin in history! That wasn't your fault, you're the one who saved me. Bad things don't happen to me because of you, they just happen. Far more *good* things happen to me because of you!"

"Do you really think so?" Nessa asked sadly. "I have always been sure that I'm useless and bad things happen around me because I'm somehow just inherently evil, you know, without even trying? Ever since my own sister turned against me and gleefully threw me down here!"

"Well… Do you know what I think? I've thought this for a while, but couldn't admit it because she was my boss. I think Jophiel is a bit of a bitch!" Ophelia's eyes widened at hearing herself swear, and Nessa almost choked on nothing, in disbelief.

"I've never heard you swear!" she grinned, finding Ophelia's surprised look incredibly adorable.

"I never have…" said Ophelia, her hand clasped to her mouth. "Maybe it's because I'm a demon now?"

"Maybe? Or maybe it's just because Jophiel *is* a bitch?" smiled Nessa.

Ophelia giggled slightly. "Now where are we?" she asked, properly looking around for the first time. "It's rather cold…"

"Oh just some hellish pit that you land in when you fall from Heaven," sighed Nessa. "I remember it like it was yesterday!"

"Thank you for coming after me," Ophelia said.

"Of course!" said Nessa. "I wouldn't let you wake up here alone..."

"You are amazing. I really don't deserve you!" smiled Ophelia.

"You deserve the universe Phee; everything! Far more than I could ever give you, but I promise I will try!" Nessa kissed Ophelia's hand, and Ophelia blushed slightly.

Ophelia glanced around again. "Do you know the way out of here?" she asked, standing and offering a hand out to help Nessa up. "I might be a demon now, but I've already seen enough of Hell to know it's not really my cup of tea... Ooh, I would *love* some tea right now! Or anything really! I haven't been able to eat for a year, and after getting used to human food, it's been torture!"

Nessa smiled as she stood beside her angel. Ophelia looked at her pocket watch.

"I think there's time for a little something before the world ends..." she said. "Not that I'm going to let that actually happen!" Ophelia looked more serious and angry than Nessa had ever seen her. She was a little concerned.

"What are you going to do?" Nessa asked suspiciously.

"We'll discuss it over tea..." said Ophelia. "Now how do we get out of here? We don't have to go through Hell do we?" She suddenly stopped. "Oh gosh, don't new demons have to stand before Lucifer?!"

"Technically yes, because you're supposed to live in

Hell at his whim, but you're not living here, and I'm not letting you go anywhere near that psycho. Demons should also seek authorisation to go to Earth, but you're with me. I have permission, *and* I've got my magic back!" Nessa grinned triumphantly. She clicked her fingers, and in a moment she and Ophelia were standing around the corner from Ophelia's cottage.

Ophelia looked a little surprised. Nessa was about to start to move towards the cottage when her angel grabbed onto her jacket collar and kissed her passionately. Nessa had to take a step back due to the force at which she had thrown herself at her. As Nessa gripped onto Ophelia tightly it occurred to her that this was their first kiss as official girlfriends, maybe that was why it felt so... Intense...

Eventually, after what felt like forever, they stopped kissing, but their faces remained close; their lips still almost touching.

"Not that I'm complaining, but what was that for?" asked Nessa, smiling. "You nearly pushed me into the road! It was so hot though..."

"You'll think it's silly," whispered Ophelia.

"You don't know that," said Nessa, gently touching Ophelia's lips with hers. "Tell me and we'll find out..."

Ophelia took in a small sharp breath. "Your kiss was the last thing I felt on earth, so I wanted it to be the first when I returned. Physical feelings are so much more intense here than they are in Heaven or Hell. I wanted to feel it again, only as your girlfriend this time... Plus I haven't seen you for a whole year and I have thought about kissing you an embarrassing number of times..."

"That's not silly," whispered Nessa. "It's beautiful... You're beautiful!"

She began to kiss Ophelia again; this time pushing *her* backwards until she was up against a wall. She thought about how full of passion and love they had both been when Nessa had shoved Ophelia against the wall to take information from her that morning. She had so desperately wanted to kiss her then, now she could pin her against the wall to kiss her, rather than to possess her, and that felt incredible.

"We really need to be quick if we are having tea *and* saving the world..." Ophelia gasped after a moment. "I promise we can kiss for eternity once the Earth is safe."

"I'll hold you to that!" smiled Nessa, breathlessly.

They rounded the corner and were about to open the cottage door when Ophelia grabbed Nessa's hand.

"Nessa?" she asked. "Do I still look the same?"

"The same as what?"

"The same as earlier, before I became a demon?" Ophelia whispered.

Nessa looked Ophelia up and down, double checking for differences.

"Yep, still the same gorgeous angel as ever!"

"Oh... Thank you!" smiled Ophelia. "But I'm not an angel anymore, and I don't think black suits me..." she said, looking down at her outfit.

"Oh it does!" smiled Nessa. "Anything would look beautiful on you; but here..." She clicked her fingers and Ophelia's outfit turned back to the pale colours it was before she fell.

"Aww, thank you!" Ophelia squeaked excitedly,

kissing Nessa on the cheek. "I know it's silly, but I don't feel ready to try demonic magic yet..."

Nessa was about to tell her that she might still have angelic magic, when the cottage door opened, startling both demons. Ezra peered out and breathed a sigh of relief when he saw it was them.

"Oh thank goodness you're back!" he said, opening the door properly. "I was getting concerned, but then I heard talking and hoped it was you. If it wasn't I was worried it might be dangerous intruders and I'd have to fend them off, like in that 'Home Alone' film you showed me. Except I don't think I'm that creative..."

Nessa and Ophelia laughed.

"Come here Little Brother, I've missed you!" smiled Ophelia, and she pulled Ezra towards them for a hug. They both gave Ezra a big cuddle.

"Thank you for helping earlier!" Nessa said. "Even though I think you enjoyed turning me into a mouse far too much!"

"Yeah, I'm really going to need the story behind that!" Ophelia laughed. "I'm proud of you, my little former spy! You are so brave."

"I wanted to help you!" Ezra said. "I think that Jophiel would be annoyed if she knew that, rather than sending me to spy for her, she was actually giving me a family! I'm so pleased that out of all the angels in Heaven she asked *me* to come here!"

"Believe me, so are we!" Nessa smiled, ruffling Ezra's hair. "No other angel would be this nice to us!"

"So, are you together now? Like, properly?" Ezra asked excitedly, like a child who had been trying to get their divorced parents back together.

"Absolutely!" announced Nessa, grabbing Ophelia's hand triumphantly.

"Very much in love!" added Ophelia, leaning her head on Nessa's shoulder.

"Oh *finally*!" said Ezra dramatically. "I was concerned that if you weren't together by now, I'd have to lock you both in a room until you kissed, or something!"

Both demons laughed.

"Well, don't worry, we are definitely together," said Ophelia. "And I really want some tea, oh and I was so jealous of those custard creams you had this morning Nessa!"

"The ones you crumbled to dust?" Nessa smiled. "*That* jealous, were you?"

"The ones I sent back here!" Ophelia said defensively. "I really am sorry about all that nonsense. I hated having to be mean to you…"

"I didn't mind, because I knew it was all an act. It was kind of fun, in a weird way…" said Nessa. "I quite like mean Ophelia…"

Ophelia raised an eyebrow at her. "I think that says a lot about you as a person…" she grinned teasingly.

"Well, I've been a demon for a long time…" Nessa laughed.

"Look, I want you guys to be together, but I don't appreciate the flirty looks you're giving each other!" said Ezra, making his sisters laugh a little. "Why don't you come inside and I'll make us tea? And coffee, don't worry Nessa, I know you don't like tea! I'm quite good at making tea now Ophelia!" he smiled.

"He is!" agreed Nessa.

"I'm glad my lovely demon colleague here managed to persuade you to consume human food while I was away," smiled Ophelia.

"Eventually!" said Nessa. "It was a long road though! Ice cream got him in the end."

"Well, if you're going to cave in, that's a good choice!" Ophelia said as they entered the cottage.

Nessa and Ophelia walked into the living room, while Ezra disappeared into the kitchen. Ophelia looked around the room and smiled.

"It's *so* nice to be home!" she sighed after a moment. "I love this place..." She glanced out of the window as some humans walked past, and her face suddenly changed. Nessa wasn't sure if it was a look of concern or anger, but it looked out of character for Ophelia.

"Are you okay?" Nessa asked worriedly.

"What if I can't save them? I helped to design the stuff that's going to kill them. What if they all die because of me? I don't have a plan Nessa, I don't have a plan! What am I going to do?!" Ophelia's voice sounded rather manic, and Nessa was concerned. She stood in front of Ophelia and held onto her shoulders, gently moving her face towards hers, and away from the window.

"Phee! Look at me. It's going to be okay..."

"I've got to stop them!" said Ophelia with a strange intense fire in her eyes that Nessa had never seen before. "Nessa, I think Hell's demonic power is taking over... I feel this overwhelming wave of evil spreading through me..."

"Err, I don't really think that's how it works?" Nessa said tactfully. "I think what you're feeling is anger. Sit down darling!" She managed to get Ophelia to sit down, but it was obvious that she was still extremely tense. Nessa sat on the arm of the chair and put her hands on her angel's shoulders. "You need to relax!" she said.

"No no," said Ophelia, sitting forward. "You don't understand! I've been angry before, many times, at many things. This is different..."

"Yes I know, it's a different kind of anger. One an angel couldn't imagine," sighed Nessa. "It's unfair, it's not right; you didn't do anything wrong, you just stayed true to yourself, and now suddenly you've been betrayed by the people who were supposed to care about you! You dedicated your life to serving God and Heaven, and they abandoned you anyway! That's real anger, my darling demon! A demon doesn't get their evil from being flooded by Hell's power. They get it by being filled with anger and hate. But you, you're stronger than that! You don't have to give in to it!"

Ophelia turned sharply to face Nessa; her face darkened with intensity and rage. Nessa gave out a small gasp, her beloved angel actually looked like a demon... How could this have happened? She had seemed so calm before, so... *herself*. Where was the angel that was just kissing her?

"Ophelia, please!" begged Nessa. "I love you! That's why you're stronger! You don't need to let the hate take over, because you have what no other demon or even angel has! Someone who loves you... Please..."

The desperation in her voice must have softened Ophelia. She lost a little of her intensity and instead a tear ran down her face.

"That's better," said Nessa, gathering Ophelia in her arms and pulling her close for a hug. "Now, let's talk about it? And enough of this 'I' nonsense, you need to let me help. I'm here for you and you'll never have to face anything alone, I promise! If you never ask for help you will just feel like a failure for your whole life because you can't possibly fix everything on your own, and that makes you quite angry and miserable. Would not recommend..."

"You could ask me for help, but you never do!" came Ophelia's muffled voice, crying into Nessa's shirt.

"I know! What can I say, I'm great at being a bad example!" smiled Nessa, stroking Ophelia's hair. "Now, talk, my angel! Your former leader Archangel Zadkiel commands it."

"You can't use that!" said Ophelia indignantly.

"I can if you won't talk to me!" grinned Nessa. "I'm also a former Duke or Prince of Hell, so whichever realm's authority you fancy obeying... Come on Phee, joking aside. Talk to me..."

Ophelia sighed. "The world will end at seven o'clock tonight. They are obsessed with sevens! They made me help to plan it all. They said if I didn't, then they would kill you! I never had a choice, I loved your idea about running away, but I knew they would come after us. Jophiel once said she wanted to take you down, specifically! Plus I knew I had to try to stop them. My conscience wouldn't let me run away knowing they would all die... The humans *can't* be destroyed! They are innocent... It's not even Hell's fault that some humans do bad things; God gave them free will and equal capacity for good and bad, so it's kind of Heaven's fault really." She stopped her panicked rant to take in a gasp of air, then continued. "Even though I've been told so my whole life, I don't think there really is such thing as proper good and evil anyway! When people do bad, they always have a reason. Like the archangels! They think in their own weird way that they are doing good by wiping out the humans, but they are actually ending up being more evil than most of the 'bad' humans they want to get rid of!" Ophelia's crying intensified and she clung to Nessa's jacket.

"Just breathe, honey..." said Nessa, gently stroking Ophelia's arm. "You are so right. That's what I've always said. Good and bad are not two separate things, it's a spectrum, with grey in the middle, and even the two ends aren't completely black and white. It would be great if life was that easy; if there were just good things and bad things, but it's not. But listen to me darling," she said, lifting Ophelia's head so that she had to look at her. "I know you're angry, and scared with the weight of the world literally on your shoulders, but you've got me! We will fix this together, I promise!" Nessa hugged Ophelia tight and kissed her on the forehead, really wishing they could enjoy finally properly being together without having to save the world.

"Nessa, I honestly have no ideas," said Ophelia sadly. "I don't know what to do..."

"Well if you helped to set it up, can't you sabotage

it?" asked Nessa. "Surely you know how it all works right? So you can undo it?"

"Maybe... But we would need to get back up to heaven, and now neither of us are angels!"

"Oh don't worry about that!" smiled Nessa. "I'm getting quite adept at sneaking around Heaven! Now, I need you to relax for a little bit, okay? We know exactly when the world's supposed to end and we've got plenty of time. Look, Ezra's coming with the tea now," she said, hearing the clattering of mugs on a tray. "Just concentrate on your tea, and Ezra will happily tell you all about his first year on Earth, okay?"

"Okay..." said Ophelia, taking a deep breath. "Thank you. I love you!"

"I love you too, my precious angel," Nessa smiled.

Ezra brought the drinks through triumphantly and placed them on the coffee table. Nessa moved off the arm of Ophelia's chair and sat on the floor at her feet. Ezra excitedly sat on the sofa beside Ophelia's chair.

"I missed you Ophelia!" he smiled. "I know we only knew each other for two months, which is nothing in our lives, but I love you! You were the first person to care about me, and you said we were family!"

Ophelia smiled and put a hand on Ezra's. "You *are* my family, you're my little brother, and I love you too!"

"Yeah, the length of time you've known someone means nothing!" Nessa said. "I've only known you for a year and I love you, but I've known Lucifer for six thousand times longer than that, and I utterly cannot stand the man!"

Ezra laughed slightly, then grew serious when he

remembered something. "What happened?" he asked. "Are you a demon now, Ophelia?"

Ophelia looked worried, and shot Nessa a desperate look. Nessa gave her an encouraging smile and Ophelia turned back to Ezra, nervously.

"Yes..." she said after a moment. "Does that make you think of me differently?" she asked in concern.

"No..." said Ezra sadly. "It makes me angry though! All the nicest and best angels become demons, because Jophiel knows what she's doing is wrong! It's been wrong since the first demon was created! Jophiel should have never been in charge and she knows it! We need Zadkiel back in charge to save Heaven..."

"I've been a demon longer than anybody, I really don't think I could run Heaven!" Nessa protested quickly. "I'm also not sure I'd want to, ironically I don't think I thrive in charge... Anyway, you sound like the one who should be in charge, Ezzy! You seem to know how it all should be run."

Ezra laughed. "I'm from admin; you learn things."

"Anyway! said Nessa. "Your lovely sister here needs to relax before we try to sort out this mess, why don't we tell her what we've been up to this year?"

"Okay!" said Ezra excitedly.

Nessa took a biscuit and held her girlfriend's hand, leaning against her leg, as Ezra began to recount the last year in painstaking detail. For just a moment everything was perfect, aside from the impending doom of course...

Chapter Seventeen
No One Survives This!

Eventually, when all the tea and coffee had been drunk and all the biscuits had been eaten, there were no more excuses, and Ophelia and Nessa had to get on with the inconvenient matter of saving the world. Ophelia had so many emotions, and they were all about *not* wanting to leave her cosy cottage now she was home. Ironically, the last year in Heaven had felt like her version of Hell, and demon or not, she just wanted to relax and spend time with Nessa, her new *girlfriend*! But unfortunately Ophelia had been made to help create this mess, so now she had to fix it.

"You're not really going back to Heaven are you?" Ezra asked worriedly. "You are both demons now, how will you get in?"

"Don't worry, I have an idea," said Nessa confidently. Ophelia wondered if she actually was confident, or whether she was pretending for her and Ezra.

"Why won't you let me come?" protested Ezra. "I

could help! I feel useless just sitting here worrying about you..."

"No, absolutely not!" Ophelia said quickly. "I already wish Nessa wasn't coming, because I will completely blame myself if anything happens to her, but she's too stubborn and determined!" She shot Nessa a look and Nessa grinned and made a face in agreement. "I can't deal with the responsibility of keeping you safe too!" Ophelia finished.

"But..." Ezra looked at Nessa, obviously hoping she would contradict Ophelia.

"I agree," said Nessa. "Sorry Ezzy, but it's just because we love you. We are about to go commit treason against Jophiel. I don't want you anywhere near any of that! I won't let another angel I love fall..." The last part seemed to catch in her throat.

Ophelia took Nessa's hand and gave it a reassuring squeeze, wishing she didn't put so much pressure and blame on herself.

"But what do I do?" Ezra asked sadly.

"You stay safe!" said Ophelia. "Maybe find a few good deeds to do, or read a book if you're bored, and if for any reason we can't save the world you get yourself safely back up to Heaven before seven o'clock, understand?"

"Okay..." said Ezra sadly. "Please be safe!" He paused. "I was going to say something, but I think it sounds too selfish..."

"What?" said Ophelia encouragingly.

"I was going to say if anything happens to you two then I will be alone again... I didn't used to mind being alone, because I didn't know any different, but now I'd be so lonely without you…" A tear fell down Ezra's face and he gasped, wiping it off and looking at his fingers as if it were something magical. "Am I crying?" he asked in a small voice.

"Yes you are," smiled Nessa. "In my experience the two things most likely to make you cry are love and loneliness. We'll be fine Ezzy! Don't worry about us. We're always okay! When we come back we'll take you out somewhere really nice to celebrate us all being together, yeah?"

"Do you promise?" Ezra asked, still crying.

"Absolutely!" smiled Nessa. Ophelia smiled encouragingly too, but she was painfully aware that neither of them had any control over whether or not they would survive their mission. Storming Heaven was never a good idea, especially when you had just been thrown out, and confessed to all your sins before that!

Both demons gave their little brother a hug and then they set off hand in hand into the city towards the lift.

When they arrived, Ophelia frowned in concern.

"How is this going to work?" she said. "In order to go up it must be summoned by an angel. Maybe we will need Ezra after all?"

"I've got it," smiled Nessa, activating the lift with angelic magic. Ophelia gasped in shock.

"How did you do that?" she asked in awe. "I knew it! I thought you used angelic magic to get us out of that Hell pit and change the colour of my clothes. You didn't even have *any* magic before, how is this possible?"

"I really don't know..." said Nessa.

Ophelia had a sudden thought. "Maybe that's why your wings are grey?" she said excitedly. "Maybe you are somehow part angel now?!"

"Maybe..." said Nessa. "Or maybe my wings have gone grey because I'm old? Like humans' hair?" she grinned.

Ophelia gave her a playful shove. "I don't think that happens to immortals!" she smiled.

"Who knows, I am a tiny bit older than you?" Nessa smiled. Jophiel and I are the second oldest things in existence after God..."

"Well, you look very good for your age, grandma!" teased Ophelia.

Nessa smiled at her, and Ophelia wondered what her amazing girlfriend was, if she was somehow half demon half angel. Was there a name for that? Ophelia was fairly certain that it was impossible to be both at the same time, but then most people would say it was impossible for them to be in love too, so you never know...

The lift arrived and Ophelia took Nessa's hand as they stepped inside. The last time they had been in that lift together, they were going down, and Ophelia had been about to face Lucifer. She wondered why Nessa never realised how much she loved her. She would do anything for her. She considered for a moment how horrible it would have been to be banished from Heaven right back at the beginning; to be the first to fall, without a loving girlfriend to wake up to. That must have been awful! It wasn't Nessa's fault that she felt unloved, or

Ophelia's for not showing it enough; it was Heaven's for throwing her out back then!

Ophelia didn't really feel like she had recently become a demon. She felt no different, she had expected to. Whilst becoming a demon was a big deal after thousands of years of fearing exactly that; it was nothing compared to the monumental moment that Nessa asked her to be her girlfriend. Now here they were facing Heaven together; properly a couple, officially girlfriends! She squeezed Nessa's hand slightly and Nessa looked over at her, love radiating from her face.

"I feel like we are properly on the same side for the first time. It feels nice." whispered Nessa.

"We've been on our own side for ages haven't we?" said Ophelia, slightly puzzled. "Since Abraham I'd say…"

"Not fully," said Nessa. "Until now."

"Because I'm a demon now?" asked Ophelia sadly.

"No! Definitely not," said Nessa, seeming almost offended that Ophelia would think that of her. "Because we are together, properly. We've admitted how we feel. We don't care what they think anymore! It doesn't matter if we are angels or demons, we are finally *us*! That's all I ever wanted…"

"Me too," said Ophelia. "We should have been together for years… I'm sorry I wasn't brave enough…"

"No no, it isn't your fault!" Nessa said quickly.

"But you didn't even know I loved you!" Ophelia insisted. "I should have somehow told you…"

"No, that's on me!" said Nessa. "In hindsight of course you loved me, it's my problem that I didn't believe it. At least we have been together since the beginning?

Even if not as girlfriends. Just being near you makes me feel like the luckiest person in the universe!"

"Yes, but now that we *are* girlfriends we have a lot of catching up to do, haven't we?" Ophelia grinned.

"What do you mean?" asked Nessa with a nervous laugh.

"I mean this!" said Ophelia, and she pulled Nessa close for a kiss, wrapping her arms around her.

It began as a gentle kiss, but then Ophelia thought about how much she had wanted to kiss Nessa since she returned after the war. She had been in love with her for thousands of years, just thinking about how many kisses they should have shared in that time made her feel like crying. Soon the kiss turned more desperate and passionate. Ophelia found herself pushing Nessa against the wall, feeling like she couldn't possibly get close enough to her. She wanted to kiss her forever. Then she realised they had already been kissing for quite a long time.

"Do lifts normally take this long?" she asked breathlessly, her lips still against Nessa's.

"Of course not!" Nessa answered, equally breathless. "I've paused time, I want to kiss you!"

"You can do that?" Ophelia asked in amazement.

"Yeah, I did it when Lucifer poisoned you, so I had time to work out what to do. It's quite useful I guess."

"You are so incredible!" Ophelia said. "And that's so romantic, stopping time to kiss me! I'm so lucky you're mine!"

"I am yours, completely!" grinned Nessa.

Ophelia started the kiss again, but a more gentle

and romantic kiss now she knew they had more time; time to be slower.

"The no scandal rule has definitely been broken!" Ophelia giggled, leaning her body against Nessa, who was still against the wall. "Two demons kissing in the lift up to heaven! I can't think of anything more scandalous than that!" She very gently ran her finger across Nessa's mouth.

"Very scandalous..." breathed Nessa, gently catching Ophelia's finger in her teeth and looking into her eyes, raising her eyebrow slightly. Ophelia gave a small gasp, her eyes widening. Nessa very gently released Ophelia's finger and she moved her hand away slowly, neither one breaking their eye-contact or even blinking.

"Oh my god I adore you," said Ophelia.

"Blasphemy? The scandal continues..." smiled Nessa playfully.

"She made us," said Ophelia with a grin. "It's all her fault really! If she somehow made us wrong, that's her fault, we can't help how we were made!"

"I feel like I was somehow made to be with you," Nessa said.

"Me too. I've never wanted anything as much as I want to be with you!" said Ophelia. She imagined inviting Nessa to live with her in the cottage; them being together like humans do, but then she remembered that they had to save the world first, and as personal enemies of Heaven, that might prove to be difficult.

Nessa restarted time and they reached Heaven. As they stepped out of the lift, Ophelia noticed that Nessa was suddenly dressed in white, obviously trying to blend in amongst the angels. Ophelia smiled at her, thinking she looked rather nice in white too. A heavenly guard stopped them as they started down the corridor.

"Hello," she said, with a serious look on her face that didn't match her friendly tone of voice.

"Hello?" said Ophelia, glancing at Nessa, hoping her face said subtly *what's her deal?*.

"Mandatory demon check!" announced the guard. "We are under strict instructions not to let any demons in before seven o'clock."

"What happens after seven?" Ophelia asked, wondering if this angel knew what her beloved Heaven were doing.

"I don't know," said the angel. "That's all they said! Come on if you want to come in."

Both fallen angels took a nervous step forward, wondering what would happen if they were found out. The guard pointed to some sort of heavenly device attached to the wall.

"This is to check for demons," she explained. "It scans for angelic energy. If you don't have enough angelic energy then you must be a demon, so you can't come in!"

"What would happen if a demon did try to get past? Would it do something to them? Just out of interest..." asked Nessa.

"I don't know, it hasn't happened yet!" the guard said with a smile.

"Right..." said Nessa, taking Ophelia's hand nervously. Ophelia gave it a reassuring squeeze, but she was just as terrified. The device made some sort of noise and Ophelia held her breath, scared to move. After a moment though, the device lit up green.

"Great!" said the guard. "That's all fine, you are free to go in! Sorry about all this, but we really can't let demons in today."

"Of course!" said Ophelia, quickly pulling Nessa past the device in case it changed its mind. She didn't know why it didn't detect their demonic energy, but she wasn't going to stick around in case it did. Perhaps the device was broken?

They walked hastily down the corridor, the kind of walk that's almost a jog, until they were far enough away from the entrance to stop and catch their breath.

"Why did it let us through?" asked Ophelia.

"No idea, but I'm not arguing!" said Nessa. "I tell you what though, that thing wasn't there earlier when Ezra and I came in. There was a guard, but no weird device. I bet they've added that to keep us out!"

"Probably," sighed Ophelia. "We might be in, but I've got no idea what to do now…"

"Well, where's this world-destroying machine everyone keeps talking about?" asked Nessa.

Ophelia thought about pretending to take Nessa's life force that morning. So much had happened since then that it almost felt like a different day.

"It's this way," she said, leading Nessa down the corridor. The room that the machine was in was worryingly close to the archangels' meeting room and Jophiel's office, it was very risky.

"Do you know how to break it?" whispered Nessa when they entered the room and faced the machine, which Ophelia had always thought looked almost as scary as what it represented.

"I think so…" replied Ophelia. "It already won't destroy Hell because it needs a demon's life force for that and I obviously just pretended to take yours, but the part that takes down Earth is still working…"

"Well then, stop it!" hissed Nessa. "Before someone comes!"

"Okay okay!" said Ophelia. "Keep watch!"

She slipped into the room and ducked under the terrifying machine. She had, regrettably, created the formula that made it work, the key was a little vial, like the one she filled with black smoke to fool the angels earlier. Only this one contained part of the Earth mixed with energy from the core of a star. She had retrieved part of one of the stars to experiment on almost a year ago, and while she was there she had taken a little piece of Jupiter to give to Nessa for Christmas, desperate for her to know that she was thinking of her.

Ophelia yanked the vial from the machine and it spluttered to a halt. She quickly pulled a few more small parts off the machine and stuffed them in her pockets, wanting to make certain that they wouldn't be able to start it up again, even though she was fairly certain they couldn't. Only she knew the formula that went into the vial, and she hadn't written it down anywhere.

"Nessa! I've done it!" she whispered triumphantly. She grew concerned when there was no response. "Nessa?" She stood up and to her horror Nessa wasn't there. She gasped and rushed out of the room.

"Ophelia!" she heard Nessa yell.

She whipped around and saw Nessa being dragged down the corridor by Archangel Jophiel herself. Ophelia was furious. She had never felt such rage before. She ran towards them and ripped Jophiel away from Nessa, pushing her to the ground and standing over her.

"Don't you *dare* touch my girlfriend!" she yelled, as commanding as if she were performing the highest level of smiting.

"Holy shit…" she heard Nessa whisper. Ophelia had to bite back a smile, it felt good to be the one protecting her darling demon for once.

Jophiel laughed at Ophelia's outburst. "You don't scare me, Demon Ophelia!" she said, revelling in referring to her as a demon. "I am the Head of the Archangels, you are a new demon, what do you think you can do to me, just push me over? That's all you have!" She stood so that she was facing the demons, a nasty smile on her face. "Tell me Nessa, how does it feel knowing your precious little angel is finally a worthless demon like you?"

Nessa's face was like thunder. "She's more of an angel than you've ever been!" she hissed.

"It must provide you with a little comfort to know that after all that, it wasn't actually you who made her fall," Jophiel went on, ignoring what Nessa said. "She betrayed us without you! But that's hardly surprising though is it; when your beloved Ophelia was actually to blame for *you* falling too!"

"What?" Ophelia said in horror. She looked desperately at Nessa, hoping she didn't believe Jophiel's lie.

"Shut up Jophiel, you can't turn us against each other with stupid lies!" said Nessa.

"Oh, but it isn't a lie!" smiled Jophiel. "Don't you remember providing us with the information that damned your dear demon, Ophelia?"

"I don't know what you're talking about..." Ophelia said nervously, wondering if she had somehow accidentally done something wrong.

"Oh, well it was a very long time ago..." said Jophiel, enjoying this far too much. "Lucifer and I had our suspicions about our dear leader, but we didn't know for certain that something was wrong, and we definitely didn't know why. That's when you helped us out. I transported you to my office because I knew that you were the only other angel that had spoken to her. Is any of this ringing a bell?"

Ophelia was suddenly filled with panic. She *did* remember what Jophiel was talking about, and it *was* the day Nessa fell... She felt sick.

"Ooh, I can tell it *is* ringing a bell!" Jophiel said with a smile that worryingly reminded Ophelia of Lucifer. "You told us about Zadkiel's feelings of doubt, you confirmed that she had strayed from Heaven. I wasn't sure I trusted Lucifer's word, and he didn't know much, but you? You provided the evidence that led to Zadkiel's banishment. Without your testimony we would not have damned her. She might still be an angel today?"

"No..." Ophelia breathed. She couldn't even tell how she felt, it was too complicated.

"Sorry to ruin your relationship, whatever it is," said Jophiel. "But honesty is so important. Isn't that right Ophelia?"

Ophelia swallowed hard and took an unsteady step backwards. She had had no idea that what she said that day was the reason Nessa fell. Did *she* ruin Nessa's life? She didn't know how she could look at her, Nessa wouldn't want to be her girlfriend anymore, she would never speak to her again! Ophelia had somehow ruined her relationship over six thousand years before it began.

She jumped in surprise as Nessa took her hand. She looked down at their entwined fingers, because she couldn't bear to look at her face, Nessa squeezed her hand reassuringly.

"All I hear is another story about you and Lucifer intimidating and manipulating people." Nessa said to Jophiel. "I know what you're trying to do, but it won't work. I love Ophelia more than life itself, you can't destroy that."

Ophelia dared to look at her sheepishly; utterly mind-blown that she was being so nice about it. Nessa gave her a reassuring smile.

"All I am doing is ensuring you know the truth about what Ophelia did to you..." said Jophiel.

"Ophelia didn't *do* anything to me!" Nessa protested. "As if she had a choice with your stupid 'angels don't lie' crap. You know full well that any angel would do anything you asked them to, because everyone is so terrified to disobey." Nessa paused and looked at Ophelia for a moment. "Anyway, if she did cause me to fall then I'm actually grateful for it!" she continued.

"You are pleased that you are a demon?" asked Jophiel, sounding disgusted.

"I think so!" smiled Nessa. "Well, I don't really want to be a demon or an angel, but if I had to choose I'd pick demon in a second! There are far too many petty, nuanced rules here for me. I can't imagine what my life would be like if I'd stayed in charge up here, but it wouldn't be the same, and I love my life right now. If I wasn't a demon I wouldn't have the life I have, so I wouldn't change it."

Ophelia looked into Nessa's eyes searchingly.

"Are you truly not angry with me?" she asked in a small voice.

"Of course not!" said Nessa. "You didn't cause my fall; and even if you did it wouldn't be on purpose. I know you'd never do anything to hurt me..."

Ophelia breathed a sigh of relief. "I honestly had no idea! But I was so scared just then that you'd leave me..."

"Phee, it would take more than that for me to leave you! In fact I can't imagine anything that would make me even consider leaving you for a moment. I've waited thousands of years for this!" Nessa gave Ophelia a hug and she instantly felt better.

"I'm sorry..." Ophelia whispered.

"You've done nothing wrong my darling!" Nessa said, stroking Ophelia's hair.

"Well, this is all very heartwarming!" sighed Jophiel. "But none of it really matters because Ophelia has committed many forms of treason over the years, and since you were foolish enough to come back here when I was willing to let you live in Hell, I think it's time for a more serious punishment. It is long overdue I'd say..."

Ophelia was right back to being terrified again. She

looked to Nessa for some sort of reassurance, but she looked just as concerned.

"Listen Jophiel, I'm sorry I had to betray Heaven, really I am. If you let us go now I promise we will never come back!" Ophelia said, knowing she had already sabotaged the archangels' plan to destroy the Earth.

"It's too late Ophelia!" said Jophiel. "The two of you are, at this moment, the biggest threat to Heaven. As the leader it is up to me to eliminate such threats. Whilst you are now a demon and should be dealt with by Lucifer, he has agreed that it is best if we execute you here in Heaven. It is more convenient for everyone."

"Don't you fucking dare!" yelled Nessa. "If you kill her I will kill you! I've got over six thousand years worth of anger towards you, I would do it gladly!"

"Nessa…" Ophelia was so scared, and Nessa threatening Jophiel was only going to make the situation worse.

"No! I'm sorry Phee, but I am so sick of her and her secret ally Lucifer thinking they can do whatever they want!"

"Lucifer is The Devil. He runs Hell and I run Heaven, he is most certainly not my ally…" said Jophiel, maintaining her annoying calm air.

"Of course he is! I know you worked together to kick me out so that *you* could be in charge! Now he's in charge of Hell, you both got the power you wanted. I've seen letters in his throne room in your obnoxiously swirly handwriting, but never really thought much of it. You must be working together!"

"I assure you I have no idea what you are talking

about..." said Jophiel dismissively.

"Anyway, does it ever occur to you that you don't actually *run* Heaven, God does!" Nessa said. "I know you are the Leader of the Archangels, but you are still *just* an angel! You need God's authorisation to do insane shit like this, and you never bother getting it. What do you think will happen when she finds out?"

"Well, The Almighty has not been seen since *you* destroyed her favourite monastery dear sister," said Jophiel patronisingly. "Sometimes we have to make our own judgments, you should know, you are good at doing that..."

"None of this is about that bloody monastery!" yelled Nessa, completely losing her cool, if she'd had it to begin with.

Ophelia felt very uncomfortable, given the threat of execution, and wished more than anything they could get out of there.

Nessa took an angry step towards Jophiel. "You once accused me of thinking that I was more important than God's plan or whatever crap you said! Well guess who thinks they are the most important thing in the universe now? You're not following God's plan! You're doing whatever the fuck you want, and somehow getting away with it!" Nessa took in a deep breath, clearly full of rage. Ophelia put a hand on her shoulder, not really sure how to help.

"Well, ask God what she thinks then!" said Jophiel. "Oh dear, my mistake, she abandoned you long ago!" Jophiel had a nasty smile on her face, just like Lucifer when he poisoned Ophelia.

"Stop it!" Ophelia shouted. She could tell that Nessa was bubbling with rage and she wasn't sure if her own feelings of anger were stronger than her fear, but it was close. All she wanted was for her and Nessa to go *home!* She wanted to ask Nessa to live in the cottage with her, she wanted them to be happy forever like at the end of a fairytale, but right now she was terrified that neither of them would make it back to Earth at all.

"Please let us go!" she begged. "You don't want the trouble and neither do we, why don't we just agree to leave each other alone?"

"Regardless of whether you want it, trouble seems to follow the two of you around wherever you go," sighed Jophiel. "You have committed treason on many occasions Ophelia. What kind of message would I be sending if I let you go now?"

"Kindness?" offered Ophelia. "Compassion? Forgiveness? All the values that angels should base their lives upon?"

Before Jophiel could respond, Archangel Gabriel came striding down the corridor with a large jug of water; holy water Ophelia guessed. Terror ran through her. She had touched holy water many times, but suddenly now she was a demon, that same stuff could destroy her in an instant...

"Thank you Gabriel. I was beginning to think that you were not coming!" said Jophiel. "Oh, and don't bother trying anything, Nessa. Magic is currently blocked in this area..."

Ophelia glanced at Nessa, who was looking down at her hand in panic, she had obviously tried to do something; perhaps stop time as she did earlier, so they could escape? Nessa looked over desperately at Ophelia as Jophiel took the jug from Gabriel and studied it, as if checking it for authenticity.

"I'm sorry…" she whispered. "I don't know what to do, I don't know how to save you again…"

"It's okay," said Ophelia, which was the biggest lie, because she was completely petrified. "I love you, thank you for being my world…"

"No…" said Nessa quietly as Jophiel readied the jug. Ophelia screwed up her eyes in fear, knowing the water was coming and knowing there was nothing to be done. At least the Earth was safe, she thought. At least she had got to finally kiss Nessa.

In a moment as Jophiel threw the water in Ophelia's direction, Nessa's protective instincts had taken over and her wings had appeared quicker then they ever had. She leapt in front of Ophelia and wrapped her wings and arms tightly around her, shielding her from the water.

Ophelia's eyes were still shut, but she gasped and closed them tighter when she realised what Nessa was doing, not wishing to witness her love's death. In a moment it felt like Nessa had released Ophelia from her grip, but Ophelia knew that meant she must be gone. She couldn't bear to open her eyes. If she opened her eyes it would be to a world without Nessa; a world where she died to save her…

"What the hell is going on?" Jophiel said, sounding equally furious and confused.

Ophelia felt a glimmer of hope, she was sure that she still sensed Nessa, she always felt her energy so strongly that surely it would be more noticeable if she was gone.

Ophelia dared to open her eyes and to her delight, saw her gorgeous girlfriend still standing before her; holy water dripping from her hair. Ophelia made a very audible gasp at the image. She had never considered that human term 'sexy', until now... Now, when her demon-angel had risked her own life to save her and stood dressed in a white suit with magnificent grey wings, dripping with holy water; steam rising from her skin. She stared, wide eyed at Nessa, she knew demons were good at tempting, but she shouldn't be *this* irresistible. Before she knew what she was doing she leant closer to kiss her.

"No!" cried Nessa, the word muffled mid way through by Ophelia's mouth on hers. Holy water had dripped down Nessa's face from her hair and onto her mouth; a deadly kiss for a demon... Ophelia realised as she felt the hot water on her lips and panic flooded her. There was nothing she could do now, she moved in closer, kissing Nessa more passionately; determined to kiss until it destroyed her. Only, it didn't...

The holy water continued to run down Nessa's face to her mouth and it sizzled between the lips of two angelic demons, as though it were boiling, but neither felt any pain; just an intense heat. After a moment, Ophelia realised that the water wasn't going to kill her. She had no idea why she survived, but she wrapped her arms around Nessa, opening her eyes and seeing steam rise when she touched her jacket. She had never felt more attracted to her.

"You know, this is where we met?" she whispered

through the kiss; delighting in saying the same thing Nessa had that morning when she led her to the prison cell. That felt like forever ago; Ophelia had had to pretend to be nasty to her beloved demon that morning, but now she never had to hide again!

"I think it's best if you don't talk..." grinned Nessa, echoing Ophelia's answer from that morning, but in a delightfully sensual way; biting Ophelia's lip gently. Ophelia took in a breath and ran her hand along the top of Nessa's wing, the water on the soft damp feathers sizzling as she touched it.

"For God's sake, how are you both so damn indestructible?!" yelled Jophiel, startling Ophelia and Nessa out of their kiss. She *never* lost her temper; not properly. They must have really got to her without even trying. Jophiel looked at Gabriel, but he said nothing. He avoided eye contact and pretended to straighten up his suit. Getting nothing from Gabriel, Jophiel turned back to the demons.

"How did you survive that?" she asked. "No demon survives that! And what's wrong with your wings, Nessa?"

"I don't know," said Nessa. "I don't know when or why my wings turned grey, but Lucifer already tried to execute me with holy water last year and it didn't work. For some reason I'm immune to it, and I guess Ophelia must be too." She looked down at the steam being produced by Ophelia's hand on her sleeve.

Ophelia looked at Nessa in horror. "Lucifer tried to execute you?! When?"

"I committed treason by saving your life when he

poisoned you," said Nessa, glancing at Jophiel who was whispering something to a concerned looking Gabriel.

"Nessa!" cried Ophelia; horrified. "Why didn't you tell me?"

"Because it didn't matter. I survived, so it's fine."

"It's not fine, Nessa I wish you'd told me!"

"I didn't want you to feel guilty, plus I didn't know what that made me if I survived holy water, a bad demon? I didn't want to talk about it..." sighed Nessa.

"I think surviving holy water makes you a bloody lucky demon!" said Ophelia. "Now we are together, please promise to actually tell me things!"

"Okay, sorry..." said Nessa.

"Make all the promises you want because you won't be *together* for long!" sneered Jophiel. "No one survives this!" She gestured to Archangel Uriel walking down the corridor holding some sort of large book, followed by Gabriel who must have slipped away without the demons noticing. Nessa gasped when she saw the book. Ophelia didn't know what it was, but as she looked at Jophiel she felt she saw pure evil in her eyes; more than she had seen from any demon, apart from maybe Lucifer.

"Is that... the Book of Life?" Nessa asked in concern.

"It is indeed! Well remembered," smiled Jophiel.

"I used to be its guardian!" Nessa said angrily. "Protecting it from mad people like you!"

"Hmm..." said Jophiel. "It looks as though Ophelia doesn't know what it does, why did you explain Nessa?"

Ophelia knew it contained the name of every single angel and human to ever be in Heaven, but what did

Jophiel mean what it 'does'?

Nessa sighed. "If they erase an angel or demon from that book, they are completely destroyed. The book contains the names of everyone who has ever been in Heaven, so erasing someone doesn't just mean they are destroyed; it alters everything so that they were never in Heaven in the first place! They never would have existed at all!"

Ophelia gulped. She didn't even feel scared; she was too exhausted to be scared. It almost felt like more had happened in that one day, than in all the thousands of years she had lived. This book thing sounded pretty final, and she felt like giving up. She grabbed on to Nessa, who simply put her arms around her; wings disappearing as she did. In their embrace, Ophelia could tell that Nessa felt defeated too.

"Ophelia, since you cannot be dealt with using normal methods, we must turn to extreme measures," Jophiel said, taking the book from Uriel.

"Why just Ophelia?!" asked Nessa desperately. "I've committed treason too, why not erase me as well?"

"Nessa! Stop..." said Ophelia, close to tears.

"Because you belong to Lucifer, I know technically so does Ophelia, but he asked me to deal with her. I am certain Lucifer may wish to deal with you in some way too, but that is not for me to decide. At least you won't remember your beloved Ophelia at all, that must bring you a little comfort? Maybe without her you would have been a less troublesome demon anyway?"

"No I bloody wouldn't!" said Nessa. "I can't imagine what I would be like without her, but I don't think you'd like it. And I do not *belong* to Lucifer you idiot!"

"There is no point in arguing Nessa..." said Jophiel. "There is nothing you can do."

"My perfect angel..." Nessa said desperately, still hugging Ophelia, tears now pouring down her face.

"Shh..." said Ophelia, pulling Nessa close so that her head was on her shoulder. Nessa cried pitifully into Ophelia's jacket, edging closer to her neck. Ophelia didn't cry, she didn't have the energy. Jophiel was determined to get rid of her. No matter what they did, she would just keep thinking of new ways, and Ophelia didn't think she could stand it anymore. Perhaps it was better if it all just ended now, she had nothing more to give.

"I know you won't remember me," she whispered to Nessa. "But I hope I have placed enough love in your heart so that deep down you will always feel loved, and always know in your heart that somebody once cared about you!"

"There's no point saying goodbye!" said Jophiel, sounding exasperated. "She won't remember you! You will never have existed!"

Ophelia ignored her. "I adore you!" she said, stroking Nessa's hair, holding her for as long as she possibly could. "Thank you for being my girlfriend for a bit..."

Nessa clung desperately to her as Jophiel ceremoniously opened the book and, with glowing archangel power coming from her fingertips, wiped her hand over Ophelia's name; erasing her forever.

Chapter Eighteen
Beautiful Love Filled Angels.

The brightest golden light engulfed Ophelia. It must have been so blinding that it forced Nessa away from her, causing her to stagger backwards, landing on the floor.

"I love you!" Ophelia heard Nessa shout. Ophelia smiled slightly; happy that that was the last thing she would hear.

After a moment the light reached its intensity and spread, pulsing through the room and disappearing. Ophelia opened her eyes. She was still there, she hadn't been destroyed! She looked down at herself, double-checking that her body was still there, even though she could tell it was. As far as she was aware, nothing had changed. She looked over at Nessa, who was staring at her with a traumatised look, tears still staining her face. She suddenly had a horrible thought. Jophiel and Nessa had made it very clear that no one would remember she existed, what if somehow she hadn't disappeared, but no one remembered her? That would be worse…

Before she could ask Nessa if she remembered her, Jophiel spoke, sending fear through Ophelia's body with her words.

"Who are you?" she asked, sounding genuinely confused. Those three words were the most terrifying Ophelia could have possibly heard in that moment.

"I'm Ophelia..." she said slowly. "Don't you remember me? You've been trying to kill me for the last, however long we've been standing here..."

"No, I don't think I've ever seen you before," Jophiel said. "Gabriel, Uriel, do you know this girl?"

"No I certainly don't," said Gabriel, and Uriel shook her head.

The book should have completely erased Ophelia; so that she never would have existed, and whilst she was somehow still there, it seemed that the archangels genuinely didn't recognise her. She looked back at Nessa, who was still looking up at her with that same shell-shocked expression.

"Nessa?" she asked quietly, almost too terrified to ask the question. "Do *you* know who I am?" She glanced back at the confused archangels for a second, filled with panic. What if Nessa *didn't* remember her? She would far rather have actually been erased. She felt like crying again. "Nessa, do you?" she pleaded, the words hardly coming out.

"My darling, I know you!" said Nessa quickly, obviously noticing Ophelia's terrified expression, as her eyes filled with tears. "You are my angel!"

"Nessa..." Ophelia breathed, now crying for a different reason, as relief flooded her body, so intense that she felt a little unstable on her feet. "I don't know what I would have done if you didn't remember me!" She helped Nessa off the floor and then hugged her tightly, never wanting to let go.

"If I forgot you, you would have had to try to make me fall in love with you again, which wouldn't be too difficult I imagine!" grinned Nessa, stroking Ophelia's hair gently.

"I was so scared…" said Ophelia, her tears sizzling as they made contact with holy water that Nessa's jacket was still drenched in.

"Me too!" Nessa signed. "How many times have I nearly lost you today? I can't bear it."

"Prince Nessa, did you bring this demon to Heaven?" asked Jophiel, interrupting their beautiful moment of relief.

Nessa turned to face her, holding Ophelia's hand. "Yeah, I did! Wait, Prince?!" Nessa glanced at Ophelia in confusion. She hadn't been a Prince of Hell for a couple of thousand years now; since she moved to York to work opposite Ophelia.

"Don't you know me at all?" Ophelia asked the archangels.

"No, why would we know some random demon?" Jophiel said with disapproval.

"But you know Nessa?" Ophelia said, trying to wrap her head around what was happening.

"Everyone knows Demon Nessa!" Gabriel said, glancing at Nessa with fear behind his eyes.

"Then who is she?" Ophelia asked, confused by who Nessa was in their strange reality.

"Err, known as the most bloodthirsty demon?" Gabriel answered nervously, as if he was afraid of saying the wrong thing. "Some say she's scarier than Lucifer. In fact, she's only ever seen when he sends her on some dark mission…"

"Exactly, so what are you doing here? How did you get past the guards?" Jophiel added. "You can't do anything up here; Heaven's frequency weakens demonic power!"

"I know, I'm not doing anything," Nessa said sadly. "So, are you three scared of me, because you think I'm evil?"

"I wouldn't say *scared*! I can handle you sister dear…" Jophiel said with a nasty smile. "This is my realm, not yours… You might be the worst demon of all, but I'm in control here."

"The worst?" Nessa whispered, glancing at Ophelia, as if for confirmation that she wasn't. Ophelia shrugged; she had no idea what was happening.

As Ophelia watched the archangels, looking at Nessa suspiciously, as if she was a completely different person, she suddenly realised something. If the angels knew a reality where she never existed, then maybe they remembered a version of Nessa that existed without her. Ophelia supposed that their lives would have been very different if they didn't have each other. Maybe without someone to love, Nessa's bitterness would have consumed her, and she might have become an evil demon?

She turned to her beautiful, kind girlfriend, who looked hurt at the angels' accusations. *Her* Nessa was the most wonderful person in the realms, and Ophelia felt quite proud if their love had helped to make her into the perfect person she was.

"Give us a minute!" Nessa announced to the archangels, and she pulled Ophelia aside, looking as confused as she felt. None of this made any sense; were they now living in a world where Ophelia shouldn't exist? If so, then why did Nessa remember her?

"This is weird right?" Nessa said quietly once they were a few steps away from the others.

"Very..." answered Ophelia, glancing across at the archangels who were inspecting the book, in confusion; obviously not remembering why they had it.

"They don't know you at all," said Nessa. "I'm so confused, I used to look after the Book of Life; it's so final, so definite. When someone is erased from it they are *gone*, they never existed! I don't understand how you are still here. I am insanely grateful, don't get me wrong, but confused..."

"It seems like the others are acting like I never existed," said Ophelia. "As if to them I was erased and they don't know me, but for some reason I'm still here and mercifully you still know me."

"I could never forget you!" said Nessa. "You are far too important to me. Without you I can't imagine what I'd be..."

"The most bloodthirsty demon apparently!" Ophelia smiled.

"Yeah, I suppose so. I guess they know a version of me without you. Shit... I always knew loving you kept me sane all these years. Without you I would just be a demon, unfairly thrown out of Heaven, that no one loves... I would probably be so angry, and I'd have nothing to live for. I don't mean that in a dramatic, suicidal way, I just mean without you there would be nothing to *try* for. You make me want to stay a good person, you always have. I suppose without that I'd have slipped into darkness..."

"Well it's a good thing you are so very loved then isn't it?" said Ophelia, running her hand up and down Nessa's arm.

"Does that scare you?" Nessa asked after a moment. "Knowing what I had the capability to become?"

"Not at all!" Ophelia smiled. "Anyone has the capability to become jaded if everyone turns against them. Without you I might be an angry demon too? Who knows, but I am in love with you no matter what you are or what you could be."

"Thank you darling, I really don't deserve a perfect angel like you," Nessa said quietly.

"You do! And I'm not actually an angel anymore, and I'm certainly not perfect!"

"You are to me!" said Nessa.

Suddenly Ophelia realised something. "If they still think you're a demon, and I never existed, then that means it wasn't my fault that you fell!"

Nessa smiled. "No, I told you that. I know now that it wasn't something you did, or even really anything I did; they wanted me out and would have found a way no matter what. I'm so sick of all their bullshit, they find nitpicky ways around all the rules." Nessa's eyes widened, as if she were hit by a sudden realisation.

"Ophelia! I've just realised, you're free!" Her eyes sparkled with excitement, but Ophelia was confused.

"What do you mean, free?" she asked.

"Heaven and Hell don't remember you; you never existed to them! Plus you're not an angel anymore, but you can't fully be a demon, because holy water didn't destroy you. You really truly have no side. You're just, you! You're free from it all! No more rules, no more guilt, no more heavenly duties, no more reports; just freedom... Phee, that's amazing!"

"I suppose that's true..." Ophelia was stunned. She hadn't thought of that, but Nessa was right! The pressure of heavenly duty had always weighed heavily on her mind. It's hard to devote thousands of years to something you don't fully agree with. Maybe she really could do what she wanted now?

Nessa had a strange look on her face. Ophelia was about to ask her what was wrong when she spoke.

"We could both be free..." she said, glancing back towards the book that Uriel was now holding.

"Nessa?" said Ophelia suspiciously. "What are you talking about?"

Nessa turned back to face her; an almost manic look of possibility in her eyes. "If I erase myself from the book, they will forget both of us, we can do what we want! They really will leave us alone, forever! We won't really be angels or demons, we will just be *us*!"

"Darling, that's insane," said Ophelia worriedly, really hoping she was joking. "That thing is supposed to erase you from existence! You said it yourself"

"But it didn't! You're still here, and I remember

you."

"True, but we don't know *why* it didn't! It's too risky. What if it does what it's supposed to this time?"

"What can I say, I'm an optimist!" announced Nessa, giving Ophelia a quick kiss on the cheek before heading towards the confused group of angels.

"What are you doing?!" cried Ophelia. "Nessa, please don't, it's not worth the risk, I can't lose you!"

"It worked with you! I can alter the book, I'm still part archangel!" Nessa shouted, snatching the book from a rather threatened Uriel.

"Nessa don't be stupid!" said Ophelia, fighting the tears that were desperately trying to spill from her eyes. "Don't leave me alone!"

If Nessa erased herself and actually did disappear, Ophelia really would be truly alone in the world because it seemed like Nessa was the only person who knew her. She couldn't imagine wandering around knowing that not one person remembered ever meeting her, and that was aside from losing the love of her life.

Ophelia rushed to Nessa, hoping to take the book off her, but it was too late; Nessa had already found the right page and pushed Ophelia's hands away. Ophelia couldn't take it anymore, she had been through so much that day; both she and Nessa had almost been destroyed so many times, and now Nessa was risking her life again for no reason! She was so full of fear and anxiety that she felt like she might faint.

Nessa erased her name from the book and was engulfed by the golden light, dropping the book to the ground. Ophelia stepped away and closed her eyes. She was desperate. She prayed to God that Nessa would be okay. She wasn't sure if God would listen now that she was a demon, or if she had ever been listening. She begged her to let her and Nessa be together after all they had been through.

Ophelia was praying so hard that she almost didn't notice when the light dissipated. Nothing had changed, Nessa was still there, Ophelia still knew her, and she was still completely *furious*! There was no guarantee that Nessa's crazy idea would work, and Ophelia had never been so angry at her.

Nessa did look worried, maybe she had realised how stupid she had been? That didn't make Ophelia any less angry though. Nessa rushed up to her, grabbing onto her arms, Ophelia tensed slightly.

"Ophelia!" Nessa cried. "Do you know me?"

Ophelia didn't answer straight away. She knew it was quite evil, but then she was at least part demon now. A horrible, angry part of her wanted Nessa to worry, just for a moment. She had made Ophelia terrified, she deserved it just a little bit... For a moment Ophelia looked at Nessa in confusion, as if she didn't know her. She slowly looked down at Nessa's hands still holding her arms.

"Ophelia?" Nessa said in panic. "Don't you remember me?!"

Ophelia looked at her, her demon had never looked so scared. She felt bad; but still so furious.

"I remember you're an idiot!" she yelled, pushing Nessa off her angrily.

"What?" said Nessa, obviously confused. "I don't

understand… Do you know who I am?"

"Yes, you're my stupid reckless girlfriend!" Ophelia said.

Nessa let out a breath. "Fuck, Ophelia. That scared me so much! What was that for?"

"Good! It was supposed to scare you!" Ophelia said. "Serves you right for being so selfish!"

"Selfish? I want us to be together forever, without Heaven or Hell. How is that selfish?" said Nessa indignantly.

"Because if your silly impulsive theory was wrong you would be gone, which wouldn't matter to you, because you wouldn't exist so you wouldn't know. But you are the only person who has ever loved me in all these years, and right now the only person who even knows me. If you left I would be completely alone. You are all I have, and even if the erasure meant that I didn't remember you, I would still be alone! So that's why it's selfish you silly girl!" Ophelia was crying again. She'd lost count of the number of times she had, just that day.

Nessa looked guilty, as if she hadn't realised just how reckless her plan was until Ophelia pointed it out. She started crying too and wrapped her arms around Ophelia, holding her tight. Ophelia was still so upset with her that she tensed a little when Nessa put her arms around her. That seemed to break Nessa's heart.

"I'm sorry my darling angel," she said softly through tears. "Please forgive me…"

"You put the thing I love most in danger on purpose without even asking me…" said Ophelia. "That's not fair…"

"I didn't think of that," said Nessa sadly. "But I did think of *you* though! I did it so we can be free, together..."

Suddenly Jophiel startled them both by speaking. Ophelia had almost forgotten the archangels were still there.

"Excuse me, what is going on here?" she asked, sounding very confused. "Are the two of you *crying*? I have never heard of a crying angel before, that's a human thing..."

"Jophiel, do you know who I am?" asked Nessa hopefully.

"No, I'm sorry I am the leader of Heaven, I don't have time to remember every single small order angel, there are millions of you! I only know the important ones..." Jophiel said. "And it's Your Highness, if you please."

Nessa smiled triumphantly at Ophelia. So her stupid plan had worked, but it easily could have destroyed her and ruined Ophelia's life.

Ophelia looked at Jophiel. The archangel really had no idea who they were. She had been so angry, and had lost her temper saying they were indestructible. Ophelia wondered what she'd think if she knew they had survived this too.

"I am so sorry to disturb you, Your Highness, we will be on our way now, back to our duties." Ophelia said to Jophiel, bowing her head slightly. Nessa copied and Jophiel stared them up and down.

"Very well. Off you go!" she said.

They didn't need telling twice, Nessa grabbed Ophelia's hand and they headed towards the lift before the angels noticed their demonic energy. As they left, they heard Jophiel demanding that Uriel pick up the book, and telling her off for putting it on the floor.

Ophelia and Nessa stood in the lift in silence. Quite a contrast to their passion-filled trip upwards. Nessa kept looking at Ophelia, but she stared straight ahead. She didn't want to be angry at Nessa; she loved her more than anything, but that's why she was so mad.

As they got out of the lift, Nessa grabbed Ophelia's arm.

"Ophelia! You can't blank me, I am the only person who knows you!"

"I'm still furious with you!" snapped Ophelia, wondering why Nessa didn't seem to understand her anger.

"But it's all okay," said Nessa. "It worked. We are both alive! We escaped, and we never have to step foot there again!"

"Don't you understand why I'm angry?" pleaded Ophelia. "You almost killed yourself! What if I'd done that? How would you feel?"

Nessa hung her head slightly, as if she had finally fully got it.

Ophelia went on, "Just today we've reunited, I became a demon, we confessed our love, and nearly lost each other countless times! That's enough without you doing stupid things like that! It was a real miracle every time we survived, you can push things too far you know? I could be completely alone right now and it would be *your* fault!"

"I'm sorry..." said Nessa quietly. "You're right,

of course you are. I'm such a mess, I ruin everything! It doesn't matter what colour my wings are, I'm still a horrible demon inside, and you are a perfect angel. I'm so grateful that you wanted to be my girlfriend, but of course it was inevitable from the start that I'd ruin this somehow…"

"No no, for goodness sake my darling, you don't get it do you?" said Ophelia, feeling rather exasperated. "I'm only mad at you because I love you so much! I want to be with you so badly, that when you put that in danger I couldn't bear it!"

"Really?" sniffed Nessa. "I thought you might not want to be my girlfriend anymore. Like I might have ruined it already, before it's even really started?"

"No, my silly demon. I love you more than anything! I was so scared I'd lose you…" said Ophelia, pulling Nessa close for a hug. "Anyway, proper girlfriends have fights sometimes. They can get really angry at each other, but it's okay because they love each other so much it doesn't matter."

"Really? On the rare occasions we argue I get so scared, because I am so sure everyone will just abandon me because I'm bad. I couldn't bear to lose you over an argument," Nessa sighed.

"You won't lose me over any argument!" said Ophelia. "Listen my love, we've known each other for over six thousand years, and I love you more with each one that passes. After all that time and all we've been through, I can't imagine anything that would make me consider leaving you for a second! We'll never leave each other, because if we haven't got sick of each other in all those years, we never will!"

Nessa gave a small laugh. "I love you, and I'm so sorry!"

"I forgive you my darling, and I love you too," smiled Ophelia. She felt Nessa shaking slightly in her embrace and frowned. "Honey, you're shivering."

"Yes, it's December and I'm still soaking wet!" said Nessa. "Holy water might not kill me on impact, but it still might if I freeze to death!"

Ophelia laughed. "You are silly!"

She used magic to dry Nessa and turn her white suit back to her normal clothes, in perhaps the flirtiest way one could, bringing her hand down slowly in front of Nessa's face and carrying on gently stroking down her body until she reached her belt, which she grabbed onto, pulling Nessa in for a kiss. Nessa made a small noise in surprise, but then wrapped her arms around her, one around her shoulders and the other lower on her back. Ophelia thought about how nice it felt to have Nessa's body against hers; to feel her mouth on hers; and for Nessa to have hold of her like that... She knew that humans were walking past and it gave her such a thrill to know that they were finally one of those couples that she was always so jealous of.

As their lips parted, Ophelia stroked the collar of Nessa's jacket. "Why do you always look so bloody gorgeous?" she whispered. "It doesn't matter what era it is, you have always looked so attractive... But you know you also looked cute in white today."

"You think I'm attractive?" asked Nessa playfully; seeming slightly shy.

"Of course I do!" said Ophelia. "Everything about you is irresistible, I don't know how I managed to be friends with you for so long without kissing you!"

"Aww, I wonder the same about you. I think you're so damn hot!" grinned Nessa. "Anyway, do you realise what you just did, my gorgeous little demon?"

"What? What did I do?" asked Ophelia slightly suspiciously.

"Angelic magic!" announced Nessa excitedly.

"Oh yes, so I did! I suppose it must be a habit. I didn't think to do demonic magic, I guess I forgot," said Ophelia.

Nessa suddenly gasped, grabbing Ophelia's hands. "Phee, show me your wings!" she said excitedly.

"What?" said Ophelia in confusion.

"Show me your wings! Please?"

"No, what are you talking about?" said Ophelia in a hushed voice. "We're in the middle of York! I am not..." she hesitated, glancing around, "showing you my wings!"

Nessa clicked her fingers and the street around them ground to a halt, looking like an eerie tableau of the city.

Ophelia rolled her eyes. "You can't keep doing that now you know!"

"Why not?" said Nessa. "Now we're alone, can I see your wings? Come on Phee! I'll show you mine if you show me yours!" Nessa's grey wings sprouted.

Ophelia felt a little bit uncomfortable. "I don't really want to..." she said sadly. "I'm a demon now, and I don't particularly want to be reminded of that by seeing my lovely wings all black…"

Nessa looked a little sad, and Ophelia realised in horror what she had just suggested.

"Not that there's anything wrong with black wings!" she added hastily. "Your wings have always been beautiful. I think I just need some time to get used to the idea of being a demon."

"But you're not a demon, that's the point!" insisted Nessa. "You survived holy water and you did angelic magic! I have a theory that we are both somewhere in between! Please, let me see. You don't have to look if you don't want to."

"Okay…" said Ophelia, taking a deep breath. She had used her wings to prove to the monks that she was an angel last year, she had no idea that would be the last time she would see them white. She closed her eyes tightly and let her wings appear. There was silence for a moment, and for some reason that made her nervous. She wished Nessa would say something, but then she felt a hand on her wing. She flinched a little, as no one had ever touched her wings before, then smiled. It felt nice. Since she had started to live among the humans in disguise, she hardly ever showed her wings. They felt like a private hidden part of herself, and for some reason it thrilled her that Nessa was stroking them gently; it felt special.

"Your wings are beautiful my darling!" said Nessa. "I think you should open your eyes, if you trust me…"

"I trust you completely," said Ophelia, and she nervously opened her eyes. She was shocked to see her wings no longer white, but also not black! Her wings were grey just like Nessa's! Ophelia stared at them in amazement for a moment, gently touching one to check it was real.

"They look like yours..." she said in wonder.

"They do!" Nessa laughed, placing her wing beside Ophelia's to compare. They were exactly the same shade; completely identical. Nessa suddenly broke down in tears, startling Ophelia.

"What's wrong?" she asked, touching Nessa's wing with hers.

"We are the same!" smiled Nessa, still sobbing. "I've always felt like I'm not good enough for you. I wondered why an angel would even *speak* to a demon like me. But now we are the same thing; so maybe I don't have to feel unworthy of your love. Maybe we really are free from everything? We're not angels or demons, we are just us. I'm sorry, but I haven't been the same as you since I was transformed into something that people called *bad*. I was told there was something wrong with me, that I wasn't good enough to be what you are, so what made me good enough to be *with* you?"

There was silence for a moment, Ophelia wasn't really sure what to say. "Nessa, darling, you have always been good enough, I have always loved you. I feel like I've said it a hundred times today, and I'll say a million more if that's what it takes for you to believe me! You were never really a demon to me, you were always just Nessa; or Zadkiel before that, but always someone I just liked! You are the kindest person I have ever met and I've met a *lot* of people."

"Thank you, I know," said Nessa. "But we can't

escape the connotations; demons represent evil and angels represent good. I've always felt evil just for being a demon, I don't have to actually *be* evil, it's just inherent. I know you loved me as a demon, but I am actually crying with joy! I'm so happy that we are the same! Look at our lovely grey wings, they match Ophelia!" She grabbed Ophelia's hands, almost laughing with joy. "I've said for a long time that I didn't want to be a demon, but I also wasn't keen on the idea of being an angel, but now finally I'm not either! And neither are you! We can be and do whatever we want and we're actually allowed to love each other, with no one to judge us! Phee, aren't you excited? Gosh, I need to calm down…"

Ophelia smiled at Nessa's joy, but she wasn't sure how she felt. While she didn't agree with everything Heaven did, she was still quite proud to be an angel, it felt important to her; it was all she had known for thousands of years. No matter how the world changed, she was always an angel, that was always a steadfast fact. If she was a fallen angel, then that was still something; not a great identity, but *an* identity. The idea that they were now something different and unique obviously excited Nessa, but it kind of filled Ophelia with an odd uneasy feeling.

"But, what are we?" she asked worriedly.

"I don't know, does it matter? You're Ophelia!" Nessa said.

"I think it matters," said Ophelia. "It feels weird to think I'm nothing…"

"Honey, you're not nothing!" said Nessa quickly. "You're something new and different!"

Ophelia wasn't sure she wanted to be *this* different, but she didn't say anything.

"Maybe God knows?" suggested Nessa, obviously noticing Ophelia's sad face.

"Maybe, but she's not going to answer…" sighed Ophelia. "No one's seen her for over a year!"

"Hey, God?!" yelled Nessa suddenly.

Ophelia panicked. "Nessa, what are you doing?"

"Shh!" said Nessa, looking to the sky. "God? It's me, Archangel Zadkiel! Do you remember me? I made those pointless stars and planets! You used to love me… The last time you spoke to me was in Eden. Even though I couldn't see you I could tell how disappointed you were seeing me as a demon, and that broke my heart because I only ever wanted you to love me… After all I've been through today, and for my whole life to be honest, do I not finally deserve some answers? Please! I have questions, but after that I'll never bother you again, I promise!"

For a moment everything was silent. When Nessa stopped shouting it felt eerily quiet, with everything still frozen around them.

"It was worth one last try…" sighed Nessa. "I guess we really are on our own…"

Ophelia was about to speak, when the sky lit up with golden light, just like in Eden. Ophelia grabbed Nessa's arm, too stunned to speak, was God going to talk to them? Would she be angry? Nessa must have wondered the same, as she gripped Ophelia's hands with her other arm, almost hurting her.

"It is always worth a try, and you are never alone,"

came God's voice. She could often be quite formidable, and at times genuinely terrifying; well, she was God! But right now her voice sounded kind. Maybe she agreed that they had already been through enough.

"Oh, shit. Hello! I didn't think you'd actually speak to me," said Nessa, then she gasped. "Oh fuck I just said shit in front of God! Oh I said it again! And fuck… Oh dear, Ophelia stop me!"

"Nessa! With all the love in the world, shut up…" said Ophelia, giving her arm a little shake. "Good evening my Lord, it is truly an honour to hear from you!"

"Yes, such an honour!" said Nessa quickly. "Believe it or not that's what I was going for…"

"Honey…" said Ophelia warningly.

"Right, yeah…" whispered Nessa.

The Almighty just laughed. Ophelia was concerned she might get angry that Nessa swore, but she oddly seemed to find it hilarious.

"You can relax, I am not angry with you," said God.

"Really?" asked Nessa meekly, like a little child hoping their parent was in a good mood.

"I promise," said God. "Now, do you wish for me to address you as Nessa? To me you will always be Zadkiel, but I don't mind calling you either."

Nessa's eyes widened. "I will? Oh, I don't mind you calling me Zadkiel. It might be nice to hear you say it when I've tried so hard to push her away…"

"Hmm… Interesting…" said God. "Go ahead Archangel Zadkiel, what was your question?"

Nessa smiled slightly. "Well, it's more *our* question. We were wondering what all this means?" She gestured vaguely to their grey wings.

"An intriguing question," said God. "And not a simple one to answer... You are now neither angel nor demon, or else you are both. That was not something I ever planned to be possible, but you created it yourselves. By Heaven's terms you are not pure enough to be angels and by Hell's terms you are not wicked enough to be demons, you are a mixture. You have the capacity for good and evil, but it's up to you how you choose to use it. Closer, I suppose, to humans. Today the archangels tried to cast you down, Ophelia, but all they did was make you more powerful; allowing you to access demonic power too. You can't become a demon because you were not really an angel, you haven't been an angel for some time now. Zadkiel had both angelic and demonic power, and now you do too. I believe that the two of you planted the seeds of this strange phenomenon when you decided to create your own secret middle ground. It was then fueled by your love and I think that you began to be psychically changed by it when Ophelia was lost during that human war, as that was when you both fully acknowledged that you were in love. You have both been most fascinating to observe over the years; angels were never made to fall in love, yet I have never witnessed love like it."

"Excuse me, my Lord?" said Ophelia nervously, but full of hope. "So you don't hate us for loving each other?"

The Almighty laughed slightly. "Dear Ophelia, it has been a *very* long time. Don't you think if I hated you for loving each other you would know about it by now?"

Ophelia didn't think that was supposed to sound like a threat, but coming from God she almost felt like it was. She had been so scared of angering God her whole life, it was odd that she was being so very kind now. She had seemed a little annoyed when Ophelia last saw her; back when she was granted permission to return to Earth after getting killed.

"Err, my Lord? Sorry, but you said I have angelic and demonic magic?" Nessa said nervously. "I know I always had angelic magic but didn't realise, but I sacrificed my demonic magic to save Ophelia, right?"

"No Zadkiel. You retained all your power," God said. "An ordinary demon would indeed be required to sacrifice their powers for such an act, but you are far from an ordinary demon. Your magic remains the same as it was."

"Oh, really?" Nessa glanced down at her hands, obviously testing her powers. "Wow, I never thought to check... I guess I didn't need to live like a human this last year!"

Ophelia smiled at her beloved demon and took her hand. Nessa looked back at her, full of love.

"How about the Book of Life thing?" Nessa asked God, suddenly remembering. "What happened there? I know that book well, we should have been erased from existence!"

"In theory indeed you should," said God after a moment. "It is complicated as this is all very new. No creatures have existed like you before. But the simple fact is that only angels and demons can be erased from the book, and as I said, you are neither. So for that reason you could not physically be erased. However, as far as Heaven and Hell are concerned, you do not exist. That also means that you no longer have any obligations to either party. You have a new start as of now and you can choose to do what you wish with it."

"Sorry for all the questions, but why can we remember each other if no one else can?" asked Nessa. "As far as I know I remember everything about Ophelia..."

Ophelia looked at her in horror, and she glanced back, realising what she had just suggested. It hadn't occurred to either of them that it was possible that they remembered things differently and they wouldn't even know.

"Yes, don't worry, you both retained all of your memories. Everything you remember is truth," God explained. "And the reason for that is that you are in love. Your love is too powerful to erase, and since the beginning you have shaped each other so drastically that if one of you never existed, the other would be unrecognisable. Most angels make little impact on their fellow angels. They don't form emotional connections, so they can easily be taken out of the picture without much fuss, but you intertwine so much that it is impossible."

Upon getting it confirmed by God, Ophelia suddenly felt excited too. They really could be together, the archangels didn't know them, even God didn't mind.

"So we really are free?" she grinned excitedly. "No

angel or demon knows us, Nessa you're right, we're truly free!"

"Yeah, I told you!" smiled Nessa, squeezing Ophelia's hand. But suddenly her face changed as she realised something. "Phee, if *all* the angels have forgotten us, what about Ezra?..."

"Oh..." Ophelia felt guilty that she hadn't realised that, but they both loved their little brother, it would be awful to go back to the cottage and have him not know them. Other than Nessa, Ezra was truly the only other person who had ever cared about Ophelia. She remembered with a pang when he said how lonely he would be if anything happened to them. They had somehow both made it, but what if he still feels alone?

"Do not worry my dear angels," said The Almighty warmly. "Angel Ezra remembers you both. You have made a great positive impact upon his life also, and he views the two of you as sister-like figures. As I said, love cannot be erased..."

"Oh thank goodness!" said Ophelia, feeling mightily relieved.

"Thank you so much for answering our questions!" said Nessa. "I really thought you abandoned me..."

"I never abandoned you Zadkiel!" said God, sounding a little incredulous. "You were one of my first angels, and by far my favourite archangel, not that I probably ought to have a favourite, I know, but you embody exactly what I wanted angels to be; kind, loving and truly passionate about everything you do. Ophelia is the same; both the model of an angel."

"But I was the first demon, I've been a demon

longer than even the bloody Devil!" said Nessa.

"I know, and that is not fair, but then not everything is fair," said God. "I believe you have worked it out already, but my dear Zadkiel, I did not cast you out of Heaven. I was rather busy, and simply asked Lucifer to keep an eye on things while I put the finishing touches on the Earth, in hindsight not my best move I know, and the next time I checked I had lost my best archangel. I did not authorise your damnation, Zadkiel. Ezra is very right; even before you began to become this mixture that you now are, your angelic power was always there. Deep down you have always been an archangel, because only I can take your powers from you, and I wouldn't do that without a very good reason."

A tear ran down Nessa's face. "If you didn't damn me, then why didn't you help me? I didn't think you cared because, authorisation or not, I became a demon and you did nothing!"

Ophelia was a little concerned, it was quite risky to speak to God like that. She wondered if she should say anything, but decided it was best not to potentially make things worse.

"You didn't need help. You did fine on your own Zadkiel. You never lost your kindness, I wondered if you would. You never lost your sense of what is good; most demons do. And most of all you had this fascinating relationship building with Ophelia. You all have free will, otherwise that would be quite boring for all of us and rather a lot of work for me. You didn't need me."

"I did need you..." sniffed Nessa. "I was so alone."

"No you were not. You had Ophelia," said God.

"Your life has turned out far more interesting and wonderful than it would have if I got involved. I did not know it was possible for angels to love each other as fiercely as the two of you do. You don't want me getting in the way, you built something incredible all on your own."

Ophelia and Nessa looked at each other in joy, despite Nessa's tears. God actually *wanted* them to be together! That felt wonderful.

"Oh, and Zadkiel?" said The Almighty. "Before I go and sort out all this unauthorised archangel activity that has been going on in my absence, I must say one thing to you."

"Yes?" said Nessa, gripping Ophelia tightly.

"Thank you for your work on the universe. The stars and planets bring me, and the humans, a lot of joy. Thank you for bringing them to be, and for designing Jupiter, which, as was often the case when working with your brilliant creative mind, was better than my own designs. It is my favourite."

Nessa completely broke down upon hearing this. Whilst she had been very emotional many times that day, this was different; it was over six thousand years worth of abandonment issues coming to the surface! She clung to Ophelia, who put an arm and wing around her.

"That was all I wanted…" sobbed Nessa. "I worked so hard on it; poured everything I had into it, I just wanted you to be proud of me, because my whole existence had been devoted to working on that."

"I know, and I am proud," said The Almighty. "I am very sorry that I did not say it before. Unfortunately

I was too wrapped up in creating the Earth and the humans, I didn't even realise that you were so upset. That is entirely my fault. I had planned to thank you and reward you once the Earth was completed, but of course it was too late then..."

"Thank you..." said Nessa, still crying. "That means so much after all these years of thinking you hated me..."

Ophelia secretly thought that God could have spoken to Nessa even as a demon to explain all this when she saw how upset she was way back thousands of years ago, but she certainly wasn't going to say anything. She supposed God was right that Nessa's life had been more interesting than other demons or angels, because of their relationship, they had found each other and life had worked out just fine without God's help.

"Thank you for speaking to us," said Ophelia, as Nessa was crying a little too much to say anything else.

"You are most welcome Ophelia," said God kindly. "You have both had quite a difficult day, thank you for saving my humans. Certain archangels seem to have some *interesting* ideas..."

Ophelia gasped. Despite what all the archangels said to her over the past year, destroying the world was *not* part of God's plan! She hadn't been betraying God at all! That made her feel hugely relieved, and less like a bad angel.

"It is nice to finally speak to you as a couple," said God. "The two of you fascinate me, my beautiful love-filled angels... Through you I have been able to watch the strength of true love, the kind that survives, despite everything that is sent to test it. I wish you happiness, and hope that you will always try to do what is right."

"We will," Ophelia said in awe, not quite believing that God wanted them together after thinking love was forbidden all this time.

"Thank you..." said Nessa, wiping her tears. And with that, the golden light vanished and the two angel-demons were left alone.

For a moment they stood there in the frozen street, their grey wings around each other. Nessa had stopped crying and was staring off into the distance.

"I think there's one thing God was wrong about!" she said after a moment.

Ophelia gulped and glanced to the sky, still rather scared to anger The Almighty. "What do you mean? The Almighty is never wrong... Be careful, she might still be able to hear you!" she hissed worriedly.

"Nothing bad Phee, don't worry I'm not going to commit heresy or anything," smiled Nessa. "She was wrong about that part where angels and demons aren't supposed to fall in love. Loving you is the only thing that's ever felt right. I think we were somehow made to be together, because I'm realising more and more that I don't feel whole without you. You know, some humans believe that they are two halves of a soul and they spend their lives looking for the other half? Their soulmate!"

"Well that's silly," said Ophelia. "Souls aren't cut in half, that would be odd, and inconvenient..."

"Darling! Not the time to be pedantic! I'm trying to be romantic..."

"Are you now?" said Ophelia teasingly. "Go on then?"

Nessa gave her a playful nudge before continuing. "Their logic might not be exact, but they have a point! I always used to feel like something was missing, but when I was with you, I didn't feel that. I feel safe and content with you, just knowing you were somewhere on the same planet as me made me happy. Whether we're trying to save the world, or just having a drink at the pub, I'm glad to be by your side."

"I suppose you're right," smiled Ophelia. "I have always felt the same about you. That's why it was so important to save the Earth, especially this time. I feel physical things much stronger here, and I want to feel you."

Ophelia turned to stand in front of her girlfriend and took both her hands, Nessa smiled, and then looked a little concerned. She released one of her hands and took Ophelia's pocket watch from her jacket, which of course had stopped, because time had stopped.

"When I start things up, there will be just over half an hour until the world was supposed to end," she said, handing the watch back to Ophelia. "Are you sure it won't?"

"Quite sure," said Ophelia, reaching into her other pocket and taking out the Earth vial. "This is what makes the machine work. Unfortunately I created it, but fortunately that means they don't know how to recreate it even if they tried. I don't think they will though, it sounds like God *definitely* doesn't approve of destroying the world."

"I'm so proud of you!" Nessa said, touching Ophelia's face. "My girlfriend saved the world!" she yelled, knowing no one could hear her. "She's the most amazing person that has ever existed! I'm so lucky!" She put her arms around Ophelia's waist and lifted her slightly, making her giggle.

"Well I think *my* girlfriend is the most amazing person in the world!" Ophelia smiled, giving Nessa a tiny kiss.

Nessa put Ophelia down and looked at her, suddenly seeming a little more serious. "I'm so proud that I can finally call you my girlfriend, but I'm not sure if that's enough..." She paused, looking as shy and nervous as Ophelia had ever seen her. "I was wondering if I could call you my wife instead?" She looked away, as if she couldn't bear to see Ophelia's reaction.

Ophelia was rather stunned. "Wife?" she whispered, the word sounding so special as she said it. "We only officially became girlfriends today, are you sure?" She wanted to be certain that Nessa was ready and wasn't just saying what she thought Ophelia would want her to say.

"No, we said it out loud today! We've been together a million times longer than any human, really. Come on Phee, after six thousand years I'm not scared anymore! A little bit nervous to ask you something so important, sure, but not scared! We survived, and we are completely free, *and* God still likes us! Now let's be together, properly! Please..."

Ophelia had never really thought about getting married to Nessa. Not because she didn't want to, but because that was a human thing. But Nessa was right; now they were free they could do whatever they wanted.

"I would love to my darling!" she smiled. "But how are we going to have a wedding when nobody knows us?"

"We don't need a wedding Phee, I'm pretty sure we're already married now anyway!" grinned Nessa triumphantly.

"How so?"

"Well, what is a wedding? It's when humans get God's blessing to be together right? Well, we just got her rather firm approval didn't we? So I think that means we are married now! If you definitely want to be?" Nessa quickly added.

"I do!" smiled Ophelia, hoping Nessa noticed the reference to what humans say at weddings. "Oh! Do we get wedding rings?" she added excitedly.

"Absolutely!" smiled Nessa.

She reached into her pocket and took out the little bottle from Jupiter that Ophelia had given her for Christmas. It made Ophelia smile that she kept it with her. Nessa opened it carefully, then gently poured a little of it out onto her hand. Ophelia watched in fascination, wondering what she was doing. Nessa put the bottle back in her pocket and rolled the piece of Jupiter in the palm of her hand with her fingers. To Ophelia's amazement, it transformed into what looked like an orange gemstone. Nessa smiled proudly and a ring formed, with the Jupiter gem in its centre. Nessa carefully slipped the ring onto Ophelia's finger, before holding her hand interlocking their fingers.

"I can't think of anything more fitting to create your wedding ring from than the place we stood together all those years ago; my former greatest creation. Now of course my greatest creation is this; our relationship! I love you my darling wife!" Nessa smiled at calling Ophelia her wife, and Ophelia couldn't quite believe she was hearing it.

Ophelia had an idea for a similarly symbolic ring. She still had the Earth vial in her hand.

"Nessa, this is a mixture of the Earth and one of your stars," she said, tipping it into her hand. "Two things we love. You showed me the stars and I'm the only angel you told about the constellations, so they are ours really; the stars. And obviously the Earth is our place too, so your ring will be made of both!" She transformed the mixture into a ring she knew Nessa would love and placed it on her finger. "It also represents the time we saved the world! Today has been the best day of my life, also simultaneously the worst, but we won't dwell on that..."

Nessa laughed. "Thank you my darling. It's perfect!"

"Not as perfect as you; my *wife*!" Ophelia's stomach seemed to leap with excitement as she said the word. It felt so special.

"May I kiss the bride?" smiled Nessa.

"No, I'm kissing my bride first!" said Ophelia, and she threw herself at Nessa, thrilled to be kissing her new wife.

"Wings," said Nessa, her voice muffled from the kiss. Their wings disappeared and Nessa clicked her fingers to start time again, as though all the people burst to life to celebrate their love.

Chapter Nineteen

On the Same Frequency.

The newlyweds walked hand-in-hand back towards Ophelia's cottage. Nessa couldn't stop smiling. She looked at her new ring, and she could feel Ophelia's on the hand she was holding. She felt like she never wanted to stop gazing at it. This morning had been the 365th day since she had seen her angel, and now suddenly that angel was her *wife*! She couldn't believe it.

"You promised we'd take Ezra somewhere to celebrate," said Ophelia. "Any ideas?"

Nessa thought for a moment. "Ooh, there's that restaurant that only serves desserts! He'd love that, we'd *all* love that. Why didn't I invent that? That's such a deliciously unholy place!"

"You invented the chocolate that makes most of the desserts," Ophelia smiled. "I missed chocolate! It's so irresistible, just like the person who created it!" She kissed Nessa on the cheek and they rounded the corner to the cottage. It occurred to Nessa that she had entered through the gate three times that day, all in very different circumstances. This morning she had been alone, then she came back with a girlfriend, and now she had a wife! That was a lot to happen in one day of an immortal's life, but Nessa hoped that now they were married, and free, they would be able to relax and enjoy life together peacefully. It was better to get all this nonsense out of the way in one day, after all. It was over now. All was well.

Ophelia opened the door. "Ezra? We are back!" she called. She glanced back at Nessa who was standing on the doorstep, waiting to be invited in. "What are you doing?" she asked.

"You need to let me in," said Nessa simply.

"No I don't. Not anymore," smiled Ophelia.

"Oh yeah! I'm not a demon anymore, and you're not an angel..." Nessa grinned excitedly.

"Well yes, but that's not the reason," said Ophelia. "You are free to come in because this isn't my house anymore, it's *our* house! You don't need permission to come into your own house do you?"

"Really?" said Nessa, slightly mind-blown.

"Of course! I'm not letting my wife go off across the city to a sad little flat every night! You are staying with me! You can't escape me now we're married..."

"Good!" Nessa smiled, stepping into the hall. "You can't escape me either. I'm the demon that will torment you forever!"

"Mmm, I can't wait!" said Ophelia. "Ezra?!" she called again. "Are you here?"

Nessa felt concerned. Why wasn't he waiting for them? Then after a moment there was a commotion from above and Ezra appeared at the top of the stairs. His face lit up when he saw them.

"You came back!" he yelled, rushing down the stairs. "Did you stop them? It's nearly seven, I was getting worried. I was trying to collect things to take if I had to leave."

Nessa smiled at seeing their little brother. Even though God had said he would remember them, in the back of her mind Nessa had been a little worried in case he didn't, but he was the same as ever.

"We did," said Ophelia as Ezra hugged them both. "Everything is okay now. We are all safe, I promise."

"And you're both staying? No one's leaving or avoiding each other? Because in the time I've known you we have been together twice, the day I arrived and today! For two people in love as much as you, you are literally never in the same room!" said Ezra.

His sisters laughed.

"Yes we are staying together now, forever," smiled Nessa, showing Ezra her ring.

"What's that?" asked Ezra.

"It's a wedding ring!" Nessa said proudly. "We are married now!"

"Really?" said Ezra in awe. "I thought you were saving the world, when did you have a wedding? And why wasn't I invited?"

"We didn't have a wedding," said Ophelia quickly. "But we got God's permission to be together, so that makes us wives!" She looked over at Nessa, putting a hand on her shoulder.

"That's so cool!" Ezra said excitedly. "I'm happy

for you. You've been in love for an annoyingly long time without telling each other. I'm the one who persuaded Ophelia to be brave enough to tell you Nessa, so you're welcome!" he smiled. "Even though she didn't get chance to in the end..."

"Yes, thank you Little Brother," said Ophelia. "And thank you for looking after Nessa for me while I was away. I knew you'd get on, and I knew you'd be exactly the kind of friend she needed."

"Shall we go and eat cake?" Nessa asked. "There's loads to celebrate, Ophelia coming home, our marriage, saving the world, surviving all Jophiel's nonsense, being free? Come on Ezzy, I said we'd go somewhere nice."

"Surviving?" Ezra exclaimed. "What did she do?"

"A lot!" said Nessa. "We'll tell you about it, go and get your coat."

She watched Ezra get his coat and thought about the mouse shenanigans that morning. That seemed like ages ago. This day had felt almost as long as the year without Ophelia.

They went to the dessert restaurant and ordered way too many things because they couldn't decide on just one cach. Ophelia kept going on about how much she had missed food over the last year, and the two of them (very quietly), recounted their dramatic trip to Heaven to a horrified Ezra.

"Nessa, you seemed confused when I said I would never lose faith in Heaven, but that's the reason!" said Ezra after hearing their story. "Heaven isn't the problem and neither is God; Jophiel is! She's really not running it properly... I believe fully in Heaven's divine mission, I just don't believe in Jophiel!"

"Sadly, not believing in Jophiel seems to be all it takes," said Ophelia. "And she's ensured that her mission *is* Heaven's mission. Though I'm not sure if that will go on much longer, given what God said."

"So, do you think Jophiel will get in trouble?" asked Ezra hopefully. "Maybe someone else could be in charge; like you, Nessa! You were always supposed to be in charge."

"You keep saying that, and it's sweet of you, but I don't want to run Heaven. I want to stay here with you two," Nessa said quickly.

"I know, but you were the best archangel! You are Zadkiel! Literally the angel I idolised for thousands of years. I know you don't want to be Zadkiel, but you are!"

Nessa smiled, still somehow surprised that Ezra felt like that, even though he had told her over and over again.

"I know I'm Zadkiel, and you know what; for the first time in a very long time I'm okay with that," she said. "I really tried to separate Nessa from Zadkiel, locking the angel away to protect her from the demon I was, but thanks to you, Ophelia, and God I've realised that I'm okay with being both. I kind of felt like they were two different people, like when I fell, Zadkiel somehow died and I turned into Nessa, but that's not true. They are just names, if I changed my name again now it wouldn't make me a different person. I guess I made myself believe they were different to protect the angel who was scared; the angel that didn't know what she did wrong..." Nessa paused to wipe her tears and stopped time so that the humans wouldn't see her cry so much.

Ophelia looked around in confusion. "Did you just stop time again? You can't just use that so flippantly!"

"They'll wonder why I'm crying, shut up and let me have my existential crisis in peace! You said I should talk about things more!" Nessa sniffed through tears.

"You're right I did. Go on..." said Ophelia.

Ezra was staring around at all the humans, frozen mid meal, but Nessa didn't feel like explaining right now. Now she had started thinking about it, it all made sense.

"I suppose Nessa really is something I made up to keep Zadkiel safe. I sort of told myself that Zadkiel was gone, she kind of stayed in Heaven, it was Nessa that became a demon. That way Zadkiel never had to feel the way Nessa did, I could pretend she was still happy..." Nessa stopped for a moment. Ophelia took her hand and squeezed it, but said nothing. "I felt like my archangel days were almost a story; something that happened to the angel, not the demon. But now you've helped me realise that Zadkiel hasn't gone, I am the same person who led the meetings and created the universe. I've had different names, but since I was created I've always been *me*... That's odd because that means that Archangel Zadkiel has done the dark things that Demon Nessa was forced to do, but then also Nessa did all the good things Zadkiel did, so I suppose it balances out."

"Nessa, I completely understand what you mean," said Ophelia. "It makes total sense to try to protect yourself like that, but I hope you can love yourself properly. Not Zadkiel or Nessa; just *you*. You could have a hundred names, you could have no name, it doesn't matter because it doesn't define you or change you. I am in love with you, and I have never for a moment thought of Nessa any differently than Zadkiel. They are not two people to me, they are two names my wife has had."

"Thank you darling. That's the thing, I think I'm finally okay with being both, especially after what God said. I'm sorry for randomly having a mental breakdown, but a lot has happened today..." Nessa sighed. "I'm just feeling a bit weird about it all..."

"Did I upset you?" asked Ezra worriedly. "I didn't mean to if I did..."

"No no Ezzy, it's not you!" insisted Nessa. "You helped me be okay with still being Zadkiel; when you told me last year that you thought I was a legend or whatever, and you said I was the same person even though I was a demon. That meant so much to me. I'm only crying now because I'm realising stuff that I've never thought about, and I'm happy because I feel okay with just being *me* for once."

"Can people cry because they're happy?" asked Ezra.

"Yes they can, but I think I'm happy and sad right now. Mostly happy though."

Ezra glanced around at the frozen restaurant. "Are the humans okay?" he asked in concern.

"Yes they are fine," smiled Nessa, taking Ophelia's napkin to wipe her tears because she had already used hers. "I stopped time. I'll start it back up in a minute."

"Wow, that's amazing!" said Ezra. "See, I told you

you were a super demon last year because you were immune to holy water, but you really are!" He suddenly gasped in excitement when he realised something. "I've read your file a hundred times! Not in a creepy way, there was never that much to do... But anyway, pausing time is part of your angelic magic! It's because you are the Archangel of Justice. God gave you that power to help protect people and stop bad things from happening. But I guess she never told you? The file said it was given to you after you created the stars and stuff."

"Oh Nessa!" said Ophelia, grabbing her hand. "Remember when God said that she had planned to reward you? Maybe it was that? Special extra powers? Because I am fairly certain that you are the only being that can do that! Back then you were wondering what your purpose was when you had finished the universe, that was it! She was probably going to get you to watch over the humans as the Archangel of Justice?"

Nessa thought for a moment, did God give her extra powers because she was proud of her work? That was nice to think, but she wished she had known; a little note or something wouldn't have gone amiss.

She restarted time, and all the humans carried on eating. Nessa looked at her ring, she felt like every time she looked at her hand it would take her by surprise, and each time she was delighted to see it.

"Hey, Phee?" she said.

"Yeah?" answered Ophelia, her mouth full of cake.

"Can I put on Instagram that we are married? There's no chance the angels will use it as evidence now, because they don't know us. I want to show off that I have a wife! I never thought I'd be married, demons just don't, so I'm so excited to call you my wife. Can I?"

"Sure," smiled Ophelia.

Nessa excitedly took a photo of their hands together, making sure the rings were in view. She was about to post it when Ophelia nudged her.

"Hey. Don't you want a proper picture? Of us?"

Nessa stared at her. "What, to put on Instagram? A picture together?"

"Yes! I'm not an angel anymore so it doesn't matter. Believe me I want to tell every single human that you are my wife just because I'm so proud of it!" Ophelia said.

Nessa smiled, completely delighted. She took a photo of them together and Ezra asked to look at it.

"You look happy like in that other picture, but even more!" he smiled.

Ophelia laughed slightly and Nessa looked at her questioningly.

"The photo on the fireplace," she explained. "When we were keeping away from each other he said that I didn't look happy like that unless I was with you. He's right."

"Well, same!" said Nessa, taking the phone back from Ezra.

"Can we take one more for your Instagram?" Ophelia asked.

"Of course," said Nessa. It was odd that Ophelia was so into the idea of posting pictures on Instagram, but she wasn't going to complain.

She readied the camera and Ophelia leant over to kiss her.

"What's that for?" Nessa laughed.

"How are your Instagram friends going to know we are in love if we aren't kissing?" asked Ophelia. "I've loved you for a long time, I want people to know!"

Nessa happily took the kissing picture, then uploaded all three, proudly telling the humans that they were married.

When they got back to the cottage, which Nessa was thrilled she could now call home, it was getting quite late.

"Right, bedtime!" announced Ophelia.

"Yes, I just need to get a new book from the library. I finished mine while I was trying to distract myself from worrying about you!" said Ezra, and he disappeared off towards the library.

"Hang on Phee, you're not actually saying you're going to sleep are you?" Nessa asked in concern.

"Of course! Why, what did you think bedtime meant?" she grinned, raising her eyebrows. Nessa's eyes widened at the suggestion. "No, I really want to sleep. I haven't slept in over a year, and today was so exhausting." Ophelia continued. "Sleeping makes you feel better when you are tired out. I know you're a demon or angel or whatever, but don't you sometimes get tired out? Living on Earth does that I think."

"Of course I do, but then I watch telly or something until I feel better."

"I don't think that's as healthy as going to sleep!" smiled Ophelia. "Come on, our bed is really cosy, I promise!"

Nessa smiled at Ophelia referring to it as *their* bed,

but she wasn't convinced. Whenever she had tried to sleep before, the nightmares had actually made her feel worse.

She begrudgingly followed the angels upstairs and Ezra closed himself in his room with the new book he had chosen, while Ophelia disappeared off into the bathroom. Nessa went through into Ophelia's bedroom. It was pretty and smelled sweet; just like Ophelia. She had never really been in there, it did feel cosy... She walked around the room looking at the cute decorations, it was neat and everything had been thought-out and placed perfectly. It was so different to Nessa's flat, which was chaotic and messy. That summed the two of them up quite well, Nessa thought. The cottage was perfect just like the angel that owned it. She hoped she wouldn't somehow ruin it by being imperfect herself.

Ophelia entered the room, now wearing pyjamas with her hair up. Nessa studied her carefully, then smiled. She looked different, she never dressed very casually, she always wore the most beautiful perfect outfits, but Nessa thought she looked rather gorgeous right now. She looked, snuggly! Nessa wasn't sure what she meant by that, but that was her immediate thought; she wanted to cuddle her.

Ophelia sat on the bed and looked at Nessa expectantly.

"Are you going to just stand in the corner of the room all night and stare at me like a creepy demon from a horror film?" she asked.

"I am a creepy demon, you know that!" smiled Nessa. "I can't sleep, I really can't..."

"Of course you can!" said Ophelia.

"Well, physically I probably could, but I won't," said Nessa. "I can't remember the last time I slept. You go to sleep, I'll wait for you..."

"Okay... But I want you to get in the bed with me, will you do that?" asked Ophelia encouragingly.

"Err... I suppose so," said Nessa, knowing full well that Ophelia was working her way up to trying to make her sleep, but not minding too much because she did want to lie next to her angel.

"You can't get into bed with jeans and a jacket on though, that won't be very comfortable," said Ophelia.

Nessa oddly felt like she might cry, there was something about Ophelia being so gentle and taking care of her when she was scared to sleep that felt really nice. Nessa loved taking care of others, especially Ophelia, but no one ever really looked after her like that.

"I don't have pyjamas," said Nessa. "I don't sleep, what's the point?"

"Well, even if you don't go to sleep they are more comfortable than normal clothes. Sometimes if I'm not going out I don't bother putting normal clothes on, I wear pyjamas all day!" smiled Ophelia. "I want you to be comfy!"

Ophelia flicked her hand and in an instant Nessa's outfit had changed. She jumped in surprise, and noticed her own clothes folded neatly on the chair in the corner. That was easily the first time they had ever been folded. Nessa looked down at the outfit, the pyjamas were light cream colour with little flowers on, but they were very soft, and they smelled like Ophelia.

"Those are my pyjamas so I know you won't like them, but it's more effort to *create* new pyjamas when there are already some here and I'm exhausted, so I hope you don't mind too much?" said Ophelia.

"I don't mind at all, thank you." said Nessa, still uneasy at the thought of sleeping.

"Now come here..." said Ophelia softly.

Ophelia got into the bed properly, slipping her legs under the quilt, and pulled back the other side so that Nessa could get in beside her. Even if she didn't sleep, there was no harm in lying down for a bit. She climbed into the bed, and Ophelia made her lay down. They faced each other and Ophelia took Nessa's hands, interlocking their fingers.

"I have often laid here and thought about how much I wished you were beside me." Ophelia whispered with a smile. "And now you're here!"

"I am..." smiled Nessa.

"Darling, why won't you sleep? Are you not totally exhausted from today, because I am! I know we don't technically need sleep like humans, but it's nice. I love settling down in my comfy bed in my nice cottage to sleep, and it makes you feel good for the next day. If there's any night we need sleep it's tonight, after what we've been through."

"I know, but I can't..." Nessa said sadly.

"Are you scared to sleep?" asked Ophelia gently.

"I suppose so; a bit..." said Nessa. "Every time I sleep I have awful nightmares. My imagination is too much sometimes! God always said I had a brilliant imagination, which is great, until it torments you in your dreams! If I stay awake forever then they won't come..."

Ophelia stroked her hair gently. "My sweet archangel..." she whispered. "You will be okay, do you know why? Because I'm here! You won't have any nightmares tonight, I won't let you. And from now on if you ever have nightmares you will open your eyes and I will be here, and I will look after you, I promise!"

Tears were falling now, inconveniently wetting the pillow that Nessa was laying on. The thought of being looked after by Ophelia was lovely, but was too much for her to handle right now.

"Why are you being so nice?" she whispered.

"Two reasons; firstly I am always nice, you know that; and secondly, you need someone to take care of you when you're scared. I know that you have been scared so many times, and it breaks my heart that I wasn't able to look after you then, but I'll make up for it now," smiled Ophelia, gently wiping Nessa's tears.

She pulled Nessa closer and the two wrapped their arms around each other. It felt wonderful to be so close to Ophelia. They weren't even kissing, they were just laying together, but so beautifully close! Ophelia's energy always calmed Nessa, but she had never felt it this close before. Her body was right up against Ophelia's, and Nessa could feel her energy spilling over into her own; perhaps the two were mixing a little. The idea that a little of Ophelia's beautiful energy might rub off on Nessa was a wonderful thought. She instantly felt calmer in her angel's embrace.

"You have the most amazing energy," she whispered

after a few moments of silence. "It's so relaxing, it feels like I'm melting into you..."

"Aww, yours feels nice too," said Ophelia, entwining their legs slightly. "I'm honoured that you are here next to me."

"Really? Are you sure my energy is nice?" Nessa asked. "Yours is so beautiful, I assumed that's because you're an angel, so mine must be a lot heavier. In fact I'm pretty sure being around a demon should make an angel feel ill after a while, because of the dark energy. I don't know how you have been able to stand being around me so much, even if you are in love with me..."

"Maybe I'm immune to you because I'm part of you? Like you said earlier we complete each other! Anyway, your energy has never been very dark. There's no way I could stand being this close to any other demon, but even a thousand years ago, long before we started to become whatever we are, I would have laid like this with you happily. Other demons feel evil, you never did."

"Never?" asked Nessa.

"No. Back in Eden when I first saw you as a demon I was a little concerned because I'd never seen a demon before, and also worried about you because you seemed sadder, which is obviously totally understandable. After a while I felt uncomfortable, and back then I thought it was because you were a demon and I was an angel, but I was wrong. I was feeling uncomfortable because I *liked* you! I was attracted to you and I didn't understand it then. Your energy makes me feel happy and safe, it's like protection. I feel like nothing can be that bad if I can feel you nearby." Ophelia kissed Nessa on the forehead and

Nessa entwined their legs more.

"You liked me in Eden? Like, you were attracted to me?" Nessa was rather surprised by this revelation.

"Yes absolutely! I had a bit of a celebrity crush on you in Heaven, but in Eden I couldn't stop staring at you! You were just so gorgeous. Your hair, your dress, your wings! At one point you were staring off into the distance and that was the most glorious image I had ever seen, which made me nervous because, despite what I ended up doing in Eden, I was trying so hard to be a good angel back then. An angel shouldn't have been looking at a demon like that, believe me! That's when it changed from a crush on an Archangel to a complete obsession with you!" Ophelia sighed wistfully a little and Nessa giggled.

"That's a lot of details for something that happened six thousand years ago!" Nessa laughed.

"It was only the third time I had ever met my future wife," smiled Ophelia. "I remember every second!"

There was silence for a moment as the two laid together, enjoying being so close.

"Anyway, our energy feels quite similar now," said Ophelia eventually. "We are the same; not an angel and demon anymore. I don't know what that makes us, but our energy is on the same frequency now. It hasn't been, since you were in Heaven, and we didn't really know each other then."

"Are we actually on the same frequency?" Nessa asked excitedly.

"Yes, exactly the same, just like our wings," said Ophelia.

"Oh I adore you!" said Nessa, trying to somehow wriggle even closer to her angel. "I would never have dared to imagine this time yesterday that I would be here with you right now. I missed you more than I thought possible. I can't believe it was a year!"

"I know; me too. But it's funny, I missed you so much and I was worried that things might be weird between us because we kissed then I left without saying I love you, but now that year doesn't feel real. It feels like I never left your side."

"Well, let's pretend you didn't!" said Nessa.

"Mmm yes…" Ophelia buried her face in Nessa's hair. "You smell nice…" she whispered.

"So do you!" said Nessa, gently touching Ophelia's neck. "You *feel* nice too…"

"Will you go to sleep?" asked Ophelia after a moment. "I'll keep hold of you, nightmares can't hurt you if you're with me. I'm half demon now, they wouldn't dare!"

Nessa smiled, feeling the happiest she ever had. "I'll try," she said.

"Good," said Ophelia, pulling Nessa down slightly, so that she had her arms protectively around her. "I'm here my darling, I won't ever leave you."

Nessa snuggled up to Ophelia, her head against her soft warm chest, and felt so very calm. She suddenly realised that she must have never been properly calm in her life, there was always something wrong in the back of her mind, but now it was just silence and the sound of her wife's heartbeat. She was truly happy.

"Goodnight my darling wife," whispered Ophelia

sleepily.

"Goodnight my love," answered Nessa, and eventually she must have fallen asleep.

She found herself opening her eyes what felt like a second later, but the winter sun was streaming through the curtains, so it must have been morning. For half a moment she was a little confused by her surroundings, but then she turned over and saw a beautiful angel fast asleep beside her and remembered it was her wife! She laid there gazing at Ophelia, she was smiling slightly in her sleep and Nessa couldn't believe how beautiful and pure she looked. She gave her a little kiss and Ophelia moved slightly, then opened her eyes, smiling at seeing Nessa.

"Good morning," she said, stretching a little.

"Good morning darling," said Nessa.

"Did you sleep?" Ophelia asked.

"I guess so," smiled Nessa.

Ophelia grinned triumphantly. "I told you you wouldn't have any nightmares with me!"

"Thank you. That's the first time I have ever been able to sleep properly," said Nessa. "It's nice..."

"Well, we can sleep here as often as you like," said Ophelia. "That is your place, it always has been. When I got the bed I thought about how maybe one day you would be there. Now you have finally taken your place beside me I can wake up to kisses, which is a lovely way to be woken up."

Nessa smiled and gave Ophelia another little kiss.

"No I've woken up now, that's not good enough!" said Ophelia.

Before Nessa could try to kiss her again, Ophelia pushed her onto her back and climbed on top of her. Nessa gasped in surprise and Ophelia gave her a cheeky smile, grabbing hold of her wrists and pinning her hands on the pillow above her head. Nessa gulped slightly and Ophelia lent down, closer to her face.

"Am I scaring you?" Ophelia whispered with a laugh, pushing Nessa's hands harder into the pillow. "I thought you were a demon!"

"I thought you were an angel..." gasped Nessa as Ophelia's mouth touched her neck.

"Bullshit! I haven't been an angel for a long time, you know that," said Ophelia, making Nessa catch her breath at hearing her swear. Ophelia gently ran her mouth along Nessa's neck then softly kissed it. "I've wanted you for ages, and you told me that you're mine now..." she said. "If I want to pin you to the bed and kiss you I can, right?"

"You can do anything you want to me..." whispered Nessa, completely at her angel's mercy. She took in a sharp breath as she felt Ophelia's tongue on her throat, sending a feeling of electricity through her body that Nessa had never felt. She had truly never imagined this, but she certainly wasn't complaining. It was so strange and exciting, witnessing her perfect angel acting like this, Nessa would have been far too scared to initiate anything of this nature, considering how frightened Ophelia had been to kiss her last year. This had taken Nessa completely by surprise, but that made it even more exciting...

"Not even demons do this..." she breathed as

Ophelia reached her mouth.

"Well, it's a good job we're neither then!" said Ophelia, moving so that she was holding Nessa's hands down rather than her wrists, their fingers entwined. She started kissing her, pushing down on her hands so hard it almost hurt, but Nessa didn't mind.

Nessa liked to be in control, if she wasn't in control she felt like something bad would happen, and it tended to; but right now Ophelia was totally in control, and it was amazing. She had let her take over the night before too, Ophelia taking care of her when she was scared. Maybe it wasn't so bad submitting a little sometimes, letting her guard down, only for her wife...

Nessa wasn't sure how long Ophelia's mouth had been on hers, but eventually she paused for breath and Nessa saw her opportunity.

"My turn!" she said, grabbing Ophelia and rolling her onto her side of the bed so that she was on top of her, causing her to squeak in surprise.

"That's not fair, you're way stronger than me," smiled Ophelia. "So I can't hold you down properly!"

"You can if I let you!" said Nessa. "But shh! Like I said, it's my turn now..." She put her arms underneath Ophelia's body, gripping her tightly, and began kissing her gently, starting at her face and moving down her neck to her chest. Ophelia gasped and gently held onto Nessa's hair. Nessa made her way back up to Ophelia's mouth and gently bit her lip, pulling it slightly. Then that turned into a kiss. The kind of kiss that makes you feel like one person rather than two; the kind you can get lost in...

Eventually they had to acknowledge the new day, rather than staying in bed together forever. Ophelia stood up and took an outfit from her wardrobe.

"Do you want pancakes for breakfast?" she asked excitedly, suddenly back to being a sweet angel, as if she wasn't just doing gloriously unholy things with a former demon.

"That sounds lovely," smiled Nessa, looking at her phone and noticing how late it was to be getting up.

Ophelia left the room, giving Nessa a little kiss on the way, and Nessa looked at the bed. She wanted to make it look nice and neat for Ophelia, everything in the cottage was neat and the bed was made before they got in it the night before. She adjusted the pillows and tried really hard to smooth out the quilt, but she got frustrated when she couldn't make it completely perfect. Ophelia probably wouldn't have minded, but Nessa was desperate not to ruin the perfection of everything in the house. Eventually she gave up and used magic to ensure the bed looked pristine.

Once she was dressed, Nessa went downstairs and followed the smell of pancakes into the kitchen. Ophelia was standing by the cooker, Nessa came up behind her and wrapped her arms around her, nuzzling her face into her hair and neck.

"Mmm, smells lovely!" she said.

"They are chocolate chip," smiled Ophelia.

"Oh, I wasn't talking about the pancakes!" grinned Nessa. "But yes, they smell alright too..."

Ophelia giggled.

They were both surprised by the sound of the front

door opening, and in a moment Ezra came through into the kitchen holding some bags which he immediately put on the table.

"Good morning!" he said cheerily. "You were still in bed when I finished my book so I went to the shops."

"Oh... Right. What did you get?" asked Nessa, reluctantly moving away from Ophelia, to allow her to finish the pancakes.

"Oh, just stuff," Ezra answered.

"Sounds ominous!" smiled Nessa, putting an arm around him. "Any interesting stuff?"

"Yes actually! I got you a present!" he said excitedly.

"Me?" asked Nessa in confusion.

"Yeah, I've seen it before, but after what you were saying yesterday I wanted to get you it!" Ezra was rummaging in the bags and eventually pulled out a photo frame triumphantly. He turned it to reveal a beautiful painting of a ginger-haired angel in white and golden robes. Nessa's eyes widened. Beneath the painting it said; *Archangel Zadkiel, Angel of Justice and Leader of the Archangels.*

"It's me..." Nessa whispered in wonder.

If she had seen that painting a few years ago, it would have made her sad, and she would never have associated herself with the angel, but now she felt proud to say it was her.

Ezra handed her the frame and she gazed at it. The angel in the painting looked *just* like her, and she looked beautiful! The only thing that had changed was the colour of her hair, so Nessa supposed she must still be that beautiful. She never really felt *beautiful*, not in an angelic, ethereal way like that. She knew she looked cool, and Ophelia always told her she was pretty, but she felt like she must somehow be pretty in a different way to Ophelia; in some demonic way. Come to think of it, of course demons are beautiful, because they were angels before, much as they may try to make themselves look scary instead.

"Gorgeous!" said Ophelia, looking at the painting over Nessa's shoulder. "And I don't mean the painting, I mean the angel *in* the painting! Though the painting is nice too…"

Nessa smiled. "I prefer my hair black, but it was nice then too."

"Always beautiful!" said Ophelia.

"Thank you Ezzy, this is a really sweet present!" Nessa smiled.

"It's from the minster!" Ezra said proudly. "I mean the gift shop, I didn't steal it from the church or anything!" he added quickly.

"Wow…" said Nessa, amazed that, after being a demon for thousands of years, humans still made and sold paintings of her in a church.

"We need to put that up in the hall!" said Ophelia. "Ooh, and after breakfast let's go and get all the stuff from your old flat and bring it here!"

It was odd to hear it being referred to as her *old* flat, but Nessa was never really that fond of it, and in fact had always felt more at home in the cottage.

"Are you sure you want all my stuff messing up your neat cottage?" asked Nessa.

Ophelia rolled her eyes. "It's *our* cottage now, of

course I want your stuff here. I want it to feel like it belongs to both of us, because it does!"

Ophelia served the pancakes and Ezra showed them some of the things he had bought while they ate. Then after breakfast Nessa and Ophelia set off to the flat.

As they neared the flat hand-in-hand, Nessa suddenly sensed some demonic energy. She glanced around and noticed Beelzebub standing on the street corner, looking at her strangely.

"Hey! Are you listening?" asked Ophelia, giving Nessa a nudge.

"It's Beelzebub," Nessa whispered. Ophelia followed her gaze and squeezed her hand a little.

Nessa gave Beelzebub a small smile, but she didn't smile back. She didn't remember her. She was her friend, they had got quite close after spending many evenings over the last year drinking and laughing about what a dickhead Lucifer was, but now Bee had no idea Nessa ever existed… She wasn't sure how she felt.

"She doesn't know me…" Nessa whispered.

"Hmm, it's almost as if a certain someone erased themself from the Book of Life like the crazy reckless thing they are!" said Ophelia.

"I know, but she was my friend… The only other one I ever had…" Nessa felt like she might cry. She hadn't realised how much Beelzebub's friendship had meant to her; the only friendly face in Hell.

"I suppose you could introduce yourself? Try and befriend her again?" suggested Ophelia. "You could maybe explain the situation? She might believe you."

"No…" sighed Nessa. "No one is supposed to know

us, that was the point. It's too risky..."

Beelzebub had been staring directly at Nessa, probably picking up some demonic energy and wondering why she didn't recognise these particular demons. However, when Nessa finished speaking, Beelzebub moved off into the shadows, disappearing completely. Nessa felt an odd sadness, but was cheered slightly by an encouraging smile from her darling wife.

At the flat, the two of them chatted happily about the future as they packed up all of Nessa's belongings, but Nessa was a little distracted. Seeing Beelezbub look at her like a stranger was weird, and it made Nessa stop to think about the severity of what she had done. After living for thousands of years, all of a sudden almost no one knew her. Every interaction she had ever had with anyone, including her only friend in Hell, was now meaningless; none of it ever really happened in a way... Whether they hated her, tolerated her, or quite liked her, everyone in both realms had at least *heard* of her before, but now they had no idea she ever existed, and that was a weird thought to wrap her head around. She was, however, free, and that was far more important. No one could take her angel away from her now. Today was the first day of the rest of eternity, and Nessa couldn't wait to spend every moment of it with Ophelia.

Chapter Twenty
Hell's Hit Squad.

(Six Months Later)

Ophelia closed her eyes, absorbing herself in the music. The room was filled with the smell of the bread she was baking, along with the candle that Nessa had angrily enchanted to smell stronger when she discovered that it no longer smelled of anything once lit. Only now the scent of 'Ocean Mist' filled the room constantly, without the need to even light the candle.

Even with her eyes closed, Ophelia could feel the warmth of the sun on her face from the open window. She had missed last summer, so she was determined to enjoy this one as much as possible. She had truly never been happier. It had been six months since that eventful day which ended in her returning home as her darling demon's wife. It had honestly been the first time that Ophelia had been able to relax, without Heaven weighing on her mind. Only, she did find it rather hard to relax when Nessa wasn't around. She feared she was a little too clingy, but if she and Nessa were apart, which didn't actually happen that often, she would feel a strange anxiety creep up on her. She hadn't told Nessa about it; she didn't want to ruin their perfect life with her unfounded concerns. She especially noticed it when Ezra had moved out a couple of months ago, and she was suddenly properly on her own if Nessa went out. However, she was trying to be okay with being on her own sometimes. After breakfast she had stayed home while Nessa went out shopping and to drop a book off at Ezra's house that Ophelia thought he would enjoy. That was several hours ago now, hence the relaxing music, to try to distract herself.

Eventually the music stopped and the room sank into silence. Ophelia opened her eyes, she didn't realise she'd been sitting there for an entire record's worth of music. She wondered at what point it would be valid to be genuinely worried about Nessa. She had been out for ages. If she was with Nessa, she would know she was okay; she could see her, but if she was out, she had no way to know where she was or if she was okay…

She picked up her phone. Nessa had gifted her and Ezra one each for Christmas, insisting that they all needed to be able to contact each other. Ophelia did admit that it was useful in times like this, when she remembered she had it. She usually totally forgot about it because she far preferred old-fashioned forms of entertainment, unlike Nessa who could occupy herself for hours scrolling on Instagram or TikTok.

Ophelia was slightly relieved to see a text from Nessa, which said;

Hey darling, I know you probably won't see this because you're allergic to technology or whatever, but I'm on my way home. Sorry I've taken ages, Ezzy sure talks a lot when he gets going! See you soon honey.

Though she knew Nessa was on her way, in the silence, Ophelia started to feel quite anxious again.

Suddenly, mercifully, she heard the front door open. She sat up excitedly, waiting for her wife. She straightened up her dress and smoothed her hair, still wanting to look her best, though she knew Nessa didn't care what she looked like.

The living room door burst open and Nessa strode in with something behind her back. She came up to Ophelia, looking rather excited, and stood behind her, leaning over to give her a kiss.

"I've got you something my darling angel!" she announced, producing a bunch of roses with a flourish.

Ophelia turned to look at her. "What's this for?" she asked, a little confused, but still very delighted.

"Happy anniversary, my sweet angel!" announced Nessa triumphantly.

"Err, darling? It's June... We got married in December..." said Ophelia suspiciously. "Not that I don't appreciate them anyway!" she added, hoping not to sound ungrateful.

"Six month anniversary!" grinned Nessa.

"Six month anniversary? You can't do that! People don't celebrate half years. And besides, that makes me look mean for not getting you anything!"

"Call it making up for all the years we should have been together!" said Nessa, sitting on the arm of Ophelia's chair with a little jump.

"Over six thousand years?" inquired Ophelia. "That's a lot of flowers... The house will be overrun, we'll drown in flowers!" she smiled.

"Well I can take them back if you don't want them!" said Nessa playfully. "I might get the money back if I tell them my wife is an ungrateful little demon!"

Ophelia laughed. She stood up and moved close to Nessa, leaning in to kiss her.

"Happy half anniversary my love!" she said, giving Nessa a light kiss, before moving away towards the door.

"That wasn't a proper kiss!" protested Nessa.

"No, good observation," smiled Ophelia. "You get a half kiss for our half anniversary!"

"Ugh, you're infuriating!" said Nessa, rushing to Ophelia and taking her by the waist. "Why are you so attractive?!"

"I think it's my angelic innocence?" said Ophelia, giving Nessa her best cute little smile.

"Yeah right!" scoffed Nessa. "I think it's the demon in you! You little temptress!" She quickly pulled Ophelia against her, her hands tightly gripping her waist. Ophelia gasped slightly.

Nessa kissed her, and in all the talk of anniversaries, Ophelia was reminded of that eventful day in December. She thought about all the desperate kisses they had shared then, and how many times they thought they were going to lose each other. As she thought about it, she kissed Nessa more passionately, more desperately, revelling in being with the love of her life, and perhaps in the back of her mind, frightened in case she somehow lost her. Nessa still had her hands on Ophelia's waist and

Ophelia's arms were wrapped tightly around Nessa's neck. After the kiss, they stayed very close; their lips still just millimetres away from each other.

"Angel, my arse!" whispered Nessa.

"What about it?" said Ophelia suggestively, raising an eyebrow playfully.

"Oh I'm definitely not an angel!" said Nessa. "There are no angelic thoughts in my head right now! Not one… And it's all your fault…" She moved closer so their foreheads were touching and gently bit Ophelia's lip, sending shivers through her body.

"The bread will burn…" whispered Ophelia.

"Let it…" answered Nessa, still touching Ophelia's lips with hers.

"No, no! I ought to take it out," said Ophelia, pulling away from the embrace. "It's your favourite!"

"So you *do* have an anniversary present for me!" Nessa smiled.

"No, I often make bread, that can't be a present," said Ophelia simply.

"I often get you flowers…" retorted Nessa.

Ophelia shot her a little look before heading into the kitchen, and carefully taking out the bread. It was almost perfect, but it was cracked along the top and had risen a little unevenly. Ophelia glanced at the kitchen door to make sure Nessa wasn't looking and quickly fixed the bread with a little bit of magic. She liked to make sure every bake was absolutely perfect; she felt Nessa deserved perfection after all this time. The only problem was, Nessa thought she really *was* that good at baking, and she was good, (not that Ophelia felt there was particularly any talent to mixing things and putting them in an oven), but things often weren't as perfect as they appeared. Nessa once said that Ophelia should go on 'Bake Off', but they eventually agreed that it wouldn't be fair on the human contestants for an angel-demon to take part, plus Nessa insisted that she would perform demonic magic to ensure that the other cakes went wrong, and Ophelia didn't think that sounded very sporting.

For a moment, Ophelia gazed at the church rooftop outside and thought about that day; the day she stopped being an angel.

Neither Ophelia nor Nessa had been able to think of a name for what they were; half angel, half demon, and that sometimes troubled Ophelia. Nessa insisted it didn't matter, but Ophelia had always been an angel, that was who she was, even when eventually she wasn't. She found it difficult to accept the idea that she wasn't anything specific anymore. The idea of having no real identity seemed to thrill Nessa, but Ophelia struggled with it. She had, mostly, lived by heaven's rules for thousands of years. Even if she didn't particularly agree with it all, it had provided her with some form of structure. Now though, there were no rules, no one reminding her to be good and pure. Of course that meant Ophelia could do what she wanted now, and that was great, but even after six months she would sometimes lie awake all night when she was supposed to be sleeping, thinking about it. She would watch Nessa, fast asleep beside her, her chest moving up and down as she breathed, and wonder how she was so content with not being anything; without an identity. Ophelia didn't particularly want to be an angel, not if it meant being beholden to heaven, and she certainly didn't want to be a demon, but she wanted to be something! Humans spend their life knowing they are humans, even each type of animal is a specific animal, but what was Ophelia? Everybody else had been created by God to be something specific, but Ophelia and Nessa had become something else. Even God didn't know what they were, so how could they? Ophelia still tended to refer to herself as an angel, and regrettably, she often still called Nessa a demon, out of habit. Though Nessa called herself a demon too most of the time, so she obviously didn't mind. Another habit was defaulting to angelic magic, like she'd just used on the bread. She hadn't actually tried demonic magic yet. She was a little scared of what she had become; not that she knew what that actually was, of course!

    She glanced at the garden, filled with summer sun. She was happy; happier than she'd ever been, so why did this bother her so much? It didn't bother Nessa, what was wrong with her? She was married to the person she adored more than anything. They lived together in their beautiful cottage and visited Ezra in the city at least twice a week. She and Nessa were having so much fun finally being together. They went on trips and held hands the whole time. Ophelia read books to Nessa as she laid in her lap; Nessa planned weekly dates, always trying to one-up the last one; and they kissed as often as possible, proudly being *that* annoying couple. Ophelia's life was perfect, so what was this feeling? Would it ever leave her, would she ever be content with it? Or would she feel a bit lost and slightly empty for eternity? That was aside from the anxiety she often felt...

Ophelia looked back down at the bread; it was cooling and she wanted to serve it warm. She would have to push down her strange feelings and carry on as she usually did. She took the loaf out of its tin and served it with jam for herself, and chocolate spread for Nessa. She took it through to the living room where Nessa was waiting for her and smiled. She always felt better with Nessa. The odd directionless feeling only seemed to surface when she was alone; when the thoughts were allowed to come.

"Here you are my love! Happy half anniversary!" Ophelia presented the bread to Nessa.

"Thank you Phee!" smiled Nessa. "You were right, this is absolutely my favourite!"

They sat down to enjoy the bread while it was still hot, but after a few minutes Nessa's phone rang, which startled both of them, as they didn't really know anyone apart from Ezra, and he never called, plus Nessa had just come from visiting him anyway.

"It's Ezra..." said Nessa in confusion as she looked at the phone.

Nessa answered, putting it on speakerphone.

"Nessa? Hello!" came Ezra's slightly panicked voice.

"Hello, is something wrong?" asked Nessa worriedly, glancing at Ophelia, who lent closer to the phone.

"I rang you because I'm never sure if Ophelia will answer, but I think I need your help..." said Ezra.

"Why, what?" said Nessa.

"There are some demons outside the shop!" Ezra said.

Ophelia instantly felt panic rise. Ezra had decided to open a sort of bakery a while ago, only, unlike Ophelia he didn't actually like baking, so he created especially irresistible treats using magic. He rather unoriginally called it 'Treats from Heaven by Ezzy.' Technically Ophelia and Nessa couldn't think of anything more demonic than creating extra tempting desserts to entice humans, but neither had the heart to tell him. Despite that, Ophelia was very proud of how successful her little brother's shop had become, but now the thought of demons turning up there was extremely concerning. Obviously none of them could enter the shop without permission, as it was owned by an angel, but still. What were they doing there?

"What the fuck are demons doing here?" sighed Nessa.

"I don't know, but when I made my report yesterday, Gabriel mentioned something about Hell planning a war! To get back at Heaven for trying to destroy them! Maybe they have come to start the war? I don't know why they are in York though..." Ezra sounded really upset, and Ophelia and Nessa looked at each other in horror. A war would be a disaster! Of course they had nothing to do with either realm, as no one remembered them, but it would be impossible for them to ignore a war between Heaven and Hell.

"Don't worry Ezzy. We'll be there soon," said Nessa. "No bloody clue what we can do about it, but we'll be there!"

"Thank you!" said Ezra.

Nessa put the phone down and looked at Ophelia. Ophelia was so full of panic, like the anxious feeling she got when she was alone, but a hundred times worse. She felt like she might cry, or vomit, or both. Before Nessa could say anything, she stood up.

"I'm sorry, I just need to go upstairs for a minute!" she said, trying desperately to seem relatively calm, so that Nessa wouldn't be too suspicious.

"Why?" asked Nessa.

"You put the bread in the kitchen and get ready to go. I'll just be a minute!" Ophelia said; dashing upstairs before Nessa could question her further.

Once Ophelia was in the bedroom with the door shut, she was able to let out her emotions. She knelt at the side of the bed, burying her face into the softness of the quilt. She was crying so hard that she felt like she couldn't breathe properly. This was a panic attack, she knew. She'd had them before, when she was worried about Nessa, but she had only had proper anxiety recently, which made no sense to her, because she had far less to worry about now than she ever had.

She spent a few minutes silently sobbing and trying in vain to control her breathing. This must have been triggered by the idea of a war, she thought. They had to somehow stop it. They had to go help Ezra, but Ophelia couldn't do anything right now, she was a total mess!

"What's wrong with me?" she whispered, either talking to no one, or maybe God. "I should be happy, I *am* happy, why do I get so scared?" She paused for a moment, then clasped her hands together to pray, feeling desperate. "My Lord, I'm sorry to bother you... I'm not asking you to get involved in whatever's going on between Heaven and Hell, but I need help. I used to be brave, I stormed Heaven to stop Jophiel's plan, even though I knew it could kill us. I went to Hell to speak to Lucifer knowing the risk, but now I can't do anything! I can't even bear to be on my own! I'm scared, God... Can you help me? Can you make me brave again? Do you know what I can do?" She knew The Almighty wasn't going to answer; she never answered prayers. She only spoke to people when it was absolutely necessary. Ophelia cried harder; feeling strangely alone, even though she knew Nessa was downstairs.

After a moment she sensed some sort of divine magic and looked up in confusion. Eventually, she noticed her book on the bed. Where it had said *'Sense and Sensibility'* it now said *'Talk to Zadkiel'*. Ophelia touched the golden letters, to be honest that was very good advice, but Ophelia didn't want Nessa to think there was anything wrong with their marriage or lives, because there wasn't; it was Ophelia that was the problem.

Another minute passed, before there was a gentle knock on the bedroom door.

"Phee? Why have you shut yourself in there? Are you okay?"

"I'm fine!" lied Ophelia.

"Well, you don't sound fine! Can I come in?" said Nessa.

Ophelia didn't say anything.

"Right, well I *am* coming in, because I'm worried about you! Plus, this is my bedroom too..." Nessa said, opening the door.

Ophelia kept her head buried in the quilt, feeling almost ashamed of being so upset for no reason. Nessa came to sit on the bed, picking up the book, to move it out of the way.

"Hang on, 'talk to Zadkiel'? What's that all about?" she asked, staring at the title.

"God did it..." said Ophelia through tears.

"You spoke to God?" said Nessa.

"I tried to, but she didn't answer, she just wrote that."

Nessa sighed, placing the book down. "You asked God for help before you thought to come to me?" She sounded quite hurt, and Ophelia felt bad.

"I'm sorry. It's silly and I didn't want to bother you with it..." Ophelia said, quietly.

"Hey!" said Nessa, putting a hand on her shoulder. "That sounds like a *me* move; not talking about things? You made me promise to tell you stuff and ask you for help, so why aren't *you*? I'm your wife, that's what I'm here for! Among other things..."

"I know. Just because I give you advice, doesn't mean I follow it myself!" sighed Ophelia. "I don't know what's wrong with me!"

"Nothing's wrong with you darling. Tell me what's up? Is it about the demons?"

"Yes! Maybe. I don't know..." Ophelia said, looking up at Nessa for the first time. Nessa frowned at her tear-stained face and slid down to join her on the floor, wrapping her arms around her.

"I don't know why we are on the floor, but it's as good a place as any for a breakdown!" grinned Nessa, obviously trying to make Ophelia laugh. "Come on, I'm listening!"

"I'm scared. I didn't used to be, but I feel scared quite often now," explained Ophelia. "I get really anxious when I'm not with you, which probably makes me super annoying and clingy, and I'm sorry if so, but I'm just so scared if I'm alone! It's been like that for months. I used to be alone all the time, what's happened to me?"

Nessa stroked her hair lovingly. "Why haven't you told me?" she asked.

"Because I want everything to be perfect! Mostly it is, apart from whatever this is. I didn't want you to think that I'm not happy, because I promise I am! Our life should be perfect; you deserve perfection..." Ophelia lent on Nessa's chest and cried into her t-shirt.

"I don't need perfection," whispered Nessa. "I need *you*! I'm trying to be perfect for you too, but I don't think we can keep that up forever, it will get exhausting. Look, I don't care if you're perfect, and you don't care if I am, so let's agree to stop trying so hard to be. My life is perfect as long as I can spend it with you!" Nessa kissed the top of Ophelia's head. "You can't be happy all the time anyway. That would be weird and kinda unnerving! Just because you're not happy right now, doesn't mean you're not happy with your life."

"But I don't know what's wrong with me! What kind of person gets anxious by just being alone?"

Ophelia asked, desperately. "I know we don't talk about it, but that day... I wasn't this scared then because if I was, I wouldn't have been able to do it... Now we need to help Ezra and I don't think I can handle it!"

"It's okay darling!" said Nessa gently. She thought for a moment. "Maybe the problem is that we don't talk about it? That day was a lot! It sounds like it might have traumatised you a bit, which makes total sense!"

"But it wasn't until a few weeks later that I started to feel like this, and everything was fine then!" protested Ophelia.

"Yeah, that's the point. Once everything was okay, you could properly process what happened. We should have talked about it. I'm sorry..."

"I didn't *want* to talk about it. I wanted to pretend it had never happened! I thought I was going to lose you so many times that day, it was awful!"

"I know, but that's why we should have talked about it. Now, in the back of your mind you are scared we might lose each other, and so am I to be honest," sighed Nessa. "We'll be okay though. Like Ezzy said, we're super demon angel things!" She smiled.

"I wish I knew what we are..." Ophelia said quietly.

"We are us, and we'll be *us* for eternity, I promise!"

"But that's another thing, I wish I was okay with being 'nothing,' like you are, but it bothers me," Ophelia said.

"Why do you think that if you're not an angel or demon, then you're nothing? If anything you're both, double the identity if you need one! But even if you don't have an identity, you don't become nothing!

You're you! You can be whatever you want, isn't that amazing?" Nessa smiled, wiping Ophelia's tears.

Ophelia wasn't sure, but smiled anyway. She felt a lot better having told Nessa about her worries, as if she could release some of the anxiety with a deep breath, where before it had been trapped deep inside her.

"All this about a war or whatever just made it all so much worse!" Ophelia sighed. "It immediately brought that day to mind and I obviously try very hard not to think about it… I know we have to stop them, but what if something happens to us? What if I do lose you this time?"

"We'll be fine. As far as I know there are only two things that should be able to destroy us, and they've already tried those. We somehow survived being erased from existence, holy water can't kill us, oh and anything containing hellfire like that poison Lucifer had, but we are too demonic to be affected by that!"

"What if they think of something new?" insisted Ophelia.

"There is nothing new," said Nessa. "I promised you back at the beginning, that no harm would come to you with me, and I've dedicated my life to that promise. Whatever happens, I will always be by your side. I will never let you go."

Nessa kissed Ophelia before she could say anything else. She had always felt safe with Nessa around. She knew how strong and fiercely protective she was, and that always felt nice; to know someone like that was on her side no matter what. Even when they were officially on different sides, Ophelia would have trusted Nessa with her life in a heartbeat, no matter how evil she was pretending to be.

"Now, are you ready to come reason with some demons with me?" asked Nessa with a smile.

"Reason with them?" Ophelia said in surprise. "Does that work?"

"Err, depends on the situation, and the demon, but it's worth a try eh? We have the advantage because they don't know who or what we are, but if reasoning with them doesn't work, I'm sure we can take them down!"

Ophelia raised an eyebrow at the idea of 'taking down' demons.

"It's fine, I was Prince of Hell once, I can deal with disobedient demons!" Nessa smiled, standing and helping Ophelia up. "Come on my love, let's go help our little brother with pest control."

"What ever happened to 'happy half anniversary'?" sighed Ophelia.

"My darling, I promise I will make it up to you later..." grinned Nessa, giving Ophelia a very flirty look, before heading towards the door.

Ophelia bit her lip slightly, then followed Nessa out.

As they set off to the bakery, Ophelia felt much better. She was filled with a new confidence after admitting her strange feelings to Nessa. She felt somehow lighter and happier, despite what they were going to face. Nessa's promise to never leave her side echoed in her head. The anxiety only usually came when she was alone, but with Nessa holding her hand as they walked, she felt she could face anything. She had taken massive risks before, when she was far more vulnerable, Nessa was right; they were quite powerful now.

They could sense demonic energy before they even reached Ezra's shop, and sure enough, standing outside were a group of seven demons, including Beelzebub who was obviously leading some sort of meeting about what to do next. Ophelia wondered what they were doing outside Ezra's shop at all. If they wanted a war with Heaven, what was this all about?

Nessa stopped in horror when she noticed Beelzebub.

"Look who it is..." she whispered.

"Yeah, The Devil's right-hand demon. Do you think you could take *her* down?" said Ophelia.

Nessa hesitated. "She's my friend... I don't want to have to hurt her."

"She *was* your friend. I'm sure she wouldn't think twice about trying to destroy you now!" said Ophelia. "Even when you were friends, she was purposefully hurting your arms when she had hold of you in Hell, so she's not the gentlest of people."

"That was for Lucifer's benefit. She had to pick his side over mine, or he'd have gone mental. I would have done the same," Nessa said.

"Well I have a feeling she won't pick a stranger's side over Hell," Ophelia said simply. She wasn't trying to be harsh, but didn't want Nessa's former friendship with Beelzebub to blind her to what was happening; right now Beelzebub was a threat, history or not.

"I know..." sighed Nessa.

Some humans walked past the demons and Nessa

frowned slightly.

"If there does end up being some sort of fight, or anything suspicious really, the humans are going to notice..."

"Hmm..." Ophelia thought for a moment. "What if we create some sort of invisibility barrier or forcefield, so that the humans don't see or hear anything that goes on?"

"Wow, that sounds like big magic..." said Nessa uncertainly.

"Says the angel who created the whole universe!" laughed Ophelia. "Anyway, it's not that big if we do it together."

"Together?" Nessa said, surprised.

"Yeah, I bet together we are very powerful!" Ophelia said, taking Nessa's hand. "Come on!"

They had never done magic together before, but as soon as they focused on creating the barrier, power flowed through their connected hands, filling Ophelia with what felt like a warm ball of energy, both demonic and angelic. Nessa squeezed her hand slightly, she could obviously feel their power too, it felt amazing.

After a moment they released each other's hands. They had done it. No matter what happened, the humans would be none the wiser.

"Phee?" whispered Nessa in wonder. "We are so fucking powerful!"

Ophelia laughed. "We are!"

"Why have we never done magic together before? Those bloody demons should be terrified of us!" Nessa grinned, before setting off towards Ezra's shop.

"Wait, Nessa! Shouldn't we have some kind of plan first?" Ophelia hissed, quickly following her, but she wasn't listening.

"Hey!" yelled Nessa as she approached the demons. "What do you guys think you're doing here?"

Ophelia cringed in concern as the demons turned to look at her, obviously wondering who had the audacity to speak to them like that. Ophelia caught up to her and the demons stared at her too, making her feel uncomfortable.

"I assume this is your operation, Beelzebub?" Nessa asked.

Some of the other demons looked at each other in confusion, probably wondering how this stranger knew their leader's name.

"No, of course not," said Beelzebub, looking Nessa up and down. "I'm Prince of Hell, but it's never *my* operation. We get our instructions from Lucifer and Jophiel... I'm just the smiling face of Hell!" she added sarcastically.

So Jophiel had managed to get some authority in Hell had she? Ophelia and Nessa weren't sure what was going on in Hell, but they got all the Heavenly gossip from Ezra. Not long after they spoke to God, Ezra had excitedly told them that Jophiel had been cast out by her. Now Gabriel was supposedly in charge, but Ezra said he wasn't handling it very well. While Heaven had no real leader, it sounded like Hell had two!

"What are you anyway?" Aaked Beelzebub after a moment.

"I'm Nessa!"

"No, I mean *what* are you?" Beelzebub snapped sharply. "You have both demonic and angelic energy, how is that possible?"

"I am something you lot will never understand," Nessa said triumphantly. "I was once described as an anomaly. That's not a bad description, I suppose... Now what are you doing on Earth? I thought you wanted to fight Heaven."

The demons looked shocked and rather concerned that Nessa knew about the planned war, apart from Beelzebub, who just gave her an odd look.

"It's none of your business, you strange half demon!" said Beelzebub irritably. "Why don't you two run along home and leave us alone?"

"It is our business if you are threatening our brother!" Ophelia joined in. She didn't know Beelzebub very well, but she had seen her on occasion. She was a far more aggressive demon than Nessa ever was, but she seemed to be oddly calm right now to be speaking to strange people she didn't know.

Beelzebub looked at Ophelia for a moment before responding.

"We are not planning to kill him," she said eventually.

"But what do you want with him?" Ophelia asked.

Beelzebub sighed. "Jophiel said that he is the angel who knows the most about Heaven. He looked after the files and records; he knows all their strengths and weaknesses. She thinks he will be useful. Plus Heaven hates a scandal, so if we hold an angel hostage, they'll probably do whatever we want? I dunno, it's not my idea, I couldn't give a fuck about any stupid war, but what can ya do? Their Majesties have made their minds up." She gave them a strange half smile.

Ophelia thought Beelzebub seemed quite sad, as if the duties of Hell bothered her, too.

"Why are you telling us all this?" Nessa asked suspiciously. "Not that I'm complaining, but we are just random demon-angels that have turned up out of nowhere. I know you don't know me, but I know enough about you to know you are highly suspicious of *everyone*, and never this nice to strangers!"

Ophelia shot her a warning look, hinting at their history might not be the best idea right now...

Beelzebub sighed. "You don't know me! Even somebody who knew me a few months ago wouldn't know me now! I've gone from one psycho boss to two! I'm sick of this shit. They argue *all* the time, and *I'm* supposed to sort it out, like I don't already have enough to do! I don't care what you know, you won't be able to stop the war anyway."

Nessa looked at her former friend in concern. "Bee, are you okay?" she asked genuinely.

Beelzebub lifted her chin so she could look down at Nessa disapprovingly.

"That's a bit informal... And in answer, of course not! I'm never okay!" She glanced at the other demons, and her face seemed to change; become evil, she turned back to Ophelia and Nessa. "Since you're here, you can help us get hold of your precious angel. We can't get to him as long as he's in there, but if he comes out, we can."

Ophelia glanced at the shop, Ezra was nervously

watching from the window. He wasn't stupid; he knew he was safe in there. He waved when he noticed Ophelia looking at him. She smiled and waved back.

"You're not going to take him!" Nessa said, her concern for Beelzebub quickly replaced by anger.

"We will," Beelzebub said simply. "You know, err, Nessa was it? We actually have you to thank for finding him in the first place. Angel dwellings are protected by Heavenly power, hence why we can't enter without permission, but it also makes them very hard to find. Until I followed your demonic energy here earlier. So thanks for that, makes my job a bit easier!"

Nessa glared at Beelzebub. Ophelia wasn't sure that reasoning with them was going to work. Nessa was ready to start a proper argument, and while Ophelia really wanted to stop her, she noticed Ezra surreptitiously beckoning her into the shop.

"One second," she whispered to Nessa, then slipped away, leaving her wife to argue with the demons.

She entered the bakery and Ezra threw his arms around her.

"Thank you for coming!" he said.

"Of course!" said Ophelia, sheepishly remembering having a panic attack and really *not* wanting to come.

"I have to tell you something, but whatever you do don't tell the demons!" Ezra whispered, glancing outside worriedly.

"What's wrong?" Ophelia asked.

"Gabriel has quit! I just got a message. He can't run Heaven properly, so he's giving up! Jophiel was so good at being a bad leader that no one knows how things *should* be done! Gabriel couldn't handle it, but now there's no one in charge! I don't know what happens now, because God needs to appoint a new leader and I don't think she knows yet, and she certainly won't be able to, before this war starts! The demons will be able to just walk right in!"

"Hey hey, it's okay!" said Ophelia reassuringly. "We are going to stop them, I'm not sure how, but we will."

"I know. I believe in you!" Ezra said, looking at Ophelia with huge admiration.

Ophelia smiled. It was nice to have someone who always thought she and Nessa were amazing, without them even doing anything. She looked out at Nessa, now face to face with one of the demons.

"You know what, Little Brother? I believe in us too!" she smiled, ruffling Ezra's hair.

She warned Ezra to stay in the shop, then rejoined Nessa outside.

"Everything alright?" Nessa asked as if she wasn't in the middle of arguing with a bunch of demons.

"Yeah, we're fine darling, how are you?" Ophelia smiled.

"I'd be better if this lot cleared off!" Nessa said, glaring at the demons. "You can't get into Ezra's shop, and he's not stupid enough to come out, so go home!"

"He might not be, but I know for a fact people do stupid things for the people they love, no matter how intelligent they are!" Beelzebub smiled.

She signalled to the demons and they advanced towards Ophelia and Nessa, some of them suddenly producing small dagger-like weapons.

"Hey, you can't use weapons! That's not fair..." Nessa sighed.

"They won't hurt you, unless they have to," said Beelzebub, as if that was particularly comforting.

Three demons grabbed hold of Nessa, while the others headed in Ophelia's direction, brandishing their weapons. Nessa struggled against the demons and the armed ones got closer to Ophelia, oddly slowly she thought.

"Are you an angel?" asked one demon.

"Err, no..." said Ophelia.

"A demon then?"

"No, I'm both!" Ophelia said, actually feeling proud of her confusing identity for once.

"You can't be both, that's impossible!" growled the demon.

"Yes, but we are unique!" Ophelia said proudly.

Suddenly, as the demons got uncomfortably close, Ezra came running out of the shop to Ophelia's side.

"Ophelia!" he yelled, clinging to her like some sort of koala.

"I told you to stay inside! They're after you," said Ophelia. She looked at the three demons standing within arms reach of her, weapons in their hands, and wondered why they weren't trying to do anything. She put a protective arm around Ezra.

"What are you trying to do, stare us to death?" she said, feeling quite confident, for someone facing Hell's equivalent of a hit squad.

"They are too scared to do anything!" Nessa called. "They can tell how powerful we are!"

"That's not true! I don't know who you think you are, but we're not scared of you!" said one of the demons holding Nessa.

"You should be though!" grinned Nessa.

"Enough! I'm fed up of this, I want to go home. Take the angel!" yelled Beelzebub.

In a moment Ophelia's arm felt burning hot on Ezra's shoulders, so much so that it forced her to let go. One of the demons laughed and grabbed the panicked Ezra, dragging him towards Beelzebub, before Ophelia could do anything.

"Nessa!" she cried helplessly, knowing that Nessa was in a worse position to try to help, but feeling desperate. Nessa suddenly broke free from the demons, pushing one to the ground and rushed to Ophelia's side.

"I don't want to hurt them, but we need to scare them off somehow! Force them to let Ezzy go!" Nessa said quickly. "Any ideas?"

"No," said Ophelia, looking at the demons standing beside Beelzebub, two holding on to Ezra, but none making a move to leave. "Don't you think they're acting odd?" Ophelia continued. "Like, why aren't they leaving? They're just standing there."

"They'll be waiting for Bee's command," said Nessa.

"Then why isn't she giving it?"

"I don't know Phee, but I'm not complaining!" Nessa said, looking over at Ezra. "Oh! I know what will scare them off!" she said excitedly. "Ezzy once pointed out that with magic we can be whatever we want; we can transform into anything! I can scare them off, I'll be something cooler than a mouse this time!"

"What on Earth are you talking about?" asked Ophelia in concern.

"What's the scariest thing you can think of?" Nessa urged.

"Err, probably a dragon? They're pretty terrifying?" Ophelia answered nervously.

"Brilliant!" Nessa said with an air of determination.

"The thing is, dragons don't exist..." Ophelia said.

"They do today!" grinned Nessa, an almost manic look in her eyes.

In a moment, to Ophelia's horror, Nessa transformed into a giant grey dragon, causing all the demons to gasp in terror. Sometimes she could be completely crazy!

Chapter Twenty One
You're Not Nessa...

"Oh... Holy shit..." Said Ophelia, stepping away from her terrifying dragon wife.

Dragon Nessa turned to look at her, probably because she swore. Everything in Ophelia wanted to be terrified. She had just named dragons as the scariest thing she could think of, and there was one before her, she had never seen anything so frightening. Yet it was still her wife, somehow! She could feel it was Nessa, but she must have still looked a little scared, because the angry dragon face softened and Nessa bowed her head down to Ophelia's level. Ophelia took in a frightened breath.

"I just told you that dragons are the scariest thing I could think of..." she whispered.

"But I won't hurt you," Nessa said kindly. "No matter what I look like, there is no one you would be safer with."

"I know..." Ophelia breathed. She nervously reached forward and touched the dragon's face, feeling her warm breath on her skin. She felt a little calmer, but still wasn't a fan of the situation. "Hurry up then, I want my wife back!" she said.

Nessa the dragon stood up tall again and faced the demons.

"Fucking hell!" said Beelzebub, her eyes wide. "Not gonna lie, was not expecting that..."

"Let Ezra go!" Ophelia yelled, hoping the image of a terrifying dragon was enough to make them run home.

"No!" shouted one of the demons that had hold of him, but his voice sounded uncertain. Nessa *was* scaring them.

"Nessa!" Ezra yelled. "Dragons breathe fire!"

"Thanks Ezzy!" said Nessa, before doing just that, causing all the demons to scream as she set fire to the ground around them. In the chaos, Ezra managed to escape and ran to Ophelia.

"Get inside!" she said. "Go up into your flat and *hide*. Don't come out no matter what!"

Ezra nodded and disappeared into the bakery.

Ophelia looked back at the burning scene before her. Nessa was advancing towards the demons slowly, causing them to back up.

"Come on Nessa, don't be a dick!" yelled Beelzebub, sounding a little uncomfortable.

"Go away!" the dragon roared, but that time it didn't sound like Nessa, it sounded terrifying. Ophelia gulped.

"If I send this lot back without the angel, Lucifer and Jophiel will go mental!" Beelzebub said, actually sounding quite frightened, Ophelia thought. "They threaten me with this pool of holy water they have all the time, they might do it, I know they are mad enough to… They might destroy me…" Beelzebub really looked close to tears now, and Nessa turned to glance at Ophelia for a moment; they absolutely *could* use the pool of holy water, they had done it before! Ophelia suddenly felt very sorry for Beelzebub, she must be softer than most demons if she was Nessa's friend, and Ophelia had heard so many awful stories about Hell and the kinds of things Lucifer did, and she could imagine that demon Jophiel was just as bad.

"Sorry Bee, we can't let you take Ezra!" Nessa said, turning back to the demons and taking another step forward.

"And I can't call them off…" said Beelzebub. "Caspian, block Nessa's magic!"

"You can't do that!" Ophelia yelled.

"Oh we can. This magic blocking powder is Jophiel's new invention," Beelzebub explained, as a nervous demon stepped forward and threw a little cloth bag in Nessa's direction. As soon as it made contact, the bag broke open and black powder spilled out onto Nessa. Instantly, she was right back to normal. It was strange to see that giant, magnificently terrifying dragon melt down to become Ophelia's smaller, magnificently beautiful wife. Nessa looked down at her hands in confusion.

"It's only temporary," said Beelzebub. "But now you have no defences!" She turned to the demons. "Seize her, and the other one if you can."

All six of them gathered around Nessa. Beelzebub was right, without magic she couldn't do anything about it! In a moment of mad protective impulse, Ophelia ran towards the demons.

"Don't touch her!" she yelled.

"No, Phee, keep away!" Nessa shouted, trying to push the demons off.

Ophelia didn't listen, she tried desperately to pull the demons off Nessa. Then she realised, Nessa didn't have magic, but *she* did! She was about to use magic to get the demons away from them, when she suddenly gasped in horrific pain. It was not unlike the feeling of getting shot that time. She looked down and her white dress was quickly turning red as blood covered it, the dagger one of the demons was holding dripped with blood too.

"Nessa?" Ophelia said in a small voice.

In a moment Nessa rushed to her side and the demons seemed to move off.

"Nox, what the fuck did you do? I never told you to stab anybody!" yelled Beelzebub, sounding genuinely furious.

"We are demons, we're supposed to be evil!" retorted the demon that had stabbed Ophelia. "You're too nice!"

As Nessa helped Ophelia to the ground, Ophelia was sure that Beelzebub was looking over at them with a genuine look of concern and regret.

"Hey, Phee! Look at me," said Nessa. "I don't have magic right now, but try to heal yourself!"

"I can't..." Ophelia said through the pain. "It's too much..."

"Then I'll get Ezra!" said Nessa quickly, starting to

move. Ophelia grabbed her.

"No!" she said. "There won't be time, or they will get him. Please stay! You promised you'd stay by my side…"

Nessa gulped back tears and took Ophelia's hand. Ophelia noted that none of the demons had tried to come anywhere near them, despite the fact they were easy targets right now. She glanced over and none of them were moving at all, as if they were rooted to the spot. Ophelia wondered whether Beelzebub was helping them for some reason, holding them off? Maybe she felt guilty? Ophelia couldn't mention it to Nessa though, she didn't feel up to it.

"I'm both, do you think I'll be sent to Heaven or Hell when I die?" Ophelia said, gasping with the pain.

"You're not going anywhere, I won't let you die!" said Nessa determinedly.

"I hope God lets me come back to you, she likes us…" Ophelia said, ignoring Nessa's desperation, as death seemed imminent.

"Stop! She won't have to! I don't know what would happen to an angel-demon, but we're *not* going to find out!"

"There's nothing you can do…" Ophelia gasped, feeling weaker. "Just sit with me… Whatever happens I will try to get back to you, I promise. I'm glad you're with me for more than the last moment this time…"

"No! I *must* be able to think of something…" Nessa said; desperation strangling her voice. She was so absorbed in trying to save her, when all Ophelia wanted right then was her comfort.

"Nessa, please—"

"Possess me!" Nessa interrupted, her eyes shining with some mad new idea.

"What on earth are you talking about?" said Ophelia.

"Neither of us are angels, our energy is on the same frequency now! You can possess me! The demon in you can!" Nessa said as if she was making an ounce of sense.

"Why would I... possess you?" asked Ophelia, really struggling to speak now.

"Oh shit, there's not much time to explain. I know it sounds mental, but basically if you are inside my body you can't die, you'll be safe until my magic comes back and I can heal you! You once asked me to take information from you to save *my* life, you asked if I trusted you. So do you trust me now?"

"I trust you..." Ophelia whispered weakly. "You're insane, but I trust you."

"Great! Take my hand, and focus on trying to take over my body. I know you're hurt, but you have to concentrate. This will work, I promise!"

Ophelia took Nessa's hand and tried to focus, attempting to block out the terrible pain. In a moment something felt very strange and the pain was gone. For a second Ophelia wondered if she had been transported somewhere upon the death of her body, but the demons were still there, staring in interest. Ophelia looked down at her hands, but to her shock, they were Nessa's hands! Nessa's mad idea must have worked. This was by far the most demonic thing Ophelia had ever done. Suddenly though, she felt full of panic, she knew nothing about possession, what happens to Nessa now?

"Hello darling." Nessa's voice sounded as if it was coming from Ophelia's own mind. "Why are you scared? It worked!"

"Nessa! Are you okay?" Ophelia asked in fear.

"I'm fine. I've never felt your energy this strongly before. It feels lovely…"

"What is this? Where has my body gone?" Ophelia asked in concern, glancing down to where she had been laying, seeing nothing but a little blood on the floor.

"If I'm honest, I'm not sure…" Nessa answered uncertainly. "I think it's kind of inside me? I don't know, it's weird and it doesn't make sense. All I know is a demon's body disappears when they possess someone because they are entering their body. That's why I knew it would keep you alive. While you possess me you don't really have a body, so it can't die, but as soon as you leave my body, yours will return… It's a demon thing, I dunno? I've never really thought about the logistics. All I know is, you're safe here with me."

"Nessa, possession is horrible! It's the worst thing a demon can do!" Ophelia said sadly. "I'm really not an angel anymore…"

"It's not horrible if it was my idea," came Nessa's voice. "The demon that possesses you isn't usually your wife; the person you adore more than anything! Other than your anxiety, which I can feel, I'm actually really calm. You are relaxing, Phee."

"Of course I'm anxious! This is freaking me out!" said Ophelia.

"Well, relax!" She heard Nessa say. "Everything's

okay. You're not in pain anymore, I'm keeping you safe."

Ophelia looked at the demons, watching in interest. She was aware they could hear her half of the conversation. She could hear Nessa's voice in her head, maybe it would work the other way around too?

"Can you hear me like this?" she thought.

"Yes," came the answer. "Now, I have never properly possessed anyone; like you said, it's usually evil and I've never had the need to. However, I do know that you can use your magic through my body; you know, my magic isn't working, your body isn't working, so together we make a fully functioning being!" Nessa laughed.

Ophelia tuned into Nessa's feelings for a moment; she was telling the truth, she wasn't scared at all. She felt oddly happy and relaxed.

"Told you I wasn't scared," Nessa said, surprising Ophelia greatly. "I can feel everything you're doing," she added, obviously realising that Ophelia was shocked.

"This is weird..." thought Ophelia. "I don't want to possess you..."

"Well it's keeping you alive, so you're bloody doing it!" Nessa answered. "Look, I should have thought of this earlier, but you can use magic to send the demons back to Hell! I used to do it a lot back in the day, when I was a Prince, 'cause sometimes they don't do as they're told."

"Okay..." Ophelia answered, looking down at Nessa's hands and feeling her power start to flow through them.

"Listen, Phee, I'm going to let you fully take control," Nessa said. "You'll need to for big magic like that, I'll just get in the way."

"What do you mean, you hate not being in control?" Ophelia answered worriedly.

"I do, but I trust you. I would happily relinquish control for you my darling. I love you, you've got this. I fully submit to you, my precious demon. You're in charge now…"

Suddenly Ophelia couldn't feel Nessa as strongly, as if her energy had faded backwards, to the depths of Ophelia's mind. It didn't really feel like she was in Nessa's body anymore, almost as if it had become hers. She didn't like it, she wanted Nessa back, but she knew she had a job to do first.

She looked at the demons, still in the same spot.

"Beelzebub, are you holding them back?" she asked suspiciously.

Beelzebub looked uncomfortable, and not because Ophelia's voice was coming from Nessa's mouth.

"Don't you *dare* tell Lucifer and Jophiel that I'm helping you!" she said after a moment. "And that includes you lot, or I swear I'll torture you for eternity so hard you'll wish I'd just killed you instead!" she said to the demons, shooting them an extremely nasty look, before looking back at Ophelia. "I'm sorry, I honestly told them not to hurt you…"

"It's okay," said Ophelia. "If *I* send them home, then you can't be blamed for going back empty-handed right?"

"I don't know. I hope not," sighed Beelzebub.

Ophelia felt so bad for her. She had hated having to go along with whatever Jophiel wanted, now Beelzebub had her *and* Lucifer to deal with.

In a moment Ophelia used pure demonic magic for the first time and banished the six demons back to Hell, leaving Beelzebub looking very confused.

Ophelia smiled at her. "I'm not sending you to face them," she said. "You don't deserve it, and believe it or not I think I trust you."

"Oh, thank you..." Beelzebub said. "You are truly kind Ophelia..."

"Nessa?" Ophelia said worriedly. "Are you still here?"

Suddenly Nessa's energy flooded back into Ophelia. "I'm here, I won't leave you," she heard Nessa say, and she breathed a sigh of relief. "Well, I can't leave, this is my body!" Nessa laughed. "I'm proud of you darling. Not just because you banished the demons, but mainly because of your beautiful unwavering kindness. There's nobody I'd rather be possessed by! It was a lot more fun than I imagined being fully possessed would be, to be honest!" Ophelia knew if she could see Nessa, she would be giving her one of her cheeky smiles, and suddenly she missed her, even though she quite literally couldn't physically get any closer to her.

"We have to fix this. We can't stay like this! I want to be with you, I don't want to *be* you!" Ophelia sighed.

"Valid," Nessa said, somehow sounding like she should be grinning. "Most of the time I haven't even wanted to be me! Though to be fair, you'd probably do a much better job of running my life than I do!"

"Hey, I think you're so amazing that I want to be beside you, I want to see you! It's awful, I feel like you're here, but you're not..." Ophelia said.

"But I don't have my magic back yet," Nessa answered.

Suddenly Ophelia felt like she was being pushed out of the way, like Nessa was rushing to the front of their minds.

"Beelzebub! How long does that magic blocker last?" Nessa asked out loud. "I need to heal Ophelia!"

"Oh, hello!" said Beelzebub, obviously surprised to hear Nessa's voice where it had been Ophelia's. "I'm not sure... I'm sorry, it was just to stop you being a dragon because to be fair, you were being quite unreasonable! It shouldn't last long though..."

"It's not your fault," said Nessa.

"Are you both okay?" asked Beelzebub. "I really didn't want to hurt you..."

"We are both fine," smiled Nessa. "And as soon as my magic comes back, I'll save her. Thank you for being nice Beelzebub, you didn't have to be."

"Don't mention it," said Beelzebub dismissively.

"We should tell Ezra it's safe," Ophelia thought. "My injury is pretty bad, we might need his help, if you can heal me at all."

"Don't say that! Of course we'll save you!" insisted Nessa. "Lead the way then, but I think this will freak him out a bit!"

Nessa seemed to move back again and Ophelia was more in control. She went into the bakery and shouted Ezra downstairs. He cautiously appeared on the stairs and stared in concern.

"You're not Nessa..." he said, very slowly

approaching. "You're Ophelia... Or are you Nessa? You sort of feel like both! Where's Ophelia?"

Ophelia explained the odd situation the best she could, with the occasional interjection from Nessa, and Nessa was right, Ezra was highly unnerved by the whole thing.

"I'm not used to demonic things..." he said when Ophelia asked him if he was alright. "I can't imagine how that works, but I want you to be separate again..."

"Believe me, so do I!" sighed Ophelia.

"Phee!" said Nessa suddenly, startling Ophelia by taking over. "My magic's back, can you feel it?"

"Yes," smiled Ophelia, realising there was now twice as much power.

"We can heal you now, will you help Ezzy?" Nessa said. Ezra nodded determinedly.

"Hang on!" said Ophelia. "Nessa, the wound is so bad, I don't know if you can save me in time. I'm scared..."

Before Nessa could respond there was a knock on the open door, they turned to see Beelzebub standing on the other side of the threshold.

"Hey? Former angel healer here..." she said softly. "Can I help? Ophelia was close to death, she will need all of us. The three of us; demon, angel, and weird mix of both; together we can save her no matter how damaged her body is." She paused. "But you'll have to let me in?"

Ezra looked uncomfortable at the idea of allowing a demon in.

"I trust her!" said Ophelia. "Let her in..."

"Okay... Come in..." said Ezra uncertainly.

"Thanks!" said Beelzebub, entering the shop. "Come on then. It'll work if we are all ready. Don't worry Ophelia, you'll be okay. I feel like this is kind of my fault, so I won't let you die."

"Thank you," said Ophelia. "Nessa, what do I do now?"

"Just imagine leaving my body and you will," Nessa answered.

"Ezra! Get here! We have to be quick!" said Beelzebub rather harshly.

"Okay... I'm coming!" said Ezra, sounding annoyed to be snapped at, rather than scared of her, as he had been.

Once everyone was ready Ophelia did as Nessa said, and in a moment she was on the floor beside her. She was pleased to see Nessa again, but she was rather distracted by the return of the horrific pain. She could hardly breathe and had to close her eyes, but in a moment she felt a flood of warm energy through her body. After a few seconds the pain eased and she felt strong enough to open her eyes. Ophelia smiled at seeing three people working hard to save her, their faces full of concentration. All three of them cared about her enough to help her; even Beelzebub, and that felt nice.

Soon Ophelia felt completely healed and Beelzebub and Ezra moved away slightly, Nessa leant closer to her.

"Are you okay?" she asked desperately.

"I am, thank you," smiled Ophelia. "I love you!"

"I love you too, my angel!" said Nessa, wrapping her arms around her. "How many times do I have to almost lose you?"

"Ideally no more!" said Ophelia with a laugh. "It's nice to see you again and be in your arms."

Nessa kissed her on the top of the head. "Ten out of ten possession, would recommend! The invasive demon was *very* nice!" she grinned.

Ezra hugged both his sisters happily. "I'm glad you're okay!" he said.

"Thank you Little Brother," smiled Ophelia. "And you Beelzebub! Truly, thank you!"

"Truly, don't mention it!" Beelzebub smiled. "I'm already going to get in massive trouble, and right now you're the enemy to the bosses, even though they don't know you." She stopped for a moment. "Oh shit, that was treason wasn't it? I helped save an angel! Well, part angel... *And* I blatantly sabotaged the mission. They *will* throw me into holy water! I'll be destroyed for this..."

"No!" said Nessa firmly. "By helping us, you joined our side, and we will always protect people on our side! We won't let you get destroyed." She took Beelzebub's hand, making her flinch in surprise. Ophelia took the other, giving it a little caring squeeze.

"You want me on your side?" said Beelzebub, slightly suspicious.

"Of course!" Nessa said. "Anyway, you're quite dangerous, I'd far rather have you with me rather than against me!"

Beelzebub smiled, but it quickly turned to a frown. "Did you feel that energy shift, demons?" she asked.

Ophelia had felt something. "What was it?" she asked.

"It's them!" said Nessa in horror.

"Yep, dickheads on tour!" sighed Beelzebub.

"*Them*? As in Jophiel and Lucifer?" Ophelia said worriedly.

"Uh huh," said Nessa.

"They can't come in!" said Ezra. "We are safe in here!"

"Yeah, but that logic relies on us hiding here in your weird pink shop forever, tormented by the overpowering smell of sugar!" said Beelzebub.

"I think it smells nice..." Ezra said defensively.

"That's because you're a sappy little angel!" laughed Beelzebub.

"Anyway!" said Ophelia, before any kind of argument broke out. "What do we do?"

"They shouldn't be in charge!" said Beelzebub. "Hell has been in shambles since Jophiel arrived, more so than usual! They can't agree on anything and they both think they run the place. Jophiel is angry that she was cast out and Lucifer found out how close Heaven got to destroying Hell, so they are both out for revenge!"

"We can't let them get to Heaven; no one's in charge!" Ophelia said.

"What?" Nessa asked in horror.

"Yeah, Gabriel quit earlier!" said Ezra. "Don't tell Lucifer or Jophiel!" he said, looking at Beelzebub as he spoke.

"Hey Kid, don't look at me, I couldn't give a fuck who's running Heaven, or *not* running it!" said Beelzebub. "I'm just a work-weary demon who has been driven to revolutionary views by my insane bosses! I'm certainly on your side here... I say take them both down!"

"Phee, we have to face them," said Nessa. "We've done it before, but now we have the advantage that they don't know our history!"

"Yeah, but there are two of them now!" said Ophelia.

"And there are two of us!" Nessa said with a look of determination. "We're way more powerful than them, they're only demons! No offence Bee..."

"None taken, freak!" smiled Beelzebub.

Nessa smiled fondly at her, before turning back to Ophelia. "Are you up for facing a couple more demons my darling? Just let's make sure to keep our distance this time..."

"They won't have weapons," said Beelzebub. "They're so obnoxious they think they don't need them!"

Nessa rolled her eyes. "Of course they are! Ooh, hang on! A demon can extract another demon's power! I remember seeing Lucifer do it once! Only God can take angelic magic, but for some reason demons can take each other's. We could take their powers off them!"

"But when Lucifer does that, he stores the power in case he wants to use it for whatever. What are you going to do with their power if you take it?" asked Beelzebub. "I'm very much in favour of this plan, I'm just asking."

"I know!" Ophelia said, realising something. "Angelic power can neutralise demonic power! If we work together we should be powerful enough to destroy their magic completely!"

"Brilliant idea!" said Nessa, giving Ophelia a quick

kiss. "My wife is so amazing! I'm so lucky!"

"Aww, so is mine!" smiled Ophelia.

"Right, okay. Go take the demons down before you make me vomit!" said Beelzebub, gently shoving them encouragingly.

"You two need to stay in here where you'll be safe!" said Ophelia.

"Okay... As long as this isn't a trick and Beelzebub is going to kidnap me again!" said Ezra accusingly.

"Nah, don't worry Kid. I'm too busy playing 'which one is going to make me sick first', their lovey dovey nonsense, or this gross sugar smell!" Beelzebub said.

Nessa laughed as they stood up. "We'll be quick. Stay, and don't argue!"

"I'm more concerned about getting diabetes by osmosis if you take too long!" smiled Beelzebub.

Ophelia and Nessa stepped out of Ezra's shop that oozed with angelic energy, and were hit by a wall of demonic energy instead. Ophelia wasn't really scared of Lucifer or Jophiel, but she was very aware that the last time she had seen either of them they had both tried to destroy her. Nessa took her hand.

"Are you okay?" she asked.

"Yes I'm fine thanks, you three are an unlikely, but brilliant healing team!" smiled Ophelia. She looked down at her dress and noticed it was still covered in blood. She quickly cleaned it with magic.

"No I don't mean physically, I mean emotionally."

"What?" For some reason Ophelia felt a little caught off guard by the question.

"Come on, is it so strange that I'd ask you how you are, given the circumstances and how upset you were earlier, not to mention the fact that you just almost died!" Nessa stared at her with a serious yet kind look on her face.

"I actually feel surprisingly okay right now," said Ophelia. "Except I want us to hurry up and sort out this nonsense so that we can enjoy the half anniversary you promised me!"

"Good! I'll make up for all this with the best half anniversary ever!" smiled Nessa. "I'm not entirely sure what we'll do yet, but I'll think of something when I'm not distracted by demons. Come on my love, let's sort out our psycho former bosses!"

They followed the demonic energy round the corner and discovered Lucifer and Jophiel standing down an alleyway, mid-argument.

"I'm literally The Devil, you should listen to me!" Lucifer was saying. "You seem to think your ideas are better than mine, but they're all shit!"

"I didn't transport us to this dark dirty little street!" said Jophiel. "Lucifer dear, I've lived in Heaven for thousands of years. I have standards!"

"Fuck off with your *standards*! You're a demon too, Miss High and Mighty!" Lucifer retorted.

"Yes, but the difference is, I have been a demon for six months, not six thousand years! Anyway, shut up, someone's here!" Jophiel walked towards Ophelia and Nessa. Nessa gripped Ophelia's hand tighter. Lucifer followed Jophiel and they both stood before them. Lucifer looked the same as usual, but it was odd to see Jophiel dressed in black. She had maintained her elegance, despite her new demonic identity, and looked as confident as ever.

"Who are you? Are you demons or angels?" Jophiel asked.

"And are you the meddling idiots who sent the demons back without completing their task?" Lucifer butted in.

"Ah! No! I've got it, thank you Lucifer! I didn't need you to join in!" said Jophiel irritably, putting up a hand as if to silence him, before turning back to Ophelia and Nessa. "Yes, what he said. Also, where is Prince Beelzebub? She did not return with the others…"

"Oh dear, that was rather a lot of questions!" said Ophelia, loving being brave enough to speak to Jophiel however she wanted, after all those years. "I am feeling generous so I will endeavour to answer them for you." She was talking to Jophiel the way she had always spoken to her, it almost felt like some kind of revenge. Nessa looked impressed at Ophelia's confidence and squeezed her hand slightly, making Ophelia smile.

"Do not speak to me in that patronising way!" said Jophiel; instantly angry, rather than staying calm as she always used to. "I am the Queen of Hell, you should respect me!"

"Yes, well unfortunately I don't!" said Ophelia, raising her eyebrows.

"Hang on, Queen of Hell?" said Nessa. "Does that mean you two are *together*, like a couple?"

"Ooh no no no!" said Lucifer quickly. "We work together, but fuck no, no no no. I would never, no!"

"Alright!" said Jophiel, elbowing him in the ribs. "You don't have to sound quite so horrified by the idea! I was the Archangel of Beauty I'll have you know!"

"Yes Jophiel, you are very beautiful, but regardless of your face, *If* I had a type like humans do, it wouldn't be you! No offence honey..." said Lucifer, folding his arms.

"Well I think you are the most annoying person I have ever met!" said Jophiel. "Anyway, you! The one in the dress, answer my questions then!"

"A please wouldn't go amiss!" smiled Ophelia, enjoying this perhaps a little too much. "Who are we? I'm Ophelia, this is my wife Nessa! What are we? We are both demons and angels at the same time, which you probably think is impossible, but we're here to prove that wrong! Yes, we sent the demons away, and we have no idea where Beelzebub is. We don't really know her. Does that answer all your questions?"

"That was so hot..." whispered Nessa. Lucifer obviously heard, as he shot Nessa a disgusted look. That made Ophelia smile even more.

"I don't appreciate the tone," said Jophiel, glaring at Ophelia. "If you are even part demon then that makes me your Queen, you should treat me with respect!"

"As if!" Ophelia said. "You are not my Queen, I don't work for Hell or Heaven. We are just here to stop you harassing Ezra. We work for no one!" After months of struggling with her lack of identity, Ophelia felt very proud to explain that she was both angel and demon, but worked for neither realm. She was enjoying confusing people with it, after all it had confused her enough!

"I've had enough of this!" said Lucifer suddenly. "Move darlings, we're off to take an angel hostage and start a big old war!" He strode past Ophelia and Nessa, almost pushing them out of the way. Jophiel sighed and hurried after him.

"What's the point in starting a war?" shouted Nessa as they followed.

"To win it!" announced Lucifer. "To get revenge on those soppy, no good angels!"

"We could take over Heaven!" Jophiel added. "I could retake my place and it could become an extension of Hell! Imagine, no Heaven at all, nothing but eternal torment..."

"I really don't think God's going to like that," said Ophelia, as they caught up to them outside Ezra's shop.

Jophiel turned to her. "Like I give a damn what God thinks! She threw me into Hell!"

"Yes, and we know why!" said Ophelia. "Totally valid, don't you think Nessa?"

"Oh yes. Too merciful if anything!" Nessa grinned.

"Shut up. No one cares about any of you or what you're saying!" said Lucifer, waving his hand dismissively. He looked at the bakery sign. "Treats from Heaven? Not very subtle is he?" Lucifer banged aggressively on the window, but Ezra and Beelezbub must have been in the back room. "Little pig? Let me come in, or whatever crap it is!" yelled Lucifer.

Nessa rolled her eyes. "He's not going to let you in, dickhead! I almost forgot how bloody annoying you are!"

"What are you talking about? I don't remember

meeting you before, I think I'd remember a weird half demon like you!" Lucifer said, looking her up and down.

"Yeah, well I would explain, but you are far too stupid to understand and frankly I don't have the patience!" Nessa said simply.

"You remind me of Prince Beelzebub. She is the only other person, aside I suppose from Jophiel, who would dare to speak to me like that! I'm The Devil, feared by all! Aren't you scared of me?"

"Not in the slightest," said Nessa.

"Me neither," added Ophelia.

"But you should be!" Lucifer yelled.

"Ooh, should we? Shame we're not then!" grinned Nessa. "You ready Phee?" She offered her hand to Ophelia, who quickly took it.

"Yeah…" said Ophelia, excited to perform big magic with Nessa again.

"What do you think you're going to do?" said Jophiel, sounding rather nervous.

"Well, at this point we are practically guardians of both Heaven and Hell, we've had to sort out enough for both sides," said Nessa. "And at the moment, the two of you are Heaven's biggest threat, so you must be dealt with accordingly!"

"Are you going to try to destroy us?" Laughed Lucifer.

"No, but this might be worse for you!" Nessa grinned.

Together Ophelia and Nessa began to extract the demons' power. Dark energy was drawn from their hands and formed an intense ball of magic between them all.

"What the fuck? I know this, I've done it before! You can't take our powers!" yelled Lucifer.

Jophiel's eyes widened in horror. "We are the leaders of Hell! Return our power at once! You shall pay for this!"

"Err... Nah!" said Nessa with a smile.

"Yeah, no thank you, we've got something better to do with it!" added Ophelia.

They focused all their light power on the demonic energy before them. Brilliant white light shone from both Ophelia and Nessa, blasting the dark magic until it was completely gone. The two former demon leaders gasped in shock as their magical powers turned to nothing before their very eyes.

Chapter Twenty Two

Soulmates.

For a moment there was silence. Lucifer and Jophiel seemed to be too stunned to speak. Nessa was so excited by what they had just done. Before today she had known that she and Ophelia were powerful, as they had both demonic and angelic magic, but she had no idea how strong they would be working together! Ophelia was looking at her; her eyes sparkling. It felt good to work together, as if they were always meant to.

"That's... Not possible!" said Lucifer eventually. Sounding the least confident Nessa had ever heard him.

"Looks like it is!" Nessa smiled triumphantly. "Don't worry, there was a time for over a year that I thought I had lost my magic, I survived! It was highly annoying, but that's kinda the point."

"And to stop you storming Heaven, obviously..." added Ophelia.

"Oh yeah, you're not going anywhere!" Nessa clicked her fingers, creating an invisible barrier around Lucifer and Jophiel, trapping them where they were.

"Ooh, that's cool!" said Ophelia as both demons put their hands against the barrier, looking equally confused and furious.

"Who even are you?" yelled Jophiel.

"Long ago I was your sister!" said Nessa. "You won't remember me, and I don't really want you to. All you need to know is that we defeated you! I guess we really are the guardians of the realms! If I was you I wouldn't really say anything else, you'll just make things worse for yourself!"

"My sister? If you were my sister, why would you turn against me?" asked Jophiel.

"Oh don't you dare!" yelled Nessa, marching right up to the barrier face to face with Jophiel. "You turned against me *long* ago! We weren't close, but I wanted to be your sister, it was *you* who traded me in for power! You two psychos have always worked together, even when you ran separate realms!"

"We didn't *work* together!" said Lucifer quickly. "I don't exactly remember how, but I helped Jophiel become the Leader of the Archangels, so she owed me! All we did was occasionally discuss ideas about how to keep our people on our sides. Provided the odd threat of potential unrest from the opposition and so on, just to keep the people obeying!"

Nessa was furious, both realms had been run using fear and manipulation for almost as long as they had been around! And that was aside from the anger she felt at Lucifer mentioning 'helping Jophiel become the leader'. He might not remember how, but Nessa sure did!

Before she could say anything to Lucifer, Ezra appeared nervously at the doorway of the shop.

"Hi? I have to ask if it's safe to come out now?" he said worriedly.

Ophelia laughed. "Yes Little Brother, it's safe. I promise."

Ezra came running out and hugged Ophelia. Nessa moved away from the demons and gave him a hug too. Beelzebub stepped out of the shop.

"Beelzebub?" said Lucifer in shock. "What were you doing in an angel's shop?"

"I was asking myself the same question!" said Beelzebub with a laugh. "The little brat made me *eat* something!" She turned to Nessa. "He practically force-fed me this chocolate cookie thing, even though I threatened to bite his bloody hand off, but now all I'm thinking about is how I managed to survive over six thousand years without chocolate cookies!"

Nessa laughed. "I invented chocolate. Welcome to the *other* dark side!"

"Sort your brother out, it's not very angelic to tempt a demon like that!" Beelzebub said.

"I don't know, I know a former angel who was *very* good at tempting!" Nessa smiled, looking at Ophelia. "Anyway, it's not very demonic of you to hide and get Ezra to check if it's safe is it?"

"I dunno, potentially sacrificing an angel for selfish reasons? That sounds quite demonic!" Beelzebub smiled.

Nessa was really happy to have her friend back. She hadn't realised how much she had missed her until she saw her earlier, leading the demons. Even though she knew Beelzebub didn't remember her, it had been surprisingly easy to get her on their side.

"Beelzebub! You traitor!" Lucifer yelled. "You have been my right-hand demon for six thousand years!"

"Yeah, and that's a bloody long time to deal with your shit!" said Beelzebub. "Just fuck off, both of you! I honestly don't care anymore!"

"You will be thrown into the Pool of Destruction for this!" screamed Lucifer, utterly furious.

"Yeah, no I don't think she will," said Ophelia. "You've seen what we are capable of. Beelzebub is our friend now, and you really don't want to mess with us! Especially since you no longer have any power!"

"You want to be my friend?" asked Beelzebub shyly.

"Yes! If you want to be? We literally only have one friend in the world, it would be nice to have another," smiled Ophelia.

All of a sudden, the sky filled with golden light, just as it did when Nessa and Ophelia saved the world.

Ophelia took Nessa's hand. "Oh God!" she whispered.

"I was going to go for 'oh fuck', but I suppose yours is more literal…" Nessa answered, realising what a total mess both realms were right now, and wondering if God would be angry.

"Shh!" said Ophelia, but she was giggling a little.

This time the light was different though, it didn't just fill the sky, it kept coming down until it touched the ground. All six of them stared in amazement, some more nervous than others, obviously. The light dissipated and God herself stood before them! Nessa's eyes widened, she couldn't believe it! The last time she had seen The Almighty like that was when she tried to ask her questions the day of her fall. She had been so nervous then, but she actually found herself feeling rather confident facing her now, she and Ophelia wouldn't be in trouble; it was Lucifer and Jophiel that should be worried.

"Just checking, is that God?" Nessa heard Beelzebub whisper to Ophelia.

"Yeah..." answered Ophelia.

"Shit..." whispered Beelzebub, and Nessa smiled.

"Would someone be so kind as to explain what is going on here?!" God said, sounding rather angry. "I was about to try to sort out the mess in Heaven, but what is this?! Zadkiel, Ophelia! Care to explain? I trust you."

It was nice to know that, while God was angry, it wasn't at Nessa. She had spent many years feeling abandoned, imagining God must have hated her. Now though, The Almighty actually trusted her and Ophelia! That felt good.

The two explained the complicated story to The Almighty, who actually had to stop Lucifer and Jophiel from speaking at one point, as they kept interjecting with lies.

"Hmm... Both realms are currently without any leadership," said The Almighty when they had explained. "That won't work at all... Both realms must be functional; they balance each other out. The humans shall soon suffer with either realm shutting down operation, never mind both..." She paused and looked at Nessa and Ophelia. "What do you think my dear angel-demons? What should we do?"

"You're asking us?" said Nessa in surprise.

"Yes Zadkiel, you are the Archangel of Justice and my most creative mind, and Ophelia is the angel most passionate about the Earth, with the most forgiving heart, and you are both so full of love for all creations. I trust your judgement."

Nessa and Ophelia glanced at each other nervously.

"I feel that, err, both realms must be run by the right people," said Nessa, feeling rather nervous. "Both could co-exist without the need of any war if they were not run by people's egos as they have been all this time."

"Exactly!" Ophelia added. "Leaders should make rules and decisions based on what is best for Heaven and Hell, not themselves!"

"Yes, and I think if the two leaders were allies, that would be helpful, if not done in the manipulative way those two did!" Nessa said.

"Indeed," said God. "You are both very wise. You know, as is usually the case with her, Zadkiel already thought of something brilliant earlier."

"What?" asked Nessa suspiciously.

"You are both so powerful, especially together, and not all of it is power I granted you, a lot of it was born from your love. I believe you should both be my 'Guardians of the Realms' as Zadkiel coined it. You are the only beings who could possibly watch over both realms, as you have both within you!" The Almighty walked up to them and took both their hands, Nessa felt like she might cry, she never thought God would come anywhere near her, let alone touch her.

"Excuse me, my Lord?" said Ophelia nervously. "Of course I would be honoured by such a title and would happily advise both realms if needed. However, I feel that we cannot be Heaven or Hell's leaders as we are neither angels nor demons."

"That's a good point," said Nessa. "I don't really think I could run either one, because I need to be here with Ophelia. I am grateful that you appointed me as your first leader in Heaven, but it is far more important to me that I live my life with Ophelia now. Sorry..."

"Don't be sorry Zadkiel!" smiled God, giving their hands a loving squeeze. "You are absolutely right, you belong together. You found your home and it is not Heaven or Hell, it is here. I am not asking you to run anything, but as my new Guardians of the Realms I would like to ask you to appoint new leaders."

"Really?" said Nessa, shocked by the responsibility.

"Indeed!" God smiled, releasing their hands and taking a step away. "First we need a new Leader of the Archangels."

Nessa and Ophelia looked at each other, they both knew what the other was thinking and smiled.

"I think we have the perfect angel for the job right here!" smiled Ophelia.

Ezra gasped, obviously realising he was the only angel there.

"I've always said you should be running things Ezzy!" Nessa smiled. "You know better than anyone how it all should work, that's why those two were so desperate to get their hands on you!" She gestured to

Lucifer and Jophiel, who were glaring at them.

"You are kind and just, and most importantly the only other angel who was brave enough to bend Jophiel's stupid rules for the sake of goodness!" said Ophelia.

"*And* you never lost your belief in Heaven or God. You saw that it was just the way it was being run, but you always saw good at the very heart of it!" added Nessa. "I lost that belief for a long time…" She glanced sheepishly at God who just smiled at her.

"That's all very sweet, but I can't run Heaven!" said Ezra. "I'm just an admin angel that became Angel of the North! I'm not even an archangel! Certainly not a leader like you Nessa!"

"Angel Ezra, we have an empty space at the archangel table having lost one a few months ago," God said, glancing in Jophiel's direction. "Jophiel's old seat is now vacant, but if your sisters have chosen you to take that space, it shall have your name upon it."

"Really?" said Ezra in awe. "So, can I *become* an archangel?"

"Yes dear angel," smiled The Almighty. "Do you accept the job and its responsibilities?"

Ezra looked over at Nessa and Ophelia, as if for further permission. They both gave him an encouraging look.

"I do…" said Ezra excitedly.

God walked up to him and took his hands, closing her eyes. Ezra hurriedly closed his too. Golden light shone through their hands and up Ezra's arms. Then, after a moment The Almighty stepped back.

"You are now Archangel Ezra, Leader of the

Archangels and of the Heavenly Order. Just as Zadkiel once was."

"I'm really an archangel?" Ezra asked, tears in his eyes.

"You are," said God.

"Nessa!" cried Ezra, running to her and throwing his arms around her. "I'm like you! I always used to imagine being an archangel like you! You're my hero! I can't believe it…"

"Guess what Archangel Ezzy? You're *my* hero too!" Nessa smiled, hugging him tightly.

"Can I run Heaven from here?" Ezra asked God. "Obviously I'll go to Heaven for work, but can I still live here at my shop? I love the Earth…"

God laughed slightly. "If you wish!"

"Who would have thought Heaven would be run from a little bakery in York!" smiled Ophelia.

"Yeah, it's not like the name's a dead giveaway or anything!" said Beelzebub, smiling at Ezra. "Congratulations. I thought I'd hate you, but you're alright Kid!"

"Thank you…" said Ezra.

"We've got our angel leader, but there's only one demon that I would ever trust to run Hell, and she's conveniently here too," Nessa said walking up to Beelzebub, who smiled in surprise.

"You really want me to run Hell?" Beelzebub said, hopefully.

"I do!" smiled Nessa. "I know you don't remember, but I've always said you should be running it! I lost count of the number of times I said that over a beer last year when you were complaining about how much of a dick Lucifer was! You don't know me, but I know you better than anyone does!"

"Nessa! I do remember! I do know you," said Beelzebub quickly.

"What?" Nessa was totally stunned.

"Wow, how thick are you?" Beelzebub laughed. "I really thought you'd have worked it out! Like you said, I'm never that nice to strangers! I mean, I risked destruction to hold the demons back when Ophelia was hurt, and I literally committed treason to help you save her; not for the first time I'll add! Of course I know you're my friend, you idiot! I could have easily taken Ezra, and you were being quite unreasonable, you psycho dragon! I was on your side as soon as I saw you! I don't want a war, I was bloody glad you came to stop us!"

Nessa wasn't sure what to say. She couldn't believe it, had Beelzebub remembered her the whole time?

"I saw you..." she said quietly. "Six months ago outside my old flat. You saw me, but you didn't know me..."

"I did," said Beelzebub. "But you looked so happy with Ophelia. You always wanted to escape Hell, I was proud of you for doing it! You wanted to disappear, so I let you..."

"No Bee, not from you! I missed you... You are more of a sister to me than Jophiel ever was!"

"I missed you too..." Beelzebub said. "I thought this would give it away straight away, but I guess you were too busy to notice." She pointed to something on her jacket.

As Nessa looked closer, she realised it was a beer bottle-top fashioned into a badge. She gasped slightly, recognising the brand.

"Don't say anything!" said Beelzebub. "I know it's way too soppy for a demon, but when you took everything out of your flat, this was all that was left of our friendship... Shut up okay!"

"I didn't say anything..." smiled Nessa, tears in her eyes at the gesture. "How do you remember us? No one should... We were erased from the Book of Life."

"Oh shit..." said Beelzebub. "I don't know. I knew no one remembered you when I mentioned you to Lucifer and he thought I was crazy, then no other demon knew you either. To be honest I was only really by your flat to check that you *did* exist, cause I genuinely worried that I might have gone mad and imagined you!"

Nessa turned to God. "My Lord, how can she remember me?" she asked.

"The same way Ezra can," said God. "Love cannot be erased. If you positively change someone, you cannot be taken from their life, because it would change who they are as a person. Plus of course she remembers Ophelia, as the two of you are too entwined in each other's lives to exist alone."

Nessa smiled and turned back to Beelzebub. "Aww, hear that Bee? You *love* me!" she said teasingly, putting an arm around her.

"Oh fuck off! I don't love you!" said Beelzebub, shoving Nessa away.

"You do! God said so, so it must be true!" smiled Nessa.

"Ugh! I can't argue with that, she's standing right there!" said Beelzebub with a sigh, and suddenly she grabbed Nessa, hugging her like she didn't want to let go. "You are the only person in Hell who has ever liked me... I missed you! I needed a friend more than ever dealing with those two!"

"I love you Bee..." whispered Nessa, holding her tight, proud to be brave enough to admit it.

"You know what, God's right, I love you too..." Beelzebub answered softly. "Do you really want me to be your sister?"

"Definitely! I want us to be family forever, now you've chosen our side. I missed you too, I'm not losing you again," smiled Nessa.

Ophelia appeared beside them and Nessa stepped away from Beelzebub.

"Hi Bee!" smiled Ophelia. "We actually never formally introduced ourselves, or even properly met! I'm Ophelia, if you're Nessa's sister, then that makes you my sister too! Welcome to our weird little family. I'm an insufferable former angel, you'll *hate* me!" She threw her arms around Beelzebub and Beelzebub actually hugged her back! She had never hugged anyone apart from Nessa.

"I know who you are!" Beelzebub smiled. "I can't wait for your relentless bounciness and optimism to drive me mad!"

Nessa felt her heart fill with joy at the two of them hugging.

"Two good choices of leader," said God. "To entrust the realms to this family you have created for yourselves is a wise choice my dears."

Beelzebub turned to Ezra and offered him her hand.

"Official rivals, eh Kid?" she smiled.

"I was going to go for allies…" Ezra said uncertainly, shaking her hand nervously.

"Bit of both?" she suggested. "As long as I can have some more of those ridiculous cookies?"

"Sure! I have plenty of other stuff too?" said Ezra with a smile.

"Yep, great! I'll take one of everything!" Beelzebub grinned.

"Oi! What are you planning to do to us?" yelled Lucifer.

God gave them both a nasty look. "That is up to the guardians!" she said.

"I vote we hand you two disobedient demons over to our new Queen of Hell!" said Nessa. "She can do what she wants with you!"

"Ooh fun!" smiled Beelzebub, raising her eyebrows at the demons.

"Are you going to execute us?" asked Jophiel nervously.

"No," said Beelzebub firmly. "No one deserves to be destroyed, not even you two! Besides, there are plenty of ways to punish you that would be way more satisfying than destroying you. I'll have to think of the perfect thing, after all you've done to me over the years. But for now, you're my first prisoners, bitches!"

"I'm glad you're finally in charge, as it should be!" smiled Nessa. "You know, humans already get Beelzebub and Lucifer mixed up anyway? Some of them think they are two different names for The Devil."

"Ugh, don't offend me!" said Beelzebub in disgust.

"Well, you have been basically doing his job for him the whole time. At least that's a bit of recognition?" Nessa smiled.

"I'll save a special place in Hell for any humans who thought Lucifer and I were the same person!" laughed Beelzebub.

"Zadkiel, Ophelia, can I speak with you a moment before I go?" God said, making Nessa jump slightly.

"Of course!" said Ophelia, taking Nessa's hand as they followed The Almighty away from the others.

"Since we last spoke I have discovered something, and I feel it is important to tell you both," said God.

"What?" Nessa asked in concern.

"No, don't worry Zadkiel dear, it is nothing bad!" smiled The Almighty. "You were correct; I was wrong when I said that you were never meant to fall in love."

Nessa gulped. "You heard that?"

"I did, and I found it intriguing. I can easily say that I never planned for this to be possible, but the way you feel and your undeniable connection is a strong indicator that your relationship is not by chance. Your analogy about soulmates inspired me to look into this further, and I now believe that you are, in a way, correct."

Nessa and Ophelia looked at each other. They had no idea where The Almighty was going with this, but Nessa somehow felt she needed to grip Ophelia's hand tighter.

"I have discovered upon reflection that the two of you *were* created to be together, not intentionally, but you were," God continued. "Long ago at the very beginning, when my first two angels were created, your entwining relationship was set into motion before Ophelia even came to be."

"How?" asked Ophelia in wonder.

"Well, creating angels is a complicated process, why do you think I have not made any new ones for thousands of years?" The Almighty said with a smile. "There are all kinds of different elements that make up an angel, and part of what makes your souls must be mixed very precisely. When I was creating Zadkiel and Jophiel, I accidentally created too much of the energy that was to make up Zadkiel's soul. So, when I created the next set of angels, I used the other half to create another angel..."

"Me?" Ophelia breathed, gripping Nessa tighter.

"Correct!" smiled God. "That means that, while you are completely different people, that deep part of your soul is made from the same energy as Zadkiel's. That is why you had a connection from the moment you met. Your souls recognised their other half within the other. I think that is why you love each other so deeply in a way no other angels do. I also now believe that your connection may be the reason you have been able to become this wonderful new mixture of Heaven and Hell. Zadkiel, I did not cast you out, but in theory, if I had, I believe you still would have retained a little of your angelic power, as your soulmate remained in Heaven. Ophelia, angels should have no reason to cry, when was the very first time you cried?"

"Well, I feel like crying now!" Ophelia smiled,

leaning into Nessa. "Err, it was when I found out that Nessa had become a demon."

"Exactly!" The Almighty said. "Since that moment, half of that deep part of your soul has resided in Heaven and the other in Hell. As soon as Zadkiel became a demon, the two of you already had a little of both sides inside you."

"That's what I said, Nessa. I've always been a bit of a bad angel!" Ophelia said, sounding excited.

"Yeah, and I've always been a bad demon, or a good one I guess?" Nessa smiled, kissing Ophelia on the cheek.

"Eden is a good example, the first time you met as demon and angel," said God. "The angel tempted a human to sin, while the demon lied to protect her. That is certainly not how most would act..."

Ophelia gasped in horror. "You know about that?!" she said, practically breaking Nessa's hand by gripping it so tightly.

"Of course I know. Despite Zadkiel's honourable attempt, you cannot lie to me. I knew exactly what happened, but I found your reactions to it fascinating."

"Then why didn't you punish either of us?" Nessa asked.

"Because that was when I first saw a glimmer of this relationship. I was excited to see what would happen if I let you be," said God, taking their hands again. "I truly never intended for any of this to be possible. I had no idea that a mistake in my calculations would lead to the two of you fascinating creatures, but I am glad that it did. I am very pleased that after all this time you are together, where you belong."

"We've always been together one way or another!" Ophelia said happily. "But yes, I feel so safe and so whole when I'm with my beautiful wife! Thank you for still loving us, even though we are different, and we've made a lot of mistakes over the years!"

"Everyone makes mistakes! Even me when calculating mass to create an angel, apparently!" laughed God. "But, as in that case, mistakes often lead to wonderful things!"

"Honestly, you have no idea how much it means to me; hearing you say these things, knowing you accept us," Ophelia said, tears now falling down her face. "I have loved Nessa for a *very* long time, and I always thought I shouldn't. Before you say anything Nessa, not because you were a demon, but because I thought it wasn't allowed. I was always told it shouldn't be possible to love anyone the way I loved her, and that was hard. In the back of my mind I always thought there must be something wrong with me. Why could I feel that way when no one else could? It's nice to know we didn't do anything wrong and I'm not crazy for being in love, that there's a reason..."

"Not only are we *allowed* to be in love Phee, we are *supposed* to! We *were* made to be together! Accidentally, but still!" Nessa smiled.

The Almighty was still holding their hands, but suddenly to their amazement, she took hold of them and gave them a hug! Nessa instantly started sobbing. She never dreamed when she was a lonely demon down in Hell, when she was so sure God hated her, that one day she would be embracing both her and Ophelia like this. Back in Heaven all she wanted was a little bit of recognition for her work, but this was so much better than she ever could have imagined. God loved her and accepted her as she was; an imperfect half demon with a load of problems, who had loved an angel for a long time. Nothing could have made that moment more perfect.

After a while The Almighty moved away, still smiling at them.

"I must thank you once again as I did in December for what you have done today," she said. "I trust you with all three of my realms; Heaven, Hell and Earth. Unsurprisingly, given what we now know, the two of you make a very good team. I hope you continue to find new strengths by each other's side. All of the realms are better places for the two of you being together. Now, I must go, but I am certain I shall see you again one day. Oh, and happy half anniversary - whatever that is! Something from Zadkiel's creative mind once again, I imagine!"

"It is indeed!" said Ophelia, smiling at Nessa. "Thank you my Lord! Just in general really..."

"You are most welcome!" said God, with a slight laugh. "Thank you in general too..."

She gave their hands a final caring squeeze and then was gone in a flash of golden light.

Nessa turned to Ophelia immediately. She felt so odd, like she wasn't sure how to feel - in a good way of course.

"I love you!" she exclaimed, with a feeling of urgency.

"Oh I love you too, my darling!" grinned Ophelia, moving closer.

"I can't believe we actually were made to be together!" Nessa grinned. "We're literally soulmates! Half of the same soul!"

"Well, a whole soul made of the same stuff!" said Ophelia.

"You're doing it again, being pedantic when I'm saying romantic shit!" said Nessa.

"Alright, carry on with the romantic shit then!" smiled Ophelia with a cheeky look, obviously knowing Nessa loved it when she swore, it somehow drove her mad. Nessa took hold of Ophelia's waist, pulling her closer.

"I'm whole with you…" she said. "Half of whatever makes our souls, half demon, half angel, but fully yours…"

"Half anniversary?" whispered Ophelia, moving closer so their lips were touching. "You promised…"

Nessa felt Ophelia's tongue on her lip and held her breath.

"I did, and I will never break a promise to you," she whispered, then began to kiss her. It was blissful. Nessa remembered the first time they had kissed; just before Ophelia left for Heaven. That connection… It was so strong! She had thought at the time that the kiss made her feel whole, now she knew that was true! That deep part of her soul that matched Ophelia's must have known she was finally home.

Ophelia opened her eyes and glanced towards Ezra's shop.

"Jophiel and Lucifer are staring at us..." she whispered through the kiss.

"Good!" said Nessa, kissing her harder, almost out of spite.

After a few more moments they rejoined Ezra and Beelzebub, who were now inside the bakery. Ezra was showing Beelzebub all the different cakes and cookies he had.

"You two finished shoving your tongues down each other's throats?" Beelzebub asked with a grin, taking the small piece of cake Ezra was offering her. He made a rather disgusted face in response; making the other three laugh a little. "Did you say you were married?" asked Beelzebub, her mouth full of the cake. "This food stuff is fucking amazing by the way! Maybe you're right and Earth isn't that bad..."

Nessa laughed. "I told you! Yeah, we are married. When God approved of our relationship that made us wives!" They both showed their rings off to Beelzebub.

"Cute!" said Beelzebub. "It's a shame you didn't have a proper wedding, because my bridesmaid's dress would have been epic!"

"I would have been the bridesmaid!" said Ezra indignantly.

"You can have more than one bridesmaid!" smiled Nessa. "Bee, I know you're Queen of Hell now, but do you want to hang out with us sometimes? I'm ready for operation 'prove to Bee that the Earth is great'!"

"Yeah I do..." said Beelzebub, sounding a little shy. "If you ever invite me to the sea or whatever again, I promise I'll come this time!"

"Ooh, it can be a *family* holiday this year!" gasped Ophelia excitedly. "You'll come won't you Little Brother?"

"I already can't wait! I want to make Nessa go on that rollercoaster again 'cause it was hilarious!" grinned Ezra.

"I don't think so! It will give me mouse trauma flashbacks!" Nessa smiled. "I'm sure Ophelia will go on it with you, I'll be the one who holds the bags!"

Beelzebub glanced out of the window. "The idiots are arguing!" she said. "I guess I should probably go deal with them... I'm glad to have my friend back, and some new ones. I'll see you guys soon!" She started walking towards the door, then stopped. "And you, Archangel of Baking, I'll need a constant supply of those cakey things! Call it keeping Hell on your side!"

"Yes, Your Majesty!" said Ezra sarcastically. "I shouldn't have made you try any, now you'll never leave me alone!" he groaned dramatically.

"I will absolutely send legions of demons for you if you don't send enough baked goods!" Beelzebub said teasingly. "Bye guys!"

Nessa and Ophelia watched as Beelzebub transported Lucifer and Jophiel down to Hell.

"They won't come back, will they?" Ezra asked worriedly. "I'm in charge now, but I don't know what I'd do if they did..."

"No, they have no magic now," said Ophelia. "They won't come back."

"Bee won't let them out of her sight now anyway!" Nessa smiled. "She's got a *lot* of built up anger towards

Lucifer, I'd feel sorry for him if he didn't totally deserve it!"

"Anyway, you don't need to protect Heaven, just run it!" said Ophelia. "We will protect it if it ever needs protecting. Right Nessa?"

Nessa took Ophelia's hand, proud of her bravery after how scared she was that morning.

"Yeah, we'll be your scary guard dogs!" she grinned. "Plus it sounds like the Queen of Hell's loyalty can easily be bought with the promise of cake! You'll be great Ezzy, I believe in you!"

"Thank you Archangel Zadkiel!" smiled Ezra shyly.

"You are most welcome my dear Archangel Ezra!" Nessa said, ruffling his hair.

"I feel left out, I'm the only one who isn't an archangel!" said Ophelia jokingly with a little pout.

"You're *my* archangel!" Nessa said, giving her a quick kiss. "Come on - anniversary time!"

"Ooh, okay! See you soon Little Brother!" Ophelia said, practically pulling Nessa out of the door.

"Bye, have fun!" Ezra called after them.

Out on the street Nessa put an arm around Ophelia.

"Come on my darling!" she said.

"Oh, hang on!" said Ophelia, noticing a human walking past. "The barrier thing!"

"Oh shit yeah, I forgot about that! Ezzy won't get any customers if they can't see the place properly."

The two of them worked together to take down the barrier, then Ophelia put her arm around Nessa.

"I like doing magic with you!" she said.

"Me too, I like doing everything with you!" Nessa

said. "I love being near you! You are my home and my heart, and quite literally my soul! You're everything!"

"Aww! Is that more of that romantic shit you were talking about?" grinned Ophelia.

"Oh it's so hot when you swear, you bad little angel!" Nessa said, grabbing Ophelia and kissing her.

"I know. Why do you think I do it?" laughed Ophelia. "Now where are you taking me for our half anniversary?"

"I know a little pub!" smiled Nessa. "It might not be seven o'clock on a Wednesday, but I think a certain table will still be free! Apparently an angel and a demon used to meet up there to pretend to be rivals, but the demon just used to gaze at the beautiful angel the whole time!"

"Oh Really?" Ophelia smiled. "I think the angel was very distracted when trying to list angelic deeds she'd done, by some rather unholy thoughts about how it would feel to kiss the demon!"

"Oh, do you think she ever found out?" Nessa grinned.

"Yeah, I think it felt alright..." teased Ophelia.

"Hey!" Nessa gave her a little shove.

"It was *everything*!" whispered Ophelia. "I love you more than that young angel up in Heaven would have ever imagined was possible! I wonder what I would have thought if I knew that day on Jupiter, that you would become my whole world one day? I wouldn't have believed it, I wouldn't have *dared* to dream of anything so incredible! You are a miracle..."

"*We* are a miracle!" smiled Nessa. "I am honoured

to be able to love you for eternity! My precious, perfect wife!"

Nessa pulled Ophelia close, and for a few moments the two soulmates stood in the middle of York, just *being* together; their energies mixing in the embrace. Enjoying the closeness, the safety, the feeling of home. As long as they had each other, everything was perfect, even if sometimes it wasn't.

The End...

Ezra and Beelzebub's Guide to Heaven and Hell

Our new Head of the Archangels and Queen of Hell answer questions about their realms.

Introduce yourselves.

B: I'm Queen Beelzebub! I absolutely *love* saying that! I'm the new ruler of Hell, or The Devil if you want. Your turn Kid.

E: Oh, err, my name is Ezra...

B: And? Come on, *what* are you?

E: An angel?

B: Ugh, for Hell's sake Kid! What's your new job, you idiot?

E: Oh yeah! I'll never get used to that... I'm Archangel Ezra! I'm the Head of the Archangels...

B: Damn right you are! My little rival slash ally!

E: What I am is absolutely terrified... You seem so confident about ruling an entire realm. Thinking about it makes me feel quite sick...

B: I'm sure you'll be fine. Nessa and Ophelia will help you if you need it. Ophelia was an angel up until recently, and Nessa used to have your job right back at the beginning.

E: I know. That's one of the reasons I'm so scared. Zadkiel has always been my hero, and it's an honour to be Nessa's brother, but now I'm supposed to basically *be* Zadkiel! That's a lot of pressure, she was amazing...

B: Maybe, but Jophiel was utterly shit, so there's that! No one's gonna be comparing you to Nessa, they'll be comparing you to Jophiel, and it'll be pretty impressive if you manage to be worse than her.

E: I'm still nervous... I'm just a normal admin angel, I've never been anybody important...

B: Well then it's about time you were somebody important! You'll do great, Kid. To me you're exactly what I think angels should be; sweet, innocent, and caring. You'll make it up as you go along, that's what I'm going to do!

E: Thank you. So you don't know what you're doing either?

B: Of course not! Sure, I did most of Lucifer's job for him the whole time, but now I'm on my own I can do what I want. I just don't know what that is yet. Take it from The Devil, Kid, if you don't know what you're doing, do it with confidence and do it with flair and nobody will question you. You'll *look* like you know what you're doing, and that's the most important thing. No one really knew that I did most of The Devil's work the whole time, because Lucifer gave off such a commanding and confident air, that he seemed like he was in control. You've got this Archangel Ezra. Let's make Hell and Heaven better than they've ever been!

E: Thank you Beelzebub, you are actually nice you know?

B: No I'm not. Shut up! What's the next question?

Describe your realm in three words.

E: Like how it should be, or how it's been?

B: Good point, I was wondering that.

E: I'll just describe it vaguely. Err, light? Ooh, busy! Everyone's always working. Erm... Holy? That one's a bit of a cop-out I know, but that was such a hard question. See Beelzebub, I can't even describe my realm! That's not a great start is it?

B: (Laughing) You're funny Kid. I like you a lot more than I expected.

E: That feels like a backhanded compliment, but thanks I guess?

B: It's not personal, I just assumed I'd hate all angels, and you were the guy I was sent to kidnap. I was supposed to torture information out of you when we got to Hell you know?

E: (Shifting away slightly) No, I didn't know that... You're scary.

B: Thanks Kid. And you're sweet. Perfect Devil and Archangel team eh?

E: I guess so...

B: Anyway, three words... Err, let's go with; dark, and that's the lighting *and* the energy; fun, at least it will be now; and laid-back, I know that's actually two words, but let's pretend it's one.

E: Very good. The laid-back part sounds nice. Angels are always so busy! It's nice to live on Earth and be allowed to slow down a bit. The thing is, angels were made to work, and so they don't know what to do with themselves if they have nothing to do. Therefore every single moment is filled with just doing *stuff* up there! I'm eternally grateful that I was chosen to come down to Earth and got to experience relaxing for the first time. It's lovely!

B: You should have got yourself damned Kid. In Hell most of the time we are just hanging around, not doing anything in particular.

E: I think that's the other extreme and I'd be bored then!

B: Well, then you do something nasty for fun. You know, something to do?

E: Or you find a hobby? I like reading.

B: Eww no. I couldn't be doing with that.

E: How about drawing? Me and Nessa used to draw silly pictures during that year when Ophelia was away. I'm not great at it, but it's fun!

B: Hmm... Maybe I'll try that Kid. If I do, I'll draw the first picture of you.

E: That's sweet, thanks.

B: I'm not sweet! Move on!

What does your realm look like?

E: Oh, it's very bright white. Like, it basically glows! There are lots of long corridors with offices. That's the part of Heaven where I've always lived. There are offices for all the archangels and the admin rooms, oh and the healing rooms not far from that, that's where you used to work isn't it Beelzebub?

B: Yeah, I did...

E: And there's also the Seat of the Archangels, which is the meeting place where the archangels come together every month to discuss stuff. They, sorry, *we*, all have fancy seats with our names carved into them around the table. That's also where the edge of Heaven is, where angels were sent to Hell... What else? Oh, there is no ceiling or roof, so above is just clouds. That's what the office bit looks like anyway, there are other bits, like where all the humans go, but I've never been there. Maybe I should if I'm supposed to be running the place!

B: Maybe just a visit to introduce yourself? Ooh, or get yourself a tannoy like I've got! I have one for demons and one for humans, to broadcast messages throughout Hell without leaving my throne room. It's not lazy, it's efficient!

E: (Giggling) I didn't say it was lazy! That's a great idea, but I don't think I'm very commanding... I imagine you sound like a fierce Queen, I'm too soft...

B: I'm running Hell, I need to be fierce. Heaven has had far too much fierce leadership, Kid, I think they could do with a bit of soft...

E: Thank you... Go on then, what does Hell look like? I actually don't know.

B: Okay, well it's dark, very dark. So my eyes are well equipped for darkness, and the Earth feels bright to me, which adds to my general disdain towards it. I dread to think how awful Heaven would be, it'd blind me! Err, we have corridors too, but they are pretty manky to be honest. The whole place smells of burning, which I love, but some people might be put off by. To me the most important bit is my throne room! I've lived there since the fall. Obviously it *was* Lucifer's throne room, but now it's mine! I've redecorated it a bit; it's all black and red, it's lovely. I also gave my new Prince of Hell a chair, because Lucifer never let me have one when I was the Prince... Oh, the main thing about Hell is we have nine layers, or circles if you want to be all official. Different stuff goes on in different layers. I usually hang out in the first layer, 'cause that's where all the cool stuff is. Plus generally speaking, the further down you go, the more shit it is! The bottom layer is the fiery pits, and that's where all of Hell's power comes from. You angels get your power from the holy energy source, ours comes from the fiery pits. We've got loads of cool stuff down there to be honest, Kid. I'd offer you a tour, but it'd make you feel ill, so it wouldn't be that fun for you. Same as how Heaven's energy would give me a headache... I guess we'll have to meet up on the crappy Earth eh?

E: I love the Earth, and I think you're going to love it too, once we show you more of it.

B: Maybe? I'm more than willing to be proven wrong about it, but so far I don't see the appeal.

E: You're already eating human food. You're halfway there.

B: Yeah, that's your fault you sugary idiot! I don't know what those things are that you make, but sorry to tell you, they are definitely not holy!

E: I know they're not. Eating human food is very unholy. I've got to be careful with Earthly pleasures, because I get obsessed with them way too easily. I resisted the temptation of food for months, even with an expert demon making it her mission to corrupt me, simply because I knew I'd love it if I tried it. I was right. In the end when I tried ice cream, I knew I'd been defeated. Earthly influence had taken me and I'd never be pure again. But then again, I realised that nothing terrible happened when I gave in, so I was actually able to relax a bit and enjoy the Earth more. That also helped me to be brave enough to help Nessa and Ophelia with saving the world. Now though, I guess my weakness has led to being chosen to run Heaven by my wonderful sisters, so it can't be that bad...

B: I'm The Devil, I'm all for breaking rules! You're cooler than I thought you'd be.

E: Thanks, so are you. I far prefer sitting and chatting with you than getting kidnapped by you.

B: I didn't want to kidnap you. If I wanted to, I would have done. We had you for a while, and I should have transported us all down to Hell, but I didn't. I wanted to let Nessa and Ophelia rescue you, because they had become more powerful than anyone, so if they saved you, I thought they might be able to stop Lucifer and Jophiel, therefore saving me too… I felt pretty low then, but it worked because now I'm happier than ever!

E: I'm very happy for you. I can't imagine working with Lucifer for thousands of years. I'm glad you've finally got rid of him.

B: Thanks Kid, I'm happy for you too, sounds like you need a bit of appreciation. Plus, as a rule, I don't like angels, but I quite like you already, so there's no one I'd rather have as my Heavenly counterpart. I feel like because we are both friends with the new Guardians of the Realms, we are kind of on the same team, which is nice. I don't want any wars…

E: Oh, neither do I! I like the idea that our realms could be allies rather than enemies.

B: An unlikely duo, eh?

Who are the authority figures in your realm?

E: Oh, well the number one authority figure in Heaven is God, obviously. She's in charge and has ultimate power over everything, but I'm pretty sure she usually just leaves us to it... In terms of angels, the Head of the Archangels is the figurehead of Heaven, which is absolutely terrifying, because suddenly, that's me! First it was Nessa who was called Zadkiel at the time, then since she fell it's been Jophiel, now it's me! As the leader of Heaven, it's our job to head up the archangel meetings, and generally run stuff, but the archangels are a team, so everyone kind of works together I guess. Under the Head of the Archangels there should be their vice-leader, but we haven't had one since Nessa's fall. Though Jophiel used to treat Gabriel as her second in command I believe. She was the vice-archangel leader when Nessa was in charge, but God never appointed another. I'm not sure why... Anyway, then there are the other archangels. Originally there were seven, but now there are six without Nessa. They all have old-fashioned archangel titles, but like I said, they are a team. There's me; I don't have an official title other than Head of the Archangels, Gabriel; Archangel of Earth, Michael; Archangel of Protection and commander of Heaven's army, Uriel; Archangel of Wisdom, Raphael; Archangel of Health and liaison to God, and there is another one, I think her name is Azrael and she literally *never* speaks, she is the Archangel of Death who looks after all the humans in Heaven and guides them when they arrive.

Jophiel used to be Archangel of Beauty, and Zadkiel was Archangel of Justice.

B: Damn, that's a lot...

E: Yeah. Oh, I forgot! For a little while between Nessa's banishment and his fall, Lucifer was the Archangel of Light, which is a pretty ironic title if you ask me!

B: Stupid bastard! Lucifer, not you! Err, in Hell I'm in charge; I'm the Queen of Hell, but you can call me The Devil; or Satan if you really want to. Other than that, I have my new Prince of Hell. His name is Caspian, and he helps me out and does any jobs I assign him. That's it really... Err, I guess a Duke of Hell has a little more authority than most demons? They are our Earth representatives, and they are also the ones who invent new temptations for the humans. We have meetings with them once a month to discuss what they've been doing on Earth.

E: So you really are running the realm all by yourself? Aren't you scared?

B: Nah! I feel like this is right; like I was always meant to be Queen. I'm excited rather than scared. This is who I am now!

E: Then Hell is lucky to have such a passionate Queen...

B: Thanks Kid!

How do you address the authority figures?

B: The Queen, or King, is 'Your Majesty', and any Princes are 'Your Highness'. Just like humans I think?

E: Oh good, I call you Your Majesty.

B: Yeah, but you're an angel so you don't need to because I'm not your Queen.

E: I still respect you though...

B: Well thanks! That's sweet.

E: In Heaven, the Head of the Archangels is 'Your Highness' and the other archangels are 'Your Holiness'. I can't be 'Majesty', because while my job is the equivalent to yours, I can't actually be named King of Heaven, because God rules over us, and it can't be suggested that I possibly outrank her. She is addressed as 'My Lord' or else just Almighty God. Oh, and small-order angels address anyone higher than them as 'Your Holiness'. So for example, when I first came to Earth to work with Ophelia, I referred to her as 'Your Holiness' because she was the Angel of the North and I was just an admin assistant.

B: And look at you now, Your Highness! You've come a long way haven't you?

E: I have! No idea how that happened... I guess I was just in the right place at the right time?

B: Maybe it's not a coincidence? Maybe you and I were made for this? We just had to wait patiently to take our rightful places?

E: Maybe? I still don't feel worthy though...

What changes do you want to make now you're in charge?

B: Where do I bloody start? The thing is, like it or not, Hell is our home, and it's been utterly shit! Obviously it's not supposed to be particularly pleasant; it's eternal punishment from God, but here's the thing. I was damned too! To me, the demons haven't done anything wrong because we all shared ideals when we started the war with Heaven, so they are just my subjects, and I want them all to live and just hang out, you know? Lucifer was on such a power trip that he used to destroy demons for fun! Anyway, my view is, Hell is a punishment for evil humans, run by my fallen angels who dreamed of a carefree life. The humans can suffer, I don't care about them, but the demons deserve to live without fear of destruction. I want Hell to be a fair place, and so far it really hasn't been. Basically, when I joined the Heavenly war, it was because I dreamed of somewhere without so many rules where we could all just exist without all the pressure that comes with Heavenly duty. Clearly those weren't Lucifer's ideals, he only cared about power for himself.

E: That actually sounds quite nice... I assumed Hell

would be horrible, and whoever ran it would be totally evil, but you're not...

B: I'm mean, I'm nasty, I'm harsh, but I'm not going to be an *evil* Queen. We've all suffered enough.

E: That's good. If I was the leader of Heaven when Lucifer was running Hell, there's no way I'd be his ally, because he represents everything I disagree with. You on the other hand, I think we can live in harmony, and that's nice.

B: I'd like that. Go on Kid, what changes are you going to make?

E: I won't run the realm on fear. Yes angels need to obey God, but Jophiel made it all about obeying *her!* Most of all I want angels to be able to make friends and love each other. My life is so much better now I have people who love me, and I think we live in too much isolation. We have always been told that we shouldn't make friends, we shouldn't care about each other, and we certainly shouldn't love each other, but that's nonsense! I think Heaven would be a much happier place if we could all just be a bit more open, you know? We live to work, and that's great, that's what we are made for, but I think we were also made to love...

B: You know Ezra? That's not far off what I was fighting for during the Heavenly war. Not the love part obviously, but I thought there had to be more to life than endless thankless work...

E: Ooh heck, do I agree with The Devil?

B: (Laughing) I think you might, my dear archangel...

What was your job before this and do you think it will help you run the realm?

E: I was an admin assistant, and then for the last year and a half I've been an Earth representative. Being from admin means I know pretty much everything about Heaven and all the angels. I think that's the reason Jophiel got you to try to kidnap me, right?

B: Yeah, she said you'd be useful. Basically if we had you as our prisoner, we could torture you and find out some juicy stuff about Heaven. You know, their weaknesses and all that shit.

E: Right... I'm not really sure how well I'd hold up under torture...

B: Do you want to find out? I'm good at torture...

E: (Shifting away slightly again) Err no thank you! Don't make me regret letting you into my shop, you scary demon!

B: (Laughing) I'm kidding! Carry on!

E: Okay... Erm, as well as knowing a lot about my realm, I also appreciate the importance of files and documentation. I'm thinking of organising a massive sort out of all of our files, but I'll give myself a few years to settle into the job first... Oh, and working on Earth recently has taught me a lot about humans and this realm. I think that's useful too.

B: Cool, you sound well qualified, and you're obviously passionate about it too. Nessa and Ophelia made a good choice.

E: Thank you!

B: I was the Prince of Hell. That prepared me for this job because I basically had to run things anyway, because Lucifer was a lazy bastard. I've been doing The Devil's work since Hell started, but now I finally get to do it my way!

E: They made a good choice with you too!

B: Thanks Kid.

What do you think of each other?

B: Well, I want to say you're an annoying little angel, but actually, I really like you! Nessa kind of gave me permission to admit when I care about people. Like, we have been friends since The Fall, but I never admitted it because we all thought friends were a human thing, until she said she was my friend out loud and hugged me. That blew my mind, and now we've gone further than that and said we are family. So that makes it okay for me to say that I really like you Kid. I'm excited to be your friend, if you want to be friends?

E: Oh I'd love to be friends! I think you're really cool. You are super scary, but I quite like that. It'd be nice to have someone scary on my side... Nessa and Ophelia are my family, and they said the other day that you are their sister, so if you hang out with them, that probably means hanging out with me too, if you want?

B: I do want. I never knew I could like an angel, or the Earth, but I'm happy to be proven wrong. Hey, Ezra? If I'm Nessa and Ophelia's sister, and you are their brother, then doesn't that make us siblings too?

E: Oh! Do you want to be siblings?

B: Yeah! I mean, I know you want to be my ally, but I'm not sure if you'd want the Queen of Hell as a sister. If you would, I'd like to be... I'm really excited to be Nessa and Ophelia's family, but I'd quite like a sweet angelic brother too? Ezra, there's something about you. I don't know why, but when they told us to wait in here while they defeated Lucifer and Jophiel, I just instantly liked you. I was pleased when we both were chosen to run the realms, and we're probably going to be hanging out anyway, like you said. Do you want to be family?

E: I do! I really want to be your brother! Thank you! That means we can run the realms as siblings. Not only is the Queen of Hell my ally, she's my *sister!* Now I have three amazing sisters. I'm totally in awe of all of you and forever honoured to be considered a brother. Beelzebub, you are one of the coolest people I'd ever met. I can't believe you like me!

B: Aww, well you're an angel, I can't believe *you* like *me!* You're not supposed to, I'm unforgivable.

E: Well I think it's clear that I'm not really the model of a holy angel am I? Nessa and Ophelia are half demons, they were both damned. I don't care if you're a demon. What I learned a few months ago is that angels don't necessarily fall because they've done something bad, and demons aren't inherently bad people, they just happened to get damned. I like you better than all the angels up in Heaven. I'm so excited to get to know you more, my sister...

B: You are so sweet Ezra. You are like sunshine. I honestly didn't know it was possible for someone to be *so* bright and sunny. I've never met anyone like you. We are complete opposites, but I quite like that. I'm very new to this whole family thing, and I've been thinking about what it actually means. I think family means I'd do anything for you. You are the most important people in my life and I vow to always be on your side and protect you forever. You have this scary demon on your team, and I'll always be here for you. That's what I think family is...

E: That's lovely. Yeah, that's family. Family is loving someone and being brave for them. I'd do anything for my sisters, even if it's scary. You know, Nessa told me all about you and I thought you were cool. Last year when

Ophelia was away, she hung out with me every week, but she was also hanging out with you, so she'd tell me stuff about you. I kind of wanted to meet you, even though I was pretty sure you wouldn't like me...

B: I didn't think I'd like you to be honest. She told me about you, too, and I thought a sweet bouncy angel would be annoying, but I was so wrong. I'm glad we chatted, and I'm glad you're my brother now. I'm excited for us to run the realms, we're gonna do great Kid!

E: Yeah, I'll do my best. Thank you for being my sister.

B: Thank you for being my brother. Do you...want a hug? I've hugged our other siblings, and I know you've hugged them too. I don't know, I thought we could, to sort of solidify our friendship?

E: I would *love* a hug! I like hugs now, so just a heads up, I'll hug my family a lot. I'll probably annoy you!

(Ezra throws his arms around Beelzebub and hugs her hard)

B: Maybe you will annoy me, but I've heard brothers *are* annoying... This isn't annoying though, it's nice...

E: It is! I'm glad I met you.

B: I'm glad I met you too...

GREY FEATHERS

Book Two Coming Soon...

About Grey Feathers

So far, being the Guardians of the Realms has been easy... Too easy...

It's been ten years since Nessa and Ophelia finally got their happy ever after, and life couldn't be more perfect, spending their days together or with their wonderful family, but maybe an eternity of peace and quiet is too much to ask for? They almost forgot about The Devil, deep in the dungeons of Hell, but he certainly hasn't forgotten about them...

When Lucifer escapes during Beelzebub's jubilee party, stealing the power of a thousand demons, discovering the power of time travel, the Guardians of the Realms are needed more than ever. Pity they have absolutely no idea what they are doing, and Heaven, Hell and the Earth are all relying on them!

Meanwhile Ezra is shocked to find himself falling in love with Caspian; the gorgeous, cool and confident, sweet new Prince of Hell. How will he navigate love, when he didn't even know it was possible for him, and then the world as they know it is falling down around them at the hands of Lucifer?

Can Nessa and Ophelia navigate the past together and try to save their future? What happens when the leaders of the realms are driven out? Will Ezra be brave enough to chase his own happy ending with Caspian? And will the realms and the family that runs them ever be the same again?

If you enjoyed Fallen Feathers

Please consider leaving a review on Amazon, Goodreads, social media, or anywhere else you like to review books! Thank you!

Nessa and Ophelia © Romy Morgan

Join the 'Fallen Feathers Fan Club' group on Facebook to chat about the books and keep up to date with news from the world of Nessa and Ophelia!

About the Author

Romy has wanted to be an author since she was a child, and was always making up stories, but she hated writing on paper. Luckily, keyboards exist!

As well as a writer, Romy is also a historian and has a Masters Degree in Museum Studies. She is also very involved in theatre; often performing in pantomimes, musicals, and plays; directing pantomimes; and designing props and posters following her degree in Graphic Design. She also sometimes works in TV.

Romy lives in the North of England (that's why all her characters tend to be reyt Northern) with her lovely family and two sweet kittens!

Follow Romy!
She'd love to connect with readers! Why not tell her your favourite character or ask her a question!

Web: romymorgan.com
Instagram and Threads: @romy.morgan
TikTok and Facebook: @romymorganauthor
Goodreads: Romy Morgan

Printed in Great Britain
by Amazon